HEARTLESS

AL-SAADIQ BANKS

HEARTLESS

THE GAME WILL *NEVER* LOVE YOU BACK

True 2 Life Publications Presents:
Heartless

Author: Al-Saadiq Banks
True 2 Life Publications
P. O. Box 8722
Newark NJ 07108

Email: alsaadiqbanks@aol.com
Twitter: @alsaadiq
Instagram: @alsaadiqbanks

www.True2LifeProductions.com

In the game of life, we can't win them all and we won't win them all.

What separates us from losers is our mindset. Losers fear losing and they play with doubt. We play to win, determined to win, but if by chance we don't, we learn. You win like a man, and you lose like a man. The best part of falling like a man is the ability to stand back up like a man and still have the respect and honor of the people. More important, to still have respect for yourself. Honestly, I don't even pay attention to the scoreboard. I just play the game. Let the people on the sideline keep score. That's what they're there for.

—Attorney Tony Austin

PROLOGUE

"YOUNG LADY, YOU have been labeled a monster, in more states than one. You sit back with no sign of emotion, no sign of remorse. How do you feel? Don't you feel any remorse for the victims that you have slain and the families that were left behind as a result of your actions?"

She gathers her thoughts before speaking. "Yes, I can honestly say that I felt remorse for a few of them after the fact, but while the acts were taking place..." She pauses for a few seconds. "I'm ashamed to admit that I didn't feel a bit of it."

"But, if you felt any remorse, how could you have murdered repeatedly?"

Angelica shakes her head with sadness. "That I can't answer. Murder is something that I never set out to do, but it's like something gets into me, and I can't control myself from that point on. I black out, and minutes later, I wake up standing over dead, bloody bodies, sometimes not even remembering or understanding how I got there."

"As civilized creatures, we should be able to control our actions and emotions," the man says with very little compassion.

"It's not in my heart to commit the heinous crimes that I've committed, but shamefully while committing them, I felt a great deal of satisfaction. I just wish I could be judged on my intentions and not my actions because I never intended to do any of the things that I've done," she claims as she shakes her head from side to side with sadness on her face and sincerity in her eyes.

"Young lady, in the world, man and woman are judged by their actions."

"But God says He judges you by your intentions, correct?"

The man nods his head one solid time. As much as he hates to agree with her, he has no choice. "Correct."

"Well, in that case, I have no worries because God knows my intentions and my heart, and that is all that matters to me. For mankind, I point out Mathew 7: 3-5: 'Why do you look at the speck that is in your brother's eye but do not notice the log that is in your own eye? First, take the log out of your own eye, and then you will see clearly to take the speck out of your brother's eye,'" she quotes the New Living Translation loudly and clearly.

The man sits back, quite shocked at the words that have come out of her mouth. He sits there for seconds without saying a word. They stare into each other's eyes without blinking. "Young lady, is there anything I can help you with? Maybe any questions that I can answer for you?"

"I sit here, confused. I understand that I have to pay for my actions, but I need to know what it is that turned me into the monster that society has labeled me. Please just hear me out, and maybe you can give me the clarity that I need. Maybe you can tell me where I went wrong in life?"

1

NEWARK, NEW JERSEY
JULY 16, 2003

THE ABANDONED HOUSE is barely standing. It is only a skeleton with beams throughout. In the kitchen area, there are what
appear to be four young boys and an older teen-age boy. The three
young boys stand around one boy, who is sitting on a milk crate in
the middle of the floor.

To the naked eye, one would think it's a boy sitting on the crate,
but it is twelve-year-old Angelica Hill. Quite naturally, she's been
nicknamed Angel, simplifying her name, but that's always been one
of her biggest pet peeves in life. One, she hates that she has a biblical name to start with, but two, for some reason, she's never wanted
to be thought of as anybody's angel. Everyone, outside of family and
friends of family, only know her as Quiet Storm, Storm for short.
The nickname is one that she's given herself. She feels that name is
the perfect comparison to her silent but violent wrath.

Her hair is in two long Pocahontas braids and is always tucked
neatly inside a baseball cap for two reasons. The first reason is to
keep fitting right in with the rest of the boys. The second reason
is because she despises her hair. For some strange reason, her hair
color has changed gradually over the past year. At one time, she had
long and healthy brown hair that flourished over her head. Then,

almost out of nowhere, the color as well as the texture of her hair changed. She has yet to get used to it.

Her hair is the color of a reddish-wheat and equally as dry and course. Her oatmeal-colored skin tone and freckles give her quite a complex. Being a freckle-faced red-head she always feels like an eye sore in a room of strangers. Despite the unique characteristics that she looks at as imperfections, she's beautiful, but she can't see the beauty. The coldness in her heart can be spotted in her eyes. What would be bright and beautiful brown eyes are really windows of a saddened soul. One of her best assets is her bright, white, Colgate smile. She rarely smiles, though, so it goes unseen.

The three young boys stand huddled around her, all watching in shock, as Snap, the older teenager, shoves an old .38 revolver into Angelica's best friend's hand. His hands tremble as he grips it loosely. "Go ahead," Snap demands. "Pull the trigger."

"I already thought I was in," Angelica mumbles with fear.

"This is the most fear that I ever felt in my life. Just a week ago, I had linked up with this group. I was brought in by my best friend at the time. I was somewhat of a tomboy with no real interest in boys. The only fun I saw in boys was roughhousing and sports.

"I was honored to be propositioned to be in their secret group. The leader of the group, Snap, would tell me how special I was to be among them, with me being the only girl allowed. I didn't see anything special about it because I saw myself as one of the guys. It was obvious that Snap didn't see me as one of the guys, though. I could tell by the way he looked at me.

"I was quite familiar with that look because I had been noticing it for the past year and a half. At eleven, I started developing, and by twelve, I had the body of a well-proportioned woman. I would wear extra baggy clothes just to hide my body and tuck my hair under baseball hats. The way Snap looked at me let me know that he could see my body underneath the garments. It was like he looked at me with X-ray vision.

"One day, while in our secret clubhouse alone with Snap, he told me that I had to be officially initiated. To my surprise, my initiation consisted of a sacrifice, and of course, it was my body which had to be sacrificed. I declined, but he took it anyway. He made me promise that I would never utter a word of what happened and even threatened to kill me if I did. My initiation lasted all of twenty minutes, and I hated every second of it. Once it was over, neither one of us spoke about it. It wasn't until this day that he ever spoke about anything of the sort. He told me the final phase of initiation was due, and that was to either indulge in this game of Russian Roulette or I had to allow the other three members of the group to have sex with me. I thought I was making the best decision at the time."

"Go ahead!" Snap shouts.

Angelica stares into the barrel of the revolver as her best friend aims it at her face. She closes her eyes tightly. She clenches her fists tightly with fear. The clicking of the trigger sounds off but no boom. She opens her eyes with surprise.

"OK, your turn," Snap says, looking downward at Angelica. The kid passes the gun over to Angelica as she gets up from the crate. She's hesitant to grab it. Snap snatches it and shoves it into her hand.

"Ain't no room for scared motherfuckers in this crew," Snap says. "Now go!"

Angelica stands up with the gun glued to her side as her best friend in the world takes his place on the milk crate. Snap grabs Angelica's wrist, raising the gun in the air. He aims the nose of the gun at the kid's head while still holding her wrist.

"Go ahead and spin the barrel."

Angelica stands there, petrified. She shakes her head. She can't do it.

Snap uses his free hand to spin the barrel of the gun. "OK, now go. You get two chances."

The kid closes his eyes tightly. Angelica trembles with fear. Snap grabs her wrist tighter to stop her trembling. He rests the nose of the gun on the kid's head. "On the count of three," Snap says. "One, two…" Angelica closes her eyes tightly. "Three."

She mashes the trigger slowly.

Click.

She opens her eyes with a look of relief. The kid opens his eyes with the same amount of relief in them.

"See, I told you it was easy. Now you get one more try. This time, you spin the barrel yourself."

Angelica looks at the gun closely before spinning the barrel. She slowly raises the gun in the air, bringing it closer to the kid's head.

"Three!"

The sound of gunfire echoes throughout the house, shocking them all.

Angelica opens her eyes and drops the gun from her hand. She stares at her dangling hand for seconds before looking to her friend who is squirming on the floor, fighting to breathe. Blood seeps from his head. His eyes are wide open as he stares up at Angelica helplessly.

She watches in shock as the kid rolls around, extending his hand toward her to be rescued. His arm drops to the floor, his eyes close shut, and he stops moving.

"A strange feeling was in my heart at that moment. I was afraid, but deep in my heart, I felt so many other emotions. My best friend lying there, dead, dead by my hands. I felt a sense of power that I can't describe, a sense of dominance. All the years of his bossing and bullying now finally caught up with him. The adrenaline rush was a feeling that I had never experienced, and shamefully, I loved it.

"Surprisingly, the memory of my actions never haunted me. It was a secret that we all kept, and it was, like, forgotten. I was able to charge it off as I got older, but I was never able to charge off that adrenaline rush or the sense of dominance I felt. I had no idea that I would be spending my whole life chasing that rush."

2

JULY 4, 2006
10:38 A.M.

A FEW YEARS have passed and Angelica has matured, not just mentally and physically, but mischievously as well. Her young life is just one big adventure, with not a boring moment. It's chaotic at times, but she wouldn't choose to live it any other way. The mischief that she finds herself in feeds the rush that she's grown to love. She's a magnet for action, and the fast life is the only life she feels is for her.

Right now she sits in the passenger's seat of the brand spanking new convertible BMW 6 Series. The beautiful paint is as thick and white as the clouds. The butter soft upholstery feels like soft biscuits under her. Her butt sinks into the seat, feeling like she's floating on clouds. The sound of Neyo's, "So Sick", seeps through the speakers at a soothing level.

She has an oversized hood on her head, along with her baseball cap, which serves the purpose of a security blanket for her. Most dudes see her as the perfect little gangster chick, not knowing that the hat and hood is to hide her hair. She has a huge self-esteem issue because of it, along with the freckles. Those qualities, along with a few other issues she has, affect her confidence in so many ways.

The slow music she sees as an attempt of the driver to create the perfect romantic ambiance. What the driver doesn't know is she is in no way a romantic. Truly she finds the music quite pathetic. The music, coupled with the huge droplets of rain banging onto the windshield, is surprisingly relaxing to her though. The driver whips through the rain, showing off the car's speed and agility. Little does he know that speed turns her on more than his choice of music.

At a couple weeks short of fifteen years of age, she's jail bait for the driver, who is ten years her senior. He's only known her for a few days now, but he has big plans for her. It's her tough edge that he likes the most about her. He sees her as the rose that grew from the concrete. He plans to take her under his wing to raise and groom her.

The driver pulls up to the gas pump of the Exxon station. He cracks the door and holds it open with his foot as he looks over at her. "You want something out of here?" he questions.

"Get some Swedish Fish," she replies.

The attendant appears at the door.

"Fill it up with unleaded," the driver says, looking at the attendant. He looks over at Angelica. He's hesitant to speak. "I'm gonna get the blunts. Should I get condoms, too?" he asks with uncertainty in his eyes.

Disgust fills her. Sex is on his mind, just as she figured. She realizes that all men and boys want is sex and that infuriates her. Foolishly, she was expecting a breakfast date out of him. Her first time being around him, and already sex is on his mind. *Typical nigga*, she thinks to herself.

"Yeah, if you plan on getting some," she says with attitude.

"Bet," he says with a spark of cheer in his eyes. "My lil Quiet Storm," he sings as he gets out of the car and slams the door behind him.

By this time in her life, she has done away with Angelica all together. Everyone calls her by her nickname. Calling her Angelica could end in a fist fight because she sees it as disrespect, if she's already warned a person. With a straight face, she tells people that Angelica died some years ago and that Quiet Storm was born to take her place.

She peeks over her shoulder as the man walks toward the convenience store. She looks to her right where the man is pumping the gas. She watches the gas pump closely as the numbers switch quickly. Her eyes go from the pump to the store where customers are in and out with no seconds in between.

Her heart pounds harder as the numbers flick slower. She sits on the edge of her seat, quite fidgety. She watches as the attendant walks away from the car to serve another customer. The numbers are still ticking as she spots the driver coming out of the store. With her adrenaline racing, she jumps into the driver's seat and before her butt can land in the seat and her foot can touch the pedal, she slams the gear into drive. She mashes the gas pedal and the tires screech loudly. The gas nozzle is snatched out of the pump as the car speeds away.

The man watches as his car races away. He stands in shock for a few seconds, not able to move. Finally he chases behind the car as Storm is steering out of the station and onto the street. He cuts across the sidewalk as if to cut her off.

She's on a super high right now, laughing to herself as she sees the look on the man's face. Running straight at the car, he draws a gun. She leans to the left, eyes on the road and on him.

Boc! Boc! Boc!

Storm swerves the BMW onto the opposite side of the street and bends the corner, watching in the rearview mirror as the man stands in rage. She speeds up the block like a bat out of hell.

Minutes later, the BMW fishtails through the narrow block, swerving from side to side, barely missing the mirrors and bumpers of the parked cars. Storm slams on the brakes and the car stops short, damn near throwing her through the windshield. She honks the horn like a crazy woman.

In less than a minute, a young girl appears on the porch. This girl is her childhood friend, Latoya, Toy for short. The name Toy fits her perfectly because she looks just like a cute doll baby. She stands at five feet, three inches tall and looks soft, squeezable, and lovable. They are the best of friends, but Storm is secretly jealous and envious of her. Compared to Toy, she feels like an ugly duckling.

Toy doesn't act like a girl who is stuck on herself, but it's Storm and her own insecurities that breed the envy. Toy's flawless yellow skin tone and long silky hair make Storm have more hatred for her own coarse hair and dull complexion. It's not just Toy that she has this deep-rooted hatred for. It's any woman that has those physical attributes. The only difference with Toy is that Storm hides her hatred toward her friend. For the rest of the women who look like Toy, she can't hide the jealousy. She hates them openly.

Storm, for some reason, can't accept that she is just as beautiful as Toy. She can't see it for herself. As beautiful as she is on the outside, it's her dark spirit and nasty attitude that have a way of shining outward and making her look ugly. She accepts her ugly attitude just as she has accepted all of the other flaws that she sees in herself. That doesn't take away her bitterness though. It only enhances it. At just fifteen years of age, she's already a cold bitch.

Toy has one backpack on her back and the other she holds in her hand. She takes her time, prancing prissy-like down the steps. "Hurry the fuck up!" Storm shouts. The way she bosses Toy around, no one would ever know that Toy is older.

Toy picks up her step and trots over to the car. She snatches the door open and plops into the seat. She drops the backpacks onto the backseat before slamming the door shut. "Storm, you is crazy!" Toy shouts with amazement in her eyes. "How the fuck did you pull it off?"

"Girl, I told you I would!" Storm speeds off recklessly. She slams on the brakes inches before banging into the parked car to her left. "We needed a ride and I got us one."

"Let me drive. You gonna kill us in here," Toy suggests.

"I can fucking drive!"

"Bitch, you drive stolen cars."

"And this shit stolen." Storm laughs. "In a matter of minutes, every cop car in Newark and a bunch of niggas gone be looking for us."

"Well, let me drive, so we can get the fuck out of Newark. We got a long way to go!"

Storm doesn't put up any more resistance. She figures that, with Toy having her learner's permit, letting her drive would be best. She gets out of the car and they trade seating positions. Storm presses eject on the CD, which is playing loudly. "Fuck that lovemaking shit!" she says with disgust as she tosses the CD out of the window. She digs into her hoodie pocket, retrieving her own CD, which she slams into the deck. The sound of Clipse's, "Riding around Shining", rips through the speaker. "Watch out, Virginia! Here we come!"

3

VIRGINIA BEACH
SIX HOURS LATER
4:46 P.M.

S TORM AND TOY must have left the rainstorm back home behind them. At around DC, it was like they drove into a different
world. The weather here is beautiful. It's a bright sunny day with
temperatures exceeding ninety degrees.

The traffic here on Atlantic Avenue is bumper to bumper. So
many European cars on both sides of the street that one can easily forget their geographic location and mistakenly think they are
overseas. People pack the sidewalks on both sides, just observing
the car show. A string of motorcycles zip past the still traffic along
the yellow line in the middle of the street.

The group of motorcyclists show off, doing stunts to take the attention away from the exotic cars that fill the block. Camcorders are
rolling as a few men pop wheelies along the entire block. Suddenly
the block is filled with smoke and the smell of burned rubber as two
motorcycles do donuts in the middle of the street. The motorcycle
show lasts for minutes, and the whole street is just one big cloud of
smoke.

The traffic opens up a little, and they are able to now cruise.

"Yo!" a group of males shout out at them.

Storm cuts her eye over and turns away from them as if they are peons to her. Truly this is overwhelming to them because they have never received this much attention ever.

Toy slams on the brakes to avoid hitting the group of men, who are crossing the street in front of them. The young men who are dressed in the flyest attire and gleaming jewelry, are staring into the car. One man stops and locks in on them, very suave and debonair-like. As he passes, he spins around and backpedals slowly with his eyes still glued onto them. He flashes a wink at Toy. "Yo, ma!" he calls out.

Storm watches Toy as her cheeks turn rosy red from blushing. Storm feels as if all the attention is on Toy as usual. She's so tempted to take the wheel just so she can shine. Before she can ask for the wheel, her attention is caught by an oncoming vehicle.

A money green Range Rover approaching on the opposite side of the street forces the men on foot out of the picture. The driver and the passenger sit up in their seats staring into the BMW with baffled expressions on their faces. Storm and Toy try their hardest to hide their desperation by staring straight ahead as if they don't see the men staring at them. The men's necks swivel as they pass.

"Damn! Whole truck on it," Toy says as she watches the Rover in her mirror. The big and awkward truck makes a wild U-turn in the middle of the street, stopping all traffic. "They coming behind us," she says like the giggly little girl she really is.

The Rover causes a scene as it comes behind them against the traffic. Just as the Rover catches up with them, the traffic light turns red. Toy stops the car on a dime. The Rover cuts into the space behind them before zipping around the right side of them. Storm looks up into the truck.

Her sixth sense kicks in and she gets a strange feeling in her gut. As she looks around at the men's faces, she gets the feeling that these men are from home. She can smell the Newark coming out of their pores. Her heart begins to pound as she remembers that the car they are in is stolen.

The driver stares at her through squinted eyes. "Shorty, where y'all from?" he asks.

"It ain't where you from, it's where you at," she replies, thinking quickly on her toes.

"Real slick. Y'all know K-Black?" he asks suspiciously.

Storm's heart skips a beat. "K-Black, who that?" She knows exactly who K-Black is.

"My man from the Bricks. He got a whip just like this."

Toy nudges her discreetly as nervousness spreads over her face. "When they made one, they made more," Storm says slickly.

"Same rims and all," the man says as he studies the wheels closely.

"They say great minds think alike, so your friend must be a great dude."

The light changes and the horns start honking.

"Where y'all say y'all from again?"

"We didn't say," Storm replies. Toy pulls off into the intersection, leaving the Range Rover sitting in the same spot. Storm watches the truck in her mirror. "Shit," she says.

"Yo! We gotta get the fuck outta here," Toy says nervously.

"Calm the fuck down. We ain't going nowhere. We here now. Fuck that!"

A group of girls dressed in skimpy bathing suits step out in front of them, taking their sweet time. Toy stops short to let them cross watching the girls in admiration of how fly they are. Storm, on the other hand, watches with envy. She immediately singles out the one high yellow complexioned girl in the pack and her rage kicks in.

She reaches over and mashes the horn aggressively. The girls ignore the horn and continue prancing slowly. "Fuck outta the way!" she yells into the air. "Run them bitches over," she says loud enough for them to hear. "Acting like they got bumpers on their ass."

The girls continue not paying them the least attention.

Before the group of women are out of the picture, a long line of customized Harley Davidsons creep along the yellow line. The hottest and best designed bike of them all stops short right next to them. The chrome blinds them. Through squinted eyes, they can see the best piece of eye candy they've seen so far. The man on the Harley is as black as the tar on the street. The wife-beater chokes his muscular frame. Tattoos cover his shoulders, back, arms and neck.

The chrome half-helmet exposes his baby face. Bulky platinum jewelry graces his dark skin like a wealthy African king.

He sits still as he revs up the bike, screaming for their attention. All focus is on him and the chopper. The entire bike looks like an all-chrome skeleton. Motorcycle lovers know this to be a hundred-thousand-dollar toy with all the bells and whistles: the rest just know it is a beautiful motorcycle.

They give him the attention that he demands, and when they do, they see his mouth moving but can't hear him over to the sound of their loud music playing. Out of pure habit, Storm pulls her cap low over her eyes just so he doesn't see her hair. She looks at him with her best look of seduction, hoping to snatch his attention away from Toy. She's so used to men falling at Toy's feet and totally ignoring her that she knows she has to go the extra mile to get attention.

With his hand, he signals for them to lower the volume. Both Storm and Toy sit on the edge of their seats, hoping to be chosen. Their desperation, they can't even hide. Suspense fills them both as they wonder which one of them he will choose. "I ain't gon' take too much of y'all time," he says as he flips a card into the car. Just as Toy is reaching for the business card, Storm snatches it out of his hand. *Custom Cycles* is spread across the top of the card. "That's my cell number at the bottom," he says as he looks back and forth into their eyes. "Y'all call me up tonight and see what we can get into. This my city. Let me be y'all tour guide. The whole night on me," he says with charm. He begins popping the throttle as he stares at them seductively. He flashes a wink at them before cruising off.

"Bitch, looks like we just hit the jackpot," Storm says, staring at the fancy business card. Toy rolls her eyes with jealousy, feeling that Storm has stolen him from her. Storm senses Toy's anger, but she ignores it. "Bitch, we at the money! Told you the money was on the road. Fuck Newark niggas. We global now."

4

HOURS LATER

I T'S A BEAUTIFUL night, eighty degrees with a brisk breeze. The chromed out Harley cruises along Virginia Beach Boulevard at a slow pace. The bright blue lights along the Harley's frame illuminate the streets for many blocks. Lights so bright, the bike looks like a carnival ride.

This bike was beautiful in the daytime, but it's twice the beauty in the dark. On the back of the bike, Toy sits with her arms wrapped around the man's chiseled frame, her hands planted on his chest for her own pleasure. A few feet behind the Harley is the convertible Storm drives, one hand on the wheel, the other on her head, sulking in jealousy.

She made the call to the man not an hour after their meeting, not even caring if they came across as desperate. Before they linked up, Toy had already decided to fade to the back, thinking Storm already had him in her web. When they got together, although his conversation was indirect, the way he watched Toy was a clear indication that his interest was in her and not Storm. As much as it bothered her, she never let it be known. She's gotten used to being the third wheel or the last choice when it comes to Toy and a few other girl associates. Even with being used to it, it doesn't take away the bitterness she holds inside.

The Harley slows down and pulls over right in front of a club. The line of people at the door, wraps around the corner. Storm double parks as the man and Toy get off the bike. He turns to Storm in the BMW. "Pull right here on the sidewalk," he commands.

Storm looks around with uncertainty. "You sure?"

"Man, pull that motherfucker right here!" He looks to the people in line. "Yo! Watch out!" he shouts with aggression. A few look at him with hatred, but they all move.

Storm pulls onto the sidewalk awkwardly and is quite embarrassed as one wheel hangs off the curb. She nervously revs up the engine, bringing more attention to herself. Finally, she gets it together and has the car parked in the center of the sidewalk. The line forms around the car.

She gets out and the attention is on her, not just because of the blooper she just made of herself, but because everyone wants to see who the woman is with the BMW with the out-of-town plates. Toy and the man wait for her at the door. He's skipped ahead of the line like the boss he obviously is. As Storm is approaching, she and Toy are wearing the same facial expression. Seeing the bouncer checking identification is a problem because neither of them are even legal.

The three of them stand at the door for minutes before his entourage appears. They are now more than twenty deep. The men chip in their money and come up with over four grand. Toy's date is obviously the treasurer because they forked every bill over to him. Both Toy and Storm notice that he hasn't chipped in a dime for his entrance or theirs. He hands the money over to the bouncer who unloosens the velvet rope for them all to enter.

At the door, a waitress greets them and leads them to the VIP section. With Storm and Toy being the only girls in the entourage of fine men, they feel and are looked upon as royalty. Storm may have lost the man she had her eye on but she has twenty-five more to choose from or rather twenty-five to choose her.

* * *

Hours later, after popping countless bottles of champagne and smoking through a half pound of weed, the entourage called it a night. All twenty-five of the men stand at the entrance of the garage. The sign on the garage reads *Custom Cycles*, which was on the business card that the man gave them. Storm looks to Toy with discomfort as the man fumbles with the keys to go inside the shop. The group of men stand at the door with perversion and desperation in their eyes as they swarm the doorway.

He looks to the group of men, and with a solemn face, he speaks. "It's over, y'all. I'm just gonna hang out with my lil peoples for a little while, and we gonna call it a night."

"Aw! Come on, man," a man sighs from the back. "I thought we all was about to chill. It's still early."

"Nah, it ain't that type of party, y'all. They with me," he says as he holds the door open for Toy and Storm to enter.

"You selfish motherfucker. You always hogging the bitches for yourself," a voice sounds off, causing all the men to fall into laughter.

"Nah, this ain't that," he says as he backs into the garage. Clowning remarks are sent back and forth before he closes the door in their faces. "Please, excuse them," he says like the gentleman that he's been all night. "They act like they never saw two pretty girls before."

Toy blushes from ear to ear as Storm turns away, not impressed by the flattery. They bang on the door for minutes, clowning and refusing to give up.

They walk through the garage, and it's nothing as luxurious as the card seemed. It's a hole in the wall garage filled with old, beat-up motorcycles, motorcycle engines and parts. The smell of motor oil in the air is sickening. He leads them into the back office, which is a lot tidier than the other room.

"Have a seat," he says as he pulls his shirt over his head. He tosses the shirt onto the old and beat up couch in the corner. He walks away giving them a full glimpse of his tatted up back. His wings spread like that of a Silver Back Guerrilla and his traps sit up like shoulder pads.

He opens a file cabinet and pulls out a bottle of Cristal. They are both impressed, especially since they have never tasted Cristal. Hell, tonight is the first night they've tasted champagne. It made them feel quite sophisticated to be sipping champagne, although it was only Moet. They both found it to be disgusting, yet they drank it, just enjoying the moment.

To them, Cristal is the big league because all the rappers speak of it in their songs. Their mouths water at the thought of it. He passes the bottle to Toy like it means nothing to him. "The cups are over there," he says, pointing to a desk.

Toy rushes to the desk to get the cups while the man digs into his pants pocket. He retrieves the Ziploc bag of weed that Storm witnessed him cuff at the club while it was being passed around in plenitude, she caught him cuffing a bag and tucking it into his pocket. She saw him as petty for the act but didn't think much about it.

He rolls blunt after blunt, stuffing them generously while the two of them stand like starving Ethiopian children, sipping cup after cup of the Cristal. Just a few cups and they are already dizzy. After three cups, they realize this champagne is no different from Moet. It's equally as nasty. The thrill is gone. They put the half-filled cups onto the desk and go on over to the couch.

They look at the coffee table where eight blunts are lined up side by side. He crunches the empty Ziploc bag and holds it over his head. He aims it precisely before tossing it at the wastebasket across the room. "Money!" he says as the bag lands into the basket.

Obviously no one has ever shared the golden rule with him when it comes to smoking weed with women because he passes them both a blunt of their own. It's a silent rule among weed smokers to be sparing with the weed when smoking with females because they will huff through all your weed greedily in no time flat. Just as the rule states, they huff and puff on the blunt until the roach burns their fingers. He's never witnessed a blunt disappear so fast. With no hesitation, he passes them another.

In less than thirty minutes, they have evaporated both of the blunts he gave them. He passes them the third one while he nurses the same one he's been puffing on the entire time. The last one he tucks under the magazine on the table, hoping they didn't see it. They immediately light up and get to puffing.

Both of them are more high than they've ever been. The first one had them at their zenith, but they smoked the other two out of greed. They are so high that they can barely lift their hands to put the blunt to their mouths. They sit there in a near-vegetated state, only able to move the arms that hold the hands that hold the blunts. The rest of their bodies, they can't even feel.

The dizziness and the heart palpitations they are experiencing make them feel like they've reached a level of high that they never reached before. They are just happy to be in the twilight zone.

5

THE NEXT MORNING

S TORM WAKES UP groggy-eyed and out of it. The room spins before her eyes as she looks around with unfamiliarity. Her surroundings are just not clicking. She can't remember where she is or how she even got here.

Baffled, Storm looks down and sees her total nakedness. She looks around at the many motorcycles, motorcycle parts, and engines lying around all over the garage. Slowly it all starts to come back to her.

She remembers linking up with the man on the motorcycle last night. Faintly she remembers meeting him here, and while he was supposedly waiting on a phone call, he lit a few blunts for them. Strangely that is where her memory stops serving her. The moistness in between her legs makes her wonder what else has happened that she doesn't remember.

A loud bumping in the next room snaps her attention away from her thoughts. The sound of a whimpering voice can be heard faintly. A female's scream pierces the airwaves. Suddenly, she thinks of Toy and she jumps up from the bed.

She races into the next room where she sees Toy naked and fighting with all of her might. She looks like a crazy woman with her hair messy all over her head. Even with the man's back to her, she can identify him as the man they met here last night. Toy is fighting so hard that she doesn't even notice Storm coming toward her; neither does he. He pins her against the wall as he tries to pry her legs open. "The fuck off me!" Toy cries as she tries to get out of his grip.

Storm looks around for the first thing to grab, and before she realizes, she has a chain with an open padlock on the end of it, gripped tightly in her hand. Toy now notices her, and with her eyes, she begs to be rescued from the madness. Storm swings the chain with all of her might, just as the man turns around to face her. The lock lands in the middle of his forehead, splitting it down the middle.

The blood gushes instantly. Storm swings over and over, not giving him a chance to react. He falls to his knees and she continues swinging the chain relentlessly. She whips him until he falls helplessly onto the floor.

> *"I blacked out and was awakened by the screams of my friend. I had never seen that much blood in my life. I have no clue how long the whipping had been going on. Apparently the whipping evolved into a more intimate beating because when I awakened the chain was wrapped around his neck. Seeing him lying there unconscious and in a bloody pulp did nothing for me but make me want to continue on with the torture."*

"Come on! Let's go!" Toy cries. She runs over to her and jumps into her clothing.

Storm looks around, not sure of her next move. She quickly locates her pile of clothes and gets dressed as well. Toy pulls the BMW keys out of her pocket and races to the door. The thief in Storm leads her over to the man. She digs into his pockets, looking for any money that he may have. No real surprise to her; he's penniless. She takes off running behind Toy.

"*I had no recollection of what took place the night before. After listening to my friend, I was able to gather that we had been slipped something through the marijuana we were smoking. It was quite obvious that he had his way with us sexually without either of our consent. That was all the justification I needed for my action. Before you even ask me, no, I feel no remorse at all. Where I come from, all cross deserves consequences.*"

Storm and Toy stand in the back of the garage. Their eyes popped out of their heads in surprise. The getaway car sits parked on bricks, stripped of the tires and rims. Now here they stand in foreign land, hundreds of miles away from home with a homicide on their hands. Not a dollar in their pockets between the two of them, clueless on how they will make it home.

6

A HOMICIDE BEHIND them, they really have no time waste. Familiarity has guided them back to the beach where all the action is. Today they seem to get less attention than they did when they were cruising the block in the beautiful BMW. They haven't turned not one head since they stepped out here.

They really don't want too much attention. Especially not from anyone who may know that they were the girls who the man left with last night. They know their time is limited. Soon someone may go to the garage and find the man they left soaking in cold blood. Storm has no clue how she is going to get the money to get home, but she knows the clock is ticking.

"I'm going to the bathroom. Keep your eyes open for the money," she says to Toy before stepping across the street. As she's walking, her eyes are scanning the area for a possible dollar. She watches the girls with the huge designer pocketbooks, wondering how much money may be in them. She envisions herself snatching one of the bags and making a run for it. She also envisions herself not making it off of the block before she's caught. She understands snatching it could easily lead to an even bigger charge and she has to count out the idea.

Minutes later, she steps out of the small store, and she spots Toy standing in the same place she left her. The only difference is she standing in the middle of a huddle of guys. Her heart races as she wonders if these are the friends or associates of the man they left in the garage. She has the thought to make a break for it while she has the chance, but she can't fathom the idea of leaving her friend.

She walks fearfully across the street with many thoughts racing through her mind. As she gets closer, she can see smiles on the men's face which, to her, is a good sign. This makes her pick up her step. She gets closer to the huddle, and the attention of the men is diverted to her. The man standing closest to Toy continues talking to her, never once looking at Storm.

"So, you gon' give me the phone number or what, shorty?" the man begs.

Storm thinks quickly and intervenes. "Phone number for what?" she asks coldly.

"I ain't talking to you, ma. I'm talking to her."

"I'm talking to you, though," Storm replies sassy-like. "Later for the small talk. What you trying to do?"

"Huh?" the man asks.

"Ain't nobody got time to waste. Let's get right to the point. You want her?"

"Want her? What you mean by that?" The man looks over to Toy, who looks at Storm more baffled than him.

"I mean what I said. Money talks and the bullshit walks. If you ain't trying to let that money talk, let us walk."

All the men sit back in surprise at her boldness.

"You selling her?" All the men laugh. "You her pimp? Y'all trickin'?"

"Nah, we treating," Storm replies. "What she worth to you? How bad you want her?"

Toy looks at Storm with confusion in her eyes. She's no whore and is furious that Storm would even put her in a situation like this. "You want to get home, right?" she whispers to Toy.

"Tap those pockets and see if three hundred in there and let's stop the bullshitting. Time is money, and if you ain't got the money, we ain't got the time."

"Three hundred?" the man says before laughing in her face. "Ma, I ain't no trick."

"OK, then she ain't no treat. Let's go," she says as she snatches Toy away from the man. As they get a few feet away, the man speaks.

"Yo! Hold up."

Storm stops with aggravation. The man walks over to them. "I ain't got three hundred but I got two-fifty."

"Deal," Storm replies.

"I got a room at the Wyndham. Follow me there."

"Money in my hand first, and we got a deal."

The man forks over the cash, and Storm and Toy follow his lead.

* * *

Two hours later, Storm is sitting in the window seat of a Greyhound bus as it speeds up the highway. Toy sits in the aisle staring into thin air. She feels like a cheap prostitute after selling her body for a bus ticket and two number five McDonald's combo meals. There is no change left over. She's so furious with Storm that she hasn't said a word to her since her pleading. Storm wouldn't take no for an answer. The fear of going to jail for murder was the incentive she used to get Toy to go along with the plan.

> *"It was that day I learned that men would pay for whatever they wanted. I also learned that the value of a woman is the price that she feels she's worth."*

7

TWO YEARS LATER
2008

S TORM SITS IN the office inside of the Mercedes Benz dealership
with an acquaintance of hers sitting by her side. She was forced
to dress up and get rid of her trusty baseball cap to better fit the role.
Being that she couldn't wear the cap, she was forced to wear a wig
that gives her the additional five years she needs to fit the role. She
feels extremely uncomfortable without her security blanket, but at
least, she's not fully exposed. Even with the cheap wig making her
look almost ten years older: She would rather that than her natural
hair being exposed.

Across the desk from them is a well-dressed, middle-aged black
sales representative. He shoves a stack of papers over to Storm. "I
just need you to sign right here," he says. "Here, and here, and here,"
he says as he flicks through the pages.

Storm begins signing her real name out of pure habit before
catching herself. She then signs Danielle Bryant at all the prescribed
places. Whoever Danielle Bryant is, she has no clue that her name
is being attached to a fifty thousand dollar car loan. The twenty-
two-year-old college student just got her license few months ago
and crashed the used car that her parents bought her.

With the loan coming up as paid, her credit is in very good standing. Danielle's information was bought from a salesman at a Toyota dealer. Her acquaintance got that file along with a few more files for a measly five bags of heroin. The man sitting next to Storm is playing the role of Danielle Bryant's father.

"Lastly, Mr. Bryant, as the cosigner, you need to sign here, here, and here."

The man snatches the papers and forges the man's signature to perfection.

"OK, great. Let me just take these back to my manager to over-look and sign off, and I will be back with your keys," he says with a smile. The man exits.

"Told you it would be a piece of cake," the man says when the salesman is out of the room. "Easy money."

Storm's stomach is doing flip flops since she stepped into the dealership. Today she learned that the adrenaline rush that she's grown to love just doesn't come with hard crime. It comes with any aspect of breaking the law.

In minutes the salesman reappears. They both are glad to see the keys jingling in his hand. "Here we go," the salesman says. The man stands up and Storm follows his lead. The salesman hands Storm the keys with a smile. She exhales in relief when the keys are locked into the palm of her hand.

"Congratulations, Danielle! You've just become the owner of your very first luxury automobile. Drive it in good health. Thank your loving father for cosigning for you. Without him, it wouldn't be possible." He looks to the man. "Daddy's little girl. The things we will do for our daughters."

"Yeah, how can you tell them no?" the man replies, hugging Storm around the shoulders. His touch irks her, and it shows on her face.

Two white men appear in the doorway. Suspicion can be read on both of their faces. The salesman looks over to them. "Y'all must be VIP because my manager and the top dog came out to meet y'all," he says with humor. "The top dog don't come out to meet nobody. Mr. Bryant... Danielle, meet the owner of this dealership, Mr. Antonelli."

The old man replies by way of head-nod. Both Storm and her acquaintance reciprocate the head-nod.

They are no fools. When the owner comes out that means something is wrong. The old white man stares at Storm and her acquaintance peculiarly without cracking a smile. He adjusts the lapel on his custom fit pinstripe suit. His diamond pinky ring glistens with every movement of his hand.

The manager speaks. "Danielle, can we just have a copy of your license? Somehow, Mr. Jones forgot to put it on file."

Storm looks to her acquaintance nervously. She's reluctant to give him the phony license because she now knows in her heart something isn't right.

"Give him your license, baby," the man says.

She fumbles in her pocket and retrieves the phony license that the man had made up. She hands it over to the manager reluctantly. Both the manager and the old man study the license closely causing her more nervousness. They both step out of the office with their eyes still glued onto the license.

The air is tense in the office, no one saying a word. She feels like running out of the room before it's too late. Her acquaintance grips her arm because he senses what she's thinking. He starts off small talk to break the tension, and the salesman falls right into his trap. She watches the salesman trying to figure out if he knows something. She can't get a reading though.

Minutes pass and the manager comes back into the office and hands Storm the license. "OK, we're all good now. God bless you and your new vehicle."

Storm finally exhales.

* * *

Hours later, inside the McDonald's parking lot, Storm sits in the passenger's seat of the tinted out convertible Jaguar XK. They watch the E-Class, Mercedes they just got from the dealership cruise off. The man already had a sale for the car. The buyer was a young drug dealer who bought the car for his girlfriend.

It was explained to him that, as long as he kept up on his payments, he would never have a problem. If he made a late payment, whoever Danielle Bryant and her father are will be notified that the payment on their car is behind and the whole deal will blow up in their faces. It was also explained that if he loses the vehicle for late payments, the fault is his own.

The acquaintance sits in the driver's seat, counting through the money he just obtained from the deal. He hands Storm a strife stack of bills, and she looks at it with disgust. "What's this?" she asks.

"A thousand dollars."

"Thousand? You crazy as shit."

"Crazy, why? You made a quick grand for nothing. I did all the work."

"For nothing? My face on that license. Anything come up wrong, it all falls back on me."

"Nothing will come up wrong. The deal is done."

"Nah, fuck that. You giving me more than that. You worked that deal and made eight grand. I ain't taking no thousand," she says as she sits up in her seat. The man can sense her threatening aura.

"All right! I got two thousand for you. I got other people to pay. Gotta pay for the paperwork, check stubs, W2s, DMV, everybody."

"I don't have nothing to do with all that," Storm replies.

She's tempted to snatch the money out of his hand, but she gives him the opportunity to make it right first. The last thing she plans to do is get played in this situation. She's sick and tired of being played by men. Since she's stepped into a life of crime, it seems as if the only role for women is to do the dirty work that men can't get away with. In the end the woman does most of the work and gets the least of the reward or pay. She's fed up with that whole business model.

She stares into his eyes with cold murder bleeding from hers. "Give me three thousand."

"Three thousand," he says with a cheesy smile.

Storm snatches all the money from his hand. She starts to count out what she believes she deserves. He reaches for the money, and they go through a slight tug of war. She allows him to win the tug of war.

She grabs her phone from her lap and begins dialing. "Yo, where the fuck you at, yo?" she says into the phone as if she's really talking to someone. She's bluffing him. She knows that he's nothing but a scammer who wants no friction, so she preys on his weakness. She looks at all male scammers as dudes that are too soft to get into the drug game. She has no respect for them at all. "Yo! Come to McDonald's on Bergen. I got a problem." She pauses as if she's listening to someone on the other end of the phone. "All right. Bet," she says before hanging up the phone.

"Word?" the man asks with nervousness in his eyes.

"Yeah, word. Fuck that. You ain't playing me. I ain't one of them dumb-ass young bitches you can play on. I was willing to take three. Now, I want it all." She peeks around quickly before drawing her old faithful .38 revolver from her waistband. She never leaves home without it.

The man jumps back with fear in his eyes. "Yo! Yo! What the fuck? Yo!"

"Shut the fuck up," she grunts as she aims the gun at his chest. She peeks around to make sure no one is watching. It's so dark out that she believes she can shoot him and get away with it.

He clumsily counts out two more thousand and hands it to her. "Here, here, yo."

"I was willing to take three, but now I want it all for you trying to play me the fuck out." She snatches every dollar from his hand.

The man can't believe he's being housed by her. "Word is bond, yo?" he says in disbelief. "I try to look out for you and put money in your pocket and this how you pay me back?" He tries to pull the sympathy card, but it's not working. "It's all good. Just go. Get out of my car, yo. We can't do more business. I tried to make sure you eat, but you on some other shit."

"Whatever," she says while pushing the door open. "Nobody don't fucking play me," she says as she steps out of the door. "Fuck outta here before I take your car, too!" The man backs up a few feet and catches up with Storm. "Don't think you're getting away with this shit. I'm gonna see you on that."

His threat sends chills through her body. "That's a threat?" she asks as she reaches under her hooded sweater.

"Nah, that's a promise." He notices her reaching for her gun and he speeds off.

She continues on along the busy street. She doesn't take his threat the least bit serious. That doesn't mean he won't have to pay for making the threat, though.

8

THREE MONTHS LATER

A S STORM RIDES in the backseat of the Lincoln Town Car, she
stares through the dark tinted windows, enjoying the beautiful
scenery of Englewood Cliffs. Luxurious homes are spread out along
the blocks, so unlike the rundown neighborhoods she's used to. Her
eyes feast on certain houses, imagining what it must be like to live
in them.

As the driver bends the corner and cruises down the block,
Storm takes a deep breath, preparing herself for what is to come.
The town car slows down before coming to a complete stop at the
lovely two-story mansion in the middle of the block. The home
resembles the White House with huge columns on each side of it.
Bright green shrubbery wraps around it with a beautifully mani-
cured lawn to match.

"Have a great evening," the driver says with sarcasm as if he
knows the deal.

An old man stands in the doorway wearing a satin robe. Mr.
Antonelli, the owner of the Mercedes dealership, is patiently awaiting her. She gets out of the car and makes her way sluggishly toward
the house. Mr. Antonelli waves at the driver, giving him the signal
to leave. Butterflies fill her belly the closer she gets to the house.

He flashes a dazzling smile at her upon her arrival. "Hello, beautiful," he says with charm. She studies his perfect dentures before focusing on the wrinkles in his face. His smoke-gray hair looks as soft and smooth as silk. Even with the wrinkles and gray, he could still pass for a man in his late-fifties and nowhere near his actual age of seventy-three.

He holds his hands out for hers. She gives him a fake smile as she grabs his hands with no real enthusiasm. He leads her inside and closes the door behind them. The sound of Frank Sinatra's voice spills faintly throughout the house, irritating her to no end.

The housekeeper looks Storm up and down, at her tomboy appearance, and disgust covers her face. She walks past Storm and shoots her a cold look before rolling her eyes. "Mr. Antonelli, will that be it for the night?" she asks as if she too knows the deal. Storm is sharp enough to pick up on that, him having young girls over must be the normal. No one seems to be shocked by her being here.

"Yes, that will be it," he replies, "Unless my beautiful guest needs something. Angel, have you eaten?"

"I'm good," she replies in her sassy tone. He calls her Angel, not knowing anything of her real name. He calls her that thinking it's a sweet name for such a sweet girl. She's expressed over and over to him how much she hates when he calls her that but still he does.

"Yes. Well, I guess that will be it. Have a good night."

"You do the same," the housekeeper replies with even more sarcasm then before, making her exit out of the room.

The old man grabs Storm by the hand and leads her through the house. She's disgusted by the feeling of his hardened and wrinkly hands. His boney, skeletal hands disgust her and remind her of how old he is. The smell of his cologne, so young and so vibrant, smacks her in the face like a breath of fresh air. The aroma takes her mind off his age. She slowly wiggles her hands free of his.

He opens the door of the master bedroom and the sound of Beethoven's "Moonlight Sonata" is blaring at full volume. The bright room is almost blinding. It's like a winter wonderland, all white everything. The pure whiteness has an effect. She feels as if she's floating on clouds. Storm takes a deep breath, taking it all in.

This is her fourth time here, and still hasn't gotten used to it. She steps through the plush white carpet, which is as soft and thick as two feet of snow. Elegant lace curtains envelope the canopy bed. It is as big as two eastern king-size beds put together. A tiny staircase sets against the base, which is a foot and a half from the floor. White satin sheets spill over the mattress, dragging the floor.

Storm shivers as she stands in the middle of the room. Her shivering has nothing to do with the winter like aura of the room. The room alone has a cold, eerie feeling, and she knows exactly what it is. There have even been unexplainable events that have taken place while she's been here such as objects falling to the floor, strange noises, and even a mirror cracking down the middle and shattering into many pieces.

The man takes a gulp of the glass of wine that he grabs from his nightstand. He stares at her lustfully as he swallows the remainder. He lays the glass back on the nightstand and then slowly opens his robe, exposing his bare chest and his tiny button sized penis. He wastes no time. He stands there shamelessly for seconds before grabbing her hand and leading her up the staircase to "heaven" as he calls it.

He lays back on the bed, back propped against the oversized headboard. With his eyes, he signals for her to remove her clothes. She lowers her gaze bashfully before pulling her hooded sweater over her head. Her breasts sit up perfectly in her sports bra.

He watches as she climbs onto the bed. The way he looks at her makes her feel quite shameful. She looks away from him as she slides her sweats down. He can't hide his excitement. She kicks her sweats off her leg and moves them toward the bottom of the bed with her foot. She's on her knees in the middle of the bed, with only her bra and boy boxers on. She hasn't removed her cap and has no plans of doing so.

Lust fills the old man's eyes. In a sports bra and boy boxers, she still is the sexiest thing in his eyes. She pulls her bra off and her perfect thirty-eight-Cs bounce vibrantly. Her nipples, tiny as buttons, are like rich-colored droplets. His heart pounds in his chest as she slowly pulls the boxers down. His eyes follow the thin trail of a bush that leads to the forest.

The lower the boxers go, the thicker the forest becomes. The sandy color of her pubic hairs is like the color of fall leaves. He stares at her young, tender body in awe. It's been many decades since he's witnessed a body so young and flawless. His heart bangs through his chest as she stands up and steps out of the boxers. Without the boxers and sports bra, he now sees all woman, with curvaceous hips, and juicy succulent thighs. He looks upward at her, getting a full glimpse of her breasts. Their eyes lock in between her nipples which are aimed at the wall like missiles.

"It wasn't all his fault. He had no idea that I had just turned eighteen. The phony license I had stated that I was twenty-two. When he called me days after we left the dealership, I thought for sure he was calling because he was on to us, but that wasn't what his call was about. He stated that he wanted me to come over to the dealership. I was hesitant at first, thinking it was a setup for me to be arrested. When I denied, he expressed to me that he knew all about the fake paperwork that we had presented. He stated that he didn't care because it was the bank's problem and not his. He discreetly made the threat that if I didn't meet with him he would report us. Once I met up with him, he explained to me how I shouldn't involve myself in such nonsense and told me how I deserve more in life than what criminals offer.

"He told me that he had bigger plans for me. I was in no way as naive as he may have thought. I knew all about what plans he had for me. Just like he was planning to use me, I was planning to use him. The first month or so, we only indulged in phone conversation and dinner dates here and there.

"It was like free money. It was like he was paying me for my time. Before even touching me, he would give me fifteen hundred a week. By the time we had any physical contact, I was already nine grand into his pocket. Then it was time for him to cash in on his investment. I was invited to his home, and he explained to me how he has needs and demands and he only expects me once a twice or month. It still wasn't as bad as it seems because all he ever wants to do is to drink from my 'fountain of youth,' as he calls it."

The old man lays flat on the bed as Storm sits on his face. He eats from her box like it's a gourmet meal. She braces herself by holding onto the throne-shaped headboard. Many mixed emotions occupy her, preventing her from experiencing any pleasure.

She sees it all as business which helps her erase the guilt and disgust that she feels. The creepiness that she feels at allowing such an old man to touch her in this way is something that she can't get past. It's gotten easier for her since their first intimate encounter, but still it's tough. She closes her eyes and just pictures money and it all makes sense to her.

As she blocks out all the thoughts and lets herself go, she finds pleasure in it all. She loosens her grip on the headboard, allowing herself to rest totally on his face. The weight of her body suffocates him and he enjoys every pound of her. With very little sexual experience under her belt, she doesn't know what it is she should be doing up here while he's doing what he does. She just sits there, feeling awkward.

He hits a high note, and her eyes pop open with pleasure. Upon her eyes opening, they land on the portrait of an older woman whose eyes appear to be looking right at her. She tries to look away, but the woman's eyes have hers magnetized. Guilt overpowers her, causing her to look away. She looks to her left and to her right and she can't shake the woman because her pictures are posted all over the wall.

"The guilt was overbearing at times, but I managed to appeal to his demands. It all was strange to me, but I eventually got used to it. He had a weird fetish that I never really tried to understand. His wife had died in his home, in that very bed a few years earlier. His fetish was to have me in the bed that they shared together, and he wouldn't have it any other way. It was as if she was watching every second of it, and in the beginning of our arrangement, it was hard for me to deal, but as time went on, it started to excite me, just as it did him. The cold eerie feeling of death was always in the air, and strangely enough I grew to love it. It turned me on!"

Her body tenses up like a stiff board. With very little control of herself, she fights to lift her body up. She stares down into his eyes as he awaits her impatiently. This is his favorite part. He looks up at her with anticipation in his eyes.

"Yes, my angel, give it to me," he begs.

With no further warning, she squirts in his face. "Nasty, old pervert," she mumbles under her breath as her box sprays the clear, sparkling shower.

He closes his eyes tight as he allows her juices to shower his whole face, taking his breath away. She stands up in the bed as the last of it spills from her. Sprinkles drop onto his mouth and he swipes them with his tongue, mindful not to miss a drop.

He watches with great satisfaction as she shivers. This is the only time he sees her lose control of herself and he looks forward to it. Any other time, she's so tough and firm. During this time, he sees her give up her power to him and he loves it. It's that power that she hates to give up which is why she fights so hard to control it.

Storm stands over him as she regains composure. Anger quickly replaces the pleasure as she faces that she has again, given up her power to him. She feels transparent to him right now and hates that he's seen her so vulnerable. The few sexual experiences she's had she's managed to retain control of herself. Her vulnerable state is never exposed. Mr. Antonelli is the first man that she's allowed herself to let go with. The only reason she lets go is because she's paid to do so.

"Over four times my age and, although the average person would frown upon it, I appreciated him. I learned so much from him. Most of our time together was spent talking. We talked about everything — life, business, relationships, and everything in between. It was like he was a father figure more than anything, as weird as that may sound. One of the most valuable things that I learned from him was that sex ruled the world.

"Before him, I had a few sexual relationships that really meant nothing to me. It was always for the gain or benefit of the man and I got nothing from it. I did it solely for them with no enjoyment of my own. With him, it was different. Although it was for his own selfish gain, he made me feel like he cared whether I enjoyed myself or not. He did everything in his power to satisfy me.

"Before him, I saw my squirting condition as a disease or a curse. I always felt like a freak of nature and was ashamed any time it happened. It was him who taught me that I had the magical fountain of youth, and just like he was willing to pay any amount to drink from it, I knew there would be so many others who would be willing to do the same.

"Never in a million years did I expect the business arrangement with the old man to last for so many years. In my mind, he was sucking me dry of my youth, and I was merely trying to suck him dry for every dollar I could get out of him. Years flew by but I never lost sight of it all. To me, he was still just a dirty old perverted man. At least I had to tell myself that just so I wouldn't catch feelings for him.

"For the next few years, life as I knew it changed right before my eyes. The lifestyles of reality television housewives and ex-wives of basketball players; I was living just like them, if not better. Expensive cars, jewelry, and clothes from designers whose names I couldn't spell. I had it all.

"What I appreciated the most, of all the gifts the old man provided me, were the vacations. A local, neighborhood girl who rarely left the city growing up as a child now had the chance to see the world. For years, I was content with doing all the things I dreamed of doing. He did everything in his power to keep my mind occupied and me entertained.

"He could never keep my full attention though because, even with all the places I traveled, my heart and soul was always in the hood. In between trips and everything else he had to give, I always found myself in the middle of some type of madness. It was like I couldn't help myself. I was always searching for that rush.

"Although he would give me any and everything I desired, I've always been the type to get out and earn my own money. I could never see myself depending solely on a man, an old man at that, who may not even be around in the next year or so. For those two reasons, I always stayed in the hood and on my grind. He was my ace in the hole, but I always hustled and made my own moves like I didn't have him."

9

INDIANAPOLIS
FOUR YEARS LATER
FEBRUARY 5, 2012

IT'S SUPER BOWL weekend, and Storm arrived this afternoon. She's here for the New York Giants versus New England Patriots game. Having the old man, Mr. Antonelli as her lover has many perks. He worked his magic to make this trip possible. It was hard getting flights here the last minute. The actual game attendance and the short notice flights are just half of the strings he pulled.

Not only was she granted the privilege of this experience, but so were Toy and another friend. Mr. Antonelli gave Storm no hassle at all. She merely told him how badly she wanted to attend the Super Bowl, and he pulled his juice card to make it happen. Earlier today the three girls were granted entrance to the NFL Awards Ceremony, sitting front row with the many celebrities.

Sitting among the many actors, models, and singers, they were treated like royalty. No one knew who they were but knew they had to be part of the elite to be there. They played the role and fit right on in. Being around all the money put them in the right position to make some.

Storm, not being a fan of football or any other sport, sees the event for one purpose. Toy, on the other hand, is ecstatic to be here to witness her favorite team in the Super Bowl. It goes without saying that she has work to do to repay Storm for the free ride. She's wise enough to know that nothing in life is free and she looks at the trip as business with the perks of personal enjoyment.

This evening she got off to a great start by raking in a few grand already with a client she met at the ceremony. She's come a long way since the first time she ever tricked in Virginia Beach. As much as she hated it at that time, she learned a lesson from it. Since that day, she has been making men pay like they weigh. She has Storm to thank for her game, so anytime Storm calls on her to make a move she's down.

Thanks to Mr. Antonelli, Storm is no newbie to travel. Being away from home is nothing new to her. Before him, she was just a local girl, but now she considers herself international. In the four years they've been together, she has had the pleasure of visiting five countries, including seven different islands. She's so addicted to travel that she gets sick if she's home for too long. Of all the places he's taken her, the trip to Paris last year was her favorite. Not only has he enhanced her passport, he's enhanced her quality of life.

Right now they are at the official after-party for the awards ceremony. Any and everybody who is somebody is in attendance. The celebrities have stripped themselves of the formal attire they wore to the ceremony and all are dressed in something more comfortable. Storm and the crew not only fit in but outshine most of the celebrities, getting much attention.

Storm is the most modestly dressed of the three, not exposing her body at all. Both her friends are scantily dressed in designer dresses and stilettos. She's dressed quite casually compared to them but still her appearance demands attention. She's wearing simple jeans and a T-shirt under her three-quarter chinchilla coat.

She has more diamonds on than the biggest celebrity in the building. The pink faced Presidential Rolex on her wrist and the diamond fluttered Wonder Woman bracelet are her most noticeable pieces for the ghetto eye. Those pieces were bought for her at her own request. The classier pieces, such as the flawless diamond pendant necklace, princess-cut earrings to match as well as the subtle but prestigious diamond rings, were all the choice of the old man.

Coming from nothing she just has to have certain things to get them out of her system, but he's persistent about showing her how to appreciate the finer things in life. Over the years, he's built her layer by layer and has shown her some things that she never imagined seeing. Although she has gained some love for him, she still doesn't call him her man. She forces herself to keep looking at it like a business situation, even when he makes it seem like more.

Storm funded her friends' attire from head to toe. In total, she's spent a few grand just to have them looking presentable for this weekend's festivities. She's sure she will make her money back a few times over, so she sees it as a small investment. She charges it all off as a business expense. She plans to, at least, triple her earnings before the weekend is done.

Storm sits at the center of the table, wearing a long, silky black wig that shows no trace of her hair. Over the years, she has done away with the baseball cap and replaced it with the wig that now acts as her security blanket. Her attention is locked on the table directly across from them. A beautiful waitress steps over to the table with yet another bottle of champagne. "This is from the gentleman over in the corner with the yellow shirt on," the waitress states as she points to the corner of the room.

The man gives them a nonchalant head-nod. The waitress sets the bottle right next to the other five that they have collected since they got here. As the waitress steps away, Storm makes a quick assessment of the man. She studies him carefully. With the extensive jewelry that he has on, *he could easily be a rapper or a ball player*, she thinks to herself. That is until he stands up and reveals his height of about five feet five inches tall. His height to weight ratio counts him out as a ball player. She also gets a close enough glimpse of his face to know that he's not a famous rapper. She quickly charges him off as another drug dealer in the building.

"He's kind of cute," Toy admits.

"Drug dealers come a dime a dozen," Storm replies not, even looking her way. She has nothing against drug dealers, but she's been carefully avoiding them all night. Their money spends just as the celebrities' money, but tonight she's in search of a bigger catch. Besides, the drug dealers come with too many headaches. They all want something for nothing, and their big egos from being the biggest man in their little cities make them hard to deal with. They feel like the woman should be honored to be with them.

Storm slams her glass of cranberry juice onto the table. "Time to make magic," she says as she cheers the women on. "The pot of gold at the end of the rainbow is right over there," she says as she points to the table where a few football players are. "Toy, you set it off since Wendy on that shy shit. Warm them up, and she will follow up."

Wendy is the newest addition to the team. She stands in height, right between Storm and Toy. She wears her hair in long *Poetic Justice* braids. She's not what Storm considers high yellow, but more of a redbone. She despises those as well.

Wendy is a cute, chunky cheeked girl with big dimples in both aspects. The cheeks on her face are pinch-able, but the cheeks on her rear just make a man want to grab as much in his hand as he possibly can. Her big, soft rear is uncontainable, no matter what jeans she wears. Her small boobs and waistline explode into a huge rear with equally thick legs, making her top and bottom look mismatched.

This is Wendy's first time attending an event with them, and she has butterflies. Her nervousness has nothing to do with trading sex for money because she's no stranger to that. She is new to getting paid what she's worth though. She's been getting cheated in the hood ever since she first became sexually active, giving up her goods to small time drug dealers only for them to shortchange her in the end and not give her a dime. She just ends up getting promised love while only getting used for her sex and her body. Storm promised her that those days are long behind her now.

Toy gets up with no hesitation. She smooths her dress over her curves and admires how the dress is fitting her. She turns around with her ass facing Storm and Wendy. "What this ass looking like?" she asks with a smile on her face.

The dress clings to her butt which looks like two bowling balls. A deep wedgie cuts right through the middle like an ax. Toy pinches the silky material and pulls the wedgie out. She spreads the dress over her cheeks smoothly.

"Looking like money," Storm replies, further boosting her confidence.

"Enough said," Toy says as she steps away from them. She glides across the room elegantly. All motion at the table freezes as she approaches them. They all look her up and down in a trancelike state.

She can't imagine what Toy's opening line must have been, but whatever it was, they opened up their circle and let her right in. She entertains the group of men like a seasoned vet. They are laughing their heads off as she controls the group. It's evident to Storm that the Ecstasy pill Toy consumed a few minutes ago has kicked in because she can tell the difference in her swagger. On E, she's super aggressive and confident.

Storm looks to Wendy. "Go on over and back her up. She's got them right where y'all need them."

Wendy has taken a pill as well, but has a total different effect on her than Toy. Right now she seems to be more dizzy than she normally is. As beautiful as she is, she's as dumb as a doorknob. All beauty with no brains.

Wendy gets up nervously. When she was back in Jersey, she was all in but now that they are here she has cold feet. Storm hates to throw Wendy out there with the sharks, but she feels experience is the best teacher. Instead of working her up to this, she's giving her a crash course.

"What to say though?" she asks in her most naive state as she fiddles with her.

"Fuck you mean, what to say? You scared of niggas now?" Storm asks with frustration.

"I mean, these ain't no regular niggas though," says Wendy. "These niggas multimillionaires."

"What the fuck that mean? All niggas is the same whether rich or poor. They dumb as shit and think with their dicks," Storm explains. "If anything, these niggas easier marks than the broke frontin'-ass niggas back at home. These niggas just started getting pussy once they got drafted. Before that they were a bunch of no game having, no pussy getting, ball players. Just think of the ugly ass goofy ball players that went to your high school."

A spark brightens up Wendy's eyes. Storm continues on, realizing that the girl gets her drift. "Yeah, now look over there. Them are the same ugly goofy football jocks you went to school with. Underneath all them diamonds and money, they still the same corny ass niggas. You can run circles around them and cash the fuck out. They easy, like taking candy from a baby."

Wendy takes a deep breath of confidence. Storm's speech has her motivated. She gives herself a once over to make sure she looks proper. She snatches her glass from the table and turns it up to her mouth. She guzzles it until it's empty. She slams the glass onto the table and steps off without saying another word. Wendy walks away with her signature stank walk. In the hood, men equate the pigeon-toed, wagon dragging switch with good pussy.

"Wendy!" Storm calls out. The girl turns around abruptly. "Make 'em pay like they weigh. Remember… These niggas loaded. Don't shortchange yourself."

Wendy nods her head with a false sense of confidence. As she walks, she gets a boost of encouragement and it can be seen in her bop. Her walk gets even stanker.

* * *

Hours later, the hotel room is a mess. The nightstands all turned over, lamps knocked onto the floor, and the sheets are off the bed. The room looks like a hurricane has hit it. The wreck is the result of a sexual disaster. Fresh out of the gate, Wendy's very first tricking job and she runs into this — a serious situation.

It's a great thing that Wendy isn't afraid of heights because the six foot, six inch, husky man has her in the air, upside down. Her legs are wrapped around his neck, clasped at the ankles for security. He grips her butt tightly as he feasts away on her twat, sucking and slurping like a hog. She bear hugs him around the waist for her reinforcement while she blows him like a trumpet, or more like a long saxophone.

The lack of condom is due to the extra few dollars he paid her. Foolishly she allowed the man to let him go raw. She gave him her price of two grand, and he asked how much would it cost to go bareback. She suggested an extra five hundred, but they settled at three.

Right now she's giving him the best mouth job he's ever had. He's not sure if the upside down effect is making the head that much more incredible or if her mouth is just that lethal. He refuses to allow her to out-mouth him. They seek to outdo each other. The more she pleases him, the more he pleases her. The blood rushing to her head from being upside down gives her a sexual rush that she's never felt. She's dizzy but still she continues on.

She holds back the orgasm that she feels brewing. She realizes she shouldn't be enjoying this so much, but she can't help it. She refuses to reach an orgasm before he does. She expected this to be easy money, but this man obviously had other plans. He's making her work for the money. She's already exploded four times to his none. She put it in her mind that this is business and she shouldn't be enjoying it, but he's making that impossible. He's fucked her so well that she almost feels bad that she's charging him.

She has to block out the pleasure just to be able to focus on pleasing him. She tries to ignore the pleasure that he's bringing to her body and soul, but his long tongue lashing makes it hard to do. He makes her lose sight of her mission as he sucks on her love button. His nose teasing the rim of her back door drives her crazy.

Before she knows it, she's in the middle of busting another one, making the score five to zero. She freezes in motion as cum oozes out of her. The taste of her juices excites him and he sucks her opening like a Hoover vacuum cleaner. His jaws cave inward as he cleans her out.

She regains her composure and gets back to work. She blows harder and harder on his rod with hopes of finishing him off but lockjaw takes place before she does so. She's blown so hard that her lips are numb. She's just about ready to throw in the towel when she feels his knees buckle, making her realize that she's found his spot.

She twirls her tongue around his tip, tongue kissing it while blowing it. She's quite talented. She blows harder and harder, pecking at him like a woodpecker. She long necks him and teases him but to no avail. Suddenly she hits that spot again, causing him to stagger. He backpedals, holding her tightly.

She continues on with determination. His feet cross and… timber. They tilt over and she holds onto his waist for dear life. They collapse onto the floor. She hops up before him and straddles herself over him in a riding position. Her pussy passes air as the last glob of her cum escapes it. It lands on his leg, melting through the skin like hot lava.

She feels that she finally has him where she needs him, and she refuses to give him a minute to gather himself. She mounts herself on top of him, hand on his chest to control her intake of him. She inserts him and gets to bucking like a wild horse from the very first stroke. He wraps his hands around her waist, holding her tightly as she bounces up and down on him. He grips her waist tightly. His index fingers sink into the dimples that set over top of her cheeks, as if the dimples were made for this reason.

She winds her hips like a belly dancer, teasing him. His eyes roll up into his head. She finds satisfaction in believing that he's almost there. She bounces that much harder.

"Got damn, girl," he says as he tries to push her off him. He's not ready for it to end. He feels he has yet to get his money worth. She slaps his hands off her as she continues to ride away. She's come too far to let him get away now. "Damn," he mumbles. "Shit," he growls. "Got damn, girl," he grunts before he uses all of his strength to throw her off of him.

She lands on her stomach, and he crawls behind her. She attempts to crawl away from him. "Don't run from me," he says in a threatening tone. "If you run," he says as he catches her by her braids. He yanks a handful of the braids and wraps them around his knuckles. He gives her one good yanking, snapping her head backward.

With her head tilted, on all fours, she looks like a track star at the starting line, waiting for the sound of the starter pistol. With a clear shot, he drives himself straight into her with great precision and accuracy. The deep, impactful stroke lifts her off the floor. Upon penetration, he begins wailing on her, giving her all of him. He digs deep as he yanks her braids with each stroke. Wendy screams at the top of her lungs as he drops all the dick that he has into her. The sound of his balls clapping against her dripping wet pussy echoes throughout the room.

She tries to hold in her screams, to keep him from knowing he's hurting her, but the screams of pleasure override the screams of agony. He pounds and wails with no compassion, getting all of his money's worth. With him still gripping a fistful of braids, he wraps his other arms up underneath her belly, so she can't escape his wrath. He drives himself deeper into her. With short and fast rabbit strokes he bangs her walls up.

Her pussy lips are already swollen and numb, and now he's doing a demolition job on her walls as if he's trying to knock them down. She tries to run from him, but he just holds her tighter. His body trembles, and she knows what is about to take place. She holds her breath and blocks out the pain to finish him off.

As he tries to back away and delay his orgasm, she backs it up on him, ramming herself onto him. The sound of her cheeks clapping against him drowns out the sound of her moaning. Her huge ass flaps, one cheek at a time like a big and beautiful butterfly flying in the air. He grips her cheeks and spreads them wide enough to bust at the seam. With no mercy at all, he pounds, straight up the middle hitting, the g-spot relentlessly. The pleasure he brings to her g-spot is worth all the pain that he delivers. She holds her breath and endures the pain, hoping to get it over with.

He growls like a ferocious lion before his whole body freezes. She hops off of him with expertise before he can ejaculate in her. In the past, she's practiced this move so much that she's become a professional at it. She prays that her vaginal sponge is working properly because she's sure he's left a trace in her. His pullout game definitely needs work.

The sound of his toes popping makes her laugh. She giggles as she pushes him off of her. He falls over with no fight. He experiences temporary paralysis, just able to move his eyes. He gasps as he tries hard to get it together.

Wendy sighs, just grateful that it's finally over. She gets right up, walking over to her pile of clothes and belongings. Although this would be the perfect moment for cuddling after the great job he's done on her, she realizes this is business. She also realizes that she has other money to get to and has wasted too much time with him already. Midway through the room, she notices the limp in her walk that tells her the man has done more damage than she realized. She looks down at her swollen lips, which seem to be pulsating and panting for air.

She slips into her thong, and as she makes her way past him on her way to the bathroom, he speaks. "Where you going? That was round one. Round two is in about five minutes. Just let me get myself together."

Oh, hell no! she thinks to herself.

"You only paid for one round. I was being nice by letting you go that long."

"You said one round. That was one round," he says.

"Yeah, and you paid for one round."

"OK, I will pay for two rounds. The money ain't nothing," he says arrogantly. "I got more money than I got dick. Long money, long dick." He smiles. "Now let's get on to round two."

Wendy is ready to submit, but for some reason, she doesn't. Maybe it's the pleasure he's brought her that has her willing to put up with the abuse again. She knows she has a long night ahead of her. She realizes that she won't be any good for anyone else tonight, so she has to up the price to make it all worth her while.

"You gon' have to dig a little deeper into them long pockets for a round two," she says, hoping that he denies, so they can end on that note. "You take too fucking long to bust." She stands with her hands on her hips, and her pigeon toes meeting.

"I told you the money ain't nothing. Name your price." He looks her up and down, enjoying the view. Her ass in the tiny thong looks like a can of Hungry Jack biscuits that have busted open, fluffy dough, spilling over the sides. He gets a chubby in record breaking time. She looks down and sees his wood growing before her eyes.

"Damn," she mumbles to herself. "Back to work."

10

LUCAS BOWL STADIUM
THE NEXT NIGHT
SUPER BOWL SUNDAY

WITHOUT MR. ANTONELLI, the girls would have been lucky to get even nosebleed seats; instead they have the best seats in the whole stadium. Storm and the crew sit in the comfort of the luxury box, right at the fifty-yard line. She's not sure what it costed him to make it all possible, but what she does know is with her not spending a dime out of pocket, everything her girls score is all profit.

In the luxury box with them are about sixty other people, not including the bartenders, waiters and other staff. Most of the people have their eyes glued onto the game, but clearly a few of them have no real interest in it. They are merely here for the partying and the experience. Bottles of champagne flow in abundance and the smell of money is in the air.

Storm heard from ear hustling that the cheapest ticket for the box today is eight grand and that is if you had a hookup or paid well in advance. The latecomers could have easily paid double and some. With that type of money spent on tickets, she's sure there is a lot more where that came from, and she plans to get it all.

Storm and the crew sit in the far end of the room, just enjoying the view of the city through the all glass panels. Her girls are sipping mixed drinks while she sips orange juice. She never drinks while working. Just as they are engaging in people watching and chitter chatter, a young woman approaches their table.

They all stare at her wondering her purpose for being in their space. They look her over from head to toe and what they all see is "cheap." Her jacked up weave, cheesy hooker looking outfit, and no-frills shoes make them all wonder how she even got in here. She opens her mouth to speak and her twisted, yellow teeth disgust them.

"My Daddy wanna speak with y'all," she says with evident attitude.

Storm looks at her like she has three heads. "Excuse me?"

She points across the room as an obese man is making his way toward them. He stands at about six foot two inches tall with a Barney cartoon character body, all hips. His aura has Storm irritated with him before he gets near her. His cocky swagger doesn't fit the corny clothing that he has on.

He's overdoing it with the excess of bold labels. Printed Gucci sneakers, printed Gucci pants, printed hat and bulky jewelry make him look like the poster boy for a counterfeit clothing stand. Storm spots his Breitling watch with the overload of diamonds from across the room, fluttered face, fluttered bezel and even bracelet. His watch fits his outfit perfectly. *So typical for a nigga who just started getting money*, she thinks.

Upon his arrival, with a snap of his hand, he sends his messenger away from the table. He stares at them one by one before speaking. Storm is already disgusted with him. "Why are you over here?"

Shocked at her response to him, he just looks at her with venom bleeding from his eyes. "Who y'all with?" he asks. "Where y'all representation at? I ain't into talking to bitches?"

"What?" Storm asks.

"I said who y'all with? I been seeing y'all making a lotta moves since y'all been here, and I ain't been notified of y'all's presence. Don't nothing or nobody move without me greenlighting it."

"Fuck is you?" Storm barks. Her girls all laugh in his face.

He's infuriated, yet he covers it with a fake smile. "Oh, you don't know? That obviously means you ain't nobody. I'm Johnny Cash. All the hoes in this spot is mine. We the only thing moving at this event."

Storm stands up with rage and her girls follow. "Fuck you calling hoes, first off?" she asks as she makes her way around the table to him. She steps right into his chest. "Second, you ain't nobody to know in my world. You watch your fucking mouth talking to me," she says, staring up into his eyes.

He's enraged that she stands up to him like this. This is something that he's not used to. He's used to women moving at his command. The disrespect he feels shows on his face.

Toy steps in between Storm and the man, with her back facing Storm. She pushes the man away. He slaps her hands off him. "Hoe, don't you fucking touch me."

Storm tries to get around Toy to get at the man. Wendy restrains her as best she can. He lifts his hand as if he's thinking of backslapping Storm. "Nigga, I wish the fuck you would," she says not even flinching. Storm is so mad that she's now foaming at the mouth. "You fucking with a bitch that will take your fucking life. You better take your ass back over there with them dirty dog ass bitches you got."

In seconds, his stable of ten young women have Storm and her crew surrounded. They appear to be ready for war. They step up to his defense and Storm becomes more enraged. "You dirty bitches will die taking up for this goofy ass nigga. Better stay in your fucking lane." She looks to the pimp. "Better put some muzzles on them ugly ass dogs."

Security appears, breaking up the chaos. "Hey! Hey!" the suit-wearing security guard says. "What's the problem?"

"He's the problem," Toy says, believing the security would be on their side being that they are the victims of this matter. Shockingly, to her, the security is aggressive toward them. Johnny Cash whispers to one of the security guards and he walks over to Storm.

"Ladies, I'm gonna have to ask y'all to leave the premises."

She loses it. "What?"

"Evacuate the premises, or we will evacuate you."

Johnny Cash smiles as if he's had the last laugh. It's obvious that he has them in his pocket and they can't win. Storm hesitantly grabs her belongings from the table, and Toy and Wendy do the same. Before walking away, Storm turns a table over. She looks over at Johnny Cash. "You just fucked up, and you too stupid to even know it."

They make their way to the exit, and Storm turns around to give him one more long glare. She nods her head up and down and all he does is smile which makes her angrier.

11

NEW ORLEANS
THE NEXT NIGHT

S TORM STANDS AT the foot of the bed while Toy and Wendy
stand on opposite sides. Stacks of money are spread out evenly
over the bed. Even though they were thrown out of the luxury box
last night not able to score a dime there, they still were able to make
a few dollars at the after-party. Although they made a profit, Storm
is pissed because they made nowhere near what she predicted. She
has Johnny Cash to blame and every thought of repaying him for
what he's done. She prays that wasn't their last time seeing each
other.

Storm takes her cut from both of the girls' money and gives them
the rest. Toy being the biggest earner of the weekend scored close
to twelve grand, while Wendy only scored about five. Both giving
Storm half of their earnings gives Storm a profit of eighty-five hundred. A hefty score for a woman who had to do nothing for it.

Storm got wind that a good number of people from the Super
Bowl were making their way here to New Orleans for Mardi Gras
and decided to make a detour. They had their flights switched and
arrived here a couple of hours ago. She figured they lost out on the
big money in Indianapolis, so maybe they could even the score here.

As they made their way through the city, looking for a hotel, which was almost impossible, they noticed the influx of people. In her mind, all she saw was dollar signs.

* * *

Hours later, they are on Bourbon Street. It is packed with people, a great deal of them dressed in costumes. It's raining but in no way are they allowing the rain to dampen their parade. Drunkards stagger and some lay out, sprawled in the middle of the street while people walk past them as if it's normal. The drink responsible for the drunken bodies on the street is the infamous Hand Grenade. The Hand Grenade is the most powerful drink in all of New Orleans.

The smell of the spilled alcohol, mixed with the throw up that covers the streets and sidewalks is stomach turning but faint compared to the smell of horse shit in the air. Police patrol the areas on horses. Every few steps are mounds of horse droppings and beautiful broken beads. The beads seem to hold more value than currency during the Mardi Gras. Storm and the girls watch in awe as women flash their breast in return for beads. They've never seen anything like it.

Storm, with her trained eye, can spot the prostitutes throughout the crowd, even though they are camouflaged. Dressed in their revealing outfits and the excessive amount of make-up painted on their faces, they almost look like the women dressed in costume. They may have the many police that are patrolling the area fooled, but she knows a working girl when she sees one. She finds the prostitutes to be quite tacky and cheap. They also seem to be high off of drugs, or drunk, or both.

Up ahead, a huge group of people are lined up along the curb, all staring up at the balcony of a row house. The people are yelling and cheering. Storm leads the way over to see what all the hype is about. When they get there, three women are flashing their boobs at the onlookers.

They put on a show as they dance seductively and tongue kiss each other. They are staggering, obviously drunk. Even police are in the crowd, enjoying the show. It's not long before the women are completely naked and humping each other sexily. They put on a ten-minute show before they end it. The crowd screams in disappointment, wanting more.

Storm and the girls wander until they end up in a small run-down bar in the French Quarter. In observance of the bar, they notice nothing but drunk trailer trash and hillbillies. They also see a few prostitutes sprinkled throughout, getting very little attention. Surprisingly to them, the attention is on the many homo-thugs that prance around. They are half-dressed, some have their shirts tied up in a knot, showing their stomachs, and others are dressed in miniskirts. They are in disbelief at how the men are receiving them. They are touching and kissing and doing everything except actual man-on-man penetration.

Storm quickly realizes that they are obviously fighting a losing battle here. "Ain't no money in here for us. We ain't what they in the mood for." Her phone rings, interrupting her. She looks at the display, and her heart beats with anticipation. She answers it immediately. "Yo?"

"Storm," the man yells with excitement. "It's time. Everything lined up and ready to go. Where you at?"

"I'm on the road right now."

"Well, you need to get here ASAP!"

This call is the perfect antidote for such a waste of a trip. Something that she has been working on for months has obviously manifested itself. "I will hit you soon as I touch!" she says before ending the call. She looks to the girls. "We out!" she says before scurrying out of the bar. She's on to better things.

12

NEWARK
DAYS LATER

THREE MEN SIT at a kitchen table, packing cocaine into tiny vials. In front of them at the center of the table is a kilo, which barely has been touched, a digital scale, and plates with mounds of cocaine and razor blades.

"It was the perfect setup. In my later teenage years, the only way I knew how to get what I wanted was by using my body and my beauty. By this time, I had learned to use my brains. I put together a master-plan. With the help of two accomplices, the plan was executed flawlessly. I was always used as the eye candy to reel the men in, so I knew enough of about that game to coach someone else through it. Like a ventriloquist, I told this young woman all the right things to say and do to catch our mark. Our mark was the lieutenant of one of the biggest drug dealers in the city."

In no way is Storm pressed for cash. Her business with the girls keeps her pockets lined, coupled with the fact that the old man gives her more than she could possibly ask for. Her being involved with robbery isn't about business. It's about the rush.

She could easily sit back and let the old man take care of her, but that would be too easy and boring. Storm tried that for a while, and she was miserable. It's the allure of a criminal lifestyle that keeps her alive. She can't even make sense of why she always has to be in the middle of the action, but she does.

She could've easily let this vick go, but the rush wouldn't allow her to. She's been working on this for weeks. In no way could Storm let all her weeks of work go in vain. It was show time.

The occupants of the kitchen all lie face down with their hands on the back of their heads. Storm stands over them with a ski-mask covering her face. A gunman stands next to a woman sitting on the floor in the corner, holding an infant in her arms. It's evident that the baby senses something because he's been crying for minutes.

"You better shut that baby up," the gunman commands. He places the gun onto the top of the woman's head. Her mouth is gagged by a T-shirt so she can't say a word to soothe her baby. Instead she holds the infant tightly as she rocks back and forth with nervousness. Tears of fear trickle down her face.

"We had the work and all the valuables that we could find, but for some reason that wasn't enough for me. I could feel the fear in the room, and that only urged me to instill more of it. It turned me on."

The man in the center of the room looks up into Storm's eyes. His rage is intensified because he knows it's a woman under the mask, yet he knows she means business "Please, please don't put my lady through this. I gave y'all everything already."

"But it wasn't just about money. It was enjoyment."

Storm kneels over the man and starts to pistol whipping him until he's a bloody mess.

"And then came my favorite part... the torture."

The three men, now completely naked, all face the wall, in squatting positions. Their backs are soaking wet, dripping with water. Storm whips them one by one with an extension cord. She doesn't stop until thick, red bruises cover their entire backs. When she stops, there is a look of satisfaction on her face.

Storm's accomplice, Man-Man steps in front of her, holding a carton of eggs in his hands. He looks over at her as she ignores his words. "Come on now. This some sick type shit you on. I ain't puttin' no eggs up a nigga ass. We got the money and the work. Let's just go."

Storm looks at the Man-Man with fury in her eyes as she bites down on her bottom lip. She lifts her gun in the air. "You don't have to. They will. But for the record, you will do anything that I tell you to do."

She grabs an egg from the carton with the first sign of gentleness since they've been here. She leans over the man and hands him the egg. He looks at her in a confused state. A demonic smile covers her face. "Between your cheeks," she says as she aims the gun at his head. He's hesitant to move until she shoves the gun up his nose. Slowly he does as he's instructed. Shamefully, he tucks the egg in between his cheeks with a look on his face that clearly states that he feels violated.

"Whatever you do, don't let that egg break. Your life depends on it. This is a fragile situation," she says with a smirk.

She hands the extension cord over to Man-Man and gives him a head nod to go on. She steps back and watches from across the room with joy in her eyes as the man is whipped like a slave. He bites down on his lip in order not to scream. The sound of the man whimpering gives Storm not only an adrenaline rush, but it gives her a sexual rush as well.

The walls of her interior rumble ferociously. Her temperature rises as her whole body heats up. Her panties moisten more with each lash. His grunting turns her on even more.

She backs up against the wall to brace herself as her insides contract violently. She tries to retain her composure, but it's too much to bear. The attention of the people in the room is not on her but on the man who is receiving the whipping. That gives her the freedom of enjoying her guilty pleasure.

He howls after the biggest lash of them all. The pain so unbearable, he can't deny it. With no surprise at all a water as impactful as Niagara Falls spills over in her panties. She fights back the trembling as her pussy squirts like a garden hose. She closes her eyes as her spraying session fulfills her.

Her euphoria is broken when her eyes pop open and land into the eyes of the woman holding the baby. Shame spreads across Storm's face as they stare at each other for seconds. She pastes an intimidating face on to scare the woman. All the while, her pussy still sprays uncontrollably. The woman looks away just as the water gushes from the bottom of her pants leg, making a puddle on the wooden floor. She stands there fighting back the tremble as another lash sounds off. Just as she's coming down off of her orgasmic high, another splash sounds off.

A bright smile spreads across Storm' face. She walks over with her wet Dickie carpenter pants clinging to her leg with each step. In seconds she's standing over the man. He looks up with terror in his eyes. Beads of sweat cover his face. He slowly looks downward in between his legs. A puddle of raw egg and broken eggshells lay in between his bare feet. Slowly he looks back up at Storm who wears a demonic grin.

She places the gun onto the man's forehead and with no words she squeezes the trigger.

Boom!

"We left all three of them dead. The girl and the baby were left to live. I couldn't bring myself to do that."

13

LATER THAT NIGHT

S TORM SITS AT the kitchen table in a tiny, cramped studio apartment. She's still dressed in her all black. Her ski mask is rolled up on the top of her head. She's quite cool and calm for a person who has just executed three men.

Piles of money from the robbery are piled on the table. She sifts through the bills with suspense as Man-Man sits close enough to sit on her lap. He watches her closely as if he expects her to do a magic trick and make the money disappear. On the opposite end of the table is another female. The coldness in between Storm and the young woman can be felt from across the table.

Storm and this woman are strangers to each other. Any contact that they've had has been through Man-Man. Storm passed the instructions of the job down to him, and he passed the information down to her. The first time the women ever met was thirty minutes before the robbery.

Storm finally finishes her counting. She separates a few piles and slides them over to Man-Man. She then slides two smaller piles across the table to the girl. The girl looks down her nose at the money with disgust. "How much is this?" she asks with her neck popping with each syllable. Her lips are puckered up high enough to kiss the ceiling.

"Six thousand," Storm replies, staring at the girl with venom bleeding from her eyes. She hates that the girl has the audacity to even question her.

"Oh, hell no!" the girl shouts. "Y'all come up with forty-six stacks and y'all think y'all gonna get away with breaking me off a lousy-ass six? Y'all done bumped y'all fucking heads!"

"Shh," Man-Man whispers. "Hold up, Kirah. Take it down."

"Take it down… my ass!" the girl continues on. "Fuck that! If it wasn't for me, none of this shit would've went down. Let me eat, too."

Storm stares at her with fury. The girl has no fear at all. The only thing on her mind is more money. She doesn't know Storm well enough to understand that he shouldn't be speaking to her in this manner, but Man-Man does.

"As pissed off as she was making me, she was right. Without her, we would have had nothing. We used her as bait for our victim. She dated him for three weeks and got all the information needed to get what we wanted. She led us right into his living room. Couldn't get no easier than that, but still I couldn't let her think she was in control."

Storm prepares herself to speak in the most non-confrontational voice that she can muster up. "We did all the dirty work. You put us on the sting, and you got your cut," she says as she points to the money. "Usually the finder's fee for a situation like this only calls for ten percent, so I think this is generous."

"But I put my fucking life on the line, too!" she says rather animated. "I walked y'all all the way through the situation. Without me, y'all would've never got the fuck in!"

Storm paces around the table a few times before stopping short right behind the girl. Storm stares over her head for seconds without saying a word. Distrust forces the girl to look over her shoulder, up at Storm.

Storm leans closer and plants her hand on the girl's shoulder. She places her mouth onto the girl's earlobe as she braces the girl, so she can't move. She whispers into the girl's ear. "You know what? You are absolutely right. I'm all about being fair, so you tell me what you think would be fair to you."

The girl attempts to wiggle out of Storm's tight grip but to no avail. This makes her even more angry. "Y'all scored forty-six. Break me off like a third. Shit. Fifteen would be cool. Hands down."

Storm stands up quickly. She leans her head back with hearty laughter. "That's not fair. That's insanity." She walks over to the window and lifts her leg, putting her foot onto the window sill. She leans back as she digs underneath her army field jacket and grabs the gun. She stares at her gun in the air, studying it from every angle. Both Man-Man and the girl watch with suspense.

"I tell you what… I got four more thousand for you. That's my final offer. Take that or take nothing at all. The choice is yours," she says, still looking at the gun.

She walks over to the girl, who sits there with her lips puckered up with attitude. Man-Man looks over to the girl and shakes his head, gesturing for her to take it and not press her luck any further. She pouts like a child before lowering her gaze onto the table. Storm places her finger under the girl's chin before slamming the gun onto the table. The girl's eyes are locked on the gun until Storm lifts her head gently by her chin. Storm stares into the girl's eyes until her pouting melts away. Her face now shows discomfort. "So we got a deal or what?"

The girl stares at the gun one last time before nodding her head in a frightened state. "Deal," she whispers.

Storm reaches over the girl's shoulder and grabs a few piles and slides them next to the other piles.

"I hate greed with a passion, but I had no real problem giving her another four grand because I knew I had a bigger plan."

Minutes later, the halogen lights of Storm's triple black Mercedes CL coupe are the only source of light on the dark and secluded block. Storm sits comfortably in the driver's seat as Man-Man stands at the window.

"Listen. We ain't got no room for no bullshit," Storm says. She looks into Man-Man's eyes. "You sure you don't want me to handle it? I don't trust that lil bitch. She run her mouth and we finished."

"I know, I know. I got you," he says hastily, in an attempt to shut her up.

"Remember, if she asks why you going that way to take her home tell her some bullshit like, just in case the heat following y'all. Pull over at the graveyard, do what you gotta do, burn the car, and hit me when you get to your sister's house."

Man-Man nods his head with aggravation as if he's tired of hearing the details. He reaches out to fist bump her hand, but she doesn't reciprocate it. "Solid. I got you," he says as he bangs her shoulder.

Storm looks over Man-Man's shoulder where a small, American economy car is parked. The girl is seated in the passenger's seat watching them nosily. Storm waves a fake, overly friendly wave at her before sliding the gear-shift into drive.

Storm slowly cruises off, leaving Man-Man standing there watching. She peeks her head out of the window with a solemn look on her face. "Oh, and make sure that ten comes back to the table."

The Mercedes speeds off, burning rubber.

14

THE NEXT NIGHT

S TORM PACES BACK and forth around the kitchen area of Man-Man's raggedy studio apartment. Rage is on her face and fury is in her eyes. She stops short. "It was simple," she says while banging her fist into the palm of her hand after each word. "All you had to do was stick to the fucking plan but no! You had a plan of your own!"

Man-Man leans over the countertop with his head hanging low in defeat. Storm walks over to him. He backs away, not trusting her rage. She points in his face, nudging him with blatant disrespect. "Now we got a situation on our hands all because you was thinking with your little head, instead of thinking with your big ass head," she says before knocking him against his head.

"My bad," he mumbles sadly.

Outrage takes over her body. Before she realizes it, both of her hands are wrapped around his neck. She chokes him out and he gasps with desperation. "Your bad? Your bad ain't gonna get us outta this! What was the fucking plan?" She loosens the grip to allow him to speak. Man-Man lowers his head in shame. "What was the fucking plan?"

"Slump her and leave her," he mumbles almost under his breath.

"What did you do, though?" she questions with sarcasm.

Man-Man stares into her eyes with sympathy. "Come on, Storm. I know I fucked up."

With lightning speed, she snatches her gun from her waistband. She quickly jams it into his mouth. An evil grin spreads across her face. "I asked you a fucking question. What did you do? I'll tell you what you did. You let a piece of hoe-ass pussy control you. Your dumb ass took her to the hotel and fucked her! I was waiting and waiting for you to call while you was in the hotel fucking!"

She hauls off and slaps him across the face with the gun. He stumbles backward. She leaps at him and strikes him again. She doesn't stop at one lick. She slaps him repeatedly as he puts his hands up to shield his face. The man in him wants to fight back, but he's witnessed her wrath on several occasions and wants no parts of that.

"That was the sweetest score anyone could dream of. It would have been the perfect getaway if he hadn't blown it. He went against the plan of murdering her; instead he took her to the hotel and dropped her off at home the next morning.

I knew I should've handled the job myself but I was testing his loyalty. I've learned that people are quicker to roll over and tell when they have very little dirt on their hands. When they have more fault, they are more likely to keep their mouths shut. With me having three murders to his none, I figured that one would be enough to keep his mouth shut.

She snatches him by the collar and pulls him closer. "Now the bitch gonna tell everything that she knows." She spits rage in his face as she speaks. "And we are going to prison for the rest of our lives."

"Nah," he denies. "The bitch gangster, I swear! I know she won't roll over on us like that. Especially if we bail her out. I just need to talk to her to reassure her that we got her." Storm shakes her head negatively with frustration building on her face.

> *"The longer I stood there, the more I thought about spending the rest of my life in jail because he went against the plan, the more furious I got. By coincidence, after he dropped her off this morning, not even a couple of hours after the robbery, homicide detectives kicked her door in. That little voice in my head kept telling me that she was gonna give us up."*

Storm unloosens the grip on Man-Man's collar and pushes him. Her forearm is pressed into his chest. She grabs him by the back of his neck and turns him around. Fear has him putting up very little fight. She bangs his face onto the countertop over and over until he's dizzy.

"I knew I should've killed the bitch myself, but you insisted that you had it. You knew all the fucking while that you had no plans of ever getting rid of that bitch."

"That ain't true!" he says with his voice muffled. "I did plan to off her. It just didn't go like that."

"I didn't go like that because you didn't want it to go like that. You wanted to spare the bitch. Do you think she gonna spare us?"

She bangs his head onto the countertop one last time before letting him go. His knees buckle from the blows. She raises her gun in the air. Just as he's falling onto his knees, she places the gun on the back of his head.

He feels the weight of the gun on his head and his fear of her vanishes. All he can think of at this moment is his own survival. He turns around and bear hugs her, forcing her backwards. They stumble as they tussle with the gun. He grips her hand and forces the gun away from his face.

Having her overpowered, he feels as if he has a chance. He buries his face into her chest, still gripping her wrist. Rage gives her a boost of strength. She knees him in the testicles, and he so fears his life that he doesn't feel the pain. She knees him repeatedly until she feels him loosen the grip from her wrist.

She snatches away and pushes him back. His eyes stretch wide open, staring into the barrel. He leaps at her with his arms wide open.

Boc!

The bullet catches his body in mid-air. His body drops to the floor. She leans over, gun aimed at the top of his dome.

Boc! Boc!

He falls over, head in between her feet. She dumps three consecutive rounds into the back of his head.

Boc! Boc! Boc!

"You murdered him in cold blood, executioner style. Did you feel any remorse at all?"

"Not the least bit," Angelica replies. "By that time in my life, I was no stranger to cold-blooded murder. There were some along the way that I kind of felt sorry about because they didn't do anything to me. But Man-Man, I felt he rightfully deserved every bit of it. If I had to do it all again, I would do him the same."

The man watches speechlessly. The look in her eyes is that of no other killer that he's ever spoken to. It's like he's watched her transform from a sweet and innocent-looking girl into the cold-blooded monster that her criminal file describes, right before his eyes.

15

DAYS LATER
VALENTINE'S DAY

IT'S AFTER BUSINESS hours and all the employees at the Mercedes Benz dealership have clocked out. The only people present here are the owner, Mr. Antonelli and Storm. Mr. Antonelli leads her into the service area by hand.

He has promised her a dinner date for Valentine's Day. She hates that it's the biggest day for lovers and the closest thing she has to a lover is a seventy-eight year old trick, but she will take that over nothing.

Today she's dressed for the occasion. For the first time ever, she's in a beautiful black dress and four-inch stilettos. Even with this being one of the few times she's been in heels, she handles them gracefully. She's amazed at how the formfitting dress accents her curves and makes her appear thicker. She feels so much different outside of her normal casual appearance.

She's even discarded her wig and replaced it with a wet and wavy twenty-eight inch weave that looks like it could be her natural hair. She's so confident with the weave that she's told herself the cap and the wig will now be a thing of the past. She's also found that a simple layer of makeup rids her of her freckle problem. Today is the first day that she actually feels sexy. That's not a word that she has used to describe herself.

"Can we just go already? I'm starving," she whines like a spoiled brat.

"Wait. Not yet. Not until I show you the other part of my surprise. Close your eyes," he says as he covers her eyes with his hand. He guides her a few steps. "You can open them now."

She opens her eyes and is speechless as she stares at the grill of the candy apple red convertible SL550. A huge red ribbon is plastered onto the windshield. "Wait," she says. "Don't play with me. Are you serious?"

"As a heart attack," he replies. "And you know how serious a heart attack is to a seventy-eight-year-old man," he says with a huge smile.

She's speechless. All she can do is reach out and hug him, damn near knocking him onto the floor. "Thank you," she utters. "It's beautiful."

"No, you're beautiful. This is merely a car, transportation. You in the driver's seat will make it beautiful," he says as he pushes her toward the driver's side. He opens the door for her and helps her inside like the gentleman that he is.

Words can't explain how she feels right now. She was astounded when he gave her the used car, but this brand spanking new hundred-thousand dollar car is something she never imagined experiencing.

"What about the old one?" she asks, having no more use for it. So typical for a young girl who gets a new toy and loses interest in her old one.

"I've already had your license plates taken off of it. I'll be sending it to my used car lot. We have no more use for it. It's old and you deserve more."

Truly, she knows she deserves less, but his words sound very convincing. It's obvious that he sees something in her that she doesn't even see in herself. She's sure he's the only one who must see whatever it is he sees because no one has ever treated her in the manner that he does. He's the only one in the whole world who has ever made her feel special. He also makes her feel something that no one else has, and that feeling is beautiful. Whenever she's around him, she feels like the beautiful woman he claims to see and not the ugly duckling she believes the rest of the world sees.

She has no words to reply with, but the smile on her face says it all. He loves nothing more then to see her happy. It makes him feel happy and rejuvenated. He's an old man, but he lives through her, draining her for her youth. That is what keeps him feeling alive. In the five years they have been involved, he appears to be looking younger instead of older which means she's doing her job.

* * *

Hours later in Manhattan, Storm yawns through Guiseppe Verdi's *La Traviata*, which she finds quite boring. She looks around in disbelief, wondering how the people could really be enjoying themselves. Her and the old man have the best seats here in the Metropolitan Opera House, front and center of the balcony. After dinner he insisted that they come here.

He constantly attempts to expose her to the finer things in life, thinking she will be impressed, but the truth; she finds no enthusiasm in most of them. She's content and happy with the minimum, and he can't understand it. Instead of giving up on her, he continues to try harder. He graces her with expensive gifts, big steaks and the opera, when all she really loves are designer purses, Chinese food, and hip hop music.

Her level of comfort and satisfaction, he will never understand. Their worlds don't even entwine, yet he still enjoys her company. She, on the other hand, finds his level of entertainment to be a drag. As much as she hated to accompany him here, she couldn't tell him no.

He does everything in his power to help her obtain happiness so she can't deny him any happiness that he seeks. Keeping the big picture in mind helps her through his boring endeavors. He gives her anything he believes she may want, not realizing that she has everything she wants at the moment. He's made her life complete at this level.

He's her ace in the hole, and she has no worries while he's here. Her fear is the day that he's not here because she's gotten quite used to the security. With him being damn near eighty, she can't help but think that one day soon she may not have that security blanket. In the five years that they've had an arrangement, she's gotten used to her lifestyle and can't imagine it being any other way.

To secure her future, he has to do one simple thing; sign her into his will. They've touched on the subject a few times. He's the one who always brings it up. She never brings it up because she doesn't want him to think that is her ultimate goal. He's promised that he will one day sign her into the will and stabilize her future even without his presence. For some reason, he hasn't found that level of comfort yet, but she tries her hardest to help him.

Mr. Antonelli looks over to her in the middle of her yawning. "Is this boring you?" he asks. "If so, we can leave."

"No, not at all. This is beautiful," she says as she grabs his hand. She puts on a great big smile, staring into his eyes. The look in her eyes makes him believe she could be enjoying herself. What he doesn't know is that look is not enjoyment. That look is her having her eyes on the prize.

The second he turns away to look at the stage, she yawns again. That yawn evolves into a deep nod. He's enjoying the show so much that he doesn't notice her sleeping away.

* * *

Meanwhile, at the Newark Police-Homicide and Major Crimes Division, the young woman, Kirah sits at the table surrounded by three detectives. The two male detectives pace the room while the female detective interrogates. They've chosen to let the woman do the job, hoping that she can gain a level of comfort with the girl.

"Listen, sweetheart, you are in big trouble. I'm just trying to help you as best I can. I'm a woman like you, so I sympathize with you. My partners don't believe your story, but I do," she lies.

The female detective continues on. "Something about your eyes tells me that you are innocent. I believe that you had nothing to do with the carjacking."

Kirah's face shows how surprised she is. From the time the detectives showed up at her doorstep, she was under the impression that she was being snatched for the murders. The carjacking the detective speaks of she was an accessory to a few months ago. She was used by an ex-boyfriend of hers to reel a man in. No murder was involved, just an assault and a carjacking. She thought that was done and over with, but apparently the man went to the police.

The detective continues on. "I believe that you were just in the wrong place at the wrong time. I've been there. I'm from Newark and I used to be in love with the bad guys, until I almost lost my freedom when my boyfriend of three years threw a gun under my seat without me knowing, after we go pulled over. Left me to take the weight for it. But you know what I did?"

Kirah is all ears. "What?"

"I saved myself. I told the police it wasn't my gun and he threw it under my seat. Now, is the only time you have to save yourself. If you tell all you know, I may be able speak to the prosecutor and get you five years for conspiracy, instead of the minimum of twenty years for carjacking."

"Five years?" Kirah cries. "I can't go to jail for five years. I have three kids."

"Well, you need to save yourself for your kids' sake."

Kirah goes into a frantic frenzy, pulling her weave. "Wait… wait. What if I can provide you with information on a robbery with three homicides involved?"

The two male detectives stop pacing. This is music to their ears. They both walk over to the table. They are more interested in the murders than they are the carjacking. A triple murder would get them more recognition than they can imagine.

The three of them zoom in on her with their undivided attention. The female detective speaks again. "Now, that can get you no jail time at all if your information leads to an arrest."

The young woman doesn't waste a second before she starts spilling the beans. The detectives let her run her mouth for twenty minutes while they jot down notes on their pads.

"There you have it. That's all I know. So can I go home now? I been here for almost a week. My kids need me."

The female detective ignores her question. "What did you say his name was?"

"Man-Man," she replies.

"We need better than that. You know his real name?"

Kirah thinks hard, back to their high school days. His name jumps out at her. "Leonard— Leonard Hall."

"And her name was what again?"

"I don't know her real name because I don't know her. That was the first time I met her. All I know is her street name. Storm. Can I go home now to my kids, please?"

"Not so fast. It doesn't work like that. We will need you to identify them in our mugshots, and we have to get out there and find them. The more you tell us the faster we can capture and charge them and the faster you can get home to your kids. So, tell us more."

She digs into her mental Rolodex and tells any and everything that she can think of that may aid the detectives. She has very little information on Storm, but she gives up everything she knows about Man-Man, except that he's dead. That, she has no knowledge of.

16

THE NEXT DAY

S TORM STANDS IN front of the full-length mirror inside her bedroom, appreciating what she sees. She barely recognizes the woman in the tight jeans, riding boots, and short chinchilla jacket. It's as if this woman has appeared out of nowhere in the past few months. She has fallen in love with the new her and has no plans of ever going back to the old her.

Her confidence is at an all-time high these days. The life she lives is a life she never knew was obtainable. Her new car, her new clothes, new attitude and even new apartment. She has Mr. Antonelli to thank. He hasn't only changed her way of thinking; he's also changed her way of living.

Although her apartment is nowhere near as lavish as his home, it's her own. She's decorated it in a cozy, vintage style that fits her to perfection. Of course, she would love a house in some rich suburban neighborhood, but for now she's content. Mr. Antonelli pays the rent way in advance faithfully and never once has he stepped foot near the apartment. The cute little garden apartment in the quiet middle class neighborhood is like crawling before she walks. She has big plans and she's sure, with her grind and Mr. Antonelli's help, she will meet those plans in no time at all.

She runs her fingers through the silky weave one good time as she spins around and takes a view of how her jeans are hugging her apple bottom. The look in her eyes is pure satisfaction. She gets onto her knees and fumbles under the bed. She stands back up holding a jewelry box. She pops the lid and there is a block of shiny white with interior scales that shine like a diamond. While looking at the block, she doesn't see cocaine. She sees promise.

She drops the block into her Chanel purse. Before locking the door, she presses the code onto her alarm system's keypad. She stands in the doorway, peeking out. Out of habit, she takes a quick survey. Her shiny red Mercedes sticks out like a sore thumb among the more common American-made cars that are spread throughout the parking lot.

She drops into the driver's seat and starts the ignition. The sound of "Hustlaz Ambition", by Young Jeezy jumps out of the speakers, enhancing her grinding state of mind. She backs out of the parking space and zips out of the parking lot. "*I came so far from the bottom couldn't even see the top!*" she sings along.

Minutes later, Storm's Mercedes sits parked on a side street, alongside the projects. From where she's parked, she can see the hustle and bustle of drug activity taking place on the other side of the gate. She notices the man who has just stepped out of the gate and makes his way toward her. He stares into the car with unfamiliarity for seconds before he realizes it's her. His eyes light up with joy when he spots her sitting in the glorious vehicle.

This young man is the oldest friend that Storm has. There's only one friend that she would have had longer. Sadly, he is dead at her hands. This is one of the men that witnessed the murder of her best friend back in their clubhouse days. They've both moved on since then, and it hardly ever comes up in conversation. They've all went on with their adult lives, but they stay in contact. They don't see each other much, but they are always, one phone call away from each other if need be.

Breezy is a slim, laidback handsome dude with a temper that doesn't fit his appearance. He can easily be underestimated, but one of the most streetwise men that Storm knows. She's a few months older than him yet she's learned a lot from him.

Breezy gets into the car, super-hyped. "Yo! What the fuck, yo?" he asks while reaching over to shake her hand. "You done came all the way the fuck up!" he shouts while looking around in the car at the beautiful interior.

Breezy takes a long stare at her, not believing what he sees. "Look at you, looking all beautiful and shit. No hats, no sweats and even got makeup on. You one of them diva bitches now, huh?"

"Absolutely not," she says sternly. "I'm the same cold bitch I always been. You can change your clothes, but that's just the top layer. You was who you was before you got here," she sings in her best Jay-Z impression. They both smile.

"I feel that, but what's up though? What's really good?"

"Nigga, it's all good," she says as she digs into her purse. She drops the block of coke in the Ziploc bag onto his lap. His eyes pop wide open. "That's like eight hundred grams right there. I need your help."

"Well, damn," he sighs as he looks at the cocaine in amazement. "What you trying to do, off it as weight? That's the fastest way."

"Nah, fuck that. Take it to the earth bottle for bottle and let's make some real money. I ain't pressed. Look at me. I'm good," she boasts.

"I see," he smiles.

"I wanna make sure you good," she says with all honesty.

"I respect that, but how the fuck you come up like this? And why the fuck you didn't bring me in to come up with you?"

"Ask me no questions, and I will tell you no lies," she says with a smile. "Fuck all that though, I'm bringing you up now. When I'm up, you up. You already know."

"I can dig it." A group of men come walking in their direction. Breezy conceals the work. "Here come, Mud ass," he says with disgust.

Mud is another one of their friends from the clubhouse days. Mud is the name people have given him because he was the dirtiest kid in the neighborhood. He's grown up and cleaned himself up, but the name never left him. His spirit has always been dirtier than his physical, so even cleaned up, he will always be the low-down, dirty slime ball that very few trust.

"What he up to?" Storm questions.

"Same old shit, pot dropping. You know he can't get right for shit. Everything his hands touch turn to shit."

"OK, with that, help him get right."

"Man, I done tried and tried wit' that motherfucker. Done went broke fucking with him, came back alive and went broke again. I had to cut him off. He waiting on me to hit him again. He only been home for a month. Just laid down for three years the last time."

"That's because you using him wrong. You know he ain't no hustler. He the muscle. You're putting him in the wrong position, like giving a center the ball and expecting him to run the point guard position. It's not possible. He's gonna lose the ball."

Storm is correct in her way of thinking. For as long as Mud has been around, he's never been a hustler and he's never been a part of a lucrative venture. He's always been their muscle. His muscle is underestimated because he has very little of them. He only stands at about five foot eight inches tall and weighs no more than a buck sixty. He has the heart of a lion, though, and the knuckle game of a warrior. If both those fail, he has the accuracy of a sharp shooter when you put a semiautomatic weapon in his hand.

All of the approaching men in the group have their eyes on the Mercedes. They recognize Breezy, but their focus is on the female driver.

"Oh, shit!" Mud yells. He steps toward the driver's side. "Oh, shit!"

A bright smile spreads across Storm's face. She rolls down the window. "Let me get outta here with this shit before the Jake come through," Breezy says as he makes his exit. He slams the door shut and disappears.

"Storm, what's good?" he yells.

Storm gets out to properly greet a friend that she hasn't seen in years. They hug for a few seconds before he steps back. "Damn! Look at you, girl? What's goodie?"

She blushes from ear to ear. "What's up, crazy?"

"You!" he shouts. "Shit! You what's up, all shining and shit." Mud looks her up and down in admiration. "It's dark on my side. Tough out here."

"Ay, Mud, you know how it goes," she replies. "When it gets tough for everybody else, that's when it's getting just right for us."

"Yo, Mud, come the fuck on!" one man shouts hastily.

"Yo, I'm in the middle of something right now, but give me your number. I need you, yo!"

"You need me? For what?" she asks as if she doesn't already know.

"Yo, I got something major I been plotting on. I just need some backing. These other niggas be flaking," he claims. "Motherfuckers quicker to feed you when they know you're full than they are when they know you're starving. What I got my eyes on will definitely be beneficial for you."

"Is that right?" she asks, already knowing his story.

"Damn right! Major paper, too, even though it don't look like you need it. But shit I do."

"I got you," she says as she leans in her car and jots down her phone number. She already knows he will blow anything that she does for him but still she can't turn her back on him. He's one of her truest friends, and she could never leave him out to dry like Breezy has. She hands him the paper with her number. "Hit me."

He stares her up and down for seconds, setting up. "Sis, let me hold something though," he begs with no shame.

She was sure this was coming next. She gets into the car and digs into her purse. She begins sifting through the bills in her hand.

"Snap was just asking about you. I was with him the other day."

She looks up from the money. She can't hide the disgust on her face. Just hearing his name infuriates her. "Oh, yeah?" she asks as if she really cares. She hands him five hundred-dollar bills and his face lights up like a kid on Christmas Day.

"Yeah, I'm gone tell him I saw you. Maybe we all get together and catch up for old times' sake."

"OK," she nods, pretending to be interested.

"But, yo, I'm gon' hit you tomorrow with all the details of what I'm trying to do. Serious money, though, you hear me?"

"I heard. Just hit me. Only if it's serious money, though. You know I love that money."

He cracks a huge smile. "Don't we all? I got you!"

17

THE NEXT EVENING

IT IS HALF an hour before closing, and the Mercedes dealership is still flowing with business. A few customers sprinkle the showroom floor looking at vehicles, and a couple customers sit before salesmen in their cubicles. The door opens and a couple steps into the showroom. They stand and take a survey of the place.

A desperate salesman attacks them quickly. "Hello! May I help you?"

The man digs into his coat pocket and flashes a badge. "Newark Police. Is Mr. Antonelli around?" the man asks with no shade. His words capture the attention of everyone.

"Uh-uh," the salesman stutters, not knowing how to reply.

"Uh-uh! Get Mr. Antonelli," the detective says with sarcasm.

"One second," the salesman replies. He slowly makes his way to the back. He shrugs his shoulders at a salesman across the room.

In two minutes flat, Mr. Antonelli appears in the doorway with a perplexed look on his face. He steps to the detectives. "I'm Mr. Antonelli. May I help you?"

"Can we go to your office?" the female intervenes. "You have customers out here."

"Sure," the old man says as he leads them through the showroom.

Once they are in his office, he offers them a seat. They choose to remain standing, keeping control of the matter. He takes a seat behind his desk. "Is there a problem?"

"Problem?" the detective asks like a wiseass. "Of course, there's a problem, or two detectives wouldn't be here in your office."

"What can I help you with?" he asks.

"Glad you're willing to help. Do you own a Mercedes coupe?"

"Do I own a Mercedes? One? I own about two hundred of them."

"OK, smart ass. Let me be more specific then. A black Mercedes CL. The license plates come back to your dealership."

"License plates? You mean the temporary plates? Like from a customer?"

"No, like to your corporation."

The old man thinks. With his old age, it takes him quite some time before Storm's old car comes to mind. "I'm sorry but that doesn't help me much. Many cars belong to the corporation."

"Well, are many of those cars accessories to murders?"

"What do you mean?" he asks with his heart banging through his chest. His face turns beet red from fear.

"We have surveillance tapes with the black Mercedes leaving a murder scene last week. Do you know who could have been driving it?"

"I have a hundred employees," he says, in an attempt to keep his love protected. "My employees, sometimes, take vehicles home. Whether it be a salesman or a mechanic. At this time, I have no clue of who could've had the vehicle."

"Well, we will need you to find out who had the vehicle," the female says. "By chance, do you have an employee that goes by the name of Storm?"

The old man swallows the lump in his throat. Although he would never call her that, he's familiar with the nickname. He tries to keep a straight face, but it's hard under these circumstances. "I'm not familiar with my employees' nicknames. All my dealings with my employees are strictly business."

"So—" the female manages to say before Mr. Antonelli interrupts.

"I would love to help you, but at this time I'm requesting that you leave my business. Leave me your card, and I will forward your information to my attorney. Anything from this point on, we will discuss in the presence of my attorney."

Steam blows from the man's nostrils. The female detective passes her card over. "Here you go."

"Thank you and have a good evening. I will forward the information over."

"Get in touch with us, or we will be here to get in touch with you. Next time we will be taking you out in cuffs," the man says in a threatening manner before they exit.

The old man exits shortly after them. He walks to the showroom door and watches them pull off. Many thoughts race through his mind. He can't believe that his baby is in the middle of such trouble. He quickly pulls out his phone and dials her.

* * *

Storm's phone rings back to back as it lay on the passenger's seat of the Pontiac. She's not in the car to answer it. Her, Mud, and Breezy are leaning on the gate of West Side Park when a tinted out Dodge Charger parks behind Breezy's Pontiac.

The driver, Snap, gets out with no hesitation. A big smile covers his face as he sees all of his old friends. He hasn't seen them all in one place in years. As he walks up, his focus is on Storm. He hasn't seen her in many years and is shocked to see her looking so grown up.

He shakes Breezy's hand first. "What up?" he asks, totally overlooking Storm.

He looks to Storm again. "And you?" he says as he looks at Storm. "All grown up, looking like a grown woman," he says as he opens his arms for a hug. "Give me a hug, girl."

Storm is irked just being in his presence. It was Mud's idea for all of them to meet. As he stares at her with that perverted look in his eyes that he always had for her, it takes her back to how uncomfortable he always made her feel as a kid. "You not gon' hug me, girl?" he asks as he snatches her into his arms. He hugs her tightly, and she doesn't reciprocate. He finally lets her go. "Damn! You ain't no little girl no more," he says as he stares her up and down in lust.

"Nah, all grown up," she says with a fake smile.

Snap finally gets to Mud and shakes his hand. "Mud, what's up, baby?"

"Same shit. Just like old times, right? All of us together."

Storm takes a step to the side as she peeks into the Charger. Once she notices the passenger's seat is empty, she sneakily draws a gun from her coat pocket. She aims at Snap who has his back facing her. Both Mud and Breezy look at her in a baffled state.

Snap spots the look on their faces and turns around to see what the looks are about. Once he turns to face her, he's staring into the barrel of a nine millimeter. "Storm, what?" he utters before…

Boc!

The shot to the face sends him flying several feet backwards.

As he falls to the ground, Storm is already standing over him. She dumps three shots into his face.

Boc! Boc! Boc!

She turns around and both Mud and Breezy stand with their hands in the air in submission. They are confused and not certain if they are next. "Let's go," she says before trotting toward the Pontiac. They drop their hands, look at Snap's body, and take off behind her.

"It was all Mud's idea for us to meet. Really, I had no interest in meeting with Snap but Mud insisted. Snap was always my least favorite of the entire group. I hated how he manipulated us as kids and controlled our minds. I hate that he was responsible for me killing my best friend. More than anything, I hate how he took advantage of me sexually. To see him look at me, undressing me with his eyes, was all I needed to go on with what I already had planned for him. Once Mud insisted on setting up the meeting, I had already put in my mind that I would go only to seek revenge for me, for my best friend, for us. And I did, with no regrets not even today."

Storm speeds through the darkness. In the passenger's seat of his own car, Breezy sits still in confusion. Him and Mud have not a clue as to what just happened. To them, this just came out of nowhere with no motive. In their eyes, they were family. Out of shame, she never told anyone what Snap had done to her.   Storm is slowly coming down off of her adrenaline high. She keeps her eyes on the road, just zoned out in her thoughts. Breezy looks over to her. He has so many things to say to her, but he's so pissed right now that he'd rather calm down first.

She feels him peeking over at her and turns toward him. "I told you I'm the same cold bitch."

"But why, though, Storm? I thought we were all family. Thought it was all love."

"He never loved us, and he never looked at us like family. He only manipulated us." She stares at Breezy without blinking. "Know the difference." She looks into the rearview mirror and sees Mud looking out of the window, very perplexed.

She pulls over and slams the car into park. She looks back and forth at both of them. Her gun is in hand, concealed on her left side. "Before we go any further, let me know if y'all got any problems with what I just did."

She looks to Breezy. "Breeze?" He looks away from her, shaking his head. She looks into the rearview mirror. "Mud?"

"Hey! For whatever reason, you did what you felt you had to do," Mud says without looking at her. He stares out of the window. "Who am I to question what you do?"

"So we all good?" she asks. They both agree. She pulls back onto the road, gun still in hand. "OK, we all good then. Nothing else to talk about. Dead subject."

18

LATER THAT NIGHT

MR. ANTONELLI SITS before Storm with his face as pale as a ghost. He's shivering and nervous, very much unlike he was earlier in front of the detectives. In the dealership, he retained his cool, but the minute he left he lost it. He's drank two bottles of wine to ease his nerves, yet they are still not eased.

"What's the emergency?" she asks quite inquisitively.

"What type of trouble have you gotten yourself into?" he asks.

"Trouble? What are you talking about?"

"Detectives bombarded the dealership today," he says with his lips quivering. He waits to see her reaction.

Her heart races. She quickly thinks of all the trouble she has behind her and wonders which it could be. She plays it cool to throw him off. "Detectives? For what?"

"They said that a vehicle from the dealership was seen leaving a murder scene?"

Her ears twitch on alert. She's confused as to which one it could be because her car wasn't used in any of them. "Really?" she asks, quite surprised.

"Yes," he replies. "Please just inform me what this is about."

"How the fuck should I know?" she snaps. "Why the fuck you didn't ask them?"

"Calm down, calm down," he replies nervously as he reaches over to alleviate her anger.

"Fuck off of me." She snatches away from him with fire in her eyes. "You questioning me about some shit I don't know nothing about when you should've been questioning them."

"I tried but they wouldn't answer any details," he lies. "They said it was the CL."

"Well, somebody must have been driving that car and got me involved in some bullshit," she says in a weak defense.

"Angel," he says in his sweetest voice.

"Don't you fucking Angel me!"

"Sorry, baby," he apologizes. He knows how bad that angers her. "That car hasn't moved since you left it there."

"So you're saying it was me?"

"I'm not saying anything. Please just calm down."

"Fuck calm down! Are you saying that I was involved in a murder?"

"I'm not. Just telling you what they told me."

"Fuck what they told you! I'm telling you I haven't been involved in shit!" She stares at him with hatred for a few seconds without saying a word. "You know what? Fuck this! I'm out!" She storms toward the door. She's bluffing him, knowing he will fall right into her trap.

"Baby, no, please," he says, chasing behind her just as she knew he would.

He grabs hold of her and she snatches away from him. "I know one motherfucking thing... you better get my name cleared and find out who at that dealership used that car and got me all mixed up in this shit."

He buries his head in between her breast. "I will do everything in my power to get to the bottom of this and get you in the clear."

"You better."

19

TETERBORO AIRPORT
THE NEXT AFTERNOON

S TORM AND MR. Antonelli pull up to the airport in a flaming
red Ferrari 458 Italia. Mr. Antonelli stops the Ferrari short, a
hundred feet away from a G4 private jet. The center of attraction
isn't the actual jet. It's the man dressed in pilot gear that is. The African-American man sports the old school short, chocolate brown
Rocky Shearling with the hat to match. His designer aviator shades,
denim button up, and army fatigue cargo pants make him look like
the hood version of a Tuskegee Airmen. Storm recognizes the hustler's signature boot; tall, cracked leather Timberlands. Spotting the
hood in him peaks her curiosity.

The man paces around until he hears the doors of the Ferrari
slam shut. Storm struts behind Mr. Antonelli, looking quite fashionable herself, draped in a full-length mink coat and thigh-high
riding boots. Mr. Antonelli is dressed in his typical pinstriped suit
underneath his black cashmere trench.

"Mr. A," the man sings. "You almost missed me," he says as he
extends his hand for a handshake. Storm can't keep her eyes off the
man, yet he pays no attention to her at all.

"Thanks for waiting," Mr. Antonelli says gratefully. He looks to Storm. "Baby, meet Attorney Tony Austin. Tony, meet my baby." Tony looks at Storm for the first time. He flashes a sly smile at Mr. Antonelli before reaching for her hand. "Baby, this is the best criminal defense attorney in the state of New Jersey and arguably the best in the entire world."

Tony smiles arrogantly. "Arguably? Listen, I'm on a tight schedule. I have reservations at my favorite restaurant for lunch. It would be my pleasure to have you both as my guests, if you have some time on your hands. That will give us more than enough time to talk about what it is you need of me."

"How can I refuse that offer?" Mr. Antonelli replies.

"With that being said," he says as he extends his hands toward the entrance of the jet. "After you," he says.

Mr. Antonelli guides Storm in front of them. They board the jet and seat themselves. Storm looks around the spacious jet in amazement. She feels like a class act. She's impressed, yet she keeps her nonchalant edge.

Mr. Antonelli and Storm sit close to each other. Tony, who is seated across from them, opens a bottle of bourbon, and just as he does, a sudden turbulence jerks the jet. The entire bottle of Pappy Van Winkle spills onto the floor. He looks down at the puddle of the bourbon, then looks at the empty bottle, and his face shows no signs of anguish. It's as if the rare twenty-three-year-old bourbon didn't cost him close to three grand.

He merely goes into the bar and grabs a bottle of Macallan, which is equally as expensive and seven years older. He pours the glasses heftily. He holds his glass in the air for a toast. "To generations of prosperity and wealth." The three of them tap their glasses together. "So what's the problem?" Tony asks.

Storm takes a sip of the whiskey and a fire brews in her mouth. She forces the liquor down her throat and fights to keep it down. "What the…" she mumbles to herself as she looks at the dark liquor.

"You okay, baby?" Mr. Antonelli asks. "Everything good?"

"Not that," she says as she points to the glass. She hangs her tongue out with no class. "Eelk… I don't know how y'all drink that shit." Mr. Antonelli looks to Tony ashamed at her lack of class. He shrugs his shoulders with a cheesy look on his face.

"Shit," Tony mumbles feeling disrespected. He chuckles arrogantly. "It's an acquired taste, dear. Maybe a little too expensive for your taste buds." He reaches over to the small refrigerator. "Let me see if I have something a little more suitable for you."

He looks into the refrigerator. "Uh, I'm sorry. Seems we are all out of pink moscato and forty ounces." He takes the attack without looking back at her. He can feel her stare penetrating through his soul, but he pays her no mind. Instead he looks back to Mr. Antonelli. "What were you about to say?"

Mr. Antonelli gives Tony all the details from the smallest on up to the biggest and everything in between while Storm sits quietly. In her mind the girl did just as she knew she would and that is tell everything. She wishes she could dig Man-Man up from the dead just to murder him again. If it wasn't for him, she wouldn't be going through this.

Had he listened to her the girl would be dead and he wouldn't be. She wonders what all the detectives know and she can't wait until the attorney gets on the case to inform her. She thinks of the witness she left behind in the apartment, the young woman with the baby. She needs to find out who the woman is.

"Baby," Mr. Antonelli says for the second time. Storm is so caught up in her thoughts that she didn't even hear him.

Storm looks at him with her brow high. "Huh?"

"He's talking to you."

She looks to the attorney who looks at her suspiciously. "Do you have any idea what this is about?"

"Not a clue," she lies with a straight face.

"Listen, I'm gonna need you to be completely honest with me. We are on the same team and have to be on the same page. The more I know, the better off we all will be."

"Didn't I just tell you I don't have a clue?"

Mr. Antonelli gives Tony a signal with his eyes to back off. Tony accepts the sign and takes a swig of his scotch.

"So can you help us?" Mr. Antonelli asks.

"Is that a trick question?" Tony asks humorously. "Haven't you helped me get every Mercedes I ever dreamed of having?" The old man smiles in reply. "Of course, I can help you."

* * *

Two and a half hours later the three of them sit inside of DiMallo's Floating Restaurant. When the jet landed, they were driven by car service to the Portland Harbor. Outside of her reason for being here, Storm is having the time of her life. All in one day, for her first time ever, she flew on a G4 and boarded a yacht. The lovely restaurant is a yacht that floats the harbor. She feels like she's starring in an episode of *Sex and the City* with her own Mr. Big.

On the table in front of them are three two pound lobsters and all the clams they can eat. The bottle of Ferrari-Carano chardonnay has the perfect twing to not only wash it all down but to complement the taste as well.

Tony listens to Mr. Antonelli babble about the situation for the twentieth time and gets a little ruffled. He flashes a smile to downplay his agitation. "Mr. A, not over lunch. Let's enjoy our meal and get back to the business once we're done."

"Okay, sorry. I just want to clear my baby's name," he says as he looks at Storm with googly eyes.

* * *

One hour later, they are all sitting back on the jet, feeling like stuffed sharks. Storm has the 'itis' and is ready to fall asleep, but worry and anxiety keep her wide awake.

"So what is this gonna cost me?" Mr. Antonelli asks as he pulls out his checkbook.

Tony places his hand over Mr. Antonelli's. "With all due respect." He smiles. "Get a grip of yourself, Mr. A. You know gentlemen never discuss finances in front of women. Let me get on the job and find out what I can and we can discuss currency later, in a more professional setting.

"For now, do lay back, enjoy the flight or do like I'm about to do and sleep that two-pound lobster off." He leans his seat back, closes his eyes for a second before he opens them to find both of them staring at him with stress on their face. "Go ahead, rest easy. I got y'all."

20

THE NEXT DAY

ATTORNEY TONY AUSTIN is busy at work on Storm's case as promised. He stands in the middle of his office, phone glued to his ear with one hand, and holding his burning cigar with the other. His tailor kneels before him, pulling at his trousers. Tony seems to be more interested in the three television screens that are posted on the wall than he is in the conversation. All three screens have different stock trading channels playing.

To the right of him stands a tall, handsome young man. His curly, wild afro makes him look a little thuggish, but his mannerisms are nothing but respectful. The young man, too, has a tailor working on his fit. This young man is Tony's protégé. Tony has taken him under his wing straight out of law school.

To the left of him stands a well-dressed man, unraveling the bubble-wrap off of a painting. He stands cool and calm in the midst of all the action.

"Yes, Mr. A," Tony says into the phone. "Don't worry. Have I ever let you down before? I will give you a call as soon as I hear something," he says before ending the call. Not once does he take his eyes off the screens. He takes a huge pull of his stogie, hoping for some relaxation in it.

"How does this feel?" the tailor asks as he tugs at the pants around Tony's waist.

"Perfect," Tony replies. He blows out a mouthful of smoke into the air. He looks over to the tailor who is at his young protégé's feet. "Nah, I know the high-water style is in, but we don't do that. The boy is six foot five for crying out loud. Let the pants break a smidgen under the ankle." He looks to his tailor. "Raphael, tell him."

The man with the painting finally steps up for Tony's attention. This man is Tony's art dealer. Tony isn't just a lover of art but a collector, and an investor. It's love at first sight when Tony lays eyes on the painting. He's speechless as he stares with his heart racing. He can't believe he's this close to having this piece. He's been chasing it for months. The passion he has for this painting can be seen all over his face.

A beautiful young woman, Tony's intern, walks into the office and steps right in front of Tony. She demands his attention. "Mr. Austin," the woman interrupts.

He places his hand in the air. "Hold up, hold up," Tony says. "Do you see what's going on?" The woman stares at the painting, not even realizing why it means so much to him. "Do you even understand what is being presented before us?" he asks as he points to the painting.

The woman looks at the painting and is in no way impressed. To her it's just a basic painting that looks as if a child could have painted it. It's not even what she considers a beautiful painting. All she sees is a pencil drawing on dirty paper.

"Let me educate you real quick," he says to the woman. "You, too, young fella," he says to his protégé. "This right here is the most expensive piece in the Andrew Turner collection. Do you know who Andrew Turner is?" he asks. "Either of you?"

Both the young man and young woman shrug their shoulders. "Nat Turner's brother?" she asks with all seriousness.

Tony smiles at her ignorance. "Au contraire, mon frère," he says while teasing a lock of her hair. "Google him," he says as he points to the phone in her hand. "That's the problem with you youngsters. You got a wealth of knowledge right there at your fingertips. Anything you want to know you can find it at the press of a button on that phone. But all you are worried about is how many pixels the camera has, so you can post your pretty selfies on social media."

Out of respect, they look at Tony with their undivided attention. They both know it's an honor to be here working with the most powerful attorney in the state. Any knowledge he chooses to share with them, they are here to soak up. They can only pray that one day they are half the attorney that he is. What Tony loves about them is their willingness to listen and learn. With him loving to be listened to, it works for all of them.

"Andrew Turner was an African-American artist out of Pennsylvania," he says with excitement in his eyes. "He died from a heroin overdose. Some consider him a junkie and turn their noses down at him. But me, I was raised by the junkies and wouldn't be the man I am today if I hadn't sat back and listened to all the knowledge they had stored. Some of the best men I've met in the world were junkies," he claims.

"I have ten pieces of his work in my home. Fine art, yes. I also see it as a reminder that we all have issues. We all are addicted to something, but that doesn't discredit the creativity and honor of a man. Just like him, society once frowned upon me and looked at me like the scum of the earth."

He points to the bottom of the painting. "See the title? *Keeping the Faith*," he says dragging his finger across the bottom of the frame. "In a nutshell," he adds as the young woman listens attentively, "that's your lesson for today." He smiles. "You got two lessons in one. Now go on and get to work.

"I need you to get on the phone with the prosecutor's office and find out what's going on with the Angelica Hill situation. I need those detectives to never enter Mr. Antonelli's business again. Let them know I have the case. Also, I need you to get me a file on that girl. She has Mr. A's nose wide open, but something tells me she's not as innocent as he thinks she is. Typical sucker for love," he says with a smile.

"OK," she replies. She quickly steps away from him onto her assignment.

"Oh, but more important!" he shouts. She stops in her tracks. "Cut this gentleman a check for one hundred-eighty thousand for this fine painting."

The young woman's eyes bulge. She believes she may have heard him wrong. "One hundred and eighty-thousand?"

"Yes," he replies. "One, eight, zero, comma, zero, zero, zero," he says with sarcasm. "If you have trouble with it, pull it up on that smartphone you got in your hand." The young woman exits the room, absorbing his arrogance. Tony looks down at his tailor. "I work way too hard," he says with humor.

* * *

Meanwhile Storm is working on her case as well. She sits in her Mercedes, parked outside of the projects. Breezy stands at the window running his mouth a mile a minute as she listens attentively. "So my peoples said, that's easy. Said he can put me directly with the lil nigga, Juice. That's her brother. Like he said, as far as he know they got most of the money to bail her out, but they short a few grand. Supposedly they got the signatures, job references and the whole shit. Broad just sitting, waiting on the rest of the money."

"Well, you gone have to work that out because I can't go no-where near them. I don't know what she may have told her family."

"Nah, seems like the streets don't really know nothing. Unless her family keeping it on the hush. All they talking about is the carjacking with them niggas from across town. I was waiting to see if your name or even Man-Man's name even came up, but it didn't. You sure she spilled her guts?"

"I mean, who else could have?" she asks.

"I feel you. Ay, it's only one real way to find out. I'm on it for you, though," he says as Mud steps toward the car.

"Thanks," she says with much gratitude.

"No need to thank me, sis. You always been there for me. It's the least I can do. We gonna get you outta this."

* * *

A few miles away, an unmarked police car swerves around the corner and bounces onto the sidewalk. All the drug activity seems to stop as everyone is caught dead to the rear. The female detective hops out of the passenger's seat and the male from the driver's seat. They run over to the dealer who stands petrified.

The female detective snatches the dealer by the collar. "Y'all get the fuck outta here or y'all going with him," she threatens. The customers take off in opposite directions. The other dealers kind of sneak away from the scene as well.

She lays the dealer onto the hood roughly as her partner starts to frisk him. He slams the bag of drugs onto the hood. "Dumb motherfucker!" the female detective shouts. She cuffs his hands behind his back and shoves him into the back of the unmarked car.

The unmarked car pulls off, leaving the scene bare. The female detective reads from the man's license. "Charles, do you have any warrants?"

The man in the backseat prepares himself for the lie. He knows he's wanted in, at least, three cities right now. "Nah, not that I know of."

She smiles. "Not that you know of, huh? Well, let me call in and find out for all of us then."

The dealer bangs his head onto the headrest, knowing damn well this will be his last time on the streets for, at least, another five years. Something told him not to go outside today, but he didn't listen and now this. "Damn," he mumbles under his breath.

The female detective grabs the walkie talkie, preparing to call in his name and have him record checked. She stalls the call and turns looking into the backseat. "Charles, before I have you record checked, are you familiar with a young woman who goes by the name of Storm?"

An image of Storm's face flashes in his mind at the mention of her name. The look on his face tells the detectives that he's most definitely familiar with her. It would almost be impossible for any street person in Newark to not have heard of her. Her name is almost iconic throughout the city and anybody who is somebody knows her.

He thinks quickly before answering the question. "I know of her but not on a personal level."

"Is that so?" the detective asks as she places the walkie talkie on her lap. "What exactly do you know of her? You know where we can find her right now?"

He quickly picks up on the game that she's playing. The young man has always been opposed to snitching but never was faced with a decision to snitch or not to snitch. He thinks of his freedom and he thinks of the no-snitch rule. He then thinks of the five-year charge that he's on the run for.

He quickly tells himself, *It's only snitching if people ever find out.* He realizes if anyone ever finds out that he gave any information up his reputation is tarnished. He debates with himself before replying. He can't go through with it. "Nah, I just heard her name. I don't know nothing else."

"First, you said you know of her. Now you saying you know nothing. Which is it? I tell you what… I'm gon' close this partition and give you a few minutes to decide if you want to help us or not. Once you decide that you want to help us, think of anything that could lead to her capture. In return, we keep your bag of goods, and you will be let out the car to be free another day," she says before slowly closing the partition in between her and him.

Minutes later, the partition slides open. The female detective doesn't even look his way. "So, you going with us or are we dropping you off at the next corner?" she asks, still staring straight ahead.

The man immediately starts spilling the beans. "Like I said, I don't really know her personally, but I know the area that she used to be in. I knew some people that know her that could probably help y'all better than I can. But y'all can't throw my name in the mix. If niggas find out I did this, I will be murdered for sure," he says with fear in his eyes.

"Of course we won't do that," she replies. "Just give me three solid names to look up, and we will shake them down, and they will never know how they got under our radar."

"Y'all sure?"

"We would never throw you out there like that. We know how deadly she is," the detective says. She attempts to ease his fears and reel him in at the same time.

"I'm trusting y'all on this one. I don't have three, but I have two that definitely know more about her than me."

The detective pulls out her pen and pad. "OK, shoot."

21

ATLANTIC CITY, NEW JERSEY
THE NEXT DAY

STORM AND THE girls just checked into the Tropicana an hour ago, and they are already out and about in the casino working. They work the Atlantic City casinos every weekend faithfully. They can always bank on making money here. When all else fails, this spot is always wide open, flourishing with potential.

Because she's not much of a gambler, Storm sits at a penny slot machine. She's paying little attention to the slot machine because her eyes are on her investments, Wendy and Toy. She watches them wander around the room, trying to get to the money. Her phone vibrates on her lap. She sees the name on the display and grabs it quickly. "Yo!" Her mouth drops open. "Atlantic City. Are you sure? I just took that ride. Please don't make me come there for nothing. All right. Bet! Hit you when I get there." She ends the call.

She races past Toy like a flash of lightning. Toy takes a double-take at her as she exits the casino. Toy doesn't miss a beat. She continues on with her work.

Toy glides across the floor elegantly. To keep shade on herself and not look like a working girl, she has her attire toned down. Instead of an evening gown and stilettos, she's in a tight miniskirt and flat sandals. The average eye may perceive her as the everyday person here gambling their money away. The men who are looking for action can spot the adventure in her eyes.

She locks eyes with a handsome older man. His gaze tells her that he wants to play, and her's state that she's ready to be played with. Once she looks down at the chips in front of him and sees a bunch of white and blue, the game between him and her is over before it even starts. The dollar chips are a turn off for her.

She's experienced working the casinos. Her eyes don't even pick up the white, blue, or even the red five dollar chips. She assumes that they don't have money and are here looking for a miracle, hoping to leave rich. She looks at the men with the green twenty-five dollar chips as misers. They may have the money, but they are too stingy to part with it.

The only way she will entertain a man with black hundred-dollar chips in front of him is if his clothing and trinkets are in order: Meaning his shoe game must be tight, as well as his suit and his watch game. Although he's playing with hundred dollar chips, he can afford to go bigger. That is his level of comfort, and he's not trying to impress anyone.

As she walks, she makes an assessment of the casino, looking for the biggest money table in the place. Quickly she locates the money table, a blackjack table with piles of purple, five hundred dollar chips and orange, one thousand dollar chips stacked high in front of every player. She realizes that is where she needs to be. The money is obviously there, but that's only half the battle. The other half is identifying who is in need of her services.

The men at this table are low-key for the most part, and are not concerned with looking like they have money. They have nothing to prove because they are confident. Their shoes are run down and their clothes are boring. The common watch at the table is the classic, gold, Day-Date Rolex, clean with no diamonds. She refers to these type of men as "old money."

She kindly makes her way over to that table. She wanders around like a tourist, pretending not to be paying them any attention. The smell of her perfume reaches the table long before her. She takes a glance, but no one seems to notice her. Just as she's about to pass, she hears, "Hey, beautiful girl!"

Toy looks over and locks eyes with a fat older man who has *ob-noxious* written on his forehead. "Come here, girl!" he shouts.

Toy walks over hesitantly as if she's shy. She stands before him bashfully. He pulls her by the hand. "Come stand next to me and bring me some luck," he says as he wraps his arm around her. "What's your name, girl?"

"Toy," she replies, batting her long eyelashes.

"Well, I'm a big kid and I love toys. He takes a long look at the cards that have just been dealt to him. Discreetly he slides an orange chip in front of her. "For your time," he whispers out of the side of his mouth.

Toy just stands there, looking pretty. She wonders if the money is to just look pretty until she feels his huge hand palm grip her ass. She then understands the grand is a down payment for what he really wants. She looks at the chips that value at about two hundred grand and realizes, if she plays her hand right, this could be a beautiful night.

22

HOURS LATER

S TORM SITS IN the passenger's seat of Breezy's car impatiently. The block is dark but busy with traffic. "Damn! What's taking them so long?" she asks.

They've been sitting out here for hours, just idle. The door of the county jail opens and Storm's eyes spark with joy. As she watches, Kirah, the girl that has her jammed up, rage overflows from within. She gets fidgety in her seat.

"There she go," Breezy sings. "So how you wanna handle it? Want me to talk to her first?"

Storm keeps every step within her scope. Kirah walks to a car that awaits her. The lights of a raggedy little car shine brightly upon her entrance. It's no surprise to them because Breezy was already aware that her brother was here waiting for her. "You gon' holler at her or you want me to?" he asks.

"Nah, just hold up. Follow them. I will talk to her, just not right here."

"Bet," Breezy says as he turns on the lights of his car.

The car pulls out of the parking space and so does Breezy. He allows the car to get up the block before he tails them. The car bends a right at the corner, and Breezy steps on the accelerator to catch up with them.

The traffic light switches to red and the only cars on the dark block are theirs.

"Pull up on the side of them at the corner," Storm instructs. The car is in the right turning lane, which is perfect for Storm. "Yeah, pull up on my side, so she can see that it's me."

Breezy pulls his car around, just as he's told. Storm rolls her window down. Just as they are side by side, she looks into the car. Both the man and the woman look into her face, not even recognizing her before she aims the gun precisely. Not even Breezy saw it coming.

Boc! Boc! Boc!

The driver's body is forced into the passenger's seat.

"The fuck yo!" Breezy shouts in shock.

Storm forces the door open and jumps out of the car, gun waving in the air. The driver mashes the gas pedal in fear of what is to come but still it comes.

Boc! Boc!

The car crashes into the mailbox, preventing it from moving. Storm rushes over to the other side where she finds the woman hiding under the dashboard. Storm snatches the door open with her heart racing uncontrollably.

"There she was… the person that had me in this mess. If it wasn't for her nothing would have led them to me. She was the only one standing in between me and my freedom, so I had no choice."

Boc! Boc! Boc! Boc! Boc!

Storm fires relentlessly, all head shots until the woman shows no sign of life. Her rage leads her to continue on, knowing the woman is dead.

Boc! Boc! Clink— Clink— Clink—.

The sound of the empty cartridge snaps her out of her zone.

She takes off toward the getaway car. Once she's inside, Breezy speeds off.

"What the fuck wrong with you, yo?" Breezy shouts. "Why the fuck you didn't tell me you was gone do that?"

Storm doesn't say a word to him. She holds the blazing gun in her hand. The smell of the gun smoke fills the air, giving her more of a rush. Breezy speeds through the streets recklessly. He's screaming rage at her, yet she doesn't hear him.

* * *

Minutes later, they arrive safely to Storm's car. Breezy parks his car in the parking lot of the projects. They get into her car, neither of them saying a word to each other. Storm starts her car and pulls off in a nonchalant demeanor that is surprising to Breezy.

"Yo! This the second time you done put me in the mix without telling me shit!" he shouts. "I been in contact with them people. I gave them the bail money. This shit gon' fall back on me," he says as he covers his face with both of his hands. "I don't believe this shit, yo!"

Storm speaks for the first time, staring at him with a blank look in her eyes. "Breeze, you know I love you like a big brother, right?" He has no reply for her. "Don't ever put me in a position where I have to choose between love and what I think may be the right thing to do."

As calm as she may sound, Breezy still recognizes her words as a threat. He looks down at the gun that she still has gripped tightly in her hands and that threat is confirmed. "With all we been through together in life, you threatening me?" he asks. "I been loyal to you from day one, Storm." Tears drip from his eyes. "You would take my life?"

"I never questioned your loyalty until tonight. I never heard you lose it like this over shit that had to be done." She fights to keep the gun on her lap and not aim it at his head. "This the second time you have questioned my decision. Understand this… as leaders we don't make tough decisions because we want to. We make tough decisions because we have to."

She stares at him as a vision of blowing his head off rips through her mind. "Please don't make me think that you are questioning my leadership skills." She clenches her jaws tight, temples pulsating with anger. "And please, don't ever make me think that your loyalty to me has an expiration date."

"Young lady, have you come to the understanding that murder is not the answer?"

Angelica stares at the man in a cold stare. "In my world, sometimes, you are faced with two decisions, and neither one of them may be a choice that you want to make. So you make the best decision based on two bad choices. Murder may not be the choice you want to make, but it's the best choice for the time being."

The man shakes his head with no words for her in return.

23

ATLANTIC CITY

SIX HOURS OF Storm missing in action and she comes back to find her original seat at the penny slot vacant. She's been sitting here dumping dollars into the machine with no real interest at all. She's quite calm for a woman who just committed a double homicide a few hours ago. She barely revisit the murders.

She's been thinking about her decision making. She's not sure if she did the right thing leaving her only witness, Breezy, alive. She's dealing with the outcome of leaving a witness, already, and the harm they can do. She's on the fence about it, not sure if she will have to go back and finish the job.

She knows Breezy like the back of her hand and knows he's no dummy. She understands that she may have lost his trust, which means he will always be on point around her from now on. She knows that if she does decide to do it, she will have to be smart about it. She's already come up with the plan, just in case she has to go that route.

One thing she knows for certain is an attack on him won't be easy. She respects his gangster to the fullest. In no way does she take those few tears as a sign of weakness or pain. With Breezy being a master of deception, she views his crying as an act. That could easily be his way of sleepwalking her and attacking her when she least expects it. She's quite sure that if, by chance, they have to get to it, they both will have to be super creative because they know way too much about each other.

As she's caught up in her thoughts, she looks up to find a young, preppy Asian man staring at her over the machine. She flashes him an intimidating look to scare him off but to no avail. She rolls her eyes with attitude. She peeks under the slots and looks at his feet. His custom trousers fit perfectly over his wingtip shoes. His custom-made shirt is tucked neatly, exposing a slight hint of his Ferragamo belt. Storm can't help but notice the Cartier Roadster timepiece that is on his wrist. She's sort of impressed with his sense of fashion.

She continues on with the machine, and through her peripheral, she sees him making his way over to her. She gets agitated at the thought of it. He stops in front of her, and she ignores his presence, hoping he will get the hint and just leave.

She looks at him with the coldest look possible. "Can I help you?" she asks rudely.

He stands there, trying to force the words out of his mouth and it shows. "You're beautiful," he says with a heavy Asian dialect.

"Thank you," she replies even more rudely. Still he stands there as if he has more to say. "OK, you said that. Now what?"

"You work here?" he whispers.

"Work here? What you mean? You see me sitting here gambling like everybody else in here. Why would you ask me some dumb shit like that?"

He's quite taken aback at her response. Her beauty and her language don't seem to match. He was expecting something totally different and a lot more pleasant. "I apologize. What I meant to ask is, are you married?"

"What the fuck does that matter?"

"If you're not, I would like to call you sometimes and maybe get to know you."

She laughs in his face disrespectfully. "Know me for what?"

She removes the ego, and she quickly recognizes his language. He obviously thinks she's a working girl. "You can't get to know me, but I have some friends that would be more than happy to meet you."

"But I'm interested in you."

Storm pulls out her business card, which has her labeled as an event planner and party promoter. "Here. Take my card, and maybe later I will have one of my friends call you. We can set up a meet and greet event," she says just in case he's a cop.

"But..."

"But nothing," she interrupts. "Call me later. Right now, I'm gambling," she says brushing him off. He walks away reading from her card. He tucks it safely in his jacket pocket.

* * *

Meanwhile, Toy has been occupied with the same client all this time. She's brought him a great deal of luck, and he's compensated her well. She's scored five orange chips and one purple chip for doing absolutely nothing. That is a total of fifty-five hundred, and all he's done is ran his fingers through her hair and palm gripped her butt a few times. Overall, it's been easy money so far. Seems like all he really wants is an ear to listen to him brag about himself. She sits there, listening attentively, pretending to be interested.

At this present moment, they are indulging in dinner at Morton's Steakhouse inside the Caesar's casino. She's sure that she's on the desert menu. The man huffs as he sucks the fat off the bone. Toy stares over the table in amazement, as well as disgust. She conceals the disgust with a false smile just not to rub him the wrong way.

"Pretty lady, you made me the luckiest man in the world tonight," he says, staring over the rib bone. "And tonight I will repay you by making you the luckiest girl in the whole wide world."

"I'm feeling quite lucky already, just being in your presence," she says stroking his ego. She runs her bare foot up his leg while staring seductively into his eyes. She plants her toes onto his crotch and feels his erection. She rubs her foot along the length of his manhood and with her toes; she teases the tip. He damn near busts through the tight trousers. She flashes a seductive wink. "Lucky me."

* * *

In Newark, caution tape surrounds the intersection. Police and detectives swarm the area as the coroner's van pulls up. The unmarked police car pulls up to the tape, and both doors bust open simultaneously. The female detective leads the way toward the area where the crashed car is on the sidewalk.

"What's the story?" the female detective asks the detective who is handling the case.

"A double homicide. Apparently a brother and sister. The sister was just released on bail and not even a mile away… this," he says, pointing to the car. "Seven gunshots to the head. The driver, two to the head and one to the chest."

The detectives peek into the car at the two dead bodies. A weird feeling takes over as the female detective peeks in. "What's her name?"

The man hands over Kirah's jail release papers. The female detective reads over the paperwork with a solemn look. She hands the paperwork over to her partner, not able to say a word. The partner recognizes the name immediately. They stare into each other's eyes, both thinking the same thing.

24

ATLANTIC CITY
3 A.M.

STORM SITS IN the luxurious hotel suite, laid back on the couch, her mind heavy. Sitting before her on edge of the coffee table is the preppy Asian. Hours ago she left the casino and went to her room to get some rest. Sleep never happened because the only thing on her mind was Breezy. Leaving him alive is haunting her.

As she tossed and turned her phone rang, and it was the Asian. She explained to him that her girls were occupied at the time, but still he wouldn't let up. His persistence irked her dearly, but it made her think of the opportunity that she could be missing. For all she knows, he could be super wealthy and she could be passing up on the chance of a lifetime.

He stares at her with a deep lust that is uncomfortable to her. He looks from her eyes to her breasts with shame. It's as if his eyes are locked onto them. Her low-cut blouse gives him just enough of a glimpse of her cleavage to make him want to see more.

She decides to play his little game with him. "So, what is that you want from me?" she asks as she pops the top button of the blouse allowing him to see more.

"I just want to talk," he claims.

"Oh, is that all you want? My time costs money."

"How much?" he asks.

"Depends on what you want to talk about and how much time it takes to talk about it."

"I don't know… maybe an hour."

"An hour is a long time." She decides to test the water. "That will cost you five hundred."

Without flinching the Asian reaches to his right and grabs a purple chip. He hands it to her with his hand trembling. She tosses the chip in the air and catches it, clenching a tight fist around it. "Let's talk. What you want to talk about?"

"What is your name?" he asks.

"We can talk about anything but my name. What else would you like to talk about?"

"How about we talk about how beautiful you are?"

"Beauty is overrated," she says, shutting him down. The man looks closely at the shiny coat of perspiration which is building on her breast, making them look like perfectly glazed honey dew melons. She looks down and notices it as well. With a tissue, she dabs the sweat trails that seep into the crease of her cleavage line.

Drool fills the corner of his mouth, and he can't help but to stare. "Snap out of it," she says with a smile.

"Sorry, it's just that your breasts are beautiful."

"So, I've been told. Would you like to see them?" He can't believe his ears. He nods his head up and down quickly before she changes her mind. "That will cost you a thousand," she says with a straight face.

With no hesitation, he grabs two chips and hands them over to her. Slowly she unloosens the buttons of her blouse, seducing him along the way. His heart pounds faster with each button opening. The more skin he sees, the more he wants to see. There her breast sit perfectly in their cups. Her butterscotch nipples peek over nosily. She allows his excitement to build before she grips the bra from the bottom and flips it over the top of her breasts. They bounce vibrantly before sitting firmly.

He stares at them in awe. The drool that filled the corners of his mouth now drips down onto his chin. Storm is enjoying this little game with him, yet she keeps the same face of nonchalance. He can't resist the urge to touch them. He reaches out to grab them, but she grabs hold of his hands. "What are you doing?"

"Sorry," he says, lowering his head in shame like a disobedient dog. "I couldn't help it."

"I thought you just wanted to talk," she says, still holding his hands. "I should let you touch them."

A spark of excitement brightens up in his eyes. "Please?" he begs.

She is well aware that she has him right where she wants him. "Fifteen hundred and you can touch them." She lets one hand go, so he can grab the chips and he does. He hands her the chips, and she grabs hold of his hand again. She slowly guides his hands and places them onto her breast. She applies pressure onto his hands allowing him to get a full grip.

Her skin feels like silk under the palm of his hands. He squeezes them gently while rubbing his thumbs over her nipples. Her nipples become erect and as hard as steel. He removes his thumbs to enjoy the beauty of her hardened nipples. Her nipples aren't the only thing hard right now. The little bump in the crotch of his trousers indicates that.

"Not like that," she says. "Like this," she whispers as she teaches him how to caress them. Just when it gets really good to him, she stops. She removes his hands. "That's it."

He's panting with a look of perversion in his eyes. He wants more. Shamelessly, he places one hand over his crotch to hide his erection. Without realizing he strokes himself. "You horny?" she asks.

He nods his head up and down. "You want me to touch it?"

"Yes, please," he whispers.

She shakes her head. "Nah, but you can touch it."

He quickly unzips his pants and fumbles inside. Right before he takes his first stroke she speaks again. "That's gonna cost you twenty-five hundred."

A distasteful look plasters his face. "That's too much," he says.

"Okay, then," she says as she pulls her bra over her boobs. He feels like his lifeline has been cut.

"Okay, okay." He grabs hold of the chips and hands them to her. She quickly lifts the bra for his pleasure. She gives him the head-nod to go on and he does. With no shame, he pleasures himself by stroking and pulling on his shrimp egg roll.

His eyes are glued onto her breasts hypnotically. He can't refrain himself any longer. He does away with the shame and continues whacking off like a maniac. He quickly erupts and makes a mess all over his trousers.

She stands up before he's even done. The show is over. She covers the beauties with her bra and buttons her blouse. She dumps the chips into her pocket and walks away, leaving him sulking in ejaculation. She feels great satisfaction in knowing that she still has the power to have a man eating out of her hand and without touching him nor barely letting him touch her. She feels like she's mastered the game.

25

MONTCLAIR, NEW JERSEY
THE NEXT DAY

WHILE EVERYONE HAS been busy at working on Storm's defense, the detectives are busy working on her capture and conviction. The detectives stand at the door of a beautiful one-family home, on the quiet, suburban block. They've knocked on the door, awaiting a response. The door opens and a ravishing middle-aged woman stands at the door. Her beauty is toned down by her moderate, homely dress. She looks like she could be in her mid-thirties, but her granny style of dress makes her look so much older.

"Yes, may I help you?"

"Mrs. Hill?" the female detective asks.

"Yes," the woman replies, not having a clue who they are or what they want.

"Newark Police. We have a few questions for you."

Her brows connect in confusion. "Pertaining to?"

"Your daughter."

"Oh, Lord. Is she okay?" the woman asks with a saddened look on her face.

"That we don't know. That's what we are here to try to find out from you."

The woman shakes her head in pity. Her husband, a tall and husky handsome man, appears and stands right at her side. "Your guess is as good as mine," the woman says. "We haven't seen or heard from that girl in six years."

The female detective stands in disbelief. This seems quite odd to her. "Six years?"

The man steps up and takes over the conversation. "What has that girl gotten herself into?"

"A huge mess, sir," the female detective says. "At this point, we would like to question her about a few murders."

The man's mouth drops wide open while the woman begins crying. The man consoles her, not knowing exactly what to say. "Listen, we have done the best we can possibly do for her. Her lifestyle, we don't condone, but she has a mind of her own. We didn't raise her like this. We have another child who is nothing like her. Never been in trouble in his life.

Her brother is being ordained to be a pastor. She's the black sheep of the family." He begins to sob as well. "I'm a pastor, with my own church. My wife here is an evangelist. We are a God-fearing family. We named her Angelica, a biblical name. That Storm name she's given herself ain't nothing but the devil."

"I'm sorry to hear that, sir," the female detective says with sincerity.

"We have done everything we could to keep her on the right track."

"I understand, sir. It happens, and sometimes it's out of our control. I'm sorry to bring this to your doorstep, but can you lead us to her? I'm trying to protect her for your sake. I would hate to come back here with news that will further break your heart."

The man shakes his head in despair. "We know nothing. We haven't seen or heard from her in years as my wife has stated." He pats his wife's back, consoling her.

"Think of anything that could possibly help us," the detective suggests. "A last known address… anything?"

The man and woman lift up from their sobbing. The look in their eyes indicates that they may have a lead.

* * *

Storm is going on about her daily business, without a clue as to how close they are on her heels. She's too busy moving onto her next business adventure to allow the thoughts of her possible demise to slow her down. Storm sits in the passenger's seat of the rented caravan while Mud sits in the driver's seat. She drops a duffle bag onto his lap. "You sure you can handle the job?"

He looks at her with a look of agitation. "Come on now. I got this."

"Cool, just checking. That's five grand right there. Gas, toll, and eat money, and the thirty-five hundred I promised you for the job."

Mud opens the bag, and on top of the money are two twin Glock 9s with extended clips. In the corner of the bag, there is the tiniest gun he's ever seen. The Secret Semmerling 5-shot .45 is small enough to get lost in the bag. It fits right in the palm of a hand. He looks at the little beauty in admiration before taking the neatly stacked money from the bag. He quickly zips it up.

She reaches over to give him dap. "You be safe. I will be calling to check on you every hour on the hour." She exits the vehicle and walks toward her car. Mud pulls off, heading for his destination, while Storm is onto hers. Her girls are waiting for her at the airport. They are on their way to the money.

26

ORLANDO, FLORIDA
TWO DAYS LATER

STORM AND HER girls are in the hotel room preparing themselves for this big weekend. Storm sits on the dresser while Toy and Wendy sit on the foot of the bed on opposite sides of the newest addition to the team, Jazz. Jazz is from the same cookie cutter mold as Toy and Wendy when it comes to beauty. She's even more gorgeous than them and, of course, high yellow in complexion. Her long, silky, natural hair against her smooth complexion gives her a more exotic look. Not only is she more beautiful than the other two, she's also more polished and classy.

One would think Storm is prejudice and only likes light skin, pretty women because that is all she seems to pick to be on her team but only she knows that isn't the case. She's prejudice for sure, but contrary to one's belief, she chooses those complexioned women because she hates them not because she loves them. She despises them so much that she enjoys the opportunity to dominate, humiliate, and manipulate them into doing whatever it is she wants them to do. In her sick mind, it's like her payback to all the women who look like them and think they are God's gift to the universe.

Jazz, which is short for Jasmine, is Wendy's best friend. Her story is completely different from Wendy's, though. She's a more uptight, bourgeois woman who is a complete stranger to this world. She's a wife and mother of two children who never had to do anything for herself until her husband was incarcerated a few months ago. Her only reason for considering this is to fend for herself and her children.

She sits here debating and having second thoughts about it all. Storm and Wendy are trying their best to walk her through and teach her the ropes. "Just block it all out and look at it as business," Wendy says as if she's a master of the game now. She speaks with much more confidence now that it's as if she just wasn't in the same boat a short time ago.

"I know you're thinking about your husband but scratch that shit," Storm says. "Where he at he good. He get three square meals and he got a roof over his head. It's you and your kids that are out here in the world that won't have those luxuries if you don't make shit happen. That's your reality right now. Shit! I'm gon' tell you like an old bitch told me… A wet pussy and a dry purse don't match."

Jazz takes it all in and accepts it as truth. She's behind the eight-ball right now with a mortgage, car notes, and school tuition on her back. The few dollars her husband left behind are depleted at this point. He calls for her help, not once asking her where the help is coming from. That thought alone makes Jazz see him as selfish, yet she never says a word about it to him. She feels that he's self-centered and only cares about his own well-being, and that is one of the justifications she uses to help her even consider betraying him in this manner. When she looks at it in that perspective, the guilt is erased temporarily.

"Look at it like this," Toy says. She pauses long enough to dump the E pill. "The reality is you are gonna have to step out on your marriage sooner or later," she says while holding the pill on her tongue. She turns the water bottle up to her mouth and guzzles. She swallows the pill before speaking. "It's gonna happen. Eventually, you are going to need some help. You can fuck with some dude and take the risk of falling in love with him and betraying your husband and eventually abandoning him. Or you can do what you gotta do from a business standpoint with no emotional ties and never have to worry about it getting back to your husband."

"That's what I told her," Wendy says.

"Look, I'm not here to get you to do nothing you don't want to do," Storm says with no emotion whatsoever. "If you want to fall back on it all, that's cool with me. Just get the money back to me that I spent to get you here and we can scratch all this. Ain't no pressure. The choice is yours. What's it gonna be?"

The three of them look to her, wondering what her response will be. Jazz leans her head back with a deep exhale. She looks at Wendy with hatred for even talking her into this. She slowly clasps her right hand over her left. She slides the glistening three-karat diamond wedding band from her ring finger and tucks it into her pocketbook. "We here now," she says softly. "Let's go."

27

ORLANDO, FLORIDA
AMWAY CENTER ARENA
HOURS LATER

STORM IS STEPPING gracefully in a full-length snow white mink, a white mink hat, and white knee-high, strappy stilettos. She's looking like Snow White without the dwarfs. She feels a bit over-dressed to be going to a basketball arena, but she wouldn't have it any other way. She also feels crazy in fur in fifty degree weather, but she isn't the only one. The huge sunglasses on her eyes make her look like a celebrity, who is trying to be on the low but still scream-ing for attention. All the onlookers gawk at her, trying to figure out what famous person she could be.

She picks up her step, realizing that the Dunk Contest has al-ready started but she has no problem being fashionably late. Up ahead she spots a familiar face standing to the side of the arena. Wendy glows like a lightning bug in the dark. Storm sees her en-gaging in conversation with a man and is glad to see her working.

As she gets closer and recognizes the man's face, her blood boils. Johnny Cash stands in front of her, running his mouth as usual. His stable of young hood mice is not far away from him. She was sure he wouldn't miss this event, and as much as she prayed for his presence, she still was not mentally prepared to see him again. The fury she felt that night they informally met is nothing compared to the fury she feels this moment.

She contains her rage as she approaches them. Wendy's back is to Storm, so she doesn't see her coming, but Johnny Cash does. As he spots her over Wendy's shoulder, that cocky smile from the other night spreads over his face. His cocky aura livens. Storm stops short right behind Wendy, who turns around with a huge smile on her face. She can feel the rage burning through Storm's sunglasses as the smile vanishes.

Out of nowhere, a crisp backhand presents itself, sending Wendy back a few steps while holding her face. All she can do is hold her face in shock before the embarrassment settles in. A few people standing close by have peeped it and are now staring. "You laughing with the enemy?" Storm asks.

Wendy stands there with her neck stiff from whiplash, nose running like a faucet and her face stinging. Storm has slapped snot out of her nose. She wipes her nose with embarrassment. She senses another backhand brewing and decides to get away before it takes place. She backs away with her head hanging low in humiliation.

Storm steps close to Johnny Cash, who is still wearing the smirk of sarcasm. He doesn't budge until he feels the bulge from her pocket jam into his gut. She holds the gun, pointed at him. "If it wasn't so many people out here right now, I would blow that dumb-ass smile right off your face and your head with it," she says with her lip trembling as if she's fighting to refrain from doing so.

He's stuck and the smirk has vanished. He looks around, hoping someone sees it, but even the people who do don't know she has a gun resting on him. She's now chin to chest with him. "I told you we would meet again, but you thought it was a game. Laugh now."

Johnny Cash's faithful, bottom-chick steps over to his aid and Storm acts as if she doesn't even see her. He looks to her with a fear in his eyes that she's never seen. He gives her a sign by simply shaking his head no.

Now standing right behind Storm is Mud and his man that he brought along for the ride, as well as reassurance. They stand behind her, heads on swivel, watching their surroundings. Johnny Cash becomes more fearful as he recognizes their presence.

Storm continues on. "Listen, take you and your dirty little bitches and y'all blow the joint. Ain't enough money here for all of us. We got it from here. Matter of fact, the next few events, we got those, too. You got a pass tonight. Take it as that. From this day on, anytime you see me in the building, recognize strength and get out of my way. Respect my handle and respect my pimping."

She slowly backs away from him, gun still aimed in her pocket. "Now y'all go and pack it up before shit get crazy out here." Mud and his man step closer. Johnny Cash wastes not another second. He steps away from them with a fake cool and calm demeanor.

Storm looks over to his bottom-bitch who is staring at her angrily. "And let me tell you something, you lil filthy bitch. The next time you step in my face, I will leave you and him right where you do it at. Since you wanna play bottom-bitch, after I smash him out, I will be sure to stack y'all two motherfuckers on top of each other, you on the bottom."

Johnny Cash wraps his arm around the girl and leads her away. Storm steps toward the entrance of the arena as if nothing has happened. Mud and his man follow many feet behind like they aren't together. She didn't have him drive here for thirty hours for reinforcement because she really doesn't need them for that.

Her only reason for having him drive here is to transport the guns because she couldn't bring them on the plane. Johnny Cash caught her butt naked last time, but that will never happen again. From here on out, she will never be butt naked again. If she covers an event in Tahiti, she will find a way to have her guns meet her. That night, at Super Bowl Weekend, she made the vow that she will never again be caught with her pants down.

28

S TORM AND TOY sit side by side in their floor seats, watching the Dunk Contest, pretending to be concerned with it. Really they are watching the audience like hawks looking for work. Wendy sits a few seats away from them with empty seats in between them. Her face is still stinging from the backhand and her anger is still burning inside. She looks at Storm through the corner of her eye, pissed to no end with her.

If she thought she could get her hit back with no repercussions she would, but Toy already warned her to take the slap with a grain of salt and just chalk it up. They haven't said a word to each other since they've been in here. Storm is curious to know what Wendy and him were talking about but hasn't asked yet because it may only piss her off even more. She feels the conversation will present itself eventually.

She feels Wendy had no business interacting with him because that could have easily given him the impression that he could infiltrate their camp. Her perception; if he can make her smile, he can make her crossover. Humiliating Wendy publicly, brought Storm enjoyment and she has no regrets. She feels the slap was beyond justified because she had to send a message to Wendy that there are consequences for going against the grain. She had to prove to Johnny Cash, her and anybody else that may have been watching and may have known what was going on that her pimping will be respected.

* * *

Meanwhile, as hard as Jazz has been trying to stay out of the way and not be noticed, it's been impossible. Her beauty seems to be outshining the beauty of the other two and attracting the attention of men the whole time. It's like her laidback demeanor is making them gravitate to her more. None of them see her as a working girl here trading sex for money.

Even without her wedding ring on her finger, they see her as the wifing type. Her true aura shines through. They are pushing up on her, offering her the world, and hoping she will give them a chance. That is until Wendy and Toy find a way to slide it into the conversation that she's for sale, just as they are.

It's surprising to her that doesn't turn them off in the least bit. In fact, once they find that out, they end up pushing up on her harder. She's passed so many of them off to the other girls, basically rejecting all offers. She hates to be doing this anyway, and even though she's sacrificing her morals, she refuses to just give herself to anyone.

As the night progresses and the thoughts of her bills back at home keep jabbing at her, she realizes she has to bust a move. Still she doesn't go for just anybody who comes at her. After many turn-offs approached her, a halfway decent man made his presence known. It wasn't necessarily his approach or his decency that had her contemplating his offer. It was that Storm was sitting right by her and heard every word, giving her no room to deny.

Right now, Jazz lie in the king-size bed in the hotel room, looking up at the ceiling with her legs spread wide open. The man pounds away at her guts with no compassion. Tears trickle down her face. Those tears are not tears of pain. They are tears of guilt.

She can't believe that she is betraying her husband. It's like an out of body experience right now. As hard as he's pounding away at her, she can't even feel him because her body may be here, but her mind is with her husband.

The nightstand rattles from the vibration of her phone. She peeks over and through teary, cloudy eyes she recognizes the number. It's her husband calling from jail; how ironic. She watches the phone the entire time it's ringing and all she can think is, *what is he thinking right now*. Her guilt makes her feel as if he knows she's up to no good. She's never missed one of his phone calls since he's been away, and she's sure he finds that strange.

The phone finally stops ringing but starts right back up instantly. Three back to back calls and he finally gives up. The tears now cover her face. She sobs with no sound. The man opens his eyes long enough to see her face full of tears. His ego shoots to the moon, figuring he's fucking the life out of her. This, in turn, makes him pound harder. Still she doesn't feel him. The pain he may be bringing to her pussy is nowhere near the pain that she feels in her heart.

29

THE NEXT NIGHT

S TORM FEELS LIKE a small child or a midget in the room of so many amazingly tall men. She's never seen so many seven-footers in her life. It's All-Star weekend and the Western Conference beat the Eastern, which is the reason for the celebration.

The smell of money is circulating through the air. Storm knew there would be an overabundance of fine, young millionaires present, and that is why she is here. Apparently Storm isn't the only one who knew the money would be in the building. The ratio is one man to every ten women. Nine out of every ten women are out on the dance floor shaking it up, hoping to attract the attention of the wealthy ballplayers in the building. Right now the sounds of Alicia Keys' "Girl on Fire" has them all on the floor, showing off their sexiest moves.

Storm locks her eyes onto the money. Directly across from them, a bunch of men are popping bottles and carrying on egotistically. The men are draped in so many glistening diamonds that it's blinding. At that table the focal point is the most valuable player of the game. Kevin Durant can barely be seen through the men surrounding him. Everyone is carrying on, treating him like royalty.

A couple of beauties approach the men and they are welcomed hospitably. Storm sees them as a threat and fears they may beat them to the money. She realizes the time is now to send her team in. "Come on, y'all. Let's get to it."

With no hesitation, Toy gets up and gets herself together. She quickly leaves the table and Wendy follows close behind. A few steps and she turns around to see Jazz still sitting. Storm looks at Jazz with a piercing eye. Jazz gets up and follows behind the girls.

Storm sits low in her seat and watches with satisfaction as her "Angels," as she likes to call them, infiltrate. Toy and Wendy operate like the perfect tag-team duo. Jazz, on the other hand, appears to be out of place, but Storm is sure she will eventually pick up some game. In minutes her girls manage to dominate the situation and take all of the attention. The few girls that were there, ease away from the table one by one. Storm sits back with pride, knowing that she's trained her girls well.

An image pops up out of nowhere on Storm's right side. She looks over with the smirk still plastered on her face. Her eyes meet with a stranger who stands at the edge of the table. She quickly erases the smirk and replaces it with her poker face.

"Damn! Why you hiding that lovely smile?" the man asks as leans onto the table. "I saw those pretty choppers from across the room," he teases. She peers into his eyes coldly without a verbal reply. "I don't mean no disrespect. I just wish I was the one who could bring a smile on your face like that one I just saw."

Storm looks away from him, making him feel like a peon, but he's persistent. "I came to buy you a drink, but from the looks of it somebody already beat me to it," he says as he extends his hands over the champagne. "You mind if I take a seat?" he asks while sliding the chair from under the table.

As he's speaking the reflection from the diamonds on his watch clash into the diamonds from her bracelet. It's like two bolts of electricity have collided; quite blinding. The glare from their diamonds bounce off each other, dancing with perfect choreography.

He can't help but to notice the quality of her diamonds. With a jewelry package like hers, he's sure she's not easy to impress. He feels obligated, to at least try. On the sly, he lets his sleeve slide up his wrist to show off his bracelet. When he does, the reflection from the diamonds ricochet off the foil on the champagne bottle and bounce onto the strobe light on the ceiling. It doesn't stop there though. From the strobe light, the reflection bounces from table to table before cutting through the mirror in front of him. He stands there glowing like a superhero.

Storm purposely looks away from the bracelet because she knows he's throwing his hand around with hopes of her seeing it. Once that tactic doesn't work, he reaches in his bag of desperation. He drops his car key onto the table face up, exposing the Aston Martin symbol. He grabs the back of the seat. "Yes, no, maybe?" he asks with a charming smile.

There's an evident brick wall in between the two of them and he loves it. Nothing is more entertaining to him than a challenge. What he doesn't know is the challenge is really just a figment of his imagination because he has her attention right now. He just doesn't know it because she doesn't want to make it seem so easy for him.

If she was on the market looking, he surely would be one that she would look at. He's just her type, smooth brown skin with the wavy hair to match. His teeth are so perfect, they are suspect to her. She assumes they have to be veneers. She's not on the market though, so none of that matters. She will humor him, though, to kill time. Another reason she will entertain him is his level of game and would love to play around with him just to keep hers tight. As they say, steel sharpens steel.

"Can I?"

"Fuck you asking me for?" she asks hastily. "This a public bar. Sit where you want," she says before rolling her eyes.

"Feisty lil one," he laughs. "I love 'em feisty. Just my type."

You took the words right out of my mouth, she thinks to herself. "My type as well," she mumbles under her breath. She looks into his eyes for the first time and neither of them blink. "You don't even dig it, though," she mumbles under her breath.

"I'm Money Sal... What's your name?"

Storm stares at him with a false disgust. It's just her normal sassiness that she displays with men, whether interested or not. She knows no other way. "Listen, all these chicks in here, you can find another to run your lil bullshit on. I ain't with it."

"Dig, I ain't about the bullshit either. I see all these other chicks in here, but I'm over here. Why we even talking about them?" he says as he cracks a charming smile. "I'm here." The fact that she seems to be unimpressed with him makes him want her even more. He prepares for a game of mental tennis, which he knows will go back and forth for minutes until he breaks her down, but he's prepared for it.

* * *

Not even at the table for a whole twenty minutes and Toy managed to catch a mark. Her and that mark eased away from the table almost unnoticed. While Wendy and Jazz are back at the club entertaining the men all by themselves, Toy is here in this hotel room in a game of one on one. From the looks of it all, she appears to be winning.

The room reeks with the smell of green rubbing alcohol, enough to make your eyes water. Just minutes ago, Toy gave him an alcohol bath and body rub. It was her idea and she pretended it was for his pleasure but truly it was to her benefit.

Pores wide open, feeling like cool breeze, he lays flat on the bed. Toy positions herself to ride him reverse cowgirl. She reaches her hands over her shoulders for him to grab. They clasp hands tightly as she glides down on him. She slides up and down his rod slowly, allowing her entrance to get used to him.

He fits her like a snug glove making each stroke highly intense. She picks up the pace, only allowing herself to take in half of him. With forward thrusts, she guides him to pecking at her g-spot. Her back arches with the perfect curve to hit her spot perfectly, yet she manages to keep her own pleasure off of her mind.

She thrusts back and forth slow and impactful. He assumes it's great pussy that has him on edge and has him feeling sensational. There may be no doubt about the greatness of her pussy, but in this case, his sensitivity is heightened due to the alcohol opening his pores. Storm passed this trick down to Toy. Told her an old school whore she met passed the game down to her.

The man lifts up off the bed as he tries to take his mind off of the pleasure that he's experiencing. It's hard for him to do when he has the most perfect rounded ass spread in his face. Toy slow grinds, teasing him to no end. She drags her fingernails from his knees on down to his ankles, causing goosebumps to pop up all over his body.

"Damn," he sighs. He mumbles more words under his breath, barely able to speak.

Toy looks back at him, over her shoulder. "What?" she asks and stares into his eyes. "What you say?"

"Girl, why are you doing this?" he asks. "I can take you away from all of this."

This isn't the first time she's heard that. *Dumb nigga*, she thinks to herself. Always talking about rescuing a woman and can't even save themselves. What they don't know is she's not looking to be rescued.

Her vibe is interrupted and she can't refrain from saying something. "What makes you think I want to be saved? Save me, then what? I commit and you cheat on me paying for pussy on the side? She shakes her head with a smile. "Nah, I'm good." She looks straight ahead and continues on with her job.

At the end of a full thrust, she leans over and grabs hold of his toes and holds on as she speeds up her grinding. She bangs as hard as she can take it. His manhood pulsating inside her tells her that he can't take her for much longer. She bangs harder.

She squeezes her cheeks tight and chokes his manhood after each thrust. His toes spread widely, which is an indication that she has him where she wants him. She arches her back and applies short, fast strokes. Her ass spreads wider and her small but firm cheeks clap harder. She stops long enough to give him a clear view of her backdoor, knowing how appealing it will be to him. She makes the asshole wink at him and he takes that as an open invite.

He rubs his middle finger around her twat to get his finger wet and juicy before he taps on her backdoor. Getting no answer, he takes it upon himself to enter. In and out of the backdoor his finger goes, deeper and deeper, hoping to please her as much as he's pleasing himself. Toy grips his ankles tighter and shoves his big toe into her mouth. She sucks the toe like a Blow pop.

He's never had his toes sucked before and sees it as super kinky. *Freak*, he thinks to himself. "Damn," he says as he lifts up in the bed to watch the show. She's not just sucking his toe, she's blowing his mind. She sucks toe by toe, never forgetting about the ride. It's all too much for him to bear. He can't hold back any longer. Just as he reaches his orgasm, Toy stops the action abruptly.

She hops off of him, leaving him trembling. She looks at him with a smile of satisfaction as he has no control of his limbs. Feeling quite embarrassed, he can't face her. He could've very well given his money away. Two thousand, five hundred dollars made in six minutes is over four hundred bucks a minute. The fastest money she's ever made.

30

THE NEXT NIGHT
10 P.M.

STORM RIDES SHOTGUN in the luxurious Aston Martin. The sound of Donell Jones' "You Know What's Up", seeps through the speakers. She can't believe how everything about this man seems to be on-point, even his choice of music. She peeks out of the corner of her eye as he sings along very sexy and animated. She's never been one for the lovey-dovey romantic songs, but she loves this one and it seems as if he's singing to her.

"*Ooh, say what, say what, say what… girl, you know what's up,*" he says as he snaps his fingers with the beat. He claps his hands, while licking his lips. "*I'm digging you, I'm feeling you… you know what's up.*" He stops at the light and as he's waiting he does a sexy little bop. "So, tell me what's up?" he says as he points in her face, teasingly. He does something that is normally forbidden and touches her lips. Even a shock to herself that she doesn't get the least bit mad as she usually does when a man puts his hands in her face.

His show is over once the traffic light changes. The song changes, and he changes back to his normal cool and calm swagger. The driver, Money Sal, the man she met last night just had to see her one last time before she left. Their cold introduction eventually warmed up. The heat got so intense that he propositioned her to stay the night with him but she rejected the offer. That was a hard offer to decline. She truly enjoyed his company.

She just didn't want to end up with him in between the sheets. The chemistry they had was a sure sign to her that she would end up in bed with him. His sex appeal is magnetic and had her wanting him. Normally she could trust herself with any man, but with him, that wasn't the case. She continued on with her game, not giving him a clue that she wanted him just as badly as he wanted her.

"Damn! It's crazy," he says as he pulls up to the arrival ramp of the airport. "I haven't even known you for twenty-four hours and I don't want you to leave me."

Storm blushes from ear to ear. She quickly regains her composure. "It be like that sometimes."

"Never been like that with me though."

"Well, there's a first time for everything," she says as she pushes the door open. She grabs her handbag from the backseat and slams the door.

He quickly gets out behind her. He runs to her, realizing the time clock is ticking. He refuses to let it end with him never seeing her again. He grabs her hand and stares into her eyes. "Tell me this is not how it's gonna end."

"It hasn't ended yet. I'm still here."

"Yeah, but once you get on that plane, is it over?"

She snatches away and leaves him with the question on his lips. "You can never tell. Life is funny," she smiles as she walks away. "It truly was a pleasure meeting you though. You got my number. Use it."

He watches her prance off sexily. She doesn't turn to face him the entire way into the building, but she can feel him watching her. As badly as she hopes this is not their last time in each other's presence, she refuses to come across as if she really cares. She knows they will meet again.

Toy and Wendy meet her at the door. The hair on both of their heads are a mess. Big bags from lack of sleep underline their eyes. In just twenty-four hours, they look like they have aged ten years.

Storm looks around. "Where's Jazz?"

"In the bathroom," Wendy replies, not even looking her way. The tension is still evident between them.

Toy attempts to ease the tension. "Girlfriend not doing too good. She taking this shit hard. She hasn't said a word all day. Eyes all puffy from crying. I don't think she cut out for this."

Storm shrugs her shoulders with no compassion. She couldn't care less. She notices the abundance of shopping bags that are mixed in with their luggage. The bags are the result of the few shopping sprees they were taken on today by a few of the ball players. Overall, it was a very fun weekend for them all. The trip also resulted in a decent score. The minimum price set was two grand per date. A few of them had to pay like they weigh and charged extra according to the power of the punch they packed.

Poor Jazz, of course, made the least money of them all. Of the twenty-five hundred she made off of her one client that wasn't enough to even pay Storm for her flight and the tickets. She's still in the rear a few dollars which means she will have to move out with them again on their next event or find a way to get the money to her. Storm has already told her that she's not taking a loss.

As cold as Storm is, she still found it in her heart to give Jazz half of the money back just so her weekend wouldn't be a complete blank, giving up her goods and betraying her husband for nothing. She hopes Jazz gets the kinks out of her system because she saw how the men reacted to her and realizes she can make a lot of money with her. She believes she will be fine once she gets over the guilt. One thing she knows for certain is starvation has a way of helping erase guilt.

As far as Toy and Wendy go, once Storm's original money spent was recovered, she split their earnings with them fifty-fifty, giving her a profit margin of a little over ten grand. The weekend was very profitable for her, and she didn't have to lay on her back not once, except to sleep. As she slept comfortably, her money was made. Sadly, Toy and Wendy can't say the same. A weekend of taking foot long dick has them tired and worn out with sore pussies. They have enough time to recover before the next event though.

31

SUMMIT, NEW JERSEY

THE SPACIOUS GOLF course looks quite bare at this time of the year. Just a few players are sprinkled along the course. At somewhere around the eighteenth hole, sits a beautiful mini-mansion on a hill, with the back facing the golf course. The deck of the house is enclosed in glass. A home overseeing the Canoe Brook Country Club, one of the most prestigious courses in New Jersey, is like a dream come true for a golf lover. Every window of the deck has been replaced due to golf balls flying through them but still the owner wouldn't trade the home for the world.

On the deck there sits Attorney Tony Austin and his guest Mr. Antonelli. Their relationship is beyond the typical lawyer and client business, which is why he feels comfort in welcoming Mr. Antonelli into his home. Tony has been invited to his home as well as golfed and vacationed with him. Although they have a few business ventures together, their relationship is built on history and not necessarily the dollar bill.

Tony dressed in satin pajamas looks like the black Hugh Heffner. He blows smoke rings from his cigar as his eyes are on the course. "Mr. A, now that we are alone, let me first start by asking you, how invested are you into this?" He turns around to face Mr. Antonelli.

"Invested?" Mr. Antonelli asks, not quite understanding the question.

"Yes, invested. I'm not speaking financially, of course. We both know the saying, 'it's not tricking if you have it,'" he says with a smile.

Tony knows one thing for certain that Mr. Antonelli is what he calls a "tender dick," which in all actuality means a sucker for love. In the past they have entertained women together while on vacation, whether for free or paid for, and Tony learned that much about him. Women that were merely for play, Mr. Antonelli has always taken seriously. Tony never judged him on it though. He just charged it to his old age.

"How much of your heart do you have invested?"

"I love her," Mr. Antonelli admits with shame.

Tony isn't surprised one bit. "I figured that much," he says shaking his head quite angered. "Can't help who we fall in love with but we should at least know who we are in love with. Do you?"

"I would imagine so. I've been dating her for close to five years now."

"Oh, okay, so you know all about her extensive record?"

"Huh?" Mr. Antonelli asks, quite surprised.

"Yeah, her record is as long as train smoke. Breaking and entering, shoplifting, fraudulent checks, assault and battery, possession of drugs, possession of unlawful firearms… and that's all as a juvenile. Robbery and assault with possession of a firearm are the lightest of her adult charges," Tony says without blinking.

The old man's face turns flush. He can't believe his ears. He knew she was a little rough around the edges but not that rough. He's speechless.

"Yeah, looks like your beautiful little angel is really the devil." Tony plants his hand on Mr. A's shoulder. "Mr. A, as your friend, I'm urging you to stay away from this one. She's not for you. You can find one that looks just like her and makes your old toes curl just as she does, but without the criminal history."

Mr. Antonelli hears him loud and clear, and as bad as she seems, he feels he knows another side of her that the rest of the world doesn't. He loves her dearly and can't imagine living his last years without her. "Tony, I truly respect your advice as a friend, but as an attorney, what do you have to say to me?"

"Well, in that case, as an attorney, I say, what I need is a ten-thousand-dollar retainer fee." Mr. Antonelli digs into his coat pocket and pulls out his checkbook. He cuts the check with a steady hand. He hands it over to Tony.

Tony grabs the check without looking at it. "Let's play ball!"

32

STORM SITS IN Mr. Antonelli's bedroom as he paces holes in the carpet. He has so many thoughts running through his mind. He's thought long and hard about what Tony told him. He hasn't slept a wink since that day.

Of all the feelings he has, betrayal is at the top of the list. He feels as if he should've been made aware of her past. He also feels afraid. Now that he knows about her past he fears her. He questions his safety around her. The little girl he fell in love with has been hiding her true self from him. He now sees her as a master at deception.

He stops short and looks at her, and he doesn't see the sweet girl that he once saw. He now sees a beautiful monster. He's thought about cutting ties with her, but truthfully he doesn't think his heart will let him do it. As part of his life, she makes his life worth living.

The suspense is killing her. It's obvious that something is weighing heavy on his mind, and she needs to know what it is. She wonders what he knows that he's not saying. "What's the matter? Talk to me," she says hastily.

"Baby," he says. "Why didn't you tell me about your criminal past?"

"What?" she barks. "Y'all motherfuckers digging into my past?" she asks, standing to her feet.

"Angel, I mean, baby," he says apologetically. "I have assigned an attorney to your case. Of course, he's gonna check into your past. He needs all the information he can get to help with your defense. Your criminal past doesn't help," he says with sarcasm.

She has no alternative but to get on the defense. "Fuck all that! You snooping around and shit."

"Baby, no one was snooping." He stares at her closer. "It's like I don't even know you. For five years, I've been sleeping with a stranger."

"Oh, now I'm a fucking stranger?" She's infuriated. "I ain't no fucking stranger when you want me in that bed with your whole face inside of me!" she yells.

"Shh," he says as he grabs her hand. He's trying to keep her calm so his housekeeper doesn't hear her.

"Shh, my ass," she barks. She grabs her pocketbook ready to make her escape, instead of facing the music. "Fuck you and that attorney! I will find my own attorney to prove my innocence."

"Baby, stop." He snatches her toward him. "He's already been paid and is on the case working diligently. He just called me right before you got here."

"What the fuck he say?" she asks curiously. "Or is that when he called you digging into my past, playing Inspector Gadget?"

"He said this has gone past questioning. They are no longer looking for you to question you," he says very sadly. "Now they are looking for you to charge you with the actual murders."

"What fucking murders? I told you, I'm fucking innocent!"

The housekeeper peeks her head into the room. "Mr. Antonelli, is everything okay?"

"Yeah, every fucking thing is okay!" Storm snaps. The woman rolls her eyes away from Storm, ignoring her.

"Yes, all is well. Please, just excuse us."

"Yeah, excuse yourself. You are fucking excused!"

The housekeeper and Storm lock eyes with nothing but tension between them. Storm has hated this woman from the first time she met her, and the feelings are evidently mutual. She disappears from the doorway without another word.

Mr. Antonelli gives it a few seconds before speaking. The last thing he needs is for the woman to hear this. He's extremely embarrassed. "Baby," he says soothingly to calm her down. "This problem isn't going anywhere. He says the detectives will not stop until they have you in custody to charge you."

"Charge me? This some bullshit. Told you he was a bullshit attorney. Can't even get me out of some shit that I don't have nothing to do with!"

"He will get you out of it, but you have to trust me. In order for him to help you, there is something you have to do first."

"And what the fuck is that?"

"You have to turn yourself in."

"Turn myself in so they can lock me the fuck up? Both of y'all fucking crazy if y'all think I'm gonna do that!"

"You won't spend an hour in custody. They charge you, and I will be right there to post the bond."

It all plays before her eyes. Her being arrested for murder and charged. She then sees herself going away to prison for life. What she can't envision is her voluntarily walking in there turning herself in to spend the rest of her life in prison. She feels like only a fool would willingly give away their freedom.

"I don't know about that shit."

"Baby, you have no choice if you want to prove your innocence. Other than that, you appear to be guilty. You are innocent, right?"

"Damn right I'm innocent," she lies with a straight face.

"Well, let's prove it then."

33

DAYS LATER

S TORM SITS ALONE in the sports bar inside of the Tropicana in Atlantic City while Toy and Jazz work the casino. Wendy had to stay home due to Mother Nature's arrival. Toy never has a guest due to the depo shot. She's been getting the shot for so long that she doesn't get a period at all. That works to her advantage because she's always in working order. She's urged Wendy to do the same, but she's been negligent in doing so.

Maybe the few days away from each other will ease the turbulence between them and give some time for the black and blue bruise underneath her eye to go away. They have been silently beefing ever since the slap.

With Wendy not here, Storm is expecting a dent in the earnings. She's glad that Jazz decided to come along. She isn't sure if Jazz is with them because she wants to be or because she needs the money, or if it's because she owes Storm. However she's here and that is all that matters to Storm.

Storm is no heavy drinker, but tonight she has been guzzling drink after drink. She's slightly tipsy, and her mind is not at ease. All she can think about is the trouble that is back in Newark. Mr. Antonelli has been pressuring her so much about turning herself in that she has started ignoring his calls. She realizes that the trouble isn't going to vanish, but she is undecided about turning herself in. At this current time, it is highly unlikely. She plans to go Ginger Bread man — catch me if you can.

As she leans her head back to guzzle the remainder of her drink, she locks eyes under the glass with one of the most beautiful women she's ever seen in her life. The woman is so beautiful that she can't take her eyes off her. She lowers the glass to put it on the table, yet they still have their eyes glued on each other. Her chocolate brown skin glistens with a haze of perspiration covering her face. Long and neat locs are twisted into a bun on the top of her head, resembling an African Goddess. Thin and silky baby hairs stream along her temples, down to her cheekbones.

She dances with a man who has his back toward Storm. The woman stares with bedroom eyes. Storm is well aware of what that look in her eyes means and finds it humorous. She isn't sure what the woman's thoughts may be, but hers is on money as usual. She's thinking of the money she can make with that woman on her team.

She would be the perfect contrast to the three she already has. Everybody's taste in women is not high yellow. Any man that has a sweet tooth for chocolate would do anything to have this piece of candy before her eyes. With this woman on the roster, she would be able to cover all angles of the board and would have something for everyone.

The big, husky, wide shouldered man moves awkwardly trying to keep step with the woman. A few moves and he obstructs their stare. The long black evening gown grips her petite but curvy frame. The woman grabs the man by the hips, slightly pushing him out of the way, so she can continue dancing for Storm.

She looks down at the woman's shoes just to see the quality of woman she is and is impressed. She recognizes the Christian Louboutin pump because she has the identical pair. She focuses on the woman's long leg that peeks through the split in the gown and she's surprised. So petite, but her legs are thick and amazingly sculpted.

The woman catches her looking at her legs and lifts the split, giving Storm a better view. She sways her hips from side to side before twirling around and giving Storm a long glimpse of her. The way her cheeks jiggle with each sway of her hips, it's obvious that her ass is bare under the dress. She spins back around and immediately locks eyes with Storm. She has no clue what the woman sees when she looks at her, but she knows all she sees when she looks at the woman is dollar signs. She's certain she could make some real money with this one.

* * *

Jazz prances through the casino when she believes her name is called. Her heart skips a beat, but she goes on, thinking that maybe she's hearing things. "Yo, Jazz!" shouts a male voice behind her. Still she continues on with her heart racing.

She can't imagine who this could be behind her calling her name. She hopes that by her continuing on without turning around he may figure he has the wrong person. She's scared shitless when she hears her name called again, but this time, the voice is closer. Her hand is gripped, and she has no choice but to turn around.

She slowly turns around and her face turns to shit when she sees a familiar face. The man is not just a friend of her husband's but he's his business partner as well. "Hey, Jeff," she says with her smile covering her fear and guilt.

He hugs her tightly. "What the hell you doing here? Smooth know you here?" he says over-protectively but covering it with a fake smile.

"Yeah, of course, he knows I'm here," she lies. She hopes her face doesn't give her away.

"Oh, all right, just checking." Still he decides to protect his partner's best interest. "Who you here with?"

"My grandmother," she lies with rapid fire. Her husband knows how much her grandmother loves to gamble, so it would be believable. "Old as hell with a gambling problem," she says accompanied by a smile. "We came here on a bus ride."

The man chuckles. "I hear that. Where she at though?" he asks looking around.

"That's what I'm trying to figure out." She pretends to be looking around in search. "She around here somewhere, losing all of her damn money."

"That's what it's for," he says. He quickly digs into his pocket. In his hand, he grips a hefty amount of crisp one hundred dollar bills. He counts out five of them and hands them to her. "You and your grandmother go on and enjoy yourselves."

Jazz is just about ready to reject the money until she thinks of all the bills that she's behind on. "Aww! Thank you."

He grips her hand, not letting go. "It's nothing. I'm just doing what I know my man would do for me." He finally lets her hand free. "Anything you ever need, don't hesitate to call me. All right?"

Gratitude covers her face. "Thank you. Now let me go find my grandmother."

"All right. Bet."

Jazz walks off and the man's eyes are glued onto her butt in the tight miniskirt that she's wearing. "Jazz!" he calls out.

She turns around and is surprised by the way that he's looking at her. "Anything. You hear me?"

The look makes her feel uncomfortable. "I hear you." She turns around quickly and continues on.

His eyes stay on her butt, which has him almost hypnotized. Suddenly his eyes are drawn to her left hand. No trace of her wedding band has him perplexed. He steps to the side out of her view, but he doesn't take his eyes off of her. He watches like she's one of his own, wondering where she's really going. Something about this doesn't sit right with him.

*　*　*

After dancing to another song and a drink in between, the beautiful woman finds her way over to Storm's table. Storm truly respects her courage. She stands across the table from Storm with a huge smile. Her bright white teeth look like those that belong in a commercial. She's even more beautiful up close than she was from across the room. Her distinctive features like her high cheekbones, pointed nose and cartoon character shaped eyes gives Storm reason to believe that she's a foreigner, but from where? She can't put a finger on it.

"I just had to come over here and tell you how beautiful you are," the woman says as she fiddles with the bun on the top of her head.

Me? Beautiful? Storm thinks to herself. She snickers taking the compliment as game. *Obviously this woman can't spot game when she sees it or else she wouldn't be standing here shooting the bullshit at me.* She decides to entertain the woman instead of shooting her down and crushing her spirits. Anyway she would love to have this woman as a part of the team.

"Thanks," Storm says with one brow raised. She chuckles inside as she looks away.

"What is your name?" the woman asks.

"Storm. Yours?"

"Ayinabeba." Her smile is dazzling. She finally has her locs out of the bun. "I know it's hard to pronounce." Storm is caught up in the woman's accent. It makes her even more sexy. "My friends just call me Beeba. I do hope to be friends." She shakes her head, to allow her locs to untangle on their own. Her hair once unloosened, falls to her waistline.

Storm decides to shoot the shit back at her for fun. "Beautiful name, matches your beauty to a tee," she says, causing the woman to blush. "What is that Indian?" she asks, taking a wild shot at it.

"No, Ethiopian. Means 'eyes like a flower, beautiful eyes.'"

"I totally agree," Storm replies, hitting her again before she could recover from the first blushing blow. "Is that where you're from? Ethopia?"

"Yes, born and raised for the most part. Been here in the states for a little over five years."

Wow, Storm thinks, *The woman could still be ripe and not yet Americanized.* That could easily work to her advantage when it comes to her game of manipulation and getting into the woman's head.

The brolic man steps over toward them. Storm gives him a quick once over as he approaches. Although he looks big and intimidating, he has a rather clean-cut edge. He carries it kind of borderline thuggish, not a drug dealer but not completely square either.

"Storm, this is my husband, Jay. Jay, this is Storm."

"Storm, it's truly a pleasure to meet you." He stops the waitress who is walking past and he places an order. He looks to Storm. "Can I buy you a drink?"

"No, no, thank you."

He flashes a big smile. "Come on, I insist."

"I said, no. Thank you," she says with agitation.

"Baby, she's even more beautiful up close, right?" the woman says, smiling from ear to ear.

"Yes, she really is. My wife couldn't keep her eyes off you. For the past half hour, you are all she's been talking about, right baby?" he asks his wife.

"Yes, I was like, I have to get over there and tell her how beautiful she is. It's not every day that you come across natural beauty. Everything today is so plastic. Don't you agree?"

This is starting to look crazy to Storm. Their whole angle is weird to her. She had no clue the man was her husband and now the two of them are here shooting their whack-ass game at her. Storm just smiles in response but her attention quickly diverts to the matching stainless steel Datejust Rolexes on their wrists. The faces and the bezels are iced out with class. Mr. Antonelli has exposed her to watches, and now that is the first thing she looks for. She doesn't know how she missed the huge stone on the woman's ring finger.

The man examines Storm closer with no shade. "Yes, baby, she's absolutely gorgeous."

Storm is becoming livid, knowing that they must think she's some slow chick that they can run game on. That is the incentive for her to play along with them. It's obvious to her that they are in search of a menagé and he sent his wife over to catch.

"Thank you. You two make a beautiful couple, too."

Now, both of them are blushing. "Storm, where are you from if I may ask?" Beeba questions.

"New York," Storm lies with the quickness. "Brooklyn, and y'all?" she asks quickly switching it. She prays they are not from Brooklyn and catch her in a lie. This woman looks like she could be the Brooklyn brownstone living, organic food eating, yoga type. She prays they don't ask her which part of Brooklyn she's from.

"Philadelphia. You ever come to Philly?" Beeba asks.

"Nah, never had a reason to before now," she says with a sexy smirk.

They both nod their heads, thinking she must understand their language. Storm smiles back at them. "Y'all wanna play? Let's play," she mumbles under her breath.

34

WENDY DRAGS HERSELF along to the door, groggy and angry. She's not a morning person and hates to be awakened, especially not during this time of the month when the cramps are unbearable. She just wants to sleep the pain away.

"Who?" she shouts from behind the door. She peeks through the peephole and fear takes her over as she sees badges hanging from the necks of the people who stand at the other side of the door. "Oh, shit!" she says nervously.

"Newark Police," the man says sternly. "Can you open the door, please?"

Wendy wonders what this could be about. She's clean as a whistle, so she's sure it's nothing that she's done, but one thing about growing up in the ghetto, the cops always seem to be against you. While those in the suburbs grow up with the mindset that the police are there as their servants, to serve and protect.

She stands there quietly, wishing she had never said a word. Then maybe they would think no one was home and went about their way. The knocking on the door this time is harder. "Open up!"

Wendy opens the door reluctantly. She stretches her T-shirt down to cover her panties as she stands face to face with the man and woman detective duo. Her heart pounds loud enough for them to hear.

The male detective has his eyes glued onto Wendy's chunky thighs. The way her hips explode, he can only imagine what the back looks like. Wendy is uncomfortable with his glare and stretches the shirt as far as she can. She doesn't have enough material on the shirt to cover herself. Even in granny-period panties, he finds her sexy.

"Where's Storm?" the female detective asks as she attempts to push Wendy to the side so they can enter. Wendy puts up resistance and pushes the door in between them.

"Hold up! Y'all can't come in my house. Y'all got the wrong house."

"Oh, do we?" the female detective asks. She pushes Wendy out of the way, and they enter the apartment. She isn't even playing the normal good cop role today. She means business. Bodies are dropping, and they need Storm in their custody.

"Do y'all have a search warrant?" Wendy asks, chasing behind them. She leaves the door wide open.

"Shut up before I arrest you for obstructing justice," the male detective says. His eyes are now fixed on her nipples through the shirt. The female detective catches him in perversion and nudges him to get himself together.

They both draw their guns and start looking through each room. They open closet doors, look under the beds and anywhere else a person can hide. The man continues on with his searching and makes sure there is no back door that she could have escaped out of.

"I'm gonna ask you again. Where is Storm?" the female detective asks.

"I don't know no Storm," she lies.

"Angelica Hill, this is her apartment, right?"

"Oh, you talking about her. She don't live here no more," Wendy says with sincerity in her eyes.

The faking of sincerity is easy because she is telling the truth. This apartment here is Storm's old apartment that she lived in before the old man upgraded her lifestyle. Storm then passed the apartment on to Toy, and once Wendy joined the team, she moved in as well. This apartment is part of the perks of being on her team. She pays the bill, allowing them to live rent-free.

"It's me and my roommate that live here now," she says still tagging along behind the woman. "That's her room there, and this is mine," she says as the woman takes liberty to go into the room. She peeks around nosily and finds a few pieces of mail lying around. She reads from the envelope. "Who is Gwendolyn Jackson?"

"That's me."

She tucks the mail in her hand and quickly walks to the next room. "You got a copy of the lease around here?"

"Listen, I don't know no Storm. Y'all can't be searching my apartment without no warrant."

"Get me a copy of that lease right now or get dressed and take a ride with us to the precinct. Your choice!"

* * *

Minutes later, Wendy is trembling like a leaf, very shaken up. She practically had to beg them not to take her down to the precinct. She has no idea what Storm is being sought for but whatever it is has to be serious. As she peeks out of the window and sees the unmarked car pulling off, she starts dialing on her phone.

* * *

Toy speeds up Route 95 in the rented Impala, while Jazz sits in the passenger's seat, just observing the scenery. Storm is in the backseat sound asleep. Toy's phone rings, and she picks it up from her lap. "Wendy, what's up?"

"Where y'all at?" she asks nervously. Y'all still in AC?"

Toy doesn't like the sound of her voice. "Nah, we on the Turnpike almost home. Why? What's up?"

"Listen, I need you to come home soon as you get to Newark. Something crazy just went down. Oh, and, tell your friend, not to come nowhere near here," she says with sarcasm but really her anger toward Storm is over. She's too concerned about her well-being right now to be mad at her.

"What happened? Talk to me!"

Storm is awakened and sits up in her seat, wondering what's going on. She watches the expression on Toy's face through the rearview mirror.

"Not on the phone, I can't," Wendy says sadly. "Just come straight here. Without her!"

35

HOURS LATER

S TORM SITS IN the driver's seat of her car, parked in Tops Diner's parking lot. Toy felt this was the best meeting spot, far enough away for them to meet safely. She drove straight here to meet Storm, barely stopping at the red lights. Toy is worried for her longtime friend. She's in the dark about any trouble that Storm could be in.

Storm didn't tell her that the police have been looking for her. She trusts Toy more than anybody else in her life but still she decided not to tell her. She knows in situations like this you can't trust your own mama because even she will bring you in. Storm never even told her about the robbery that all this is behind. She only believes that the only people who should know your business are the people you are partaking in that particular business with. Toy knows none of the things that Storm has involved herself in unless she too was involved in some type of way.

"They had your mugshot and everything, she said," Toy advises.

"That's crazy," Storm sighs, as the only thing she can say. She can't think of how they possibly knew to go there.

"They even took a copy of the lease with them. Now they got my name on file. Now they gonna be looking for me."

"That ain't nothing though. Me and you have no criminal history together so that won't affect you," Storm says with no real concern of that.

"So, you can't think of nothing that they could be looking for you for?"

Storm shakes her head slowly as if she's really thinking. "Nah, nothing." Storm's phone rings and when she looks at the display she sees Mr. Antonelli's number. Curiosity makes her want to answer. She wonders if he has some more news about the detectives. She's considering answering but doesn't because he could easily be calling to get her to turn herself in. That is what every call to her has been about. She's been telling him that she has some things to handle before turning herself in, but she's already worn that excuse out which is why she hasn't answered his calls in days. She wonders if maybe not answering is not a good idea because he may have some pertinent information

"Well, they not playing. Whatever it is has to be serious. She said they was trying to take her down to the precinct for a lie detector test."

"That was bullshit. They were just trying to scare her up." Storm starts to think harder. She wonders what exactly Wendy may have told them out of fear. She wonders if maybe she gave her up and that is why they didn't take her. "Yo, you think she gave me up?"

"Nah, I don't think so. She was too scared for you. I can tell her concern was genuine."

"But you know she still salty with me about what happened, All-Star weekend. I don't trust no emotional bitch. I need to talk to her myself, so I can look in her eyes."

"You can't go to the house though. They may be watching."

"Nah I ain't going nowhere near there. Get her on the phone so we can meet. I don't want to call her from my phone. I don't trust it."

Toy gets to dialing. "And don't tell her that I'm coming. Tell her you want to meet with her."

"OK," Toy says as she listens to the phone ring.

"I'm telling you ahead of time though," Storm whispers. "If I get the slightest feeling that she said anything, she done. I ain't gon' hesitate to blow her brains out."

Toy looks over at Storm shocked at what she's just said. She wants to hang up the phone, but it's too late.

"Hello?" Wendy says.

Storm looks at Toy with threatening eyes. "Tell her to meet you at McDonald's on Bergen Street." She takes the gun from her pocket and places it on her lap. "Tell her you will be there in ten minutes."

Toy is speechless and in disbelief.

36

AKRON, OHIO
DAYS LATER

N OT TWO WEEKS have gone by and Storm and Money Sal from
All-Star weekend have reunited. He stays beating her phone
line up almost all day every day, especially the past few days. She
even gave in a little and reciprocated the energy. She hasn't called
him as much as he called but she has indicated that she's interested.

From the time she landed in Jersey he had been desperately trying to fly her into his city to meet with him. She held off for as long
as she could before giving into his request. The moment she did, he
made the arrangements for her first-class flight. He wouldn't have
it any other way, he believes she's worthy of.

With the detectives on her heels back in Newark, this was the
perfect opportunity to get away to clear her head and strategize her
next move. During the meeting the other day with Wendy, Storm
couldn't find any reason to think that she had given them any information. Wendy even cried and told her that she loves her which
was shocking to Storm and Toy. She's just as worried about Storm
as Toy is. Both of them are still very much in the dark about it all.

Storm arrived in Ohio a few hours ago, and Money Sal was
there to welcome her with open arms. After lunch, he had a full

itinerary laid out which consisted of all the things that she loves to do — shopping, the spa, a movie, and lots of weed smoking in between. This is by far one of the best dates that she's ever had. It's not just the things they did that makes it the best date, it's his overall company. He's so cool that she would enjoy herself with him, even if they were doing nothing at all.

She isn't shocked by any of this because she felt his energy back in Florida. The resistance that she put up had everything to do with her not being in touch with her true emotions. It's easier for her to deal with a man that she doesn't like than it is for her to deal with a man that she does like. Any time she has met someone she liked she would end the relationship for the smallest thing just to have an escape. It's been easier that way and she could protect her heart and her feelings.

In no way has she fallen for Money Sal, but his charm is winning her over. She's never been charmed by a man like this, except by Mr. Antonelli, but he doesn't count because she still considers him business. Well, at least that is what she tells herself. Because he's business, she denies any feelings she may have for him.

After all the money this man has spent and the hospitality that he's shown her, she felt that he deserved the opportunity to cash in. It wasn't all about the dollar amount spent though. A great deal of why they've ended up in his bed has to do with she couldn't wait to give him some. The anticipation was at an all time high for her.

Storm lie back in the enormous bed inside of his spacious loft. She stares up at the high ceilings gasping for air as he licks her body in its entirety. She fights hard to restrain her urge to orgasm, but it's bubbling inside of her. Their chemistry is so strong that she could cum just staring into his eyes.

They indulge in a passionate kiss while he grinds away at her. He fumbles for her breast and her nipples harden at the thought of his lips touching them. She arches her back, poking her breasts up at him and he drops his head in between them. He squeezes them together before sliding his tongue between them. He licks like a frisky puppy, not missing a spot. The feeling of his hot breath on her breasts makes her pussy pulsate.

He drags his tongue down the path to her navel. He french kisses her navel while pinching her hardened nipples. He plants soft wet kisses over her abdomen and down to the sexy V line of her pelvis. He nibbles gently on her side, dripping saliva from his mouth like a thirsty dog. Surprisingly his spit turns her on, which is strange for her because she hates the thought of a person's spit on her.

His tongue slides over her abdomen to her treasure. She looks down and becomes seasick as her eyes roll over the waves that flow over the top of his head. She can't keep her hands off of him. She rubs his hair and the ripples of his deep waves gets her more excited. Her kitten throbs violently.

He lifts his head and takes a long look at the beauty of her kitten before introducing his mouth to it. Just when she thinks he's about to go in for the kill, he detours and begins kissing on her thighs. This is forbidden land for her, one of the only spots that makes her weak. She wiggles away from him, trying to keep him from hitting her spot but to no avail.

"No," she moans as she grabs his head and tries to force him away. Her rebuttal drives him wild. He snaps his neck and frees his head from her grip. He sucks on her inner thigh, right on the bullseye.

A violent orgasm brews inside of her and she fights like hell to keep it from exploding. She grips the pillow with one hand while waving the other in the air, looking for something to grab. The lamp is the closest thing in her reach. She snatches it from the nightstand by the base and flings it. It breaks into pieces after crashing into the wall. He's so caught up in pleasuring her that he pays it no mind. He continues on teasing and licking and sucking at her spot. "No, no, stop," she begs. Suddenly her body tenses up and with no further warning, it happens… Her levee breaks.

She blasts off and her juices splash onto his chest. She sits back, mouth wide open in shock. She stares at him with embarrassment on her face. She can't believe it happened. He jumps back in awe. He looks down at her juices that are plastered all over him.

"What the fuck?" he asks in rage.

"Sorry," she says being the only word that she can come up with.

"Fuck yo!" he says as he snatches the sheet from the bed and wipes himself dry. He looks around at the puddle on the floor and on his bed and he gets even more enraged and disgusted.

Now she's beyond embarrassed. She wishes she could just disappear right now. The vibe has been destroyed. Reacting in this manner makes her even more embarrassed and has her feeling like the freak of nature that she's always felt when it comes to her sexual response. The man slams the sheets onto the floor and stomps out of the room, leaving her there to sulk in embarrassment.

* * *

An hour later, Storm lie back, wrapped up in the sheets feeling horrible while the man lie on the opposite side of the bed. He lie hanging off the edge as if he doesn't want her near him. He doesn't know exactly what to say. They haven't said a word to each other since he stomped out of the room. His silence is because he feels bad about how he reacted and made her feel.

"I apologize for the way I acted," he says as he turns to face her.

"It's cool," she lies.

"Nah, I'm sorry. I just never experienced nothing like that, ever. I mean like, I heard about squirters but never had one. That's like some weird shit that I wasn't ready for."

"I said it's cool," she says with evident anger.

"Like, you should've warned me, so I could be ready. That shit… I mean that almost went in my mouth."

As much as he's trying to make things better he's really making her feel worse as if he's disgusted by her. "I said, it's cool. Just leave it alone," she says sternly.

He can sense that she's getting angered. "Damn, I just wasn't ready."

Storm turns around facing the wall. "Don't worry. It will never happen again. Never!"

37

THE NEXT MORNING

TWENTY MINUTES AGO, Storm was left sleeping in the bed while Money Sal made a breakfast run. Away from home and uncomfortable had her sleeping light. She woke up soon as he closed the door behind him. The moment his car pulled out of the parking space she got to nosing around. She's curious as to who he is and what he's about. She's sure she will find some clue.

The first thing she checked was his medicine cabinet to see if he had any prescription drugs. That could mean he had or has an STD, even though she should've checked for that before. Doesn't matter at this point anyway because after the scene that took place last night she's positive there will never be any sexual relations between them. Last night he didn't make any attempt to touch her sexually after their episode. He did try to cuddle with her, but she charged that off as him trying to butter her up after how he treated her.

She could see the sincerity in his eyes when he apologized but that didn't make up for the embarrassment she felt. The squirting is the reason she has never fully embraced her sexuality. She always fears men will react the way he did and that is why she has only limited sexual experiences. When she does indulge in sex, she doesn't let herself get turned on enough to squirt, except with the old man.

With anyone else she has managed to turn herself off. With Money Sal it was different, and she couldn't control it. He has the power to turn her on without even trying.

Storm's nose tingles as she slides the mattress over. She knows what this tingling is when she feels it. She looks in between the mattresses and finds nothing… But the tingling gets more intense. She sniffs the air like a bloodhound.

Her eyes land onto his dirty clothes hamper and her heart races with anxiety. She turns it over, emptying all the clothes onto the floor. The tingling becomes more intense and the adrenaline intensifies. A plastic bag reveals itself underneath the dirty clothes and she picks it up quickly.

To no surprise she feels stacks of money inside the bag. Her senses have never failed her. She opens the bag and finds what was expected. She can tell by how the money is stacked that it's drug money. She figured he was a drug dealer even though he never admitted it or made any reference to what he did for a living. Game recognizes game so she already knew. She also figured that he must be heavy in it since he kept his business so secret. Through her experiences, she's learned, it's the ones who are barely making money who talk about it the most.

She flips through the stacks and finds all twenties in what she estimates to be a thousand dollars a stack, with about thirty stacks. Her heart bangs in her chest as many ideas run through her mind. She quickly runs over to the dresser and grabs her clothes. She gets dressed hurriedly as she watches out of the window to make sure he's not pulling up.

While getting dressed, she thinks of an escape plan. She steps into her sandals while dialing four-one-one for a cab company number. She quickly realizes that she doesn't even have a clue of where she is right now. She runs out of the room and grabs her shopping bags and luggage from the living room floor on her way out. She exits the loft and slams the door behind her. No clue of her destination but she does know that she has enough money in hand to make it back home from anywhere in the world.

* * *

Forty minutes later, the man steps into his bedroom, bags of breakfast in hand. He was expecting to find her still sleeping so the empty bed surprises him. He assumes she must be in the bathroom. "Storm!" he yells as he places the bags on the nightstand. "Yo, Storm!"

* * *

Storm stands at the ticket booth, giving the agent an extremely hard time. She has disguised herself by discarding of the black wig she was wearing. Her natural hair stands up in a nappy afro. Her eyes are covered by huge sunglasses. Her insecurities are not even on her mind. "Listen, I understand your policy but I have a family emergency. I need to be on the next flight," she says with attitude.

"I'm sorry about your emergency, but the next flight is filled already," the woman says politely.

"I need to speak to a fucking manager!"

* * *

As the man makes his way toward the bathroom, the turned over dirty clothes hamper catches his attention. He double-takes before stopping in his tracks. He leans over and starts fumbling through the clothes with no sign of the shopping bag. His heart rate speeds up. He tosses the clothes to the side and still no sign of the bag.

"Yo, Storm!" he shouts again. He runs to the bathroom and throws the door open and is not shocked to find it empty. He then runs to the living room and notices that all her bags are gone. He puts it together quickly. "That bitch got me." He feels like a total sucker right now. "Fuck!" he says.

He wonders where she has gone to but figures she couldn't have gotten far. She told him she knew no one in Ohio, but he wonders if that's the truth. He dials her phone, knowing damn well she won't answer. Straight to voice mail, just as he figured. He paces around for minutes before coming up with the idea of going to the airport. He set the return flight so he knows her flight isn't until tomorrow night. He races out of the house and jumps in his car. He speeds off, hoping to catch her.

* * *

Storm plops into the aisle seat of the plane. This isn't equivalent to the comfort or style that she flew here in but it has to do. The manager couldn't change her flight so she took a loss in a sense. He explained to her that he had seats on this JetBlue flight and she accepted. She had no problem taking the loss on the flight because she gained over thirty large so it all pans out.

The plane ascends into the air and she feels a sense of relief. She looks at the purse that is on her lap and a smile spreads across her face knowing it's thirty-thousand dollars heavier. She can't help but to think about how all this has turned out. It seems to always go this way when she finds someone that she halfway likes.

She will never realize that most of the time she looks for something wrong and that is why she finds it. The entire time she was there enjoying his company she kept telling herself that eventually he would do something that would turn her off. She never imagined that it would be the other way around. It was her that turned him off but that was the perfect reason for her to escape before her feelings got involved.

38

NEWARK INTERNATIONAL AIRPORT
HOURS LATER

S TORM PACKS HER bags into the trunk of her car, gets in and pulls out of the parking garage. Her mind is clouded with many thoughts. While in Ohio she didn't have the luxury of thinking of a plan because he kept her mind consumed. Now she's here right back in the middle of the madness, not knowing her next move.

As she cruises through the airport toward the exit she turns her phone on. Eight missed calls from Mr. Antonelli are at the top of the list. She listens to her messages and the sound of his voice irks her. In between messages she hears the voice of Money Sal. She listens closely to his words. She presses two to repeat the message and turns the speaker on.

"You filthy, thief, ass bitch! You fucking stole from me? You got that off though. Don't worry about it though, it's all good. Don't spend it all up because you will need it to pay for your funeral once I catch up with yo' ass. It's a small world, bitch. Should've never fucked with your lil, strange faced, ass anyway. You and that nasty ass reject pussy you got."

She deletes the message just to not listen to it again. Hearing that message has made her livid. The name calling hurts a little, but it's the threats that bother her the most. He obviously has no clue that those threats can cost him his life.

She honks the horn like a maniac. She peeks around the van in front of her to figure out why it's stopped so far away from the light that is green. She notices a long string of still traffic in front of the van. "What the fuck," she says while resting on the horn. "Move that fuck outta the way."

The traffic starts to creep along. Just as she's about to speed up the traffic stops again. She slams on the brakes to avoid banging into the back of the van in front of her. She peeks around the van and what she sees causes her spirit to sink.

Orange cones are lined up, diverting traffic into a single lane. Police stand at the yellow line. She recognizes the last thing she needs to be in the middle of at this time and that is a spot check. "Holy fuck," she says as she thinks of the reasons why she needs no trouble with the law right now. "Shit," she says remembering the gun in her glove compartment.

She snatches the key out of the ignition and tries to open the glove box. She fumbles with the key in the hole nervously. Now the horns are blowing behind her, causing a scene. She's sweating bullets.

She grabs the gun from underneath the papers and quickly tries to figure out where she can hide it. She doesn't want to leave it in the car just in case they are searching cars. She also doesn't want to put it on her just in case they ask her to step out of the vehicle. The horn sounds off again, breaking her train of thought.

She quickly starts the car back up and inches forward with the gun still in her hand. She considers tossing it out of the window but with so many people around she's sure someone will see it. She has no choice but to tuck it in her pocket and pray that they don't find reason to ask her to step out. With the gun so tiny it can barely be seen in her pocket but still she buttons her coat up for reinforcement.

As she gets closer to the corner, she sees K9s on both sides. Her freedom flashes before her eyes. Her heart races as the Port Authority cop walks toward her car. As he reaches the car he signals for her to roll her window down.

Thoughts of running him over and making a getaway flood her mind, but she realizes there's no way she could get past all of them before they gun her down. With that in mind, she slowly reaches over and hits the power button. "License, registration, and insurance card," the officer says sounding like a robot.

She reaches over to the glove box and grabs hold of the paperwork. She hands it over to him with a false sense of confidence. He stands there holding the documents with no contentment. "License."

Her heart stops beating. "Oh, I didn't give it to you?" she asks, trying to buy herself sometime. She wonders if just presenting the paperwork will be enough for him or if he will run a check on her. She's sure once he runs the check she will be leaving here in handcuffs.

It's then that she remembers something that could possibly prolong her freedom. "Hold up, one-second please. I'm just getting off my flight and haven't had time to get myself together. Can I look for it?"

"Take your time," he says but the lack of patience shows.

She fumbles throughout the glovebox and the middle console. "Who is Donovan Antonelli?" he asks reading over the registration and insurance.

"Uh, my boyfriend," she replies. Even saying that feels weird to her.

The officer looks at her peculiarly. "Your boyfriend is seventy-eight years old?"

She ignores his question as she locates the small Bible in the console. She skips to the middle of it and finds what she hopes to be her lifesaver. She hands him the license and he reads the name aloud. "Danielle Bryant. Twenty-seven years old with a seventy-eight year old boyfriend?"

"I," she says as she almost gives herself away about to defend her age. She's totally forgotten that the license states that she's five years older than she really is. "Is that against the law?" she asks with an irked tone.

"Uh, a few years ago, it would have been," he says with sarcasm. "License in good standing? No tickets or suspensions?"

"No," she says with confidence. The expression on her face doesn't support the confidence though.

"Well, sit tight for a minute and let me go and take a look," he says with a sarcastic smile.

As he walks away she goes into a panic attack. She has no idea if that license is in good standing. She doesn't even know if the license is even in the system. When it was created to get the car from the dealership years ago they never discussed if the license was legit with her face on it, everything else officially belonging to the girl or just a complete phony one. She has every mind to bust out of this door and run for her life but the cop comes walking toward her. She tries to read his face to see what the outcome is going to be but he shows no sign.

He stops at the door. "So, Mr. Antonelli is your boyfriend you said right?"

"Uh, yeah," she replies while looking him in the eyes. She covers her fear well.

"So, we can call him and he will say the same?"

"Absolutely," she replies with enormous confidence.

The appearance of another officer coming their way causes her alarm. Just as he's about to speak the officer steps away from the car to meet him. They stand there whispering. She can't hear a word or even read their lips to see what they are saying.   Her body goes numb from fear as they both make their way over toward her. They stand at the window just looking at her for what seems like an eternity. "Danielle," he says.

"Yes?" she asks in suspense. She can already hear her rights being read to her.

"You have a nice day." He hands her the paperwork. "Sorry for any inconvenience."

She sighs relief. Before they can even get out of her way, she pulls off, paperwork still in her hand. As she looks at the many police as she passes, she thinks of how close of a call this was. It all could've went another way and that way was her in the back of the police car on her way to face murder charges. She looks to the sky and does something that she hasn't done in years. "Thank you, God!"

39

A S STORM PULLS into her assigned parking space at her complex, all she can think about is getting into her bed and sleeping
for hours. She can only hope that when she awakens she will have
forgotten all about the terrible weekend she's had. She grabs her
purse and drags herself sluggishly across the parking lot.

Her phone rings and it's no surprise to see Money Sal's number
flashing across the screen. Between him and the old man she's about
ready to toss her phone into a river. It seems as if they are taking
turns calling her. She's equally tired of both of them.

She tucks her phone into her pocket and grabs her key, just a few
doors away from hers. She sticks the key into the lock and before
twisting it, the door parts. She stands there baffled, knowing damn
well that she locked the door before she left. Normal response sends
her running into the apartment.

Her eyes bulge when she sees her living room turned upside
down. She thinks break in and runs straight to her room. She prays
the money is still there. The bedroom is equally ransacked. The
dressers and the bed is turned over.

The cold and empty feeling in the room tells her that she's been
wiped out. She has little hope that her money is still here. She runs
to the closet only to find the shelves have been ripped off the wall.
Her fur coats are gone and so are her shoes and her dresses. The
whole closet has been cleaned out including the safe that her money was in. She looks onto her dresser where her jewelry box used to

be and the tears of rage slowly stream from her eyes, burning a hole in her face.

Her first thought is to call the police, but quickly remembers they are the last people she can stand before right this moment. She races to the doorway with no starting point leading to the people who could be behind this. She snatches the door open, and there stands a man assuming the position to knock.

"I was just about to knock," the superintendent of the building says.

"Somebody broke into my apartment," she says frantically. "Did you see anybody strange around here?"

His face saddens. "No one broke in. About fifty detectives just left here not even a half hour ago." Her mind races frantically. She can't speak. "They came knocking on my door asking me if I knew you. They forced me to let them into the apartment. I tried to stall them but they were persistent.

"They had your picture and everything. I didn't recognize you at first because hair color and freckles threw me off," he says staring into her face looking for the freckles she has covered with makeup. He stares at her hair as well. This is his first time seeing her natural hair.

She's furious right now. "You let them into my fucking apartment? What did you tell them?" she asks as she steps close enough to wring his neck. She has to take her rage out on someone.

She feels his heart banging against her chest. "Nothing, nothing at all. I pretended that I just started and hadn't met all the tenants yet." She stares into his eyes and senses he can be telling the truth. She knows he has a huge crush on her and maybe that saved her.

"They gave me this and told me to call them when you showed up," he says as he flashes the detective's card. She snatches it from his hand. "So, are you gonna call them?" she asks with a flirting eye.

"No, I would never."

"Fine," she says as she digs into her bra. She gives him a long glimpse of her breast, just enough to lead him on. "Here," she says counting a few hundreds out. "Take this. I trust that you will keep your eyes on my apartment while I'm gone." She backpedals away from him. "Lock my door, and if you see them snooping around here or they come to you again, don't hesitate to call me." Right before she gets to the staircase, she sends him a flirtatious eye. "Thank you and I will pay you back for this one day."

He stands there googly-eyed as she disappears. She damn near twists an ankle or two leaping down the stairs. As she lands onto the last step, the heel of her left boot breaks in half but that doesn't stop her. She runs like a peg-legged pirate to her car. Storm hops in and speeds off, burning rubber.

40

LATER THAT NIGHT

STORM SITS AT her normal penny slot machine while Toy and Wendy work the casino. Jazz didn't come along this trip and explained to that she can no longer work the casino. That run in with her husband's partner was enough to understand that Atlantic City is dangerously close. She told her that she has no problem going on the out-of-town ventures but nothing local.

Storm had no choice but to respect that. She's happy that Jazz has made her mind up to work with them, even under those terms. She knows she will be all right once she learns how to separate herself from the guilt. Any successful working girl knows how to separate business from personal.

Storm has been attempting to drink her problems away, but those problems haven't gone anywhere. She feels the walls closing in on her. For the life of her, she can't figure out how the detectives found her apartment. She can't even say it's an inside job because the only person that knows where she lives is Toy, and of course, the old man. She questions if he told them but she highly doubts it. He's still calling and she still hasn't answered. A few times she's considered answering just to hear him out to ease her curiosity. His voice messages kind of give her a feeling that he knows nothing about them raiding her home.

He spoke of wanting to see her because he misses her. She's sure what he really misses is drinking from her fountain. It's been almost two weeks since he's quenched his thirst. That's the last thing on her mind right now.

Not only have they found her hiding spot, they've also taken all her prized possessions and over a hundred grand of her savings, one hundred and fourteen to be exact. That money was money she earned on the road with her girls. She feels like the police taking her money is karma for stealing Money Sal's in Ohio. Karma is something that she really doesn't believe in but it did cross her mind.

Now all she has in her possession is the money she stole from him. She originally saw it as a come-up, not ever thinking it would be her last. She has no choice but to think if she hadn't taken the money, she would've been assed out now. She sees it as a blessing in disguise and that is how she's able to justify it. Now, the only money she has is that money and the few dollars Breezy owes her from their move. She hates that she has to start all over but she charges it to the game.

It's the fact that right now her hard earned money is gone. To make herself feel better she looks at the one hundred and fourteen thousand as bail money. They got the money but not her and that wouldn't be the case had she not gotten caught up in that spot check at the airport. That delay helped her to remain free a little bit longer. She counts the blessings that she's received throughout this storm.

She looks up to the ceiling, feeling the need for a second time. "Thank you, God."

The vibrating of her phone captures her attention. She exhales frustration as she sees the old man's name, once again. While it's ringing she feeds a bill into the slot machine. She looks back at the phone and the red light indicates that he's left a message.

She's eager to hear his message. She dials and listens closely. Maybe she can get some type of read from him to indicate that he's the culprit who gave her up.

"Baby, it's been days since I've heard from you. I haven't eaten or slept. I'm making myself sick, worrying about you," he sniffs. It's evident to her that he's crying. "Please, just pick up the phone and call me. I need to hear your voice and know that you are okay. Please, baby," he says before sniffing again. "I will be waiting for your call. I love you," he says before ending the call.

She stares at the phone in her hand. Strangely she feels something for him that she's never felt for anyone. It is compassion. She quickly tries to flush that feeling out of her system, but it goes nowhere.

She feels someone standing over her shoulder and turns around abruptly. What Storm sees almost causes her to faint. The gun in the holster, on the hip of the man in a suit is enough reason to panic and she does. Two more men in suits approach from nowhere. The three of them surround her, giving her nowhere to go even if she tried. She stares at the three six-footers and realizes that there's no way she could possibly fight her way out of this. *They got me*, she thinks to herself. Mentally, she prepares for all else to follow.

The man in the middle opens his mouth to speak. "Excuse me. We are going to have to ask you to evacuate the premises."

She's baffled. She was expecting to hear her rights read to her; instead they are asking her to leave. This can't be what she thought it was. She realizes that they are cops but not the cops she thought. These men clearly are Vice cops who work for the casino. "Evacuate? Why?"

"What are you doing here?"

"What the fuck it look like I'm doing? I'm gambling."

The man shakes his head in disbelief. "We have reason to believe otherwise."

"What the fuck are you talking about? You see me sitting here putting my money in the machine," she says while holding the vouchers in her hand.

"That's not what you're really doing here. There's no sexual solicitation inside of the casino. We are asking you to leave."

"Sexual solicitation? I ain't no fucking prostitute," she says irately. She's now causing a scene and everyone in the area is watching.

"You're here every couple of days, and we have you on camera to prove it."

"On camera doing what? Gambling like everybody else? Run your camera back because that's all you gon' see me do," she says with confidence because she's never done anything else besides the time with the Chinese man. She's sure that isn't what they are refer-ring to. "Y'all can't throw me out for no fucking accusations."

"Ma'am, we have the right to be selective," he says, pointing to the sign. "Can you please exit before we have to force you out?"

She feels disrespected that they are accusing her of being a pros-titute and making the people around them believe the same. "Fuck that! I ain't going nowhere. I'm here gambling like everybody else."

The man in the backdrop takes his handcuffs from his belt, and it's then that she comes to her senses. She can't stand a prostitution charge. It's a misdemeanor, but that is enough to get fingerprinted, and that is the last thing she needs at this time. She knows she's lost this battle.

She kicks her chair over with rage before walking away. The cops follow her through the casino, humiliating her for everyone to see. As she reaches the door she spots Toy who is looking at her with sadness in her eyes. Seeing her being escorted by three detec-tives leads her to believe the worse.

She sends Toy a quick reassuring look to let her know that it's not what she's thinking. The detective holds the door open for her to exit. As the door closes behind her, she kicks it with all of her might, hoping to shatter the glass. She can't believe that she's been kicked out of the premise for being a whore. What's harder to be-lieve is that she's banned from her old faithful money spot. She looks at the cop who stands behind the door, and it feels like the window of opportunity has been closed in her face. And just when she thinks things can't get any worse... they do.

41

PHILADELPHIA
THE NEXT DAY

T HEY SAY WHEN it rains, it pours, and right now Storm feels like she's standing in the middle of a cyclone. She's been living in the matrix the past few days with the series of events that have taken place. It's back to back drama with no break in between. Her life is full of pandemonium at this point. She is in need of a few days away from all the turmoil. Maybe then she can get her mind right and think about her next move or two.

Staying at her apartment is out of the question because she's sure they will return. Last night she stayed at the Trump Hotel in New York, just to be out of Jersey. This morning she received a call from the Ethiopian Princess, the nickname she's given the girl she met in Atlantic City. Beeba begged her to come to Philly to visit her.

She wasn't really for it with all that she has going on, but she figured the timing was perfect. Going to Philly is good for her now that she can't stay at home. In addition, this will give her time to cut into the girl to see if there's anyway she can add her to the team. Her husband seems to stay glued to her hip always, but she's sure if she can get her away from him, just for a few minutes, she could work her magic.

As Storm cruises through the Philadelphia, she gets a strange feeling. Even though she's two hundred miles away from home, she feels like she belongs. The pulse of the city makes her feel quite comfortable. Of all the places that she's ever visited, this seems to be a favorite for some strange reason.

It's not the beauty of the city because truly there isn't much beauty that she's seen so far. It's the same old ran-down ghetto that she's used to back at home, just with row homes. What attracts her to the city is the feeling of familiarity. Strangely she feels as if she knows her way around.

This is her very first time here, yet she navigates through the city as if it's her own. Some landmarks are memorable to her and even the names of streets. Riding through certain blocks, she experiences deja vu. It's perplexing to her and mind boggling. She's not sure if she's visited here as a kid or not, but things just seem to stick out for her. It's peculiar to her how certain blocks even give her a creepy feeling. The whole twenty minutes that she's been in the city has been one staggering experience.

She picks up her phone and dials. As she turns the corner she listens to it ring. "Beeba, I just turned onto Passyunk Avenue."

"Okay," Beeba replies. "I'll be standing right in front of the spot waiting for you. Keep coming down. You'll see me. You'll see a Porsche right in the front."

The chrome four-door Porsche Panamera stands out boldly. It's the only car on the block. Storm admires the beauty, having never seen anything this sick. "I see you," she says with her eyes still glued onto the car.

"Okay," Beeba replies before hanging up the call. She looks around wondering which direction Storm could be coming from. Storm is displeased immediately once she sees the woman's husband getting out of the driver's seat. She was hoping that the woman would be alone, even though that was a far-fetched idea.

Storm honks the horn to catch their attention. Both of them are a bit surprised to see her riding in class. She was dressed down the day they met her, and both being super materialistic, they kind of judged a book by its cover. It's a chance that they thought she was just some ordinary, young, naive, around-the-way girl that they could take advantage of. Now they are both reassessing.

Storm parks, and before she gets out, she digs into her bag. She sifts through the stacks of money that she obtained in Ohio. With nowhere to stash it, that she trusts, she is forced to bring it with her. She slides her faithful little friend, the palm sized .45, out of the way until she finds her lipstick in the corner of her junky purse. She applies her lipstick and gets out.

She creates a spectacle as she prances across the street like a supermodel. Today she has on her favorite and now, thanks to the police, her only fur coat. Had Toy not borrowed the coat a couple weeks ago, this too would have been in the custody of the police. The Russian Golden Sable full length is the most expensive animal in her zoo, as she refers to her fur collection. Mr. Antonelli bought it for her and spent forty-seven grand for it.

The two materialistic label whores know the price of the seventy-thousand dollar coat so they charge it off as a fake. As they scrutinize her jewelry and the rest of her trinkets that thought vanishes from their mind. She now has them both stunned. They are questioning what they have stepped into.

Beeba opens her arms to welcome Storm. Storm leans in for the hug and Beeba kisses her on the cheek. "Hey, Storm." She looks into Storm's eyes with that same flirtatious, seductive look that started it all.

The man stands with open arms, awaiting her. She ignores the invitation and offers a fist bump in return, which offends him. He fist bumps her with a sneer.

"Look at you, girl," Beeba says, looking Storm up and down. "You look like a million bucks."

"So, do you," she replies out of respect, but truly she's not impressed in the least bit. She may think she's killing it, but all Storm sees is a mixture of designer labels thrown together to look like class.

"You ready?" Beeba asks as she grabs Storm's hand and leads the way.

Storm follows with very little trust. She unzips her purse for easy access to her gun, just in case. Beeba leads her to the doorway of the building that they are in front of. No sign, or canopy on the building, creates suspense.

When Beeba invited her here to show her the city, she asked if she had anything in particular she wanted to do or see. Storm denied and left it up to her. She told her she's a chameleon that can adapt to anything. At that point, Beeba knew exactly where she would take her.

After a few taps on the odd-looking door, it opens. A bouncer stands behind the door, and once he recognizes Beeba's husband, Jay, he pulls the door open wider. This tells Storm they must be regulars here.

"Welcome to Pleasure Garden," the bouncer says to Storm with a smile, recognizing this is her first time here.

Once they are inside Storm looks around curiously. They walk down the long and narrow, dimly lit hallway. At the end of the hall, they enter a large space. The bar with the stripper pole makes her think it is just a typical strip joint. She laughs that this is where they chose to bring her.

There is also a buffet inside. Tables and booths fill the other side of the room. She's surprised to see couples spread throughout. They are the only Blacks in the whole spot. She wonders what kind of strip bar this is with no stripper on the pole.

A look of confusion crosses her face as she sets eyes on couples making out in different areas of the bar. Porn is on every flat screen posted on the wall. Some of the customers have obviously gotten caught up in the heat of the moment because a few women are dancing in the middle of the room topless, boobs exposed.

"You good?" Beeba asks, trying to feel Storm out.

Storm shrugs nonchalantly. "I'm always good." She doesn't want them to see her lack of comfort confuse her with a square bitch. She laughs to herself again, thinking of how slick they must think they are. She's sure all of this was Beeba's husband's idea, but she will play along with their little game.

The man takes the lead and heads in the direction of the bar. He pulls the seat out for Storm first, then his wife. *How disrespectful*, Storm thinks to herself. They both take their seats and he orders for him and his wife. He looks to Storm. "Last time, you wouldn't let me get a drink for you. Tonight, I'm not taking no for an answer," he says with a bright smile.

Storm flashes a fake smile back at him. "Virgin daiquiri."

"Awl, come on, live a little," he says.

"I don't drink," she lies. The truth of the matter is she will never drink among strangers. Plus, in a place like this she doesn't trust anyone. The last thing she needs is for someone to slip a Mickey in her drink.

"Come on! Lighten up," Beeba says. "Embrace yourself," she says sexily.

"I'm embraced. A virgin daiquiri."

The bartender brings the drinks back, and as Jay is about to pay, Storm interjects. "Please, let me," she says as she digs into her pocket and grabs her credit card. She feels by paying for the drinks she takes control.

"No, I can't," the man insists.

Storm hands the bartender her American Express card. "It's too late. You already did." She smiles.

In less than a minute, the bartender comes back with a displeasing look. "I'm sorry. That card didn't work for whatever reason. Do you have another?"

Storm sinks in embarrassment. "Didn't work?"

The bartender doesn't humor her one bit. "Do you have another card?"

This is impossible, she thinks to herself. This card has a twenty-five thousand dollar limit on it and the total balance gets paid every month by Mr. Antonelli. "Try it again. There is more than enough money on it," she says proudly.

"I already tried it three times," the bartender says, shutting her down.

"Don't worry. I got it," Beeba's husband says while digging into his wallet.

"No, don't worry," Storm says digging into her purse. She pulls a hefty stack out of the purse and makes sure they see it. She peels off a few twenties and hands it over the counter. "Keep the change. I'm sorry for the inconvenience. I will call them in the morning." She wonders what the problem could be with the card, but she tries to show no sign of concern on her face. This doesn't sit well with her at all.

42

HOURS LATER

A FTER A FEW drinks, Beeba and her husband have gotten loose with their mouths and have started telling all of their business. Beeba, who is twenty-six, has been married to Jay for four years. He, basically, caught her straight off the boat from Ethiopia. A naive foreigner who won over using his money and American Charm.

Jay was a professional football player with the San Francisco 49ers before he got injured. Now he's a businessman with a few restaurants and a host of real estate property. Beeba is a housewife with no income, which allows him to control her with his money. It was also confirmed that they are swingers.

Once they were good and tipsy, they took Storm on a grand tour of the rest of the club, which was very interesting, to say the least. They took her to the members only, private section of the club, where they showed her many rooms with couples and even groups of people having sex in them. Some were discreet and had the doors closed, but you could peek inside the window. In other rooms people are having sex with no shame as the doors were wide open.

It wasn't long before Beeba and Jay began going at each other like two horny dogs right in front of her. They put on a show for her to watch. She sat back, cool and calm, as if this was normal for her. They even had a bag of tricks that was bought from the novelty shop downstairs. From motion lotions to vibrating dildos, the couple displayed how each toy worked. It wasn't long before Jay took his shot. Storm watched as he whispered to Beeba to invite her into their little game.

They both were pleased that she agreed to join in. She could sense that he was more enthusiastic about it than Beeba was. Storm is sure that he expected to see his wife and herself indulge in some girl-on-girl activity. The strap-on that he bought was evidence he believed she would submit. Neither of them expected she would use his own weapon against him.

Beeba is bent over the Jacuzzi, doggy style while her husband is hunched over behind her. He attempts to please his wife, hitting her with close and fast rabbit strokes. He's highly distracted by Storm who stands behind him, equipped with a strap on, wailing on him with no mercy. He denied at first, but Storm told them she was willing to play only if they played by her rules first. He gave in with no resistance when she presented her rules to him. He expected that he and his wife would turn her out; instead, she's flipped him.

She hasn't even given them a glimpse of her body. The bottom of the long dress she holds gripped in one hand, the other hand on Jay's shoulder, ramming him. Her panties, underneath the strap-on are soaked with her own juices. So disgusted with it all that she doesn't even notice.

Beeba looks over her and her husband's shoulder into Storm's eyes. Never has she imagined anything of the sort, but the sense of dominance that Storm portrays turns her on, intensely. Eventually, Jay gives up on trying to please his wife and just takes the abuse that Storm is dishing out. One would never know that Storm is disgusted by the whole act as she's doing it so well. To see a man willing to give up his manhood like this confirms how weak some men can be, moreover how they will do anything for a woman. The thought of this infuriates her and she takes out her rage on him.

She pounds on him like a mad drummer while he screams at the top of his lungs like a shameless porn star. His screaming can be heard throughout the whole floor, she is sure. As much as she hates it, the torturing has her cumming uncontrollably. The more he screams, the more her pussy sprays. Puddles of her juices cover the floor, her feet and her Jimmy Choos, that she still has on.

A couple peek in the room through the window and enjoy the show without Storm knowing. Beeba, feeling neglected by her husband, slides her body from under his. She crawls into a corner and watches in a fetal position as the man of her life is manhandled like a little bitch. For the first time ever, she sees her big, strong superhero as a mere weakling who has been crushed. He's been broken down by a twenty-three-year-old, hundred and forty pound young woman, and from the looks and sounds of it, he loves it... Man-down.

The initial thought of it aroused her, but now that the heat of the moment is over, she's bothered by the sight of it. It's weird to her to see her husband in this position and haunting to see him enjoying it. As much as she would like to blame it on the liquor, she can't. With the way he's howling, she isn't sure if he's in pain, or if his howls are of enjoyment. Either way, she's disgusted right now. The sight has her ready to throw up. The tears drip slowly down her face.

This act can be equated to the days of slavery when the slave-masters would beat the men in front of their wives and children to reduce their masculinity. Seeing the head of their household broken down into submission would make them lose respect for the man and make them gain even more respect for their master. As Storm wails on him and she sees the hurt in Beeba's eyes, she realizes that she has taken away the power he had over her. There's no doubt in her mind that she now has the juice.

* * *

One hour later, Storm sits in her car, still parked in front of the spot. Standing at her door, blocking her so she can't pull off are Beeba and Jay. "Why take that long drive tonight when you don't have to?" Beeba asks with desperation.

Jay stands to the side letting his wife do the begging. He hasn't said much and seems to be heavy in thought. He's staring into space, looking crushed and broken down in spirit. Storm knows he's pissed with himself because of what he allowed her to do. The worse part of it all is her reneging on her end of the deal.

She never gave him what he originally wanted which was the girl-on-girl activity. When it was over, he stood there with a look in his eyes that said he had been played like a cheap whore. His cocky demeanor no longer reveals itself. He hasn't been able to look her in the eyes since.

"I got an early morning appointment," Storm says as she looks at her watch. "Nine o'clock meeting," she lies.

Jay stands in despair. "You can sleep at our house. Get a couple hours of rest and leave early," he suggests with desperation. Storm realizes his persistence has everything to do with him wanting to even the scales. She's sure he feels like a sucker because he's given up his manhood to her for nothing in return.

Storm gets a kick out of watching him squirm. He was suave, debonair and arrogant when they originally met and now this. Storm is sure this is routine for them, looking for young girls to turn out. Judging by how they are acting right now, this must be the first time the tables have been turned and flipped on them.

Storm starts the ignition and their faces sadden more. They realize it's over. Storm turns the wheel to the left and inches up a little. "Excuse me, y'all."

Jay nudges Beeba to beg a little more. "Please, Storm. Why you can't just stay?"

Storm is now getting irked with them. "I already told y'all. Now excuse me."

Beeba backs away, giving her room to move. "Beeba, call me," she says, overlooking the man.

Just as she pulls out of the parking space, Jay speaks again. "Storm." Storm looks to him with frustration on her face. "This all stays between us, right?" he asks. His eyes are filled with defeat.

"I don't know... does it?" she asks with sarcasm. She cruises off. "Beeba, don't forget... call me," she says before speeding up the block.

Jay watches as the owner of his manhood speeds up the block. Beeba looks at her husband in a total different light. Once the car is out of sight, Jay attempts to stand up like the man his wife once knew. What he doesn't know is she will never be able to see him as that man again.

As she looks at him, the words of her deceased father echo in her mind: "A man that bends is a man that will break." She hears this loud and clear in her head. It's as if her father is speaking to her from the heavens while watching over her. She heard him say this so many times as a kid that she can never forget it. Her husband has been broken.

She never quite understood what he meant until right now. Of course, when he told her this he wasn't referring to what she just witnessed, but still it can apply. Her once king, strong in stature, is now shattered into pieces. The respect she once had for him she may never regain.

43

IRVINGTON, NEW JERSEY
THE NEXT AFTERNOON

S TORM SITS IN the stylist's chair, getting a new weave. Last night's episode at Pleasure Garden destroyed her hairdo. She's done away with her shoes and her dress as well. They could've been cleaned, but she will never wear either of them again. She wants no memories of that night. The smell of his ass, and his perspiration mixed with his cologne made her want to vomit.

As Storm stares into the mirror, many thoughts race through her mind. The pace so rapid that she can't hold one thought before another comes. So much is happening in her life all at once. She loves the rush of the fast life, but this is too fast for even her. She studies her eyes and is happy to see that the stress doesn't show in them.

Her phone vibrates in her lap, underneath the styling cape, and she gets agitated. Her phone has never rung this much... ever. For days, it was Mr. Antonelli and the dude from Ohio calling her back to back, but both of them have fallen back. Her problem didn't stop with them though. Beeba's phone calls have replaced theirs. She seems to be calling more than both of them together.

Once Storm got to her hotel in Center City last night the phone calls would not end. They called her every ten minutes, and she didn't answer not one of them. Today has been the same. They've been calling her all morning and afternoon. Her reason for not answering is her disgust for him, and her at this point.

Just as she's getting out of the stylist's chair, the phone rings again. Out of rage, she answers. "Yo!" she shouts into the phone. "The fuck?"

The beautician watches Storm nosily and so do the other women who have heard her.

Beeba is taken aback by her tone. "Storm?"

"Yeah, what up, what up?" Storm lowers her voice. "Y'all hitting my line like crazy. What's good?"

"We were just checking on you. We were worried about you. Wanted to make sure you were good."

"I told you I'm always good."

Jay can be heard, pestering Beeba in the background.

"Hold on for a minute. Jay wants to speak to you." Storm notices that for the second time ever she refers to him as Jay and not her husband as she normally does. Last night, before the revolution, everything was her husband this and her husband that. Now he's just plain old Jay. "Here," she says sounding quite frustrated with him. Storm takes it that Beeba has lost all respect for him.

"Hey, lady," Jay says quite cool and calm. He sounds as if he's feeling better about himself.

"What up, what up?" she asks hastily, not even trying to sugarcoat her aggravation and disgust with him.

"I just need to kick it with you about something."

"All right. Kick it."

"Like, that lil shit that happened last night. That was the first time that ever happened. I mean, that ain't my twist at all."

Storm chuckles into the phone, humiliating him more. "Okay."

"Nah, I'm dead serious."

"Listen, that's neither here nor there. I ain't the judge," she says coldly.

"I just want to make sure that stays between us three and never goes nowhere."

Storm chuckles again, further embarrassing him. "Your little se-cret is safe with me. What happened in that room, stayed in that room. No worries."

"Cool," he says, sounding like a man in broken spirits who has been defeated and conquered.

"Anyway, do you think I'm proud of that?" she asks, further hu-miliating him. He has not a reply. Just passes the phone back over to his wife.

"Storm," Beeba says as she gets back on the phone. "Are you still in Philly?"

"Nah, I broke out this morning. Why? What's up?"

"We wanted to link up with you for lunch or something."

Jay is coaching Beeba in the background on what to say. It's obvious that all of this is his idea. "Nah, I'm home."

"When you coming back to Philly though. Or, we can even come to you this time."

Storm decides the time is now to test Beeba's chin. "I don't re-ally know when we can link up again. I got shit to do. Do me a favor though." She pauses for a few seconds. "The next time we get together, leave him at home. I need to talk to you on some one-on-one shit. Is that possible? He be in the way of some real shit hap-pening. You get me?" She sits back and waits for Beeba's reply. This right here will tell her where Beeba stands at this point.

"Totally," Beeba whispers.

"Cool, so when we gone make that happen?"

"Soon, real soon," she says discreetly, trying not to let her hus-band know what they are talking about. "We'll call you," she says rushing off the phone. Her husband is in her mouth and trying to hear the details of the conversation.

"No... You—," Storm stresses, "call me," Storm says before end-ing the call.

* * *

After paying the beautician, Storm makes her exit. She steps out of the backdoor of the beauty parlor, into the parking lot. She walks in the direction of where she parked her car. As she lifts her head up, she notices an empty parking space where she thought she parked.

She stops in her tracks, looking around. Maybe she didn't park where she normally does. Her mind is so crowded that she doesn't remember. She looks around the entire lot, and there's no sign of her car. Her heart is pounding as she stands in the middle of the lot, confused. "The fuck?" she mumbles to herself.

She walks back toward the beauty parlor, thinking of retracing her steps. She turns back around, looking all over the lot, and it's evident that her car is no longer here. The first thing she thinks is it had to be stolen while she was in there. Then thoughts of the police creep into her mind. She stands there stranded like Gilligan on that little island. Without even thinking, she starts to dialing.

Mr. Antonelli picks up on the first ring. "Yes?"

With no introduction, she just yells into the phone frantically. "Somebody stole my fucking car! I'm here at the beauty parlor, and I come out, and my shit gone! I'm here stuck like a motherfucker!" she yells. Her mindset changes and she looks around expecting the cops to swarm in on her any second now.

"I haven't heard from you in weeks," he says calmly.

"Did you just hear what the fuck I said?"

"Yes, I heard. Did you hear me?" he asks like a wise ass.

He never speaks to her in this tone, and it's pissing her off even more than she already was. She's used to having him wrapped around her finger. "Look. Are you going to do something about this? I can't call the cops. So are you?"

"Why haven't you been answering or returning my calls?"

"Yo, listen!"

"No, you listen," he interrupts. "Is that what it takes for you to call me? To need something? I figured that. Look, nobody stole your car. I reported it stolen. Just as I put a hold on your credit card. And just as I figured, you called."

"Look, motherfucker, I ain't got time for your childish-ass games! You a grown-ass one-hundred-year-old-ass man and you playing kid games? You got twenty minutes to get here and pick me up, or else! You know where the fuck I am. Get the fuck here!"

44

THE CADILLAC ESCALADE pulls in front of Mr. Antonelli's house. Storm gets out and leaves the door wide open. She stomps to the house angrily. She expected him to come and pick her up, and she had all plans to let him have it. Instead he sent his driver to get her. The anger only built up more throughout the ride here.

The housekeeper opens the door for her and walks away to not have to see Storm or even deal with her. That may be best at this time for her own good. Storm stomps throughout the house to his room. In his room, she finds him standing there with a stern look on his face.

She doesn't hesitate to let him have it. "Motherfucker, you playing with my freedom? You reported my car stolen? What if they would've pulled me over and locked me up for car theft?"

"Car theft would be a misdemeanor with all you have going on right now."

She's shocked at his response. She's never experienced this much abrasiveness from him. He normally folds at the first sign of her anger toward him.

"So selfish of you. You're only worried about yourself. I didn't know what was going on with you, and I was worried."

"Worried about me? For what? I'm the one that should be worried, not you."

"We have been together for five years. I don't hear from you in weeks, and I'm not supposed to be worried about you?" The word, together plays over and over in her mind, but still she's in denial. "Where have you been all these weeks?" His face turns cherry red. "You weren't with me, so where have you been?"

"What?" she asks, noticing his possessive demeanor. "Oh, now I have to answer to you? Where's all this coming from?"

"Where were you? Were you with another man?" he asks.

"Fuck a man! I got shit on my mind and a man ain't one of them."

He continues on with his streak of jealousy. To her surprise, his jealousy is turning her on, instead of pissing her off. "I only gave you one clause to our relationship and you are to never forget it," he says with a demanding tone.

"What clause?" she asks, clearly knowing what he's speaking of. She just wants to hear it come out of his mouth. His jealousy is doing something to her.

"You know the clause, and there's no need for me to remind you."

The clause he speaks of is the one rule he gave her back when, in his mind, they first became an item. He told her he would provide all that she needs in life as long as she never let another man enter her. She's never forgot it and she's never breeched their agreement. She's stood firm, partly out of loyalty and the other part being that she hasn't found a man that she sees worthy of having her sexually.

Well, Money Sal was almost an exception to that, but he blew his chances. So because of that, she can say with all honesty. "I haven't had sex with no other man! I been away just trying to get my mind right. I ain't thinking about no fucking nigga!"

"Well, now that you have had your time away to clear your mind, now what? Are you ready to do what has to be done?"

She huffs and puffs. He's been able to break her down and bring her right back to the place that had her avoiding him. Her silence leads him to speak again. "The problem isn't going anywhere. You can't just ignore it."

"I know," she says sadly. "Did you know they raided my apartment and confiscated my shoes, all the jewelry you bought… and my coats?" She purposely left out the mention of the money. She's sure, if he finds out the amount of money that was in the apartment, there will be many questions to be answered, even though a hundred and fourteen thousand is a drop in a bucket to him, but for her, that is unexplained wealth.

"How would I know if I haven't spoken to you? When?"

"Days ago," she whispers.

He's saddened at hearing this. "Baby, they won't stop until they get you. You can't run forever. Tony says you are only making it harder for yourself and him. The longer you run, the angrier they will be and the harder they will make it for you… for us," he says as he grabs both of her hands and pulls her closer to him.

He stares down into her eyes. "He's informed me that, if they catch you on their own, it will look like you were never going to turn yourself in and your chances of posting bail will be slim to none. Turning yourself in will look good on your behalf, and he can get you in and out. At this point, the choice is all yours. You must decide, right here right now."

45

NEWARK
HOURS LATER

STORM STANDS IN front of the Franklin Street Police Precinct
building with horror rippling through her body. She can't believe
that she's allowed herself to be talked into this. This goes against
everything she believes. The only reason she's here is because the
walls seem to have closed in on her, giving her nowhere to run. She
just wants to end the chase, so she can get back to her normal. She's
been promised it would be in and out. Once she posts bail, she can
get back to the money without ducking and dodging.

She's dressed down in her war gear, ready to meet her problem head on. The Chanel sweatsuit and matching sneakers have
her looking incredibly fashionable for a woman on her way to jail.
The huge hood swallows her head. She looks very low-key, like she's
hiding from paparazzi.

Mr. Antonelli paces back and forth with the phone in his hand.
They've been standing here for over thirty minutes waiting impatiently. Just when he's about to dial Tony again for the twentieth
time, a beautiful Bentley GTC pulls in front of them. The stainless steel beauty is filled with a creamy caramel colored middle that
erupts over the convertible top. Driver, disguised behind pitch black
shades, nods his head at them, announcing his arrival.

Attorney Tony Austin gets out of the Bentley and crosses the street toward them with a cocky bop. Dressed in a full-length burgundy shearling, fitted distressed jeans, a huge overlapping cashmere turtleneck sweater and Giuseppe three-quarter sneakers. He looks like he's been ripped from a page of a men's fashion magazine.

He walks past them with no formal greeting. "It's show time," he says as he holds the door open for them to enter.

Storm steps in behind Mr. Antonelli. She's still in disbelief that she's here. Where she's from gangsters hold court on the street and have the 'catch me when you can' mentality. As she walks through the doors, she feels like she's already crossed the point of no return.

Tony steps in and takes the lead. As he presses the button for the elevator, he looks at Storm for the first time. "You trust me?"

"I don't know you to trust you," she says with a cold aura.

"That will change," he replies arrogantly. "Lift your head up though. You're on the winning team. As winners, we take our losses the same way we take our wins... head up and chest out. Erase that doubt from your face. It says you're not sure if you're innocent," he says as he stands to the side for her to enter the elevator. "Ladies, first."

Tony steps to the front desk confidently. He removes his shades as he looks at the woman behind the desk.

"I'm looking for a Detective Sykes," he says.

The woman looks him up and down before speaking. "You are?"

"Tony Austin. Attorney Tony Austin," he replies.

"Hold on." She gets on the phone and whispers into it.

In minutes Storm watches a well-dressed, beautiful woman walking from the back. Finally she sees the woman who has been making her life hell the past few weeks, and she looks nothing like she expected. From across the room, the detective recognizes Storm's face. The soft and pleasant demeanor of the woman disappears and is replaced by a rough and edgy one.

Storm has every mind to make her escape right now while she still can. Instead she watches as two other men come out behind her. The female detective stops short right before them with her eyes on Storm. The other two detectives stand by her side for what looks like reinforcement.

"Detective Sykes," the female detective says while looking at Tony with an arctic blast.

"Detective Sykes, I'm Attorney Tony Austin, and this is my client, Angelica Hill. She's turning herself in, as promised."

Rage spreads across all of their faces, but not a one of them say a word in reply. Storm is surprised at how Tony handles them with no regard but still somewhat respectful.

"This way, please," the detective says, leading them all to the back.

* * *

One hour later, after an extensive interrogation, Storm continues on with her innocence. They've all listened with no emotion on their faces. She's sure there is so much more they want to say but are not because of Tony's presence. She now respects his stature.

Detective Sykes finally stands up and says the words that Storm has been dreading to hear. "Angelica Hill, you are under arrest for murder."

That's all she hears before her ears go deaf. The detective continues to read her rights. Storm stares at Mr. Antonelli as if she expects him to save her. Seeing the helpless look in his eyes makes her look to Tony for help.

"Please, empty your pockets and remove your shoelaces," the detective demands.

Tony looks at Storm. "Do as they say. It's all procedure."

She follows the instructions and hands her possessions over to Mr. Antonelli. As the handcuffs are brandished, her life flashes before her eyes.

"Please assume the position," says the detective.

Storm lifts her head high despite the feeling of confusion and defeat that's in her heart. She turns around slowly and is cuffed and escorted away. She looks back at Tony with one long glare, hoping for reassurance that he has her back.

"Despite your allegations," Tony says sternly. "I suggest you handle my client with care. She will not utter a word without my presence, so no need attempting."

The detectives ignore him and continue walking to the back. Once they are out of sight, tears of sadness fill Mr. Antonelli's eyes. Tony plants his hand on the old man's shoulder. "Don't worry. Bail will be set in the morning, and you will take it from there and I will do what I do," he says with his normal amount of cockiness. "Go on home and get some rest. You look like a train-wreck. I got it from here. See you in the morning."

46

ESSEX COUNTY JAIL
HOURS LATER

S TORM STEPS INTO the cell, washcloth and towel in hand. After hours of being processed, she's finally in the system. Her natural hair stands on her head in a messy, coarse puffball. She was forced to remove the weave from her hair. She was handed a pair of scissors and the guard sat and watched as she cut the weave out with no mirror. She hasn't seen what she looks like, but she's sure she looks a mess. She's quite happy that there are no mirrors, so she doesn't have to face what she's been hiding from for so long — her natural self.

This is like a bad dream for her. As the gate is closed behind her, she realizes this is not a dream. It's her reality. She can't believe that she's even here. She didn't picture herself here. She never envisioned this because she expected to be bailed out long before making it to the county jail.

The best part about it is she has a cell and she's not forced to sleep in the dayroom with a bunch of women that she doesn't trust. She quickly looks to the bottom bunk where her new cellmate sits hovered in the corner. Dressed in all black Muslim garb, it's safe to assume that she is Muslim. The excess of mixed oils flow through the air, confirming that as well. The oils are so pungent that Storm's stomach does flip-flops. Her allergies are immediately triggered, causing her eyes to water.

The sound of Arabic recitation plays faintly from the MP3 player. The woman peeks up at Storm with only the whites of her eyes showing. Her face and head, which are covered in Niqab, makes the woman appear spooky to Storm. Without saying a word, she looks away and continues reciting along with the voice coming out of the MP3 player.

Storm has been in the presence of Muslims before but never in this close of space. The mystique of the woman all covered up in here in the pitch darkness gives Storm a ghostly feeling. Storm climbs up to the top bunk and plops onto it. She grabs hold of the thin pillow and throws it over her head to drown out the noise of the woman and the MP3 player. She hopes for sleep and that by the morning, all this will be over.

* * *

Two hours later, Storm was awakened by bubble-guts a few minutes ago. She hasn't eaten in two days now, and dehydration is kicking in from the diarrhea. As she lie there, she stares at the wall, butt-cheeks clenched tight, both hands enveloping her abdomen. She can't even fathom using the bathroom in here.

If it was up to her, she would hold it until she's released. Maybe she would be comfortable with it if the woman was asleep, but she's not. Storm was able to steal a few winks of sleep throughout the night, but each time she awakened the woman was up reading, reciting, or praying. Seeing the woman walking around in all black in the dark with her head covered creeps Storm out.

The woman has now been praying in silence for the past hour, it seems. A violent spasm rips through Storm's stomach, letting her know what is to come. She gets off the bunk and slides past the woman, careful not to touch her. With shame, she drops her jumper and panties around her ankles, and she takes a seat on the toilet. How uncomfortable she is with the woman standing with not even two feet in between them. Her head hangs low, eyes closed with both her hands clasped over her belly. Her mouth moves with no sound. Storm peeks up, wondering if the woman is looking at her on the sneak-tip.

Her stomach rumbles, and she tries to silence it but it rips loudly. She is embarrassed it sounds as if she's shitting through a bullhorn, loud enough for the whole tier to hear. One after the other, like rapid fire, she rips with shame, unable to control it. She looks up at the unaffected woman who continues to pray.

The woman is now on her knees, still mumbling to herself. She prostrates one long time, head onto the floor. Her head is less than a foot away from Storm's feet, way too close for comfort. She sits back on her romp, knees still bent. With her eyes closed, she turns to her right. "As Salaamu Alaikum Wa Rahmattullah," she says out loud for the first time. She turns to her left. "As Salaama Alaikum Wa Rahmatullah!" The woman gets up slowly. She takes one step which has her standing over Storm. Her eyes glow in the darkness. Not being able to see the rest of her face leaves one to focus on her eyes. Her eyes have a violent glare in them, but her body language seems to be at peace. The woman doesn't blink. "The next time you see me praying, and you take a shit, we will have a problem."

The woman's threat doesn't sit well with Storm. She hated to have to take the shit here in the first place, but to be called out on it makes it even worse. "What?" Storm asks as she sits up, erect. She sits on the edge of the bowl and cleans herself as best she can under the threatening terms. After a half-ass job, she stands up, pulling her jumper up over her waist. She holds her hands to her side, ready to fly if need be. "What I'm supposed to do? Shit on myself?"

"I don't know what you supposed to do, but I do know if you sit your ass in front of me taking a shit while I'm praying, that'll be the last shit you take." The woman turns around and plops onto her cot.

The threat sends Storm into an irate frenzy. She loses it. She feels the woman is testing her. She knows, if she allows the woman to get this off, her days in this county will be tough. She's ready to nip this problem in the bud and any other problem that comes her way.

She stands over the woman, who now has her Quran in her hand. She reads from it as if Storm isn't standing over her. She appears to have no worries. "Was that a threat?" Storm asks. The woman continues reading and ignoring her. "Oh, I thought so."

The woman finally looks up from her book. "That wasn't a threat. Take it as a courtesy."

"I don't need your fucking courtesy. If I have to take a shit, I will take a shit, simple as that."

"Understood," the woman says a she looks back to her Quran.

Storm turns to the sink, eyes still on the woman. She has to have the last word. "I fucking thought so."

"Okay, you've been warned," the woman says humbly.

"Fuck your warning."

47

THE NEXT MORNING

THE COURTROOM IS packed. Family and friends of the three men who were killed in the robbery are spread throughout the room. A few slick remarks and threats have been made to Storm. It's taken everything in her to sit quietly as they have made threats against her life. All the spectators aren't strangers to her. A few of them are mutual friends of her and Man-Man.

At this point, she's not sure if they are there to support her or there out of love for him. Either way she's taking note of every face present just in case. There are only three people she knows for certain who are here for her support. Toy and Wendy who stand on the side in clear view for her to see, while Mr. Antonelli sits close to the front. He peeks around nervously at the angry family members present. He's quite ashamed to be a part of this.

She sits before the judge for her arraignment. Dressed in an oversized jumpsuit with her hair in two Pocohontas braids, she looks like an innocent young girl. It all plays like a courtroom television series. The only difference is she's the defendant and she can't get up and turn the station when she chooses to. Even with her always living a life of crime, she's never envisioned herself in this situation. Like many other criminals, she's always seen herself as too smart and slick to ever be in this situation.

About thirty minutes ago, she stood up after hearing the prosecutor run off her charges. Of course, she pleaded innocent. Now she sits back, listening to them go on and on. All she's interested in is hearing what her bail has been set at, so she can get out of here.

She damn near loses her mind as she hears the words that come out of the prosecutor's mouth. She prays that she's hearing him wrong. "Your Honor, we strongly recommend denying bail because the nature of the crime. We are talking about four homicides."

She wishes she could get up and choke the prosecutor right now. She looks to Tony, who is now speaking. "Your Honor, the above mentioned charges are alleged. She hasn't been convicted of a crime. She's been charged with a crime. My client poses no threat to the public."

"No threat?" the prosecutor interjects. "We are talking about four murder victims."

Tony looks to the judge. "Your Honor?" he says with his hands high.

"Sustained," the judge says.

Tony speaks. "As I was saying, she has ties to the community," he lies. "And she will undergo monitoring as a condition of bail."

The prosecutor continues on, just in case the judge is thinking of setting a bail. "Your Honor, we ask that, in event that you do grant a bail, we would like a source hearing date set, so we can make sure that all funds presented are legal."

All Storm heard is *date* which means they are trying to not let her go today. They are trying to hold her longer. She's heard of instances like this where they want to check out the money and the sources who have put up the money just to make sure she's not being bailed out with drug money. She knows this can take weeks.

"Granted," the judge says. "I hereby set the bail at two million dollars cash. No bond, no ten percent," he adds. He's sure she would never be able to make a bail of this magnitude. The people in the audience cheer at the thought of her not being able to make bail.

Storm's heart sinks. She was expecting to hear a bail of no more than a million in which she could've gotten out with a hundred grand with a bail-bondsmen. In no way was she prepared for a bail like this, and with no ten percent. She sees that they are doing everything in their power to hold her.

Storm looks to Tony, hoping he has a defense for her and this outrageous bail. "Your Honor," Tony says, "my client is prepared to make that bail today." The judge, the prosecutors and everybody else are in shock. "Can we proceed onto the source hearing today?"

"Your Honor, we are not ready to proceed with the source hearing right now," says the prosecutor.

Her hopes of being freed today sink once again. She looks at the judge, hoping for a miracle. "Okay, we will set the source hearing date for one week from today." He bangs the gavel and exits the room. The bailiff walks over to Storm and escorts her away from Tony. She looks back at Tony with helplessness that turns to rage. In no way was she expecting this and neither was Tony.

48

LATER THAT NIGHT

IT'S BEEN A long day for Storm. After court she returned to her cell. She still hasn't eaten. She's so pissed at herself for turning herself in that she has no appetite.

She and her Muslim cellmate have not said another word to each other. Storm has sat on her cot, tossing and turning while the woman goes on with her normal regimen. She prays and recites all day long. Storm is tired of her praying and the sound of the recitation. She's heard it so much that she now knows it by heart. Covering her head with the pillow doesn't work. Being on guard prevents her from sleeping as well. She's sat up, one eye open, just in case the woman decides to make a move. Seems that she submitted too easily, and because of that, Storm doesn't trust her.

As harmless as she would like to believe the woman is, she has to keep in mind that she is here on the murderer's floor. That does mean that even if she hasn't committed murder, someone believes that she has the ability to commit murder. She can't be taken lightly. She can't let her pride and ego blind her and allow her to underestimate the little woman dressed in all black. Also, something about the woman's crying while praying makes Storm believes she is begging for forgiveness for something major.

Just as Storm finally dozes off, the sound of shower slippers awakens her. She sits up, startled, ready for war. She looks around, and the woman is not there. The sound of the slippers shuffle across the floor outside of the cell.

"Yo!" the woman shouts from the bottom bunk. She gets up and runs over to the gate. "Ay yo!" she shouts more aggressively. The sound of the slippers shuffling stops. "Come here for a second," the Muslim woman demands.

Storm watches from underneath the pillow as a young butch-looking, heavyset girl appears at the gate. "What's up?" she asks cocky-like.

"Listen, I'm in here trying to get some sleep and the sound of them damn shower slippers wake me up every morning. Next time you walk past my room, pick your feet up. I don't want to hear them slippers no more."

Storm snickers to herself. *The nerve of this chick*, she thinks to herself. Storm is familiar with her type. She's like a little Chihuahua, all bark and no bite. She awaits the response of the woman on the other side of the gate, wondering how this will play out.

"Whatever," the woman says with disrespect. She walks off, slippers shuffling across the floor even louder than they originally did.

The Muslim woman says not another word. She lie back on her cot, and in seconds, her loud snoring sounds off.

Storm laughs to herself, believing the woman is just all mouth and harmless. She's able to catch some ZZZs with no further worry.

49

ESSEX COUNTY JAIL
TWO DAYS LATER

MR. ANTONELLI SITS in the visiting hall, feeling like a fish out of water. In all his years he's never been on the opposite side of the law. The only law he's ever broken is speeding five miles over the speed limit in his Ferrari. He's never had to visit a jail because no one he knows has ever been inside one.

The process of being searched and talked down to is an experience that he will never forget. As he sits in the room among criminals and criminal lovers, dressed in his suit and tie, he's looked at as an attorney and not the lover of an inmate. All of this has him frustrated but missing his baby has him comfortable outside of his element.

As she steps into the room, her rage fills the empty spaces. Once she spots him in the corner, her fury heats the room up even more. She stomps toward the table, staring at him ferociously. He hates to see her like this, dressed like a criminal in a prison jumpsuit.

As she reaches him he stands up for a hug. She seats herself with no hugging, not even a smile. "I thought you said I would be out the next day! You and your fake-ass model attorney bamboozled me."

The people in the surrounding area all watch as she creates a spectacle. She talks down to him in a humiliating manner.

"Baby, baby, calm down," he says with embarrassment as he peeks around at the people.

"Baby, my ass. When the fuck I'm getting outta here?"

"The attorney is working. We can't do anything until the source hearing. He says they are just playing hardball to make you pay for running for so long. They see you as a flight risk."

"Man, fuck all that! Money talk and bullshit walk. Put that money up and get me the fuck outta here!"

"Baby, speaking of money… why didn't you mention the one hundred thousand dollars they found in the apartment?"

"Because it was my money. Had nothing to do with you."

"But they will want to know where the money came from."

"Tell them you gave it to me. That's where I got it from."

"But I didn't," he replies with helplessness in his eyes.

"How the fuck they know that? Did you tell them?"

"No, I didn't tell them anything."

"Good!"

Mr. Antonelli sits back, wondering what he's gotten himself into just. The unexplained money coupled with many other things has him questioning her innocence. He now fears for himself, not knowing if he will be involved in her madness.

"I don't know how you're gonna do it, but you need to get me out of here," she says with rage. She walks away from him and makes her exit from the visiting hall, leaving him standing in embarrassment with no words.

50

DOVER DOWNS CASINO, DELAWARE
LATER THAT NIGHT

EVEN WITH STORM locked away, business still must go on. Of course, she appointed Toy in charge to watch over the girls and make sure everything moved accordingly. She sent Mud along to watch their backs since she couldn't be there. She trusts him to be all the muscle they need in case somebody steps out of pocket.

At this moment, Toy and Wendy are on the floor, trying to catch while Jazz has already caught. Jazz felt partly sure that no one she knows would come this far just to gamble. For days she contemplated as she expected her husband to call and ask about her being in Atlantic City, but to her surprise he never did. She even threw Jeff's name around just to see if she could get a reaction out of him.

He's stated that they have been in their normal contact and he's been putting money on his books every week as he normally does. There was no mention of anything else. What does surprise her though is that his friend has been calling her. His calls to her all seem to be reaching, but she takes it as him checking on her as if he may know that she was up to no good that night in Atlantic City. His calls only increase her guilt, but as Storm stated, guilt won't get the bills paid.

Right now Jazz drags along behind the middle-aged white business tycoon as they step down the hall of the luxurious hotel. While inside a restaurant, they met this man and he paid for their meals. His generosity didn't stop there though. He dragged them along to the casino with him and gave them all a few hundred to gamble alongside of him.

As the night progressed, Wendy decided to pass this one off to her friend, knowing it was money in the bag already. With Jazz still new to the business, she knew it would be harder for her to get another, while she could blink and catch another one. Hours and hours of gambling with no luck whatsoever, Jazz watched as he lost close to eighty thousand dollars. Just minutes ago, he decided to stop, understanding that tonight isn't his lucky night. Neither he nor Jazz had to state the details of what the rest of the night was hitting for. It was said without being said.

Just as the man stops at his room and staggers back and forth with the key in his hand, Jazz's phone rings. She prays that it's not her husband before looking at the phone. She looks at her watch and realizes it's many hours past the phone time so in no way could it be him. She exhales relief at the thought of it and looks at the display.

Seeing Jeff's number at such a late hour takes her by surprise. Her first thought is to ignore it, but she considers that maybe something has happened. Her curiosity leaves her no choice but to answer. The man stands at the door waiting for her to catch up. He rocks back and forth like a drunkard.

"Go on in," Jazz commands. "I have to take this call," she says as she falls back further. She steps away from the man and accepts the call. "Hello?" she says in a fake groggy voice as if she was sleeping.

"Jazz," he says with uncertainty. "Did I wake you up?"

"Yeah, but what's up? What time is it? Is everything okay?"

"Yeah, yeah, everything cool. I was just in the area and wondering if you was all right?"

In the area, at this hour? Jazz says in her mind. She's no dummy to game and this seems quite weird to her. She gets it now, totally. Her husband has been keeping it quiet but using Jeff to keep tabs on her. "Yes, I'm okay," she replies well aware of his little game.

"You sure? I got a couple dollars for you if you need it. I'm like two blocks away from your house. I can slide right through."

"Jeff, I don't need anything. Plus, it's one in the morning," she says with no sleepiness in her voice. Her voice is now filled with anger. One, she's mad that her husband and him are playing this little game, and two, she's angry that she put herself in the position to be played with from the beginning.

"You sure? I'm right here. Why don't you come down anyway? Five minutes. I just have something to say to you."

"It's one in the morning," she says with evident anger. "The hour is not even decent. Come tomorrow and you can tell me."

"All right. Bet," he says with defeat in his voice.

"Let me get back to bed. I have things to do in the morning. Talk to you tomorrow."

Just as she's about to hang up, he yells. "Yo, Jazz. Do me a favor and keep this between us. Like, bro don't have to know that I be calling and checking up on you to see if you need something. You know him and that pride. I don't ever want him to think that I'm crossing the boundaries and getting into his personal business. Like I know the money ain't there no more, but I ain't trying to make him feel like less than a man."

Jazz becomes extremely angered now. She reads right through the play on words. In no way is he calling on her husband's behalf. He's calling on his own. She realizes that he obviously knew she was up to something that night, and he's using that as leverage to make a pass on her.

She's sure he has no clue what she was really doing, but he does know she was up to no good. Now he feels comfortable in shooting his shot at her, knowing that she can't tell her husband. Clearly this is blackmail to get what he wants from her. It hurts her that she saw him as a real friend to her husband, but it hurts her even more that she can't tell her husband.

"Bye!" She hangs up without waiting for his reply.

She looks up and finds the doorway empty. The man has stepped inside. She steps into the room only to find him shirtless, lying back on the couch, comfortably. It's obvious that she's wearing her emotions on her face right now because he stares at her peculiarly, through drunk eyes.

"You okay, sweetie?" he asks, slurring his words.

She wipes the angered expression off her face and puts on a huge fake smile. "Yes, I'm fine."

"Okay, because I can make you feel better," he says flirtatiously. His remark makes her smile a real one. "Come on over and let me whisper something into your ear."

She walks over slowly with the butterflies floating in her belly. He grabs both her hands and guides her onto his lap. The feeling of his manhood pressed against her makes her uncomfortable, but she still continues on with her smile. He places his finger on her chin and turns her ear to his mouth. "How much is this gonna cost me?" he whispers into her ear.

She swallows the lump of fear in her throat before speaking. "One thousand," she whispers with embarrassment.

He leans back, staring into her eyes. "And what does that include?"

"Everything, I guess."

"What is everything?"

"Well, not everything." She's made a vow to herself that she will never put her mouth on these men. No way she could ever kiss her children after oral sex with a complete stranger. She may be disrespecting her husband and their marriage, but she will never disrespect her children. "My mouth is off limits."

"Party pooper," he says teasingly. "So, is it okay to put my mouth on you?"

The thought of that bothers her as well, but she realizes it's all a part of the business. She simply shrugs her shoulders in reply.

"Okay, good enough," he says as he digs into his pocket. His trousers are so tight he can barely pry his hands inside. He lifts up from the seat and gently pushes her off him. He gets up, digging into his pocket. He staggers back and forth.

Jazz watches as he grips the fancy leather wallet in hand. Instead of digging in for the money, he flips the wallet open. "You are under arrest for the solicitation of sex," he says with no sign of being drunk. It was all fake.

Her mouth drops open. As she stares at the badge, she hopes this is a joke. He reaches under the cushions of the couch and handcuffs appear in his hand. She's speechless. He grabs her hands to cuff them in front of her.

"No, please, no," she pleads. "I'm sorry. Please don't do this to me."

He smiles at her with no compassion for the tears that are dripping down her face. "You've done this to yourself." He pushes her back onto the couch. She sinks deep into it. He walks over to the nightstand and pulls the drawer open. The walkie talkie in his hand solidifies that this is no joke. She's really being arrested for prostitution.

* * *

Jazz is escorted through the casino in cuffs by vice. The undercover is nowhere to be found so that his cover is not blown. Wendy spots Jazz, but her head is so low in humiliation that she doesn't notice. This has to be the worse day of her life. The closest she's ever been to breaking the law is spending the money that her husband gives her so to be in handcuffs is a nightmare for her. All she can do is pray that this news never makes it back to New Jersey.

51

NEWARK, NEW JERSEY
TWO DAYS LATER

D ETECTIVE SYKES AND her partner step out of the apartment
building with all the attention of the neighbors on them. Walking in between them is Breezy. The neighbors watch, wondering
what trouble he has gotten himself into. Although he pretends to
not know what they are here for, he knows the exact reason.

He predicted this would happen and was just counting the days
down until it came into fruition. Because he knew they would come
for him, he made sure to keep his house clean of anything illegal.
He actually expected the police to come in riot gear with K9s and
knock his door down. So being escorted out of his house with no
raid, is good.

* * *

Meanwhile, Storm holds the jail phone to her ear listening closely
to Toy who is on the other end. "Straight caught her in the act.
Luckily, Heavy Bottom stepped off on them, or she would've been
jammed up right with her."

Heavy Bottom is the code name they use for Wendy when using her real name isn't appropriate, and this is one of those times. They both are well aware that this conversation is being recorded. Heavy Bottom is the best description they could come up with, being so tiny with such an enormous ass.

Storm is sad to hear this news, which is shocking even to her. Despite her jealousy she holds for her girls, she still has some feelings for them and would hate to see them in bad situations, especially in a situation where their freedom is compromised.

These past five days feel more like five years to her and have been hell on her mental. Each second of the day that passes that she's still behind bars she hates herself more for allowing them to talk her into this. She's experienced a few bumps and bruises with the law that have had her at the precinct for a few hours but never has she spent damn near a week in custody. After this experience of being locked down, she doesn't wish jail on her worst enemy.

"Yo! Go snatch her ASAP. Don't let her sit another minute."

"She's already been snatched," Toy replies. "I grabbed her the next day soon as she got a bail. I wasn't leaving without her."

"Good," Storm replies. She's quite proud of the leadership that Toy has exerted. Toy has always followed her lead, so she's never witnessed her make boss decisions without consulting with her first. "What the bail was looking like?"

"Super light, like fifteen hundred."

"Okay, cool. What she saying though?"

"Oh, Married with Children is distraught," she says using Jazz's code name. "I haven't talked to Married with Children, but Heavy Bottom said she told her she done for sure this time. Said she will find a way to get that money back, but that ain't for her."

"Hey, everything ain't for everybody," Storm replies with no real concern.

"What's up with you though? No word on a bail?"

"Nothing! I'm a sitting duck with no clue of what's going on. I'm in here on some bullshit that I don't know nothing about," she says crisp and clear, so there is no confusion for anyone who will be listening to this recorded call. Her hopes are when they play this call back they believe her innocence. "Santa Claus, says the lawyer told him they just fucking around with me because they mad and don't really have nothing on me. I'm innocent."

* * *

Breezy sits in the interrogation room with the detectives leaning over the table on both sides of him. The questions from both of them are coming at him like rapid fire. He's been holding it down no matter how intense it has gotten. He's not new to interrogation and is a seasoned veteran with it.

"Listen," Detective Sykes says. "Storm has already admitted to the murder of that girl," she lies. "We already know that your role in it was to play the liaison and speak to her family and give the bail money to them so when she got out Storm could kill her."

Breezy looks at her with a straight face that shows no indication of the thoughts running through his mind. Hearing this almost makes him question if she really told them that. Knowing her, he can't imagine her rolling over, so he quickly washes that from his mind. He twists his lips at the detectives in disbelief. "Why would she tell y'all a lie like that?"

"Right now she's trying to save herself because she knows with another two murders she will never see daylight again."

"So, just admit that she used you to put all this together," Syke's partner interjects. "Conspiracy is better than murder."

Breezy sits there unbothered with all of this. Sykes fires away with no pause in between. "You know she has the best attorney in the state of New Jersey, right?"

"Yes, Tony Austin," he says.

"And you know what that means for you, right? That means he will do his best to make her appear innocent in that courtroom. Prosecutors will then throw both murders on you. At the end of the day, she never spoke to Kirah's brother, you did. And you're the one who gave them the money to bail her out."

Breezy's facial expression changes for the first time. He can very well see it all playing out just as she says it will. He's heard of cases that the attorney has beaten with men who have been caught with their hands in the cookie jar. The streets have labeled him a magician in the courtroom.

The detectives notice the change of body language and feel like they have him where they need him. "The only way we can help you is if you help us right here, right now," Detective Sykes says. "So, did Storm use you as the liaison?" She can see the thoughts ripping through his mind, and she thinks she sees a sign of victory.

"Like I told you from the beginning… Yeah, I know of Storm, but I haven't seen her in five years. I haven't even spoken to her. The money I gave that girl's brother was a loan. He came to me for the loan. I knew him from gambling with him and that's it."

Detective Sykes and her partner laugh simultaneously. Breezy wonders what they are laughing about. Maybe he fucked up somewhere in his story. "Are you sure about that?" the partner asks. Breezy thinks hard on what he just said and wonders what Storm's story may have been. Did she say she saw him more recently than what he said?

"Listen," Detective Sykes says, interrupting his thought process. "We are gonna walk out of this room so you can think all of this over. When we come back, we will allow you the opportunity to try again because that is not the story we got from her or the family of the murder victims."

Sykes and her partner make their way to the door. Her partner holds the door for her to exit first. She looks back at Breezy. "You got five minutes. Get it right."

52

ATLANTIC CITY
TWO DAYS LATER

TOY STEPS INTO the casino ready to punch the clock, another night at work. Over the past few days, she has gotten used to being in charge. Even without Storm here to watch over her, she makes sure that she and Wendy work as hard as they would as if she was here. In fact, they are working harder. She misses Storm so much and hates that she's going through what she's going through. She hopes to ease her struggle by having a hefty bag of money to give her once she's free.

She peeks around the casino, just to see what she's working with. The casino is packed, just the way she likes it. The more people present, the better the opportunity. As she's strolling through, her eyes land on a poker table which is filled with purple and orange chips which tells her that is where she needs to be.

Just as she wanders in that direction, she feels a tapping on her shoulder. She turns around and is face-to-face with two huge men in suits.

"Excuse me, ma'am," one of the men say with unusual politeness. "Come with us."

Toy recognizes the men as casino vice. The looks in their eyes tell her that her cover has been blown.

"Come with you where?" she asks, just trying to play it clueless.

"Save the bullshit," the other man intervenes. "We know exactly what you are here doing, so save yourself the scene and the embarrassment." He snatches her by the hand. "Let's go."

* * *

Detective Sykes sits on the corner of the table, directly in Storm's face. The other detective stands in the cut, just watching and letting Sykes handle it because he knows how much of a hard-on she has for Storm. The hatred they have for each other is mutual. Detective Sykes can see the hatred written on Storm's face and it causes her to egg her on more.

As Storm looks up at Detective Sykes, who is in her face, she can't figure out if she hates her more that she's a cop or for her skin color. Sykes is not a high yellow complexioned woman, but still fits the lighter skin, long pretty hair, mold that Storm despises.

"So you and Man-Man together pulled off the robbery which turned into a triple homicide. Or was homicide part of the original plan?" Detective Sykes asks sarcastically. "Why did you murder Man-Man though? Just so there would be no witnesses?"

Wow, Storm thinks. She had no clue that they were attempting to link her to Man-Man's murder. She thinks that maybe this is why they have been holding her, just so they can get enough information to charge her for his body as well. She's sure the only person that could link her to his body would be, who else but Kirah.

She looks the detective square in the eyes. "May I please call my attorney?"

"Shakirah Jenkins was used as the bait, correct?"

Just as she figured, Shakirah is the source. Again, she regrets that she didn't off the girl herself that night. If she had, none of this nightmare would even be taking place. She flutters her eyelashes while staring into the detective's eyes. "My attorney instructed me to answer no questions in his absence."

"Why did you murder Man-Man? Just so there would be no witnesses?"

"I wish to make no statements without the presence of my attorney."

"Now Shakirah is dead… which means no more witnesses are alive to testify against you, huh?"

Storm's ears stand up on alert like a K9, but still she wears the same emotionless face.

"You're quite crafty, I must admit. Had that girl bailed out, so you could murder her. I guess the money you spent was nothing and your freedom was well worth it, huh? Smart to an extent. You didn't expect her family to put it together that you had your longtime friend, Breezy aka Donald Jackson, give them the money to bail her out so you could murder her, huh? You did have him give them the money, so you could have her murdered right?"

"I wish to make no statements at this time without my attorney," she says while looking away from her rudely.

"You don't have to make any statements because Breezy already made them all," she says with a smile.

Storm quickly thinks of the way that Breezy reacted in the car that night and can't help but wonder if he rolled over on her out of fear of losing his own freedom.

"So, are you ready to admit to us that you murdered Shakirah and her brother on that night?"

Storm huffs with frustration. When she does, spit flees from her mouth. A few drops of spittle land on the detective's face which drives her mad. She reaches over the table and grabs Storm by the collar and draws her face close enough to bite her head off. She's been waiting for a reason to do this. "Bitch, you spit on me?"

Just as she she's about to wrap her hands around Storm's neck the other detective steps in between them and pries her off. Storm sits back calmly, and this makes the detective even angrier. "You little, funny looking, freckled-faced bitch you! Orphan Annie face-ass bitch!" the detective says. She's so mad that her professionalism and her adult go out of the window.

Storm is no longer unbothered. The detective has struck a nerve. Those words cut through her already hole-riddled self-esteem. This is something she hasn't heard in years and the rage she feels right now is more than she felt as a child.

She's now equally as pissed as the detective is, if not more. Venom bleeds from her eyes. "Fuck you, you yellow bitch!" she barks with rage as she stands up, ready for war. The male detective stands in between them again as they try to get to each other. He pushes Storm and she lands onto the floor.

"No, you lil ugly bitch." She realizes the impact of what she said and uses it to get her rowled up. "Nappy head, freckled-face bitch!" She smiles with satisfaction as Storm steams with rage. "It ain't 'fuck me.' It's 'fuck you and your attorney'! I promise you are going to jail for the rest of your fucking life!"

* * *

Toy is in the middle of her own heated situation as she sits in an office surrounded by a bunch of vice squad.

"Here's the deal," the chief says. "We have video of you using this casino as a place to solicit sex. We have searched through videos for as far back as six months. We even have under-covers that you have offered sex for money," he claims as Toy sits back with a face full of guilt. "You can either admit to the charges and go to jail for prostitution or you have another option that can help us as well as help yourself."

"And what is that?" she asks, eagerly wanting to help herself.

"Are you willing to help us?"

"All depends on what helping you consists of."

53

DAYS LATER

S TORM AND TOY sit across from each other in the visiting hall. Toy has never seen Storm look so depressed. She's known Storm to be high in spirit regardless of what she is up against. For the first time during their friendship, she sees Storm look worried.

She looks like she has lost ten or more pounds in just the few days that she's been here. Seeing Storm like this saddens Toy, especially since she believes that she is innocent in all of this. She has more news that she's sure will make matters worse. She hates that so much has gone wrong since she's been in control. She feels as if she's let Storm down.

What Toy also sees is Storm's self-esteem at an all-time low, but she doesn't realize it though. She confuses it all with depression. Storm, with her nappy hair and freckles exposed, makes her feel naked. Over the years she has managed to bury her complex but not now. In here, she's forced to face it with no way to hide it. She can barely look Toy in the eyes.

Toy exhales, preparing herself to drop the bomb. "So, Atlantic City's over with," she says sadly.

"What you mean over with?" Storm asks with a baffled frown.

"The other day, as soon as I stepped into the casino, I was surrounded by vice. They took me into the office and told me they'd had me on video for months and even had some undercovers that I supposedly had conversations with."

Storm shakes her head with disgust as she thinks of her money spot being blown up. That was her lifeline. She rubs her hands over her face. "Shit! If it ain't one thing, it's another," she grunts. "So, they locked you up?"

Toy shakes her head negatively. "They gave me an ultimatum," she says sadly. "They said I could either admit it and get locked up or I could help them."

Storm automatically thinks that helping them meant bringing her in and telling on her, revealing that she was the mastermind behind it all. "You're here, so is it safe to say that you helped them?" A smirk spreads across Storm's face. "So, you gave me up, huh?" She chuckles with disappointment.

Toy laughs in her face. "The same thing I thought they wanted. But no. The other option was coming to work for them." Storm has no clue what she's talking about. "They like my style and said I have a gift. Said they want me on their team at the casino."

Storm assumes that means working for the casino selling sex. "Figures. I always knew they had their own girls on the payroll, and that's why they so hard on the independents. Getting in their way and cutting their money."

"Yeah, but not on the ground level. Like on some bigger shit. Their money's on a different level, like tricks paying twenty and thirty-thousand for a night."

"Wow."

"Yeah, they not even talking about me working like that. They want to give me a real position. Floor Manager."

"Oh, that's what they call it?" Storm asks maliciously.

"Nah. I don't have to work in that way no more. My job will be to entertain the big money clients that come to the casino. I pick them up from the airport when they arrive and I would be in charge of them their entire stay. I set them up with everything that it takes to keep them entertained — food, plays, and partying. My job would be to make sure they spend all of their money before leaving that casino."

Storm sees the spark in Toy's eyes and realizes that she may have lost her number one girl. "So did you accept the job?"

"Nah, my loyalty is with you."

"Listen, you know I would never hold you back from doing what you wanna do. Them other girls are business to me, just pawns on the board. Me and you are friends with years of history together."

"I know that, but I'm thinking this could work out for both of us."

"How so?"

"Like I said, I would be in charge of keeping them entertained in every sense. The casino has their own escorts that are called in for the entertainment. What we can do is slide a few of our own girls in there, and we can bust the bread down the middle."

The bigger picture plays right before Storm's eyes. She would be losing her best girl but would have free range to move other girls through the casino pipeline. A smile pops onto her face. "I like that."

"Millionaire motherfuckers dropping it like it's hot. Tens of thousands of dollars for one night. So, what you say?"

"That's a no brainer. I say take the gig and let's go."

"I thought so," Toy says with a smile. "Right now all we got is Wendy though. I been trying to think who else we could get, but I ain't got that gift you got. You know you have a way of getting in their heads and making a bitch do what she don't wanna do," she says looking at her with a side-eye and a smile.

Storm stares into space and what she sees is promise and opportunity. She rubs her hands together like a mad scientist. "Don't worry about that. I got it from here. Once they bust this gate and let me out... it's on!"

54

4 A.M.

WITH THE CASINOS now out of bounds, Toy had to find another source of income for them. Storm's hustler mentality has rubbed off on Toy over the years, so she knows how to get to the money. Didn't take her long to come up with a plan. Earlier today after leaving the county jail, she set up in the Holiday Inn near the airport.

They've been in their room for hours now. She's posted on Craigslist and the customers have been coming in by the hour. Wendy has entertained twelve dates already, all paying a minimum of four hundred dollars. Toy's only job was to answer the calls and set up the appointments. She screened the calls, making sure that all the clients were white men. With no security, they need no friction, so she wanted no young, black, drug dealer clientele.

The entire day she turned not one trick, letting Wendy do all the work while she played the Madame role. That was until she received a call from a man who requested two girls. With no other girl on the roster, Toy had to join along to fill his request.

Wendy stands at the door, butt naked as the middle-aged Caucasian man steps inside. He walks past her, cool and calm, not taking a second look at her nudity. Toy sits at the head of the bed, dressed in fine lingerie. They both examine the man and see no sign of him being a cop.

Instead he looks like the typical respectable business man dressed down on the weekend like a soccer dad. The wedding band on his finger makes them erase the word *respectable* from his description. He catches them eyeing it and removes it. His honor is restored in their eyes and they see him as just another married man in need of some fun to break the monotony of a boring marriage.

Wendy locks the door and follows behind the man. He stops at the sink and Toy walks over to greet him. She rubs her hand over his clean-shaven face. "Hey, handsome." Wendy hugs him from the back, arms around his waist, checking for a hint of a gun or a walkie-talkie. She finds neither. What does pique their attention is the Poland spring water bottle with what appears to be beer inside. They both consider that he could be drunk and that could mean hours of sex without him being able to cum.

"So, you ready for a good time, handsome?" Toy asks as she's extra touchy-feely.

"That's why I'm here," he replies. His aura says he's not new to this.

"What you doing up at this hour?" Toy asks. "Couldn't sleep? Did morning wood wake you up?" she asks as she rubs her hand over his crotch. She juggles his manhood in her hand and is shocked that her magic touch has no magic in it. He remains limp.

Wendy is now at Toy's side. They stand there like double trouble. "So, you requested two girls. Are you sure you can handle that? You got enough energy for two of us."

He cracks a smile for the very first time. "I think I can muster up enough energy." He reaches out and twists Wendy's nipple in between his fingertips.

She grabs his hand. "Not yet. Money first," she says before flashing a wink.

"Tell mama what you need." She kisses him on the cheek, hands on his crotch.

He gets to digging in his pocket for his wallet. He peels the bills from his wallet very neatly and meticulously.

* * *

In the Essex County Jail, loud snoring from the Muslimah on the bottom bunk rips through the air quite rhythmically. The outside of the cell is peaceful and serene until the shuffling of slippers against the floor breaks the peace. Storm is awakened.

"Hmphh," she sighs with aggravation.

She's just dozed off for a few minutes… and now this. She shakes her head with anguish as she lifts up and looks out onto the tier. Through the glimpse of light she sees the woman walking by, dragging her feet as she always does. The shuffling seems so much louder being that it's the only noise around.

The Muslimah's snoring ceases, and she can be heard fidgeting around on her cot. She sighs in aggravation as well. Her eyes can be felt burning through the bottom of the top bunk. The shuffling of the slippers fades the further away the woman gets. Once it's no longer heard, the Muslimah's snoring starts up again. Storm is not as fortunate to find sleep. She's stuck in a state of insomnia. Another long night.

* * *

Back in the hotel room, Toy and Wendy have been surprised with the weirdest request ever. In this business, they have come across many weirdos, but this one here exceeds the weirdo meter. They almost take it as an insult that, as beautiful and as sexy as they both think they are, he doesn't want sex with them. He hasn't even touched them in a sexual manner. What he's paid them to do is strange to them.

He lays in the bed stark naked, spread eagle as Wendy stands over him. With all of her might, she drops a fist full of her most powerful punch onto his testicles. He grunts with agony. Satisfaction fills his eyes. "Harder," he begs. Before he can ask again, she drops an even more powerful punch. "Agghh," he grunts as he rolls over onto his side. He slowly rolls over onto his back with agony but no satisfaction. "That's not enough. Harder, please," he begs.

Wendy looks to Toy helplessly for she has done her very best. They have taken turns on him, yet he seems not to be content. Toy steps up to bat, once again, as she thinks of what she can do to bring him the pain that he desires. "Stand up!" she commands.

Once he stands up, with no warning, she grabs his testicles in her hand and squeezes them like she's squeezing an orange for fresh orange juice. His tongue hangs from his mouth and he's not able to utter a sound. He drops to his knees with pain while his eyes light up with pleasure. "Yes!" he grunts. "Don't stop! Squeeze harder!"

Toy, feeling like she has him at his breaking point, uses her other hand for reinforcement. With both hands, she squeezes the life out of him. He screams a high note as he reaches his peak. They back away from him, staying clear of the ejaculation that erupts like confetti in the air. Never have they seen anything like this. To be paid two hundred and fifty dollars apiece for this is probably the strangest money they ever made, but it doesn't stop there.

The man stands up and with a spark in his eyes he speaks. "Now for the grand finale."

"That's it," Toy replies.

"Don't worry. I have more money," he says. He reaches over to his pants that are on the nightstand and digs into his pocket. He peels through his crisp bills and hands them both another three hundred.

They await his request, not sure of what it could possibly be. They are almost afraid to ask, but they have to. "What is the grand finale?" Toy asks.

The man cracks a smirk. "You, beautiful, I would like you to urinate on me." He looks to Wendy. "And you," he says as he slaps her ass for the very first time. "I want you to drop a doozy on me?"

"A what?" Wendy asks.

"Yes, a number two," he says with guilty perversion on his face.

They look at each other in shock at his request. They then look at the three hundred dollar bills in their hand. "Okay, I got two more hundred apiece." He quickly gives them the additional money and lays onto the bed, not thinking of taking no for an answer.

"You first," he says as he pulls Wendy to him. He guides her over top of him, planting her exactly where he wants her. She straddles him, ass onto his stomach, looking at Toy with embarrassment on her face. She leans forward and buries her face on the bed in between his feet to cover the shame she feels for even entertaining such a thing. She grabs his ankles tight as she strains, trying to fulfill his request.

Toy, not wanting to witness the act decides to fulfill her obligation and make her exit. "She steps close to the bed and with the most sexiness she can muster up under the circumstances she asks, "And where do you want me, handsome?"

He hangs his head off the edge of the bed and positions her wherein she's standing straddled over his face. With his eyes closed, he worships Wendy's glorious ass with his hands. He massages her slowly in attempt to make her more comfortable. His fingers seep into the softness of her fluffy cheeks. A few loud slaps leave her with a stinging that lasts for seconds. "Come on. Give it to me," he begs as he gives her a deep tissue massage. Just as she's about ready to drop the load he's begging for, he slaps her again and breaks her concentration.

Suddenly his focus is broken as the golden shower floods his face, taking his breath away. He opens his eyes and mouth wide. Enjoyment spread across his face as the shower revives him. Toy allows the few tinkles she has left to drip before she backs away and watches from the distance. She's sure no night will ever match this one and if it does, she doesn't want to be a part of it.

Twenty minutes later, and Wendy has finally been able to meet her job description. She gets up from the bed feeling dirty and disgusting. She leaves the man, lying on the bed, a shitty mess, and by the look on his face, he's in heaven right now. He lays back in pure ecstasy.

Wendy walks toward the bathroom, legs spread apart, careful not to let them touch. As she passes Toy, she lowers her head in shame. "Damn, girl! You stink," Toy says with her lips turned up to her nose. "Bitch, you need a detox," she teases. Wendy rolls her eyes and steps into the bathroom, slamming the door behind her. The shower water sounds off immediately.

Minutes later, all have cleaned themselves up, but the stench is still blaring in the air. The man now fully dressed has reverted to his soccer dad disguise. "Thank you, ladies," he says as he takes a sip from his water bottle. "I've enjoyed myself." The familiar smell of Listerine rips from his mouth.

He places his wedding band back onto his finger with no shame at all. He guzzles the mouthwash like water, attempting to wash away the evidence of his fetish. If only his wife knew about his secret fetish, maybe they wouldn't have such a shitty marriage, or maybe they would.

55

I N THE MESS hall, Storm sits at the table alone in the far corner of the room. On a tray in front of her are three globs of slop. She's disgusted by it, but she's starving so she prepares the slop the best way she can by sweetening it and adding excessive salt to cover up to the taste. She hasn't eaten in days and has been filling up on only water. She can no longer get by that way and has no choice but to be here.

This is her first time stepping foot into the mess hall, and as she figured, the room is quite tense. Clusters of women are spread out throughout the room, all in cliques. A table full of dykes across the room have their full attention on her. They watch Storm with lust in their eyes as the table full of divas at the next table watch her with jealousy. Storm's attention is on the table full of Muslim women to the left of her. She appears to not be paying them any attention, but truly she keeps both eyes on them. Venom has been coming from that table ever since she stepped foot in there.

It's obvious to her that her cellmate must have told them about their beef. Her cellmate sits at the center of the table. Storm can't keep her eyes off the woman for this is the very first time she has saw her without her face all covered up. The woman is totally the opposite of what she expected.

She expected her to be an old, hard-faced woman, maybe an ex-drug addict. For some reason that is what she thinks the women who are covered up must look like underneath the garments.

She always believed that, for them to hide like that, they must be hideous. She automatically assumed that had to be the case for her cellmate.

The woman has a youthful look in her eyes that she couldn't see with the black cut-out around them. The material made her eyes look cold and creepy. Her skin glows and is flawless. She looks young, but her mannerisms and her laidback and mature aura makes Storm estimate her at around her late thirties.

The woman's position at the table and how everything revolves around her indicates that she must be their leader. Storm peeks up, and the table full of about eight women have their eyes locked in on her. The cellmate is pretending to be focused on the food on her tray, but it's evident she's saying something about Storm. They all watch her blatantly.

Storm gets the feeling that something is going to go down in here. She's worried, but she retains her calm swagger. In no way is she worried about fighting. She's been fighting all of her life. She's not even worried about them outnumbering her. She's been there before as well. Being jumped on by more than five girls is less abusive than two girls because they all can't get to you. What she is worried about is being cut in the face. That's always been her biggest fear in life. A buck-fifty razor mark in the face will only add to her already super low self-esteem.

Storm is so focused on the Muslimahs at the table that she doesn't notice the table full of young women in the corner to her right. They notice her though. "That's her right there," the young girl whispers to her group.

"You sure?"

"I promise you that's her. Yo Big Bruh labeled that bitch food, and I'm gon' eat. On Bs," she says with passion. The 'Big Bruh' she refers to is the cousin of one of the murder victims that Storm left behind at the robbery. "Big Bruh promised me bail if I rock this out for him."

"Let's move then. What you waiting for?" a woman asks. She's being the instigator because she loves the drama.

"Nah, not right now. The shit gotta be done right. He want the bitch smashed all the way out, so it can't be in the wide open like this."

"I heard. Say that."

"Big Bruh said the bitch dangerous. Like she thinks she some type of Mob Wife or something. Said be careful with her. I told him, 'Fuck that bitch. I'm dangerous, too.'"

"More less," the instigator says, cheering her on.

The woman takes the battery charge from the instigator and gets up from her seat.

"Matter of fact," she says as she walks toward Storm's table.

All the girls sit on the edge of their seats ready to watch the show and also ready to join in. They are just waiting for her to set it off.

As the young woman is making her way over, Storm's attention is captured by a more than familiar noise. The sound of the shower slippers shuffling across the floor, which has become a part of her everyday life, and it annoys her to no end. She looks to the doorway where the butch-looking woman has just come into the room. She drags her feet lazily across the room.

Storm is caught by surprise when she feels a tapping on her shoulder. She flinches as she stands up from her seat. Storm looks to the young woman who has her hand planted on her shoulder. She wears a grin of sarcasm as she looks at her. "You Storm, right?"

After studying the girl's face and realizing that she doesn't know her, Storm slaps the girl's hand off of her shoulder. She stands in defense, ready to square up. "Who you?"

The young woman smiles in mockery. "Relax. The homie Big Face said you wasn't easy to touch. I just wanted to put a hand on your shoulder to prove him wrong."

Storm has no clue who Big Face is. She's sure this has something to do with the robbery and homicide. She's correct in her thinking. Big Face is a high-ranking Blood. One of the men she killed in the house was Big Face's cousin.

The young women from the table all make their way across the room toward them. The woman stands cool and calm as Storm jolts from around the table positioning herself, back against the wall. She's ready for whatever is about to come her way. Before they are halfway across the room, the young woman sends them a signal to halt and they do.

The young woman then backpedals away with her eyes glued on Storm. Storm bops her head up and down with a smile. "You fucked up," she mumbles, allowing the girl the ability to read her lips. She seats herself, eyes still on the woman.

With her attention on them, she hears the shuffling of the slippers in the backdrop. She cuts her eyes at the woman who drags along with her tray in her hand. Just as she passes the Muslimah's table, Storm's cellmate gets up from her seat. The play can be read if the woman was paying attention, but instead she's busy eating, from her tray. She picks the food from her tray greedily while walking.

The Muslimahs get up from their seats and all disperse in different directions. Just as the woman is about to sit down, Storm's cellmate leaps at her, jumping on her back. The woman tumbles forward, dropping her tray. The woman flips and flops like a huge hog, but the Muslimah manages to hold on. By now everyone is running over to get a front row seat of the action. Storm watches from afar, mindful not to put herself in the center of the room where she could be next.

The Muslimah rides the woman's back as she bucks like a mechanical bull. She holds on tight with one arm wrapped around the woman's neck. With the other hand, she appears to be dropping punches onto her neck. It's not until the blood starts to gush that it becomes evident that she's not punching her. She's jabbing her with a shank.

The woman screams bloody murder at the top of her lungs. The Muslimah continues to poke at her, not just in the neck but everywhere. When the screaming stops, so does the movement of the women, but the Muslimah continues poking. The woman bleeds profusely like a cow in a slaughter house. The spectators watch in awe as she stabs her mercilessly.

The corrections officers bust in the room, dressed in riot gear. At the sight of them, the inmates disperse. The Muslimah looks up from her dead prey and doesn't flinch at the sight of the many officers. They surround her, ready to attack, but she drops her shank and submits. She places her hands high in the air, as she stands up. She turns around slowly and places her hands behind her back to be cuffed. Paramedics rush into the room, and at the sight of the woman, they realize they are already too late.

Storm watches closely as the Muslimah is shoved out of the room. Her demeanor is calm and easygoing, as if she hasn't just committed cold-blooded murder over the noise of shower slippers. It dawns on her that she has been living with an extremely vicious woman. Chills run through her body as she thinks of how she's slept in her cell not knowing how dangerous the woman really was.

She asks herself how she didn't detect the viciousness of this woman. She realizes she most definitely slipped on this one. They say you should never judge a book by its cover, but this woman had no cover for her to judge in the first place. The black covering hid her viciousness well.

She considers that she could have easily been the one lying out on the floor in cold blood right now. If she had ignored the Muslimah's request, she would've learned the hard way that the Muslimah was about her business. *Better the other woman than her*, she thinks to herself. She counts this as another one of her blessings in disguise. She walked in this jail on point, eyes open, but now after witnessing this, she won't close her eyes, not even to blink.

56

TWO WEEKS LATER

M ANY DAYS HAVE passed, and Storm has been able to keep herself safe and out of harm's way. Her cellmate was shipped to a maximum prison, which got her a new bunkie. The new roommate is a young girl who is in jail for the first time. She wouldn't bust a grape in a fruit fight but has gotten locked up for conspiracy to a murder. She's the codefendant, along with her children's father.

The woman came into the cell a nervous wreck. Storm felt sorry for her and tried her best to put her at ease. She kept the girl close, just so nothing could happen to her. In all reality she could barely keep herself safe with all the tension she had around her, but she was able to keep it cool and keep them both safe. Storm protecting her was not about her being a good Samaritan. As she looked at the young cutie she saw the bigger picture. By protecting the young girl today on the inside, Storm hoped to capture her mind and take their bond to the outside and make some money together. She's always working.

Storm is sure one day her safety would eventually run out and they will get heart to make their move. It's too late now because they will never be able to catch her in a position like this. They didn't make their move while she was on the inside, and she promises that is the biggest mistake they could ever make. She has plans on making them pay for that mistake, starting with the homie Big Face. She hated to have left the young girl alone to fend for herself, but she charged it to the game of life.

Storm also found out the story on her own cellmate. The woman was already facing murder charges. Not murder like murder as result of robbery murder, but psychopathic murder. The woman drowned her three babies in the bathtub and waited for her husband to come home to see them in the tub, dead. This was done after finding out that her Muslim husband of twelve years had had a stripper side-chick, for years. The worse part of it all was the three year old son, the man and the stripper had together, behind the woman's back.

She felt more betrayed because she converted to Islam for him and dedicated her life to it. As she covered herself up totally and was home dedicated to the religion her husband was out chasing the women of the world. The pressure of all she found out caused her to snap. Once he came home and witnessed the surprise she had for him, she stabbed him. She left him alive though to live with the consequences of his actions.

Goosebumps pop up all over Storm's body when she thinks of how she slept in a room with a psychopath. She already knew her life was over, which was why she had no problem committing more murder. All of this has been an eye opening experience for Storm, but now it's over. Well, at least, it's over for the time being. She can only hope that the attorney has the juice that she heard he has and she's able to beat the charges. She will deal with that when the time comes, but for right now, that part of it is over.

The Source Hearing that was supposed to be held a week after the arraignment was finally held two days ago. That was after the prosecutor requested a two-day extension and on that day he couldn't make it because he was supposedly held in contempt of court on another case. Once the prosecution couldn't duck and hide any longer the judge supposedly had a medical emergency. Tony informed Storm that all of that was game playing just to keep from releasing her.

They searched through Mr. Antonelli's financial history as well as his personal history and hated that he was as clean as a whistle. They dug as far back as the first million he ever made. It baffled them as to why a White senior citizen was willing to put up two million in cash for a poor black criminal. They subliminally made accusations that she was one of his prostitutes or escorts.

That is after they asked him if she or anyone else had made any threats to him if he didn't post the bail. When all failed, they attempted to scare him out of posting the money by stating that she was his responsibility while out on this bail, and if any other crime is committed, he would be charged, along with her. Not fully knowing what any of this was really about he became worried until Tony explained to him that, in no way, was that legal.

Right now both Storm and Mr. Antonelli are just happy that phase of it is over. They know that is only half of the battle and the hardest part of the fight is to come. During the time of her incarceration Mr. Antonelli had some time to think. This situation leaves him with so many questions.

He's started to doubt her innocence in all of this. He can't force himself to believe that she's a murderer, so it's easier to convince himself that maybe she's guilty by association. The motive he can't understand because he provides for her. He's sure it has to be more than money that has her wrapped up in this. He just doesn't know what.

"You know the lawyer told me that they questioned you about three more murders, right?" Mr. Antonelli asks, looking over at the passenger's seat.

"I'm sure he did," she replies, not even looking at him. She continues to look out of the window, not even interested in his conversation.

"Ang—," he starts but can't fix his mouth to say it. He can no longer see her as an angel. "What is going on? All this is too much for me. I'm an old man. You're gonna give me a heart attack. Please just come clean with me, at least."

"Wow," she says with a smile. She's quite stunned. "Look, I came clean but you don't want to believe me," she says still looking out of the window.

He leaves it at just that, realizing that she's sticking with her story. They continue on with their drive, neither of them saying a word. His mind is filled with questions that he may never get the answers to, from her, and her mind is just all over the place. She has some questions that she needs answered as well, and as soon as she's showered and changed she plans to hit the streets and get those answers.

* * *

Hours later, Breezy parks behind Storm's rental car on the outskirts of the projects. He gets out holding a shopping bag with a sneaker box peeking over the top. In his right hand, he grips his .9mm inside of his coat pocket. The money inside the sneaker box is the last of the money that he owes her for the work.

In total he scored a little over sixty grand off the kilo she gave him. She hasn't applied any pressure on him for the money because she wasn't in dire need of it. But now with her being a hundred and some change in the arrears from the police raid, she's now in need. The money she's lost with Toy and the girls just adds to her financial distress.

Storm looks in the mirror at herself, through her dark shades, and it's like a blast from the past for her. Her hair is tucked neatly inside of the baseball cap. Her appointment isn't until the end of the week, so until then, the hat will be glued to her head. Her baggy track suit has her looking like the tomboy she hasn't seen in some time. The only difference from back then and now is the coat of make-up that covers her face.

She watches closely as Breezy makes his way toward the car. She grips her .9mm under her left thigh. She hasn't been able to sleep a wink since the detectives questioned her and made accusations that he told them some things. Now she plans to find out what exactly he told them.

Breezy gets into the car and takes his hand off his gun just long enough to close the door. He looks over at her, and although she has dark shades over her eyes, he can still feel the coldness bleeding from them. "What up?" he says.

She takes notice that he didn't greet her with peace, which means obviously he's not at peace with her. He taught her that many years ago, and she's never forgotten it. She also notices that his right hand is still in his pocket. She wonders if it's guilt that has him on guard like this.

He hands the bag over to her. "That's thirty-two grand. I crushed the whole thing on the ground in nickel bottles and scored like sixty-four. I gave you an extra four for your patience with me."

"That's honorable of you," she says with sarcasm.

Breezy notices the sarcasm and cuts his eye at her. He says nothing though. "Yo, you know they came to my crib and snatched me, right?"

"Yeah, I know," she replies. "They told me when they questioned me. So, what they ask you? Better yet, what did you tell them?"

That comment pushes him past his boiling point. "Yo, we not even gone play this game. Fuck you mean, what I tell them?" he asks while gripping his gun tighter. The grip he has on his gun is two-seconds behind the gripping of hers. In fact, she's managed to slide hers to the edge of her seat without him seeing it.

"When you ever known me to talk the police?" he questions with authority. "At eleven years old I didn't run my mouth. I was a fucking kid and I didn't say shit when they questioned me. Fuck I look like talking as a grown ass man?" he asks with spit flying from his mouth. "You know how the fuck I feel about snitches." His rage builds at the thought of what she's insinuating. "I will die before I ever tell a cop any fucking thing."

"Ay, you never know. Niggas change every day. All I got to go on is how you reacted that night."

"You know what? If it's gon' go down, we might as well do it right now on some Jesse James shit. You draw yours, and I draw mine, and may the best man win. I ain't playing this game with you. I ain't gon' be watching over my shoulder while you call yourself sleepwalking me.

"I know you and you ain't gon' run up behind me when I think shit all good and over with. On some real shit, you know how I get down, just like I know how you get down. And the only reason I ain't go is because I love you like a sister. But right here right now, if what we built don't mean nothing to you, let's go!" He stares into her eyes with a violent streak. His body language tells her that he's ready to go if need be.

She sits back, cool and calm. "First of all, when you ever known me to shoot a motherfucker in the back or in the back of his motherfucking head?" she asks calmly. "That's coward shit," she says, raising her voice a tad bit. "Any nigga I ever took the fuck up outta here, we looked each other in the eyes before I did it."

Breezy's rage has him sitting on the edge of his seat while she sits in her same calm position. "Me, too!" he shouts. "I ain't never doubted your gangster but don't doubt mine either!"

She finds his rage funny in a weird way. If this was anybody else, his head would be splattered on the window by now. Deep down, she knows that he would never roll over on her. She raises her gun, and with a flick of the finger, she hits the lever. The cartridge falls out of the gun and lands in the console. She lays the gun on top of it. She raises both of her empty hands in the air for him to see. He takes his gun out of his pocket and lays it on top of her gun.

"Cool. Now that we got that outta the way, let's talk like brother and sister," she says with a peaceful tone.

She removes her shades from her eyes, and the sparkle in them is comforting for him. He reaches over and hugs her. "Girl, you know I love you more than I love my own family," he whispers in her ear. "Don't ever put me in a situation where I have to think about going against you. It's us against them. Whatever we gotta do to wipe them the fuck out, I'm here. Anybody... niggas... police... whoever!"

57

NEXT DAY

STORM IS ABOUT to indulge in some retail therapy. Her spirits have been in the dumps these past few weeks and she hopes that this will help her a little. This morning, she hit the old man up for a few grand to sponsor her trip to the mall. He gave it to her with no problem as usual, but what was unusual to her, he hasn't hit her up for any pleasure of his own. She could care less about engaging with him in that manner, but she does find it weird that he hasn't tried. She's charged it off as him caught up in his feelings about all of this.

Storm strolls along Fifth Avenue in Manhattan, both hands full of bags. Alongside of her is the Ethiopian Princess, Beeba. Once Storm got her phone back from Mr. Antonelli, she saw that she had nearly a hundred missed calls and fifty voice messages. The messages were from Beeba and her husband, well, at least, most of them. In the messages, Beeba was practically begging her to call back. There were also many messages where clearly she could hear Beeba's husband in the background coaching her on what to say, to get them to link up again. To her surprise, there were a few calls from him without Beeba. That was strange to her.

Beeba is in awe of New York City. She walks around with her head in the clouds like the tourist that she is. This is her first time in the Big Apple. Storm met her on the parkway this morning and showed her the little that Newark had to offer before bringing her over the water.

When Storm made the call to Beeba and told her that she wanted to link up without her husband, she didn't know how that would go. However, she had managed to do it. Storm didn't even ask, but she does know that he's been calling her every twenty minutes asking of her whereabouts. She's not much of a liar and has made up all kinds of lies. Not once has she mentioned Storm, though. Beeba lying to her husband to be with her, is a good sign to Storm.

* * *

Shopping until it became boring, they end up at the Cafeteria. Their table is at the window, which gives Beeba the pleasure of eating while watching the busyness of Seventh Avenue. Storm has shown her a lovely time and has even spent a few dollars on her. She has money of her own, but Storm wouldn't let her spend a dime of it.

Storm has treated Beeba like the perfect date, which has Beeba confused. She doesn't know if this is an actual date or just friends shopping and chilling. She's caught Beeba looking into her eyes many times, as if she's actually feeling her in an intimate way. Beeba hasn't said anything to her because of her confusion.

Beeba's puzzlement has a lot to do with that night at the Pleasure Garden and the act that took place. Before that night, when they originally met in Atlantic City, she thought she saw lesbian in Storm's eyes, and she thought they had a common attraction to each other. She was thrown off at Pleasure Garden when they had all the opportunities in the world to go at each other and Storm didn't touch her. Not only did she not touch her, she brushed off any advances that Beeba made toward her. The truth, Storm has no feelings for her in a girl-on-girl way. She knows Beeba feels her that way, so she continues to play the mind games with her. Beeba doesn't understand it all, but one thing she does know is, if Storm is any way thinking of being with her in that way, she's all for it. Storm is in no way attracted to women, but she knows how to play the game to get what she wants.

As they are enjoying their meal, Storm's phone rings. The two-six-seven area code floating across the display leads her to know that Beeba's husband is calling her once again. She wonders if maybe he's calling to see if they are together. She lets it go to voice mail, just as she does all of his other calls. A few seconds pass and the message alert goes off. She quickly dials and listens to the message.

"Hey, pretty lady. I got some time on my hands, and I was wondering if we can link up, just us. I'm willing to make it worth your while. Just name your price." He pauses for a few seconds. "That was my first time on that type, but I ain't gon' lie, it was all right. I been hitting you crazy because I'm comfortable with you. I can't be moving out like that with just anybody. Hit me up and let me know if we can get together. I can come to Jersey, or if you don't want to come here. Just call me back."

Storm presses the key to replay the message. She hands the phone over to Beeba. "Listen to that."

Beeba slowly places the phone to her ear, and in no time, her mouth gapes open. She can't believe her ears. The betrayal is only a fraction of what she feels compared to the disgust. To actually hear her king begging to be tossed up breaks her heart.

He always made her feel like their little sexual fantasies and ménage a trois were for them as a couple. He told her doing things with other women turned him on because he knew it turned her on. Foolishly she believed that those ménages were for her. He said it would only strengthen their relationship. To hear him begging to play that position, without her involvement makes her question if any of it was ever for her. She hands the phone back to Storm, not able to listen to another word.

Storm realizes this is the perfect time for her to go in while she has her on the ropes. "I got about twenty-five messages from him, all similar."

Beeba drops her fork onto the plate. She's lost her appetite. Storm looks past the hurt in Beeba's eyes and can see that she's lost any respect that she had for him. If this was a game of tug of war, he's just let his end of the rope go. She's won the game.

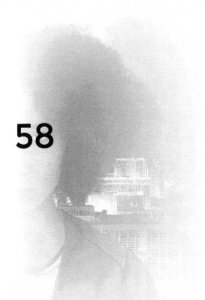

58

IRVINGTON, NEW JERSEY
SLICKS GO-GO BAR

T HE STRIP BAR is dark but live with action. The smell of Victoria's Secret mixed with funk floats throughout the air. Walking in with a fresh nose, the smell could knock you unconscious. The dancers all look the same, Beyoncé knockoffs, all with, at least, thirty inch long cheap weaves. The ones who aren't wearing weave are wearing even cheaper wigs.

Storm, Toy, and Wendy are not here for enjoyment or pleasure. Their reason for being here is all business. They've been hitting up strip bars all over the city this week scouting for talent. They've hit the lowdown raunchy bars and lock-doors where it all goes down. They've also hit the Russian bars where very little goes down. Storm has picked the best of them all and hopes to put together a solid team of women.

They sit in shock at how these women have the confidence to get up here and dance in front of men damn near naked. Another thing that most of these women have in common, besides weave, is the lack of an exercise regimen in their lives. Rows of stomach overlap each other with their breasts sitting on top of the rows lifelessly, just flopping lazily. Their bodies are covered in enough sweat to fill up a sauna suite.

Their weaves are matted against their faces from perspiration. Layers and layers of cellulite cover their thighs. Storm has even counted a few bullet hole wounds on some of them. She has nothing against big girls because she has seen some beautiful, well put together, and polished plus-size women, but these women here are not them. What shocks them even more is how these men are reacting. They seem to have no problem with any of it.

"Look, look," Wendy says, pointing rudely at the man a few seats down from them. "Look at that look in his eyes. Like a damn rapist."

The pitch black, big bellied, big bearded, big watch, big jewelry wearing man has big money written all over him. His snagged tooth smile exposes his cherry red gums. Lips so red it looks as if he's been eating red Kool-Aid out of the pack. He watches with his tongue hanging out of his mouth as the plus-size dancer crawls around the bar. She rubs her hand over his bald head as she continues to crawl past him. Just before she gets out of arm's reach, he wraps both hands around her waist and pulls her back to him, butt to face. He buries his mouth in between her cheeks and begins to feast as his friends cheer him on.

Storm can't take another second of this. She gets up and her girls follow. They've seen more than enough. As they are making their exit, a dancer steps in front of Storm in the aisle and doesn't move.

"Y'all leaving? I was just on my way around to y'all," the dancer says.

Storm looks her up and down, and this has to be one of the better ones in the spot. She's tall, thick, and juicy, with a lil pudge around the gut but still sexy to say the least. Storm peeks around at the girl's butt with no shade whatsoever.

The dancer toots her ass up in the air and turns to the side, so Storm can get a better view. Storm can't believe her eyes. The young woman's ass is the size of a full grown cow's. All three of them stare at the girl's butt in astonishment.

"Y'all gonna stay a little while or what?"

"Nah, we out," Storm says as she digs into her pocket. She flicks her business card to the girl, holding it in between her fingertips. "Lose half of that ass and call me. I can take you away from this shit and make you a lot of money. Ain't no money in them big gigantic asses. Lose all of that," she says, pointing to the girl's butt. "Then call me," she says walking around the girl.

The woman has never heard anyone tell her that she had too much ass, it's all new to her. She is quite intrigued as to what Storm meant by, make a lot of money. She's not sure if she's ready to rid herself of her most valued possession, but she will call to find out the details. She stares at the business card for a few seconds before watching them exit the door. She sees strength in how they are rolling. Judging by how they move, they seem to be into something heavy. She most definitely has plans on finding out exactly what.

The girls giggle on their way out of the bar. As they approach the doorway, a man intentionally obstructs their pathway. With her head still turned facing the girls, Storm bumps into the man, knocking her back a few steps. She turns around where she finds the man standing there, as if he doesn't intend to move.

"Excuse you," Storm says sarcastically.

He doesn't say a word, just stares into her eyes with his head nodding. Storm looks the man up and down. She charges him off as young and dumb and quite ugly. He looks like a black Rottweiler with a full Sunni beard. He has a head that would fit a three-hundred pound, six foot five man, yet he weighs about one-sixty and stands five foot seven.

"Fuck is your problem?" Storm asks as the rage builds inside.

An off-duty officer spots the problem at the door and walks over. As the man peeps the officer, he slides out of the way, not wanting to make a scene. He moves, but he doesn't take his eyes off of her. They indulge in a stare-off full of hatred.

Toy wraps her arms around Storm's shoulders and pulls her along. "Come on, girl. Later for that shit. He's probably suffering from broke, ugly nigga problems," she says to ease Storm's rage. "Ain't nobody got time for that," she adds as she steps out of the bar.

Storm makes her way to her car parked directly across the street. Toy and Wendy get into the rented Impala. The man has now stepped outside of the bar. He pays close attention to both cars. Storm pulls off without noticing him. Toy speeds off right behind her.

The man stares at Storm's license plates until it's locked into his head. Another young man steps onto the stoop. Both of them watch the cars speed up the block. Storm has no clue that she was this close to the homie Big Face. Had she known it was him, it all would've made perfect sense to her.

"Damn, big bruh! You should've just let me at her right here. Could've got this shit smooth over with," the young man says.

"Nah, it's about patience," Big Face says. "I wanna see what else we can get out of the deal. Heard the bitch eating. This shit gon' be worthwhile. Kill two birds with one stone. Smell me?"

The young man understands exactly what he's saying. "No doubt."

They are always thinking of ways to make a come-up and looks like they just found a new one.

* * *

Hours later Storm and the girls are receiving a great deal of attention at the Emigrante Men's Club. The attention has very little to do with them being women in a strip bar, although they are the only female patrons in the spot. The attention they receive is mixed, good and bad. Racism can be felt in the air, and it's all aimed at them being the only blacks here.

This bar is the difference between night and day compared to the three neighborhood spots they just visited. The girls are prettier and much more polished. The music is completely different, too. Even the patrons are different. They are either Puerto Rican, Portuguese, or from some South American country.

Storm is here in search of some Latin flavor for her roster. Of all the spots she's hit so far, she has had an eighty to ninety percent success rate. The ten percent that she didn't get was at the Russian bars. She hasn't been able to crack that market yet, but she plans to. She's seen, in those bars, the most beautiful green-eyed, six foot plus, all legs, Russian women, that she's ever seen in life. She's sure those women could score a lot of money on the road and supply the strictly white women lovers.

Toy has the perfect, classy look that can reach that crossover market. She's beautiful and just the right size that is not intimidating to white men. Wendy, on the other hand, is pretty enough for the white men, but her huge ass keeps her pigeon held. She's right in the middle, pretty enough that the white men want her, but once they see her huge ass, they become disgusted or intimidated.

Once Beeba is added to the team, she will be able to take Toy's spot. With Toy and Storm partnering on other business, there will be a void that Storm is sure Beeba can feel. She's beautiful enough and thin enough to fit in any market. She has the perfect mass appeal. Her dark complexion and locs will accommodate any white man who has jungle fever.

Storm even picked up a few bottom feeders, big, ghetto booty, weave head chicks from the past couple raunchy bars. There's a market out there for them as well. The young drug dealers love the ghetto booties, the bigger the better for them. All in all, she's just trying to put a brand together that has something for everyone.

A tall Latin brunette struts sexily across the bar. Her hair extends down to the middle of her thighs. Dressed in the cheesiest two-dollar outfit and five-dollar white platform shoes, she's still super sexy. She winds her hips as she glides across the stage.

She catches Toy pointing at her from across the bar. She stops short and puts on a dance show just for Toy and the girls. Her lips pucker up as she blows a sexy kiss across the bar. She turns around and drops it like it's hot.

She bends over, pulls her long hair to the side to show the tiny handful of cheeks that she has. She slides into a Russian split and lays the top half of her body onto the floor. Then like a worm, she wiggles across the bar before turning over onto her back. She wraps her legs around the pole that extends from the floor of the bar to the ceiling. Using her legs, she pulls herself closer to the pole. She grips her legs tighter around the pole and humps it like a cat in heat. She leans forward, just enough to grab the pole. With one hand, she pulls herself onto her feet and, from there, puts on the sexiest pole dancing show.

"Yo! That's the one right there," Toy says with no doubt. "She a bad bitch."

Storm looks over at Wendy. "What you think?" she asks, expecting her to say no.

They both have their own taste when it comes to women and haven't been able to agree on many during this scouting phase.

Storm has peeped that Wendy is a bit jealous, and any woman that she feels threatened by she finds a problem with. One woman she disagreed on because her pinky toe was just as long as the rest of her toes. It was then that Storm realized that she had to take Wendy's opinion lightly because her they were based off of envy.

"That bitch is bad," Wendy says, mouth gaped open. Storm is shocked at her reply. For Wendy to admit that, this woman must be supermodel status.

"Wow! Y'all finally agree."

"That's definitely universal beauty right there, hands down."

The woman comes walking toward them after her pole dance. The lack of ass she has is made up by the super-sized breasts that bounce vibrantly with every step she takes. She stops in front of them and puts on a special show just for them. The anger can be seen on the racist patrons, hating that the black women who they don't even want here are getting all the beautiful woman's attention.

Storm reaches for the woman's hands. She grasps them gently and pulls her toward her. She stares into the woman's big and beautiful eyes. "You're beautiful," she says with charm. The woman winks at her as a reply. She can't stop blushing. Storm leans in closer to whisper in her ear. "What country are you from?"

"Mexico," the woman says in the strongest Mexican accent.

"What nights do you work?" Storm asks. "I would like to come and see you sometimes."

The woman looks at her kind of starry-eyed. She's confused, but she tries to retain her sexiness by keeping the seductive smile on her face. "Me no speakie Ingles."

"Oh," Storm says. She grabs her card from her pocketbook. "You understand money, don't you?" she asks as she rubs her fingers together, signifying money.

The woman nods her head up and down with a smile. Storm hands her the card and points to her phone number. She places her phone to her ear. "Call me and we make money," she says, rubbing her fingers together again. She can tell the woman understands her clearly. Just like her beauty is universal, so is money. Everybody understands it. "*Mucho, mucho dinero.*"

59

BEEBA AND HER husband cruise their city after a delightful dinner. He's so stuffed that he can barely keep his eyes open behind the steering wheel of the Range Rover. Beeba, who is in the passenger's seat, fell asleep minutes ago. The ringing of her phone awakens her. She sits up, startled. A burst of energy shoots through her body when she sees Storm's name on the screen. The husband looks over with jealousy, wondering who could be calling her at this hour.

"It's her," she says with joy. It's rare to see her call.

"Word?" he says with a spark in his eyes as well. Both of them are hoping the same thing. Well, maybe not the same thing, but they both want her equally. Hopefully she's calling to tell them she's in town and is finally ready for part two to their sexcapade. "Hurry, hurry, pick up."

"Hey, Storm!" Beeba answers, not able to hide her enthusiasm. She has a supernatural effect on Beeba and knows it. She idolizes Storm.

"Yooo," Storm drags. "What's up with you?"

"Nothing much. Just leaving dinner."

"I heard. What that pussy doing though?"

This catches Beeba by surprise, and she can't stop the blushing. She really doesn't now how to answer. "She chilling, I guess." She giggles like a goofy little girl. "Me and Jay just headed home," she says, trying to give away the hint that she's in his company.

"I ain't ask about him. I asked about that pussy. Later for him."

"What she say?" he whispers only loud enough for Beeba to hear. "See if we can hook up."

Beeba places one finger in the air. "One minute," she whispers to him. "Where you at though? What you doing?"

"Wondering what that pussy doing? That's what I'm doing." Hearing this come out of her idol's mouth has her box tingling right now.

"Watering," she whispers, hoping he doesn't hear her.

"Is that right? Got your panties wet?"

"Ain't none," she admits.

"Nah? What you got on? I need a visual."

"Long black dress and pumps."

"Ask her," Jay demands with excitement in the background.

"Put your hand up that long black dress for me and play with it." Storm is curious to know how much power she has over her and over her husband.

"Huh?" she asks, totally shocked at her request. "Right now? I can't."

"You telling me no?" Storm asks sternly.

"Nah, not no but —"

"But nothing. Put your hand on it for me."

Beeba discreetly puts her hand on it. "Uh-huh," she whispers.

"Palm it for me."

She peeks over at her husband, hoping that he doesn't notice what she's doing. "I did," she says in a normal tone to throw her husband off. Her pussy is throbbing at the fact that she's doing something this sneaky right under his nose.

"How wet is it?"

"You have no idea," she says, squirming in her seat.

"Give me an idea then."

"Gushing," Beeba whispers.

"Is that right? Pop that clit for me."

"I can't right now," she says with great disappointment.

"Can't what?" Jay asks nosily. He's so eager he can't hide it.

"No such thing as can't. Put me on speaker and do what I ask."

Beeba places the call on speaker as demanded. She's torn right now, really not knowing what to do. "You on speaker," she says, looking at her husband.

"Yo, Storm! What up?" he shouts.

"Chilling, chilling," she says barely having any rap for him.

"What you up to?" he asks.

"Right now... trying to get Beeba to play in that pussy for us."

He's stunned by her response. The word *us* sounds like music to his ears, to his own selfishness, hoping that this is leading to them getting together. He looks to his wife and gives her the head-nod to go on. "Do what she asked."

Beeba lifts her dress over her belly, but she's hesitant to touch.

"Give me the visual. Tell me what you doing," Storm commands.

"I'm just sitting here in the passenger's seat with my dress pulled up to my stomach."

"Cool. Now put your left leg on the dashboard."

Beeba does as she's instructed. "Okay. I did it."

"Now tease that clit for us, slowly though."

Beeba's pussy is on fire right now. This whole scene has her steaming hot inside. She wastes no time doing what she was instructed to do. As her clit hardens, her teasing evolves into full blown petting. She's so hot she can pop right now. She leans her head onto the headrest and closes her eyes. She quickly forgets that her husband is watching and loses herself in the moment. She gasps loudly with arousal.

Jay, is turned on right now. Seeing his wife this hot and aroused turns him on crazy. He can barely drive. His eyes are off the road and on the action.

"With your left hand pinch that clit gently. With your right hand I want you to two-finger my pussy," she commands.

Referring to Beeba's pussy as hers sticks out in his mind. He's noticed that it went from ours, to hers. It doesn't sit well with him, but he rolls with it, hoping this will reel Storm into their trap. He watches as his wife squirms in the seat uncontrollably. The gushing sound of his wife's wet pussy swishes loudly over the music that's playing. He becomes jealous that someone else has her like this. He's never witnessed her so wet. He can't help but touch it himself, too. He rubs his fingers through her juices.

"Can you fit three fingers in?"

"I can try. It will be tight though," she says as she's inserting her fingers. "They in."

"It's tight?" Storm asks.

"Yes, really tight," she says. She fingers herself slow and passionately to loosen herself up.

"Now wind your hips for me."

"I am," she says as she winds like a belly dancer.

"How my pussy feeling?"

"Horny as shit," she grunts. "I need to cum. Can I?"

"Tell me you wanna cum for me."

"I wanna cum for you," she gasps. "Can I? I need to, right now."

The man sits back with envy. The fact that another woman has control over his wife, over the phone with no physical contact is a blow to his ego. "Yo, Storm, where you at? We trying to get with you."

"Pound that pussy with your three fingers for me and make it cum," she says, totally ignoring the man.

Beeba ignores his presence as well and does what she's commanded to. She loses herself and pounds her pussy. "Here it come," she screams. "Here it come. I'm cumming! Ah, yes!" she sighs. The orgasm controls her.

Storm smiles with satisfaction. She realizes that she has total control of Beeba at this point. She's controlled her pussy like a remote control car. The satisfaction comes from knowing that she now has control of her mind. Deep down inside, Jay knows this as well. He sits back in defeat, knowing that he has lost control of the one thing that he had total control over.

With desperation, he speaks once again. "Where you at, Storm?"

Storm ends the call, leaving Jay angered, while leaving Beeba panting for more and in more awe of her.

* * *

Meanwhile, Homie Big Face pulls his Jeep Cherokee in front of the Seventeenth Avenue precinct in Newark. The passenger, a young woman dressed in a police uniform, leans over for a kiss. She sighs as she dreads going into work. She still isn't used to working the overnight shift.

As she steps out of the Jeep, Big face speaks. "Yo, do me a favor," he says as he digs into the cup holder. He grabs a sheet of paper and hands it to the young woman. She reads it and identifies it as a license plate number. "Run that plate number and get an address for me." The license plate number is who else but Storm.

No, this young woman isn't a cop. She's a dispatcher. It's all the same though for him. Having a plug inside of the police department has many perks. Using her to get home addresses of drug dealers gets him right to their doorsteps. He scored a few hundred thousand this way, in the few months the woman has been on the job. She's his secret weapon.

"Get on that ASAP," he demands.

"I got you."

60

DAYS LATER
11:57 P.M.

STORM CRUISES THROUGH the dark streets of the Portuguese section of Newark. Her business here is to link up with the beautiful Mexican girl from Emigrante. Araceli is her name, and she called Storm earlier today. With the aid of a translator, she told Storm how anxious she is to hear about any business opportunities that she may have for her. Storm, being the business woman that she is, didn't hesitate to set up their meeting.

Storm stops at the intersection for the red light. She spots Araceli and another woman standing in front of the bar, just as they said they would be. "There's a parking spot, right there," Toy says, pointing up ahead. Storm parks the car and they get out with no hesitation.

Araceli's eyes light up as she sees them coming across the street toward her. She points at them for her accomplice to see. Before they get onto the sidewalk, Araceli rushes her and gives her a huge hug. Storm is kind of uncomfortable with a stranger hugging her like this. She thinks very little of it because she knows many Latin women who are overly affectionate.

"Hello," Araceli says with her raspy but sexy voice. "Happy to see you again," she says slowly as if she's practiced saying this. Storm has to wiggle out of the hug because Araceli seems to not want to let go. A shadow appears over Storm's shoulder. When she turns to look in that direction, she sees two short Hispanic men only a couple of feet away from them. Both of them dressed in all white, they glow in the darkness. They're dressed identically in white sneakers, white T-shirt and white sweat pants. Their body language and their eyes tell her something isn't right.

She quickly thinks to reach for her gun just in case, but it's already too late. Both men have their guns drawn and aimed at her. She backs up with her hands in submission, thinking that maybe it's a robbery. She looks over to Araceli and the guilty look that is displayed on her face is a dead giveaway that she set all of this up.

Storm studies their faces and tries to lock them both into her memory bank. They've caught her with her pants down right now, but she will surely get even with them. She pays key notice to their features and quickly comes up with the assumption that they must be from El Salvador. The shape of their heads is a clear indication, coupled with the flat-top, faded on the side, haircut one of them wears. The other one is bald-headed with tattoos all over his neck and some on his face. This seems to be the most aggressive one.

She pays notice to the colored bead necklaces they both wear, wondering what they symbolize. The bald man grabs Storm while the other one grabs hold of Toy. They push the two of them in the same direction, down the block. The man who has Toy utters some words in Spanish, and Araceli and the other woman go into the bar. Toy is a nervous wreck and it shows. Every few steps she peeks over to Storm, hoping that she has a way to get them out of this.

"Just take it all," Toy says as she shoves her pocketbook in the man's face. She's heard so many stories of these men raping and robbing and murdering that she can already see the end results. "Please, take the money and go."

The man shoves the pocketbook, clearly letting them know that money isn't what he wants. That leads her to believe he has plans of doing all she has heard of. She looks to Storm, who wears a cool and calm look even under this pressure. She has no time to be scared because her mind is too busy trying to figure out how she will get her hands on the gun that is in her bag. She knows this will be risky and things may get ugly, but she'd rather take her chances than to be at their mercy later.

The men push them into the dark alley. The one with the flat top takes the leadership role. Clearly he's the boss and the other one is just the enforcer. "What do you want down here?" he asks. His speech is shocking to them. With the strongly accented El Salvadorian features one wouldn't expect him to be able to speak English at all.

"You been down here three times this week passing out your business cards," he says as he holds a stack of her cards in his hand. "You must don't know the rules to this shit. These girls belong to me. They're mine. They will never go anywhere with you," he says, throwing the cards in Storm's face.

"I should blow your fucking head off, both of you," he says as he points in her face. Storm can't help but to notice the tattoo on his hand. She recognizes the M with the one and the three inside of it as a sign of the MS-13s. Seeing this triggers of thoughts of a possible way out of this.

With desperation she reaches into her bag of tricks and hopes that it works. "Cypress? You know Cypress?"

Hearing the name catches him off guard. Cypress is a high-ranking Latin King that she met many years ago. He took a strong liking to her just as she did him. They've done lots of business together over the years, but she hasn't seen him in some time. Cypress is a Latin King, but he's one that the MS-13s have a great deal of respect for. Anytime there's a beef in between the two gangs, Cypress is the only one that can get it squashed.

"What about him?" the man asks.

"Just wondering if you know him. If by chance you do, ask him about me," she says arrogantly.

"I don't care to know about you," he barks. "And if I catch you down here getting in my way again you won't be a problem to nobody else." Storm flashes a cocky smile that frustrates the man. "You think this is funny, huh?"

He says a few words in Spanish, and the other man starts dialing on his phone. He has the phone in his hand and the gun in the other. "He's calling Cypress right now, and if he doesn't know you, I'm gonna show you how funny this is. Since you think it's a joke," he adds.

"Yo," the man grunts into the phone. The man indulges in a conversation in Spanish before looking over to Storm. "Who are you? What's your name?" he asks.

"Tell him this Storm, Quiet Storm."

The man on the phone lowers his gun as he listens. He looks to his partner and speaks in Spanish. He lowers his gun as well which tells her the desperate attempt worked. The man hands her the phone. She grabs it with the same look of cockiness on her face that infuriated him.

"Yo?" she says into the phone.

"Storm, what up? Fuck you doing down there?"

Her face lights up when she hears his voice. "You better tell this nigga about me, waving guns in my face and shit," she says with no filter. She feels confident, knowing that they evidently want no trouble at this point.

"Nah, nah, don't worry about that. I got that."

"You know that's a violation," she continues on.

"Nah, Storm, just cool out. Dude the real deal. Let me just handle it. We'll all get together and talk this one out. Because shit can definitely get crazy, feel me?"

"I'm the real deal, too," she says in defense of her gangster.

"You know I know that. Just breathe easy, though. Let me handle it. Give him the phone. And come by the store tomorrow, so I can set this meeting up."

She sighs with agitation. "All right," she says before passing the phone back over to the man. He speaks in Spanish on the phone. What he says they have no clue but what they do know is he's leaving the alley and he's instructed his partner to follow.

The girls walk out a few steps behind them. Right now, Storm has free access to grab her gun and bang his brains out through his face. She laughs to herself that he could be such a fool. It's obvious that he doesn't know what type of bitch she can be.

She doesn't take that clear shot for two reasons. One reason, she prides herself on never shooting a man in the back of the head like a coward. The second reason is that Cypress put his seal of approval on her. To bust a move like this after a man has vouched for her would be very dishonorable. Regardless of the things that she's done in life, sacrificing her honor isn't one of them. She won't take the shot tonight but that doesn't mean she won't take it on another night.

*　*　*

Just as Storm has gotten out of one sticky situation, another one is in the making. The homie Big Face pulls up a few houses away from Mr. Antonelli's house. He looks to the man in the passenger's seat. "Look at all them cars. Look like a fucking car show."

"Bitch eating like that?" a young man asks from the backseat.

"Nah," Big Face replies. "I did my homework. She fucking with some old white motherfucker. He own a Benz dealership. Old motherfucker fully loaded with that gwap. See what I always tell you about patience? Look how this shit fell right in our laps. We gon' get revenge for my cuzzo's death and we gon' get some M's out of it, too. I already got the perfect plan. Patience is the name of the game though."

61

THE NEXT DAY

S TORM CRUISES ALONG Bloomfield Avenue in the North Newark section. This section is predominantly Hispanic, and it is evident in appearance. Food trucks selling *arroz con pollo*, pushcarts
selling fruit and *cohito*, corner bodegas with colorful and bright can-
opies and Spanish music blaring loudly makes the entire community look like it's not even a part of the rest of the city. The traffic is
even different. The small, older model compact cars with loud pipes
and dark tinted windows fill the streets, making Storm's Mercedes
stick out like a sore thumb.

She parks right in front of the custom rim and tire shop. She
gets out and steps into the store. The chiming of the door breaks
the attention of the men who stand around in the store. She is
dressed very casually today, yet she still looks like a boss. The only
sight of glitter is the diamond stud earrings she's wearing. Her distressed jeans, tight fitted sweatshirt and Gucci flats have her ready
for physical battle, if it comes to that. She's dressed for a fist fight
even though that's something she rarely does. She's always skipped
over the fist fights and went right into the gunplay.

She quickly spots the El Salvadorian dudes from last night,
both still dressed in all white. It appears they haven't changed their
clothes. She snarls at the sight of them. They engage in a stare-off

until the door chime sounds off again. She removes the dark sunglasses from her eyes, so they can see the savageness in her eyes.

Mud and Breezy walk side by side until they get to Storm. They post up on opposite sides of her. A tall, thin Puerto Rican steps from out of the back room. He immediately feels the tension in the room. "Storm, what up?" he says, trying too hard to warm the coldness of the room.

Storm looks at the man, and she can't help but smile at him. "Cypress, what up?" She quickly looks back to her enemies. It takes all the strength in her not to start an all-out war. Out of respect for Cypress and his store, she refrains.

Cypress doesn't know exactly where to go from here. The silence in the room is broken when Storm speaks. "First and foremost, if it wasn't for the respect I have for Cypress, I would leave both of y'all right here."

"Yo, yo, Storm, nah," Cypress interjects, trying to keep the peace.

Both of the men smile deviously with fire burning in their eyes.

"Nah, you better let these motherfuckers know I don't give a fuck about no Ms13s, 14s or 15s. Ain't a nigga walking the earth who has waved a gun in my face and lived to talk about it."

The enforcer has become enraged while the other man stands cool and calm. Cypress steps over toward Storm. Before he can get to her, both Breezy and Mud stand in front of her like guard dogs, protecting their master.

"Storm, I told him all about you. Breathe easy. I want to get this squashed right here, right now. Let's just talk about it," he suggests. "What started all of this?"

"She came down to my side, throwing her business cards around, trying to take my girls home without coming to me first," the man says. "She must don't know the rules."

"Take your girls home?" Storm asks furiously. "I ain't no fucking trick! You got me fucked up!" As angry as she is, it all makes sense to her now. This man is their pimp. Madame to pimp, she respects his handle, just not his delivery. "Yo, on some G shit, I didn't know those girls belong to you. That's all you had to say that night and not wave no gun in my fucking face. That shit will get you killed."

"Talking a lot about murder today. Not last night though."

"Motherfucker, I'm the same bitch today that I was last night. You caught me slippin'. I ain't gon' lie. I wasn't thinking like that, but if I was and I could've got to my gun in my purse you or him wouldn't be standing here today!" she says, forcing her way in between Mud and Breezy.

Cypress steps in front of her before she can get into their faces. "Storm, let me talk to you," he demands as he wraps his arm around her and snatches her away. Mud and Breezy are left with the enemies, all staring coldly at each other, ready to go any second.

* * *

Minutes pass and Storm and Cypress make their way back into the room. He's managed to calm her down by explaining to her that he has the perfect proposition that could make both parties some money.

"First let me formally introduce the two of you," Cypress says while standing in between them. "Storm, this is Esto. Esto, this is Storm." Esto nods his head at her while she looks away from him with no verbal reply.

"Esto, Storm explained to me what she was doing down your way. After hearing it, I thought of a way that money can be made. At the end of the day, we all like money, right?"

"Of course," he replies.

"Her reason for being there is trying to get hold of some girls. She's into the same line of business as you. And I know you got all the girls. So, I'm thinking maybe you can slide some her way and everybody can eat."

"If she needs them for a night, we can work something out. My girls don't come cheap though. You need them for how many hours? And how many do you need?"

Storm looks to Cypress. He quickly wraps his arms around the man. "Let me talk to you over here for a minute." They walk off far enough away to be unheard. Esto listens with a disturbed look on his face, but Cypress continues to talk until the expression changes. Cypress reaches for a handshake and Esto reciprocates it. They make their way back to circle.

"We can work that out," Esto says. "Let me first tell you, I never do this type of business with people of your color, but you come from a good reference." He speaks in Spanish to his enforcer, who exits the store quickly.

I have over a hundred girls to choose from. I have another ten coming in this week that have never been used yet. All shapes and sizes, young and old, light and dark. Whatever you need, I have or can get. It will cost you, though, and I don't know if you can handle the price. I told you, my girls don't come cheap. Some are virgins, never been touched. Of course, they cost more."

"How much we talking per girl?" Storm asks.

"Because you are vouched for by a good man, the prices start at ten thousand a girl. I don't own them one hundred percent. A part of the money will go to my partner. It's like you will be buying them out of their deals in a way. After you pay, she's yours forever to do whatever you want with her."

"If I give you my ten grand, how do I know that these girls won't slide off on me?"

Esto smiles. "You must don't understand this business at all. I guarantee you they will never slide off. Nothing or nobody can get them to cross you. You will be their owner. You see how my girls gave me your cards? It's because going against me puts them and others in big trouble."

Esto's enforcer comes back into the store, holding a photo album. He hands it to Esto, who hands it to Storm. "Look through that and pick which ones you like."

Storm flicks through the album, and she sees some of the most beautiful Mexican women that she's ever laid eyes on. Some of the girls appear to be as young as twelve and thirteen years old. Seeing them touches her heart a little, but she understands it is business.

"As you can see, whatever you need is in that book. I will leave it here with Cypress, and when you get your money together, you let him know who you want, and she's yours."

He reaches for her hand. They clasp hands with a firm grip. "If you're serious, call me."

62

ONE WEEK LATER

THIS HAS BEEN the longest week ever for Storm, except for the days she was locked up. She hasn't been able to sleep due to anxiousness. The thought of the money she will make has been on her mind day and night. For some reason, today feels like one of the biggest days of her life, making one of the biggest investments of her life. If all goes as well as she plans it will, she will be investing much more.

Storm's heart beats with anticipation as her and her whole team — Mud, Breezy, Toy, and Wendy step through the dark alley. Cypress leads them through the darkness. On both sides of them are what appear to be quiet, little, neatly kept, one-family homes. In the backyards, there are a few rundown cars.

The stairs creak through the silence as they step onto them. Cypress taps on the door, and in seconds, it opens. An older Spanish woman holds the door for them to enter. She pays very little attention to Cypress, but she stares at the rest of them suspiciously as they pass her.

The back porch is dark and cold and the only source of light comes from the small table which has a few candles and a many small statues of the Virgin Mary and Baby Jesus. A huge picture of Jesus is propped neatly against the wall behind the statues. Even with the hint of religion of the display, it still gives off a creepy aura. Storm understands the display to be Santeria, which is a religion practiced by people of the Caribbean. The display at the doorway is believed to keep the house guarded from evil and evil spirits.

They round the display quite uncomfortably and advance into the house. The smell of cheap booze slap them in their faces. They maneuver through the cheaply furnished kitchen, and at the end of the corridor, a Spanish man stands with a few playing cards in his hands. The cards serve as confirmation of payment of the entrance fee. The man extends the card to Breezy. "Forty dollars," he says sternly.

Cypress stops him. "Nah, they with me."

They step into the living room, which is equally cheaply furnished. Sitting and lying around on the old, rundown couches are beautiful Mexican women dressed only in lingerie. At the sight of the strangers at the door, they all sit up on their best behavior, waiting to be chosen.

It's as if someone must have made the money call because women appear from everywhere. In seconds, there are about twenty women in this one little room. Storm and her crew all watch with amazement, having never seen anything like this before. The women are picture perfect, like the models from the Miss Universe Pageant.

Esto and his enforcer creep through the darkness like two ghosts. Cypress has explained to Storm their reasoning behind them always always being dressed in white clothing. The white is a symbol of their religious practice, the religion of Santeria'.

Esto and Cypress shake hands at the doorway. Esto speaks in Spanish to his enforcer, who opens the side door. He yells a few words of Spanish up the stairs. Not even seconds after the command, the sound of heels banging eventually leads to the sight of beautiful long legs in stilettos coming down the stairs.

The man holds the door for the women to enter the apartment. They step inside with fear of the unknown covering their faces. In the back of the pack is the woman Araceli from the bar. She holds her head down in what appears to be fear. The women all stand behind Esto obediently.

"You got the money?" he asks.

After looking through the photo album over and over, these are the four that it is narrowed down to. There are so many drop-dead gorgeous women with bodies to die for that it was hard for Storm to choose. Although she wants many more of them, she had to settle for the best four because that is all she could afford at this time. She debated about asking Mr. Antonelli for the money, but lately he's been acting so distant that she chose not to.

It pisses her off that her money was caught up in the house raid because she would have much more money to work with. She's so confident this investment will make her wealthy that she would have blown the entire hundred and fourteen thousand on it. She understands that, in business, it takes money to make money which is why she has no problem investing almost every dime she has into this. She's scraped up every dollar that was owed to her just to make this happen.

Her biggest fear was these women deviating once they are in her possession but Cypress explained to her the process and guaranteed her that is the least of her worries. He explained that these women all come from Tenancingo, which is a small town in Mexico. Tenancingo is known as the town that sex trafficking built. Tenancingo is the major source of the sex trafficking pipeline to the United States. They send these women here as sex slaves.

All of them are here unwillingly. Some have been kidnapped and sent here while others have been manipulated, by what they believed to be their lovers. The predators of these women who are called Romeos are handsome men. These Romeos pick up the women from parks and bus stops. They pretend to be wealthy businessmen and they seduce the women into following them.

The Romeos even impregnate the women, tell them they love them, and even promise to marry them. They never have a clue of what's going on until they go away for vacation with their lovers and their lovers take them to their new owners and tell them from there on they will be sex slaves and do whatever their masters command them to do. The incentive for keeping them in check and not running away is the babies that they have left behind in Mexico. They are threatened that, if they flee or tell the police, they will kill the babies as well as their family back in Mexico.

Back in Tenancingo, this is a family trade, multigenerational. You have families where the grandfather, father, son, and grandson are all engaged in trafficking. They pass down the tricks of the trade. Many kids aspire to be traffickers.

As Storm looks into the eyes of these women and sees the fear and helplessness, she kind of feels sorry for them, but it's all business. She made sure that all the women she chose were of age because she couldn't stand doing this to young underage girls. She knows exactly what it feels like to be taken advantage of as a young girl, and she would never do anything of the sort. But these grown women, she has very little compassion for. She justifies it all by saying to herself that these women are better off with her than with these men who will only mistreat them.

Cypress has told her that these type of houses in Tenancingo are called 'Calcuilchil' (Houses of Ass). In these houses, women are forced to have sex with approximately sixty or more men a day. When they don't meet their quota, they are beaten like dogs. The price for sex with them is a measly forty dollars for fifteen minutes. Of the forty dollars, twenty of that goes to the house and the other twenty goes to the girl. Her earnings are sent back to the Romeo back in Mexico.

Storm plans to take better care of them. She will introduce them to another world where they can make thousands at a time and keep more of their earnings. She believes the men of Mexico obviously don't know the value of sex to sell it for so cheap. She does, which is why she's sure she will get rich in no time.

"You got the money?" Esto asks, cutting to the chase.

Storm hands over the bag. He speaks Spanish to the women and they all go into another room. When they return, they all have small overnight bags in their hands. Storm is amazed that all of their possessions are packed in such small bags.

Esto steps next to the woman in the middle. He looks to Storm. "This here is Maritza, the one I told you who speaks English. The other girls can't speak much English, so she will be your translator and keep all the other girls in check.

Storm walks around the girls, looking them up and down, examining them, like a plantation owner inspecting a new shipment of slaves fresh off the boat. She wants to make sure they look like they did in the pictures. They look better in real life. Their bodies are perfectly sculpted without a blemish in sight. They stand there for her to view them like the slaves that they are. This whole experience would be unbelievable to Storm and her crew had they not witnessed it for themselves.

Storm signals to Esto that she is completely satisfied with the work. Esto then looks to the three other girls. "This is your new owner," he says in English. The woman translates word for word to them in Spanish.

"You are to respect her, just as you have respected me. You will do whatever she tells you or suffer the same consequences." The translator translates word for word. "When you are sent onto jobs, you are to call her and report to her every hour on the hour, just as you did with me. All the same rules still apply. If you break any of the rules, I will be contacted, and I will make the call back home, and you know the rest," he says with threatening eyes. The fear that these girls display is saddening.

Esto shakes Storm's hand. "Thank you for the business, and I look forward to more business in the future." He turns around and exits the room.

Storm is now the proud owner of four grown women, as crazy as it may sound. They are her own personal pets who have to obey her every command. They are hers to do whatever she wants with, which seems unbelievable to her. Now that the ownership has changed hands, there is one thing left to do.

She steps in front of Araceli, face to face. She looks to the translator, Maritza and points to Araceli. With all of them awaiting Storm's word, she hauls off and backslaps Araceli. Araceli stumbles back dizzily, holding her face in shock.

"Tell her, that is for what she did the other night. She put my life in danger, and if she ever does anything like that while under my ownership, the punishment will be worse." Maritza translates quickly. "*Comprende?*" Storm asks.

Araceli nods her head with the same fear in her eyes that the rest of the women possess. Although she understands that, while under Esto's command she had no choice but to report to him, her life was put at risk. She can't forget that. That loyalty that she displayed to Esto is the reason that she was chosen.

There were many women in the photo album equally as beautiful as Araceli, and some were more beautiful. That loyalty to Esto out-shined her beauty. The reason for the vicious slap was partly for revenge. The other part was she knows she had to instill fear into the women outside of the fear that they already have due to the circumstances of their ties back at home.

In no way does she want them to show her any different respect than they would an owner who has direct ties to their original traffickers. In order for her to get the best out of them, she knows they must fear and respect her. She has no plans of ever mistreating them as they have been mistreated. Her only plan is to make money with them and lots of it.

63

ONE WEEK LATER

TOY SCURRIES THROUGH her and Wendy's apartment with her phone glued to her ear. She looks like a sexy librarian today, dressed in a pinstriped suit. She had the skirt taken in super short to keep her sex appeal. With her hair in a bun and tiny square framed glasses.

"Okay, we are on our way. I truly apologize for any inconvenience," she says into the phone.

She hangs up the phone. "Selena, vamos, mami?"

Toy peeks into the living room where all the Mexican women are lounging around. Three of the women are dressed in dingy T-shirts, no frills jeans, and run-over, no name sneakers. In their casual gear, they look like financially challenged women from their poor country, so unlike the drop dead gorgeous women that were bought at Esto's place of business.

Selena, on the other hand, is dressed to the max, looking even more beautiful than she did that night. Storm, Toy, and Wendy all donated some of their old clothes to the women. All they had was lingerie and sexy underwear since that is all they needed for business. Now that they are going out on calls, their presentation is important.

For now the women live right here with Toy and Wendy, sleeping on the couches. The crowdedness of the apartment is nothing new to them. In prior situations, there had been up to twenty of them in a one-bedroom apartment. For Toy and Wendy, six women in a two bedroom, one bathroom apartment is hell. The only real benefit in having them here is how tidy they keep the place. Having them here is like having live-in maids, and they use them as such.

Toy and Selena are on their way to meet a client at the airport. The wealthy business tycoon has flown in from Dubai for business. Toy is doing well with her new job and loves it. Just as they predicted, she's great at it. She gets to dine, shop, and be entertained by these wealthy men and not drop her panties for them once. Shamefully they were quite a few of them that she actually wanted to drop her panties for, but she didn't. When it came time for that, she called one of the girls in.

As Toy and Selena are making their way through the living room to the front door, Wendy appears. Her attitude is evident. She stops short, blocking them. Her body language speaks volumes. "So you really taking her and not me?"

"Wendy, we already talked about this."

"Bitch can't even speak English," Wendy blurts out with disrespect. Not once does she look in the woman's direction.

"She doesn't need to talk. She can give him what he wants without saying a word. She could be a deaf mute. You know how this game goes."

"I thought I knew how it goes," Wendy replies. "I thought we looked out for each other."

"Wen, the man told me his type. It's my job to get him what he wants."

Wendy turns her back and steps away from them. "Don't forget we started this shit together."

Wendy has been tripping since the first day the girls arrived. The new franchise seems to be working for everybody but her. She feels that she helped build this thing and is the only one not reaping the benefits of her labor. She feels left out.

Toy is getting paid from both ends — the casino and a cut of the girls' money. Storm is making a hefty score from the girls. The girls are making more money than they've ever made. Meanwhile she's not making a dime.

The casino is off limits for her now that Storm and Toy have the inside connect. They don't want to blow this thing by having Wendy freelancing. She hates how they act like they are a part of the casino and have the casino's best interest at heart. It wouldn't be so bad if she was getting sent on these dates with the men coming from out of town, but she has yet to get one of those jobs.

*   *   *

Fifteen minutes pass and Toy sits at the ramp in her brand spanking new snow white Audi A7. The Audi is the company car, just another one of the many perks. Life couldn't be going any better for her than it is right now. Just a few months ago, she didn't have a pot to piss in.

At times she thinks back and feels like a fool for selling herself short for so long. She wasted so many years with fronting-ass drug dealers who used their money to entice her, but rarely giving her a dime. Every time she thinks about it, she thanks Storm for getting her started. Without her she would still be in the hood chasing fake drug dealers who are chasing fake drug dealer dreams.

Toy dials Storm, and she picks right up. "Yeah, we here waiting on him now."

"Cool," Storm says through the intercom.

"Yo," she says changing her tone. "Heavy Bottom is bugging! She met us at the door talking about, you really ain't taking me. Even called Selena a bitch and said she can't even speak English. She said we started this together. I have to send her on the next one. She will be okay."

"She better be," Storm replies coldly. "I hope she don't think she gone fuck up my business. If she do, she got another thing coming."

"Let me hit you back. The trick, I mean, my client just arrived."

The well-dressed man standing on the curb throws her off. She was expecting a sheikh in a white throbe and sandals. Instead he's dressed in a fine business suit. She honks the horn to get his attention. The suspense of wondering how much money she will drain him of, overtakes her. Time to get to the money!

64

LOUISVILLE, KENTUCKY
WEEKS LATER
MAY 5, 2012

M R. ANTONELLI AND Attorney Tony Austin lounge around in the Horsemen's Suite, which is exclusively for horse owners. The owners all have their own suite where they can watch the races from. Today is the biggest day of the year for horse racing. Nervousness and anxiety run through both of their bodies. To have their horse in the Kentucky Derby is a great accomplishment for them.

Two years ago, Tony had a client who was strapped for cash, and in an attempt to get back on his feet, he was willing to sell all his possessions. When he offered Tony his horse for sale, Tony immediately thought of Mr. Antonelli. He knew how much Mr. Antonelli enjoyed horse racing. Mr. Antonelli is the one who introduced him to that world. The two of them would go to races just to bet big money.

Tony, being the hustler that he is, saw the opportunity to make some good money. They each put in two hundred and fifty-thousand and bought the horse. The three-year-old, one thousand, one hundred pound Arabian Thoroughbred has already earned them $1.7 million dollars in the two-year period that they've had her.

The hundreds of thousands they've spent on maintenance and travel expenses still has them up a quarter million apiece, which makes it a great investment, just as Tony predicted.

Tony towers over the four foot eleven inch, ninety-pound Mexican jockey. The Lucchese Cowboy boots that Tony sports gives him another couple inches in height. The Caiman Crocodile boot is perfect for the occasion. His dark blue stone-washed jeans drape over one boot while the other pants leg is strategically cuffed just enough to show off the red leather upper with the handcrafted design. The shreds on the bottom of the jeans and the few distressed holes are just enough to add the fashionable sense to the outfit.

The sagging of his jeans, his fitted white V-neck T-shirt and his New York Yankees hat propped on his head to the back gives him a thugged-out edge that separates him from the rest of the horse owners. Around all the old money present, the elite may see Tony and believe that he doesn't belong here. That is until they catch a glimpse of the crocodile band Patek Phillipe Minute Repeater Tourbillion Perpetual that he wears on his wrist, and their minds change immediately. Although he's bought the watch pre-owned at four hundred grand, any timepiece connoisseur at the event knows this watch is worth every dime of nine hundred grand. With close to a million dollars on his wrist, he's really the biggest horse at the Derby.

The jockey listens attentively as Tony drills her. "Listen, we here," he says as the lit seven inch San Cristobal cigar dangles from the corner of his mouth. "We didn't come this far to lose. I have total faith in you," he says in an attempt to build her confidence. "We got three million cash riding on this one."

The jockey understands all that is on the line. The three-million-dollar purse really means nothing to her financially, being that she's only paid forty thousand a year, win, lose or draw. For them, it's business and about the money. For her, it's about status. If she can pull this off, she goes down in history.

"You like money, right?" She nods her head with a smile. "I thought so. Now listen… if you pull this off, we got ten percent for you. That's three hundred grand." The jockey smiles from ear to ear. "You ever seen three hundred grand before?"

"No."

"Okay, win tonight, and you will go home with three hundred grand of your own money."

* * *

Storm steps through the aisle in the normal seating area. Dressed in simple jeans and a designer T-shirt, Storm would look peculiar at home due to the big and floppy church hat that she has on her head. The black hat with the huge flower on the side is one of the simpler hats in all of the Derby. It's a tradition for the women in attendance to wear the most standout hats they can find. Some of the hats worn are eccentric and others are elegant. The hats almost all come with some combination of feathers, flowers, and ribbon, and the finished product is believed to bring good luck to gamblers at the races.

Mr. Antonelli has brought her along for the experience. Knowing how much money is involved in this race, she had to get a piece of the action. Although she's here with him her agenda is totally different. She's had her whole team flown here for the event.

Toy had work to do back at the casino, but she couldn't blow this opportunity. She knows the money will be endless here and wouldn't miss a chance to get her some of it. Even though she has her new job, she still loves the game. She doesn't have to sell herself anymore, but like Storm, she loves the rush and that is what keeps her in the game every chance she gets.

Storm finally gets to her seat where her team is already seated. It's an honor for them all to be at the actual race, witnessing it in real life, unlike the people they know from the 'chitterling circuit' as she calls it. The people of the chitterling circuit are the people from the hood who travel all the way to the derby, or any other big event and not actually be in attendance of the event. They only come for the festivities and bragging rights to say they were present.

The girls, with their hats they look like respectable Southern Belles and not the sex-selling prostitutes they are. Storm sits right next to the Mexican translator girl and all the Mexicans look at her, awaiting their instructions. Over the past couple weeks, they have become more comfortable with her. The money that they've made with her has given them new life.

To actually split their earnings with her is unbelievable to them. The few hundred they send back home doesn't even put a dent in the thousands they've made with her. With Storm and her generosity, they almost forget about the pressure they are under back at home. They feel more like business women than actual slaves now.

"I know this is different for y'all," Storm says slowly to the translator. She translates word for word. "But it's not as hard as it looks. Just follow their lead," she says. She points to Toy and Wendy on the other side of her.

Toy smiles invitingly at them while Wendy rolls her eyes. She's been nothing but abrasive since the day they joined the team. Her jealousy of them is more than obvious. Instead of realizing that there is enough money in this game for all of them, she sees it as them cutting into her business.

Beeba walks up the aisle, holding sodas and goodies. The way she's dressed is totally out of tradition for the Derby. While all the other woman are dressed like classy Southern Belles, she looks like a woman from a Southern porn skit. Her long legs in the short cut daisy duke shorts look amazing. Her thick nipples which poke through her almost transparent T-shirt makes her look sleezy. The combination may have her appear to be a cheap slut, but it's the way she rocks the all black straw Fedora that gives her a touch of class. The big yellow flower on the side of the hat adds just the amount of pizazz needed to clean up her image. Her long locs swing freely down her back.

When Storm invited Beeba here with her, she didn't hesitate to accept the offer. She was even willing to pay her own way. It was her pleasure just being invited. Of course, Storm funded it all which opened her up more. As far as right now, she has no clue of what is expected of her. Storm is confident that she won't have to work hard to sell her on the idea.

The fact that Beeba is here is all the reassurance she needs to know that she has total control of Beeba's mind. She's here, thousands of miles away from home, without her husband even knowing where she is. He foolishly believes that she's away with her family.

Never would he believe that his wife is in Kentucky with a For Sale sign on their pussy.

Just as Beeba gets to their row, Wendy gets up from her seat and walks to the aisle. She bumps Beeba on her way by. Beeba doesn't understand Wendy's attitude toward her. She stands there cluelessly. Storm shakes her head angrily. She prays that Wendy gets it together before they have another problem.

* * *

Tony and Mr. Antonelli are on the ground watching the race before theirs. They look like the odd couple, with Tony dressed in a cap to the back with a white T-shirt. Mr. Antonelli, as usual, looks quite traditional, dressed in a seer sucker suit and white suede bucks on his feet. The straw boater hat on his head has him looking like every other old man at the Derby.

Tony watches the horses closely. He's placed a few grand on this race. "Damn!" he shouts as he watches the winning horse hit the finish line. "Fuck!" Tony is such a sore loser, and that's all he seems to be doing tonight. He's already lost close to twenty grand.

As he's looking down at the card, Storm comes over to them. He doesn't even acknowledge her presence. The energy between them makes it evident that they aren't too fond of each other. For him, it's not personal, only business. He hates the fact that the old man is so open for her because he's sure she means no good for him.

The announcer calls for the owners of the next race. It's time for them to prepare. When he hears their horse's name over the loud speaker, a strange expression crosses his face. Their horse's name is Storm and not until now did he realize that Mr. Antonelli named the horse after his young lover.

"This can't be good," he mumbles to himself. He already saw her as a bad luck charm in life, so when he found out she was coming along, he didn't think it was a good idea. Now that he knows the horse is named after her, he's sure their chances of getting that three million are over. "Fuck," he whispers as he walks away.

* * *

Thirty minutes later, the race is starting, and Tony is too nervous to watch it. Instead he listens from the horsemen's suite. Mr. Antonelli stands at the window watching. Tony's stomach does flip-flops as the shot sounds off.

Trevor Denman, the track announcer speaks. "And they are off... in the Kentucky Derby," he says in his English accent. "A Beautiful Night in the City gets off to a great start, while Dinner for Two tails behind. Lonely Old Geezer creeps around the bend, Storm coming up the opposite side. Lonely Old Geezer and Storm run side by side. Love At First Sight cuts in between them."

Tony sits up on the edge of his seat. He looks at Mr. Antonelli in awe. He can't believe how the names of the horses in the race seem to match real life. Not sure if it's coincidence or a sign. He listens closer. Mr. Antonelli is in quite a shock as well.

"A One Night Stand takes the lead with Whatever You Do Don't Cuddle close on the heels with Sucker For Love close behind. Make My Toes Curl runs on the outside. Sucker For Love takes the lead. We Don't Love Them Hoes on the far outside." Tony shakes his head in disbelief.

"Storm and Devil In Disguise run side by side. Lonely Old Geezer tries to cut through the middle, running neck and neck until Sucker For Love steps into the race at top speed. Forty-one and fifth second. A One Night Stand and Looking for Love clash and Lonely Old Geezer trips over them. Start of a Romance takes the lead. Storm running strong with Lonely Old Geezer on her heels. Pandemonium catches up to them and Lonely Old Geezer stumbles. We Don't Love Them Hoes breezes past Lonely Old Geezer.

"Tender Dick is beginning to come alive, and stays in the middle of the action, causing Lonely Old Geezer to trip up. Honey I'm Home takes the lead. Catastrophe At Its Finest going strong in the red, white, and blue is racing in the inside and passes them all. Lonely Old Geezer can't keep up and topples over. He attempts to get up but Heartbreak tramples over him."

Mr. Antonelli's face is now as red as a cherry with embarrassment. He turns away from Tony with shame. Tony rubs his sweaty palms over his jeans. He knows the race is coming to an end and he can't handle it. The money at stake has him a nervous wreck. He gets up and paces circles as he listens carefully.

"Storm continues on ahead of them all until Karma catches up to her. Storm and Karma run side by side as they race up the final. Catastrophe steps in and passes them both. Catastrophe At Its Finest takes the lead as they continue down the final furlong. Hold up!" the announcer screams. "Looks like I'll Have Another has come alive in the end. He passes A Devil in Disguise and A One Night Stand with ease. It's Catastrophe At Its Finest, Storm, and I'll Have Another running neck and neck."

Tony shivers with nervousness. Anxiety rips through him. His palms and underarms are sweating, but nowhere near the bullets of sweat that cover his face. He watches the race, as hard as that is to do right now.

"I'll Have Another shoots at a clear lead as they come down to the finish. Storm scores for second place. Tender Dick finishes in third. Finishing up in fourth is Karma. Lonely Old Geezer comes in last. The winning time is 2.02 flat. The jockey riding, I'll Have Another is Mario Gutierrez, for the win."

Tony snatches his hat off his head and throws it onto the floor. "Dumb ass Lonely Old Geezer!" he shouts. He storms out of the suite.

65

THE NEXT NIGHT

TONY LAYS BACK on the bed in the hotel room. He's so sick that he hasn't been able to get out of bed all day. He can't believe they were so close to that three million and it slipped through their hands. At this moment he's ready to take Storm, Mr. Antonelli's lover, and Storm, the horse, out back and take them all out of their misery. He blames all the bad luck this weekend on Storm. The race with their horse isn't the only loss he's taken. Normally he has so much luck when going to the track betting the horses, but this weekend he's lost more than fifty grand. He's won not a single bet.

* * *

In the same hotel on a different floor, victory is in the air. All the girls are happy and satisfied with their earnings, even Wendy. She was able to walk away with forty-five hundred after giving Storm her cut. Making a few dollars for herself helped ease the tension between her and the rest of the girls.

Toy, on the other hand, is not as pleased with herself. With all the wealthy, old men here, she thought this would be one of the biggest weekends of her career. Tonight, for the first time ever, she raked in the least money. To only have earned fifteen hundred during an entire weekend is an embarrassment to her.

She's never been the lowest on the totem pole and hates how that feels. She was cold and couldn't seem to warm up. This weekend has her doubting herself. She believes that she may be losing her touch being that she isn't using her skills as much.

The Spanish women, after working the kinks out, maneuvered well. They navigated through with expertise. With the presence of so many ethnicity groups at this event, they felt at home and not so much of an outcast. The fact that Latin American jockeys dominated the Derby made them feel right at home. Between the four of them, they brought in over fifteen grand.

This was an easy weekend for the girls being that the most of the men they entertained were senior citizen. Because of that not a great deal of sex took place. A few kisses on the cheeks, sitting on laps and heavy conversation was all the old men wanted. For the most part, all most of them wanted was to be listened to as they bragged about themselves and their abundance of riches and success. The ones who wanted to talk about their unhappy, long-term marriages were the easiest to please. All they really wanted was their egos stroked and made to feel appreciated.

Even Beeba did well. Once she wrapped her head around what Storm expected from her she did everything in her power to impress Storm. The last thing she wanted to do was disappoint her idol. And she didn't. She managed to bring in close to five grand. Not bad for her first night as a working girl.

Storm is the happiest of them all. Overall she had a fifteen thousand dollar weekend. Unlike the rest of the girls who may have selfish plans for the money, Storm has plans of investing. She already knows the exact girl that her money will be spent on. She can't get back to Esto fast enough. She's already called Cypress to put the deal together.

* * *

As Tony is checking out at the front desk, he spots Storm walking among her group of girls. This was bad timing. She had no clue she would see him here at this time. He and Storm lock eyes, and when they do, she falls back, allowing them to proceed without her. The look on his face is a dead giveaway to her that he has suspicion. He watches the group of girls as they pass him, wondering what their connection can be.

Mr. Antonelli comes out of the bathroom and walks right over to her. She prays that he didn't see her with the girls. Her guilt causes her to hug him right in the middle of the floor. As she hugs him, she looks over his shoulder and finds Tony staring at her with disgust.

She realizes that he can possibly be a problem for her. Before Tony came into the picture, she had the old man wrapped around her finger. She has all reason to believe that the distance that is now between her and the old man has everything to do with Tony. It's obvious to her that he hates her and that makes her question if he will defend her fairly. He's like double jeopardy to her. Her freedom is in his hands just as her livelihood and that causes all type of thoughts in her head, none of them good.

Tony and Storm stare at each other over the old man's shoulder with a hatred that freezes the room. If looks could kill. Or can they?

66

DAYS LATER

S TORM CRUISES THROUGH Philadelphia on her way to see Bee-ba. Strangely she finds her way through the city without the need of her GPS. It still boggles her why she's so familiar with a city that she's never been in. A little voice in her head tells her exactly where to go.

Her heart races when she rides through certain neighborhoods and she doesn't know why these blocks haunt her. There are other areas that she drives through that give her an insane rush. One particular abandoned house in North Philadelphia stood out to her.

She was so attracted to the house that she had to pull over and look at it. It wasn't a beautiful house that demanded attention, either. It was an abandoned shack. She sat there observing the house, wondering what it was that had her captivated. She eventually pulled off but she still couldn't figure it out.

Storm parks the rental in the peaceful residential area. This area of Philadelphia, West Oak Lane, is so much different from the rest of the city. Until now she never knew that Philly even had a suburban area. She looks over into the passenger's seat at Breezy and points at the huge one-family house. It's an older house but well kept.

"This it right here." She picks her phone up and dials. Beeba picks up on the second ring. "Yeah, we here." She listens quietly. "All right bet." She ends the call and lays the phone on the middle console. "Come on."

Breezy snatches his gun from his waist and slides the safety lever. Mud, in the backseat, tucks his gun into his hoodie pocket and pulls his hood over his head. Storm snatches a Louisville slugger from the backseat. They get out and follow Storm as she leads them through the dark alley that separates the houses.

As they are stepping through the alley they hear a tapping on the second window. They look up and behind the window is Beeba. "She said the windows are nailed shut," Storm advises. She lifts the bat into the air. "We gone have to break the window."

Breezy laughs. "Damn! The sucker-ass nigga gotta nail the windows shut to keep his hoe inside?" he whispers.

"Yeah," Storm replies. "And that's why I don't respect his pimping."

"Fuck the bitch right and he won't have to lock her up like a caged animal. Let me fuck that pretty, long leg motherfucker and I will keep her in check for you."

"Dick don't keep no bitch," Storm replies. "That's where y'all dumb-ass niggas get it fucked up."

Storm signals Beeba to back up from the window as she raises the bat.

"Hold up, I got it," says Mud. He takes the bat and bangs on the glass until it shatters. He then uses the bat to shift the broken glass out of the way. Beeba climbs through the window with the help of Breezy and Storm.

Storm takes notice to Beeba's face and gets an instant attitude. Both of Beeba's eyes are swollen shut. Her lips are swollen double the actual size. She feels responsible for the beating, so she feels obligated to repay him. She looks away from Beeba, not able to look at her like this. The beautiful face she knew has been destroyed, for now.

Once Beeba returned home from Kentucky, her lies didn't add up. Her husband gave her the whooping of a lifetime. Her radical rebellious behavior didn't start until they met Storm, so his gut feeling told him she must have snuck away to be with her. He beat on her until she admitted it.

He believes that she and Storm are having some type of affair. She went along with it, never confessing what she had really done while away. She felt that was an easier pill to swallow than the truth: She had given herself to strange men for money. Ever since her return, he's been fighting her every time he thinks of her betrayal. He doesn't trust her alone, so whenever he has to leave the house for business, he locks her inside.

Breezy climbs into the window and grabs the bags filled with some of Beeba's clothes. She packed all she could for her temporary escape. She has no plans of leaving him for good, just long enough for him to feel sorry for what he's done to her. This escape is rage driven, but it gives her time to do what she really wants to do, and that is to be in the company of Storm and her new friends. Friends are something that her husband has always forbidden. For as long as they've been married it's been just him and her. Now that she has what she considers to be friends, she realizes what she's been missing all the while.

They all grab a bag or two and start through the alley. Storm looks at Beeba. "You know I can fix all of this for you, right? All you gotta do is give me the word."

"Fix it how?" she asks naively.

"We can sit out here and wait for him to come home, and when he does, I can make it where he never lays his hands on you again," Storm says as she lifts her shirt. Beeba sees the gun on her hip and she understands exactly what she's insinuating.

"No, no. I don't want anything like that to happen to him. Let's just go." She walks away hurriedly. She's angry with her husband, and yes she's lost a great deal of respect for him, but she doesn't want anything to happen to him. Regardless of it all, she still loves him. All that she's doing now is just an act of rebellion.

They pack the bags into Beeba's Range Rover, and she climbs into the driver's seat. Storm slams the door behind her. "Are you sure? You know, the ass whippings not gon' stop here, don't you? Let me just fix this shit and move on. We can just make it look like a robbery. No one will ever know."

For the first time, Beeba sees another side of Storm. The viciousness in her eyes and the rough edge about her makes Beeba slightly nervous. She wonders what she has gotten herself into. But at the same time, it is a turn on that Storm is so ready to do such a thing for her.

All this plays like one of the urban fiction novels that she loves to read. She can't believe that she's living it in real life. This new-found excitement in her life is a bit overwhelming at times, but it's broken the monotony. It's a rush that she's never felt, and she loves every second of it.

67

TWO WEEKS LATER

S TORM AND THE old man sit in the salesman's office inside of the Bentley dealership. He thinks they just happened to pop in here window shopping. He has no clue that all this was calculated. She dragged him along for what he thought was a lunch date, knowing damn well this was her desired destination.

When she got here, it was love at first site when she laid eyes on a black Bentley Continental GTC that was sitting on chromed out twenty-two inch factory wheels. She came in looking for a white one, but the black one snuck in and stole her heart. She feels the black more fits her personality. After taking the car for a test drive, they ended up in the office.

Mr. Antonelli's nonchalant attitude about it all causes her some real concern. She damn near had to force him in here. His attitude toward her has been different the past few weeks. He barely calls her, and when he does, the only rap he has for her is about her court case. She knows Tony is the blame for his behavior. She's been noticed the distance between them but was so busy with her own ventures that she hadn't had the time to address the matter. Besides, the three grand direct deposits have yet to be late, so she disregarded it all.

The salesman looks over the paperwork in front of him and reads from it. "The vehicle plus the rims, plus the luxury tax, we are looking at a buck eighty."

Storm looks to Mr. Antonelli with her signature puppy dog eyes that she displays when she wants something. He looks back at her with a blank stare that confirms that distance between them. Normally he would be pulling out his checkbook right now. She nudges him under the table. "Babe, I want it," she whispers while rubbing his leg.

Seeing him shake his head no bothers her, but it's nothing compared to what comes out of his mouth. "No," he whispers sternly. He looks away from her, not able to look into her eyes.

"Sir, can you excuse us for a minute, please?" she says to the salesman. She flashes a fake smile, but underneath it she's livid.

"Of course," he replies. He gets up and exits.

As soon as the salesman is out of the office, she goes directly at the old man.

"What do you mean no? That's what I want for my birthday."

"I'm not buying a hundred and eighty-thousand dollar car. You just got a brand new car a few months ago. Besides, I can't afford it right now. I'm two million dollars in on bail money. Or have you forgotten?"

She tries to conceal her rage. "How the fuck can I forget when you bring it up in every conversation? I want that car," she says as she pouts like a child.

He turns away from her, unbothered. Nothing she says seems to penetrate him. For the next five minutes, she begs and does everything in her power except throw a temper tantrum and nothing works. He's solid in his stance.

The salesman comes back into the office. "So, have we made a decision?"

"Yes," she replies before the old man does. Mr. Antonelli looks at her shocked at her answer. She ignores the tension that is coming from him. "Let's work the numbers out."

"I'm not buying that car," he whispers.

"You don't have to. I got it." The old man is even more shocked now. "How much we need for a down payment?"

"Depends on the credit and what kind of payment expected."

"We got fifty thousand for the down payment."

The old man looks at her speechless. The salesman gets to working on his calculator. "With great credit," he says, looking to Mr. Antonelli. By analyzing the matter he's sure that Mr. Antonelli is the source of credit. "We are looking at two thousand a month for seven years."

Mr. Antonelli's face goes stone as he thinks of a seven-year commitment, not with just the car but with her. He really can't see that far down the road.

"Good enough," she says. "We need another five minutes alone."

Once the man leaves, Mr. Antonelli loses his cool for the first time ever. He stands up enraged. "Where the hell are you getting fifty-thousand from? I'm not putting a dime up for that car."

"You don't have to!" She hates that he thinks she needs him and he's doing her like this. She feels betrayed like she's been played. *All these years of being intimate with his old wrinkled ass and now this*, she thinks to herself. "I'm taking that twenty-five thousand cash limit off the credit card you gave me and I got twenty-five thousand to put to it. All I need is your name."

"My name?"

"Yeah, you heard me. I didn't stutter. All these years I never told you no, and now you telling me no?" she asks, trying to pull the guilt trip on him. "I want that car for my birthday next week, and I'm getting it! I'm not taking your no for an answer."

* * *

Hours later, Storm stands behind the Bentley with butterflies floating in her belly as the salesman places the temporary tag in the window. She practically forced the old man to sign his name. He hasn't said a word to her since he signed. Right now, he stands to the side, face plastered with fury. The steam can be seen coming from his ears.

She admires herself through the reflection in the side window. She's not sure if she appears thicker through the window or if she's filled out so nicely. Either case, she likes what she sees. The sales-man steps to the side of her and catches her in the act of loving herself. He hands her the keys. "She's yours."

"Thank you," she says with a cool demeanor as if she isn't the happiest person alive right now.

She gets into the car while the salesman is shaking Mr. An-tonelli's hand. He's grateful for the hefty commission he's just made. While they engage in conversation, Storm flips the visor down and applies a coat of her shiny and glittering lip gloss. She grips the steering wheel, head tilted to the side. She admires herself through the rearview mirror.

She poses as if the neighborhood paparazzi are snapping pic-tures at her. She can't believe she's not only sitting in her dream car but she owns it. Today is the happiest day of her life. She's ready to shit on the world.

As the old man is making his way over to the driver's side of the Bentley, Storm speeds off with rage. She leaves him with a face full of burned rubber smoke and embarrassment.

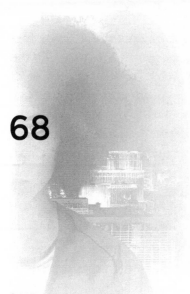

68

ONE WEEK LATER

STORM IS HAVING the time of her life. A great deal has taken place in less than a month. One thing she learned from watching others in the drug game is that life can change overnight if you happen to land the perfect racket. She's witnessed dirty dudes land a solid, dope connect and take off right before her eyes. It's always been somewhat unbelievable to see a person dirt-poor today and ghetto rich the next.

For many years, Storm played the sideline, watching dudes pop off overnight. A solid run changes it all. Although this past year has been a very lucrative year for her she wouldn't necessarily say it was a run. What has happened for her since she came home from her short couple weeks of incarceration is what she considered a run in the making.

Storm steps out of the front door of her new home. The thirty-two story, high rise apartment building here in Fort Lee, New Jersey, overlooks the Hudson River. Being on the twenty-sixth floor she has the perfect view of New York City. This apartment is a dream of hers and worth every dime of the forty-five hundred a month that she will be paying. It's still surreal to her.

Less than a week, and she already has the apartment fully furnished. One would think she hired an interior decorator with the way she's put it together. Her living room looks like a page out of a magazine with pure white tufted love seats which sit on a plush white fur area rug. She's stolen that idea from Mr. Antonelli himself. The room is decorated with black and white photos of old movie icons. Each corner of the living room is accessorized with tall crystal candle holders. Despite her aggressive demeanor she loves feminine elements in her home. As hardcore as she carries herself, stepping into her apartment, one will know that she's all woman.

Just as she steps through the double doors, her Bentley cruises around the path and stops short in front of her. Luckily she has on her sunglasses because the bright rims reflect brilliantly. The red interior demands attention. She's nicknamed the car "Bloody Murder."

The valet attendant gets out and holds the door for her to get in. "Thank you," she says as she seats herself. He gently closes the door, and she cruises off.

She thought the Mercedes, SL was the ultimate automobile until owning this one. The attention she gets in this is like the SL to the tenth power. After driving this around, she now sees the SL as an introduction to the Big League. This car here is the real deal. The Mercedes she looks at as a low-key get-around car and that is what she plans to do with it.

What makes her feel even better about this car is that she bought it on her own. Originally she wasn't expecting to buy it herself. The word "no" sounded completely foreign to her coming from his mouth. Him saying no to her and his cold distant demeanor is starting to worry her.

Ever since he bailed her out, they haven't been intimate, not one time. In no way does she believe the bail money put a dent in his savings. She believes that Tony has gotten into his head and turned him against her. She has plans of showing him that she doesn't need him, and hopefully he will fear losing her and come to his senses.

She now worries that her game isn't working because he hasn't called her not once since the day she pulled off on him at the dealership. She was sure that by now he would be calling her off the hook. Normally when she's angry with him, he calls her back to back, trying to get on her good side but not this time. Now that her rage has vanished, she's now concerned with his actions. She has a gut feeling that she has lost control over him.

Storm flies along Route 280, doing more than half of the dashboard. The speedometer wavers between one hundred and ten and one hundred and fifteen of the two hundred mile per hour maximum. The music that rips through the speakers rejuvenates her soul yet has tears trickling down her face. This song reminds her of her childhood and gives her a sense of closeness to her parents and her brother that she hasn't felt in so long. On Saturday mornings, her father would walk through the house singing this song.

"*Someone asked the question?*" she shouts with Kirk Franklin. With the way she's bopping to the beat, no one would ever expect her to be listening to gospel music. This CD is her little secret that she keeps tucked in the stash. She pulls this CD out whenever she is missing her family. This is one of the few things that she holds as a memory of them and over the years it has managed to help her get by.

"*You're the reason why we sing,*" she sings along with the chorus. She sings as if she's a part of the concert. "*I sing because I'm happy,*" she shouts. "*You're the reason why I sing.*"

She peeks into the mirror and wipes the tears that are dripping from underneath her sunglasses. She's happy she can't see her eyes right now because she knows they are overflowing. The song and the memories of her family coupled with her menstrual period has her a wreck right now. Her emotions are all over the place. The sadness she feels in her heart is addicting. She replays the song over and over again until her face is flooded with tears.

It takes all of twenty minutes for Storm to reach Toy and Wendy's spot. She pulls to the back of the house and parks. Before getting out, she wipes away any trace of her crying. She gets out with a lively step that in no way reflects her true feelings today. Before she can get to the top of the short flight of stairs, the backdoor is opened partially. She slips through the entrance and the door is slammed behind her. She daps the man at the door as she passes him. He stands at his post.

Storm has made a business decision to emulate the house that she visited where she originally bought the Mexican women from. She even has the Santeria setup at the door to make the women feel at home. Although she has no knowledge of it, she allowed them to set it up at their request. They claim they need it there for the protection of evil, as if selling sex for money is not evil in itself.

She thought long and hard and decided that having the girls working the house in between events makes perfect business sense. It's a way for her to keep money coming in every day. She figured, what's the use of having access to everyday income and not take advantage of it? As soon as she opened the doors for business, they've been selling sex faster than candy is sold at a candy store next to an elementary school. She has no idea how the patrons find out about the house with no advertisement. The power of word of mouth has tricks coming in by the handfuls.

The Mexican women lounge around on the leather couches looking dead tired. Their faces are worn out, so one can only imagine how worn out their bodies are from being abused by many strangers. No matter how tired they are they never complain. They just go along with what is required of them.

In total, there are seven of them. Since the original purchase she's added three more to her roster. Their work day ended an hour ago and now they are just waiting for her permission to retire for the night. Together they averaged about twenty tricks apiece. Some more, some less.

She feels they've been short changing themselves, so she's raised the price. At sixty dollars a trick, she makes about nine grand a day on a regular weekday. On the weekends that nine doubles. Their clientele during the week are mainly the local drug dealers. On the weekends, the Mexicans who do work for hire all week spend their hard earned money on the women. With them being so far away from home and lonely, this house serves as their home away from home.

Storm walks past them without acknowledging them. In the dining room at the table are Wendy and Beeba. They count through stacks of money like bank tellers. She will never allow them to lower their stock and turn tricks for a lousy sixty bucks but she has other work for them.

The two of them run the house and keep track of the finances. She moved Beeba and Wendy into her old apartment. Toy now has her own apartment. The Mexicans live in this house but upstairs. Storm paid the tenants upstairs to relocate, so she can have access to the whole house. At first she was hesitant about leaving them alone, thinking they would escape, but just as Esto promised, she's never had a problem with any one of them making a break for it. They have too much at stake to even consider it.

Wendy stacks the money into a bag and hands it over to Storm. "Today was a good day. That's eleven grand."

Storm nods her head with satisfaction. "Very good day."

He's listened detail by detail to the adventure that Angelica calls her life. He's mind-blown to say the least. "So, let me ask you," he says while looking over the table at Angelica. "With you being a woman, you had no compassion for these women? Holding them captive and forcing them to sell sex for your selfish gain?"

"Honestly, I really didn't see it like that," she replies. "I only saw it from a business standpoint, and besides I treated them better than they were being treated. If you ask me, it was a blessing for them to be working for me as opposed to those other guys," she says with sincerity.

"You see, this was nothing new to me. At a young age, I was appointed to being the overseer of a bunch of girls. My job then was to watch over the money," she says while staring into space. She thinks back to her childhood and the vision plays clearly in her mind.

"It was a rainy summer day in 2003 and me and three other girls from the church were hanging around in the house of our preacher. We weren't there with him. We hung there with his daughter while he and his wife were at work. She was seventeen and we all looked up to her like a big sister.

"I was the youngest, and I was only eleven. The other girls were already twelve years old, but I was more advanced than them, so she made me her second in command, like her lieutenant. Her dad left at three on the dot for work every day. No matter what we were doing at three-ten p.m., we made our way over to their house.

"She told us if anyone ever asked us what we were doing over there, we were to tell them we had to work on our project. No one else was allowed to come with us. She explained to us the importance of trust and how she trusted us. We were honored. We never really worked on a project though. That was just the secret code for what it was that we were really doing.

"When I think back to those days, I can still hear the thunder roaring loudly as if I was there. The house was dark and the only source of light was coming from the floor model television set. The moaning coming from the television was so loud it was like the porn stars were in the room with us. All eyes are on me, not the porn, and I'm the center of attention.

"While I was sitting back on the couch, with both feet sinking into the cushions, Valerie, the preacher's daughter is on her knees. I was the project that she was working on at the time. She worked on me with her hands and her mouth and sometimes both. She knew all the spots to hit to make my 'water fall,' as she called it.

"It was with her the first time I ever squirted. I was too young to know the difference at the time, but she always told me I would be special because I could do something that most girls could not. In my mind all I did was pee on myself and was embarrassed about it. She told me I was her favorite because I could do that special thing but that didn't remove the shame. She worked on all of us one by one every day and no matter what she tried the other girls would never squirt. "It brought out jealousy in them toward me that eventually led them to ridicule me.

"Two hours would pass, and just before it was time for her mother to come home from work, she would let us all shower. She said what we were doing was top secret and we had to clean any trace of it. After every one was all showered, it was my job to supervise."Valerie would ask. 'Angel, did everybody wash their money?'

"The money was code word for the private parts. Sometimes she would call it money and other times she would call it 'our pocketbook.' My job was to watch each girl as they showered and make sure they cleaned their pocketbooks good. She told us grown folks could smell that fragrance a mile away. She also threatened us if anyone found out we could all go to prison for life. With that in mind, I made sure all the money was clean.

"So, none of this is new to me. As a kid I was taught that the woman's private part was equivalent to money and I have never seen it otherwise."

He looks at Angelica with water in his eyes after hearing such a heartbreaking story.

Storm hands Wendy and Beeba their weekly pay of two thousand dollars. They accept it graciously. She pays Mud and his friend two thousand a week as well. Their jobs are to stand at the front and back doors all day as security. The hardest part of their job is roughing up a Mexican dude who has had way too many beers to drink and may have gotten unruly.

She makes her way into the living room to pay the girls. She pays them weekly as well. Giving them four thousand in one shot at the end of the week seems so much better to them than receiving sixty dollars a trick. It seems to take forever to build up four grand, sixty dollars at a time. So happy to have so much money in hand, they don't realize that their turning many tricks for free.

Storm's weekly expenses total at thirty-eight thousand after paying everybody. After it's all said and done she's left with a minimum of forty-thousand for herself on a slow week. Last week was her best week of the three, wherein she profited fifty-five grand. The monthly rent for the spot and the utilities only set her back another two grand.

As Storm is handing Araceli her pay, the sound of loud voices at the back door startles her. She runs to the kitchen and peeks at the backdoor where Mud is standing, blocking the door. The image of another man trying to get past him is alarming.

Mud pushes the man with all of his might, and the man doesn't even budge. "Fam, I told you we closed!"

"Fuck that!" the man shouts. "Where my fucking wife at?"

Storm looks closer and realizes that the man is Beeba's husband, Jay. She rushes to the door. At her heels is Mud's buddy, the other enforcer. He's coming to Mud's aid.

Jay spots Storm, and with rage, he forces Mud out of the way. He rushes her like a mad bull. "You bitch! Where's my fucking wife?"

His hands are already clenched ready to wrap them around her neck. Just as he gets within arm's reach of her, Mud's buddy steps in between them with his gun drawn. He strikes Jay across the forehead with his gun and he falls flat on his back. The man dives on top of him, sitting on his stomach. He places the nose of his gun right in between Jay's eyes.

Right before he squeezes the trigger Mud pushes him off. Mud aims his gun precisely. The tug of war over who pulls the trigger is all due to Storm. She's informed them that they get a bonus of five thousand if they have to shoot someone in the line of duty. If by chance they have to smash someone, meaning kill them, that's an automatic bonus of ten grand. Both of them have been hoping for this day and want their hands on the ten grand.

Beeba and the rest of the women come running into the room due to the uproar. When Jay sees his wife accompanied by half-naked women, he becomes livid, forgetting all about the gun that is aimed at his head. They fight to restrain him.

Beeba races over and lays flat on top of her husband like a shield. "No!" she cries. "Please! No!" she pleads.

Both Mud and his buddy aim around her, trying to get a clean shot at his head. "Don't shoot," Storm says. She has no sympathy for the man, but she doesn't want Beeba hurt in the process. Also she doesn't want them to murder him in here and blow up her spot. The last thing she needs is the cops shutting her business down and her getting another murder charge.

"Don't shoot," she commands as she pulls Beeba from the floor. Both of the guns are still aimed at his head. Beeba is crying like a baby as she tries to get away from Storm. "Rough him up and teach him a lesson," she instructs as she leads Beeba away.

The abuse can be heard from the other room. Beeba cries harder with each whimper she hears from her husband. She feels responsible for all of this and the guilt is unbearable. She wonders how he knew to find her here.

Not once does she think that the OnStar navigation on her truck is what led him here. She misses her husband dearly but was having the time of her life, so she never went home to him. They would talk on the phone throughout the day and that only made her miss him even more. She finally admitted that she was with Storm but never mentioned any of the other details. He begged and begged her to come home and after no success he finally made his way here.

Storm walks back into the kitchen and stops the beating. Jay lays there a bloody pulp, both eyes closed shut, the same way Beeba's eyes were when she rescued her. She stands over Jay, who looks up to her helplessly. "The only reason I spared your life is because of her," she says, pointing to Beeba.

"If you ever come near my business again I will let them loose to do what I should've let them do tonight." She helps him onto his feet. "Now leave before I change my mind."

Jay looks to Beeba with desperation. "Come on." His eyes are glassy, but the blood that's leaking from them conceals the tear buildup.

Beeba stands in confusion. A part of her wants to go, but she fears the ass whooping she will get once he gets her home. Storm looks to Beeba. "You going with him?"

They all eagerly await her answer. She shakes her head from side to side. "Not right now, Jay. Just go home and calm down first."

"Let's go," Jay demands. The tears are now trickling down his face.

"You heard her," Storm says. "Now go!"

Mud and his friend grab the man by his arms and shove him toward the back door. Mud places his gun onto the man's temple. "Get the fuck in your car and get the fuck outta here. Cause any more ruckus and she not gone be able to stop me," he threatens. Mud opens the door and they shove the man down the flight of stairs and slam the door shut.

Jay sits around for a few minutes wiping the bloody tears from his eyes. They watch from the window as his Porsche cruises out of the backyard. It's now etched in stone that he's lost his bitch to another bitch.

69

MAY 28, 2012

TRAFFIC IS TIGHT on Route 280 East. The very first car leading the traffic is Toy's Audi. At a speed of ninety miles an hour the next car in line is twenty car lengths behind it. Toy maneuvers the Audi like a skilled racecar driver.

Loud engine roaring sounds off causing the traffic to veer over into the middle lane. As the Bentley speeds along the highway, swerving in and out of the lanes the only thing the drivers can see is her personalized license plates from the back. They don't know who "Storm" is, but they all agree she is most definitely showing off. Evidently, she's having the time of her life right now.

Storm stomps on the gas pedal, sitting on the edge of her seat. The only thing in her sight is the white Audi. She has the fast lane to herself except for the one car that is up ahead. She sings along with Jay-Z and Jermaine Dupri's "Money Ain't a Thing." *"In the Ferarri or the Jaguar, switchin' four lanes. With the top down screamin' out, money ain't a thing!"* Storm shouts out with determination in her eyes.

Beeba sits in the passenger's seat, head glued to the headrest with her eyes shut tightly. She's gripping the seat, both hands. She's scared to death at the way Storm is driving. She holds onto the seat for dear life, like she's on a roller coaster.

Storm catches up to the car in her lane in seconds and damn near smacks into it. She's glued to the bumper of the Cadillac which is hogging the lane. She rests on the horn as she presses the Cadillac. The driver is confused as to what they should do.

With aggression, Storm swerves around the Cadillac into the middle lane. She sticks her middle finger up at the driver before stomping harder on the gas. Just barely past the Cadillac and she cuts back into the fast lane. The driver has to slam on the brakes to prevent hitting the Bentley.

Storm stretches out in the wide open lane. *"Jigga, don't like it if it don't gleam gleam and to hell with the price 'cause the money ain't a thang!"* she shouts with one finger pointing in the sky. She walks the Audi down until another car cuts into the lane. She switches into the middle lane with no blinker or warning. Horn blowing sounds off behind her. She flies the bird into the air through the sunroof.

She cuts to the slow lane and back into the middle lane and finally back into the fast lane. She watches as the Audi takes the curve with expertise. Storm gets into the lane behind it and walks it down. Bumper to bumper she stays, putting the pressure on Toy.

As Storm is about to cut over and go around her, she's blocked by a string of traffic. Toy takes a huge lead on her. Caught up in the middle of a traffic storm, Storm is pissed as she watches Toy gain a bigger lead on her. Toy reaches the toll booth with two cars in front of her.

Storm sweeps over into the very next lane, which is wide open. Anticipation rips through her palms, both wrapped around the steering wheel. She pulls up beside the Audi and slams on the brakes. She rolls the window down, taunting Toy as she holds up the EZ Pass lane. Wendy pulls up on the left side of Storm in the next lane. She's in Storm's Mercedes.

Storm rolls both windows down and *"Bubble hard in the double R, flashin' the rings! With the window cracked, holler back, money ain't a thang!"* blares through the speakers.

Storm lowers the volume, so they can hear her. "Let's go bitch!" she says to Toy. "I gave you a head start and you still can't shake me. Now we starting even Steven!" Toy is smiling from ear to ear.

Storm looks to her left at Wendy. "Bitch, you not even in the race. You wasting all my horsepower!"

Storm cruises side by side until Toy pays the toll. Storm lets the car roll on its own. With no hesitation, Toy slams on the accelerator and the Audi takes off. Storm stomps the gas pedal and catches her quickly, while Wendy is still at the toll both.

She rides side by side as she sings along with the song. "*Come on, y'all wanna floss with us,*" she sings. The wind is blowing fiercely and she can't be heard but still she continues singing as if they can hear her. "*Cause all across the ball we burn it up. Drop a little paper, baby, toss it up,*" she says as she flies a few dollar bills into the air.

They continue side by side. "*Ya slackin' on your pimpin'… turn it up. See the money ain't a thang!*" she says before taking off. She stretches on Toy, giving them the ass of the Bentley to kiss. Wendy is so far behind that she can't even be seen.

She looks over to Beeba, still spitting the verses. "*Put it down for my dogs that's locked in the bing. When you hit the bricks, new whips, money ain't a thang!*" Beeba cheeses from ear to ear. The look in her eyes and smile on her face is clear indication that she's never met a cooler chick than Storm.

Today is by far the best birthday she's ever had in her life. Big Apple, here they come!

* * *

Diamonds glisten from under every glass case of the store. This store in the Diamond District of New York is like heaven for any woman. The bright lights from the ceiling make even the diamonds of the poorest quality gleam dazzlingly. Millions and millions of dollars worth of jewelry all in one room.

Storm holds her wrist out as the jeweler fastens the watch onto her wrist. She flips it over and appreciates every detail of the diamond bezeled, white gold, pink-faced Pearl Master Rolex. Diamonds are not only on the bezel and in the face but lined long the middle of the band as well. This is the day that she has been waiting for. She's been dropping a few grand at a time on the watch for the last few weeks just so she wouldn't have to bust such a huge nut today.

Although Mr. Antonelli has been acting weird with her lately, she believes she could have gotten him to buy her the watch. He's bought her a couple other Rolexes, but she wanted to get this one on her own for self-accomplishment. She loves the sense of independence she feels when she buys herself something that she never thought she could ever buy. It makes her feel as if she's bringing her own dreams to reality.

"Y'all like it?" she asks as she turns around to show the girls.

"Damn," Wendy says as she stares at the watch with her mouth wide open with admiration. Toy is speechless.

"Looks great on you," Beeba admits.

Storm takes one more glance before going into her purse and pulling out stacks of money. The money has been counted five times already, so she slides it across the counter with confidence. "Excuse me, y'all," she says.

Nosiness prevents them from excusing themselves right away. They don't leave until they get a glimpse of the thirty-six thousand dollar price they see printed on the bottom line. The girls walk away and find their way to the other cases, just peeking inside.

"That's the fourteen."

The man begins counting through the crisp one-hundred dollar bills quickly. Once he's done, he slams the receipt book onto the case and signs paid. He hands her the receipt. "Happy birthday to you," he says with a smile.

Twenty minutes at the glass case with just Storm and the jeweler and she calls the girls back over. As they stand before her, she hands both Toy and Wendy a small box. They admire the twin Rolex Oyster Perpetuals. There aren't nearly as many diamonds in these watches as hers, but still they find them beautiful. "What y'all think? Y'all like them?"

"Nice," they both agree.

A smile of satisfaction spreads across Storm's face. "Just a little token of my appreciation," she says with sincerity. "I know I be hard on y'all, but I want y'all to know y'all hard work doesn't go unrecognized. I just want to say thanks."

Wendy places her hand over her mouth, unable to speak. Tears well up in Toy's eyes. In all the years she's known Storm never has she said anything as sentimental as this.

"You gone make a bitch cry," says Toy. Tears of sentiment are dripping down her face.

"Go ahead, girl. You know I ain't with that mushy shit," Storm says. She tries to keep her hard exterior but tears are welling up in her eyes as well. She walks away before they can see one of them drip down her face. She passes Beeba who stands in the backdrop appreciating the moment.

One thing the streets have taught Storm is to never eat in front of your team without making them a plate as well. She realizes that builds envy and resentment, and both can ultimately lead to disloyalty. Disloyalty always ends in the crisscross. The watches are only ten thousand apiece, only a third of the price of hers, but it's the gesture that counts. By giving them these watches, it gives them the incentive to work harder to get the watch she has or the equal of it. Giving them the gravy gives them the taste of the meat without actually having it. To give them the meat would only make them content and lazy.

* * *

Minutes later, Storm sits in her car inside of the parking lot. She looks over to Beeba who is looking into the mirror visor, applying her lipstick. She places an open box in between Beeba's face and the visor. "For you," Storm says.

Beeba turns toward her in shock. "I couldn't give it to you in front of them. It wouldn't be right. I gave them their watches be-cause of all of their hard work. They would resent you knowing you got a watch and didn't put in half of the work they have. I'm giving you this though because I'm sure you will eventually earn it," she says with a sly grin.

Beeba's heart melts. She's no stranger to Rolex but to get such a gift from Storm is special to her. What she doesn't know is the watch didn't cost Storm a dime. The jeweler gave her the pre-owned watch practically for free for spending close to sixty-grand. A free watch, but the gesture speaks volumes, and she's sure it will go a long way.

70

LATER THAT EVENING

THE CRAVING FOR seafood led Wendy to the seafood store, smack in the middle of the hood. Just a few minutes more, and she would have missed out. She walks out of the store, bags in hand and they close the gates behind her. Storm's Mercedes gleams like a demon in the darkness.

Wendy gets inside the car and the smell of the seasoning rips through her nostrils. She can't wait to get home to eat, so she digs into the bag of hot steam. She throws a shrimp in her mouth and pulls out of the parking lot. At the exit of the lot, a Nissan Maxima stops short to allow her to exit. She waves a "thank you" as she cruises on to the red traffic light at the corner.

The Maxima pulls alongside of her, and through her peripheral, she can see the passenger trying to get her attention. She looks straight ahead, still eating. The car gets so much attention that it gets overbearing at times.

The attention wouldn't be bad if it was from the right sources. It just amazes her how a car so prestigious could attract so many bums. She can't understand how a man with nothing feels so comfortable in attempting to push up on a woman in a car that values at a hundred grand. Although it's not her car, it's now obvious to her that men really don't know when they are clearly out of their league.

The light changes, and she turns onto Central Avenue. The Nissan is still on her side, not giving up. The passenger hangs his hand out of the window, waving to get her attention. "Damn," she sighs as she reaches another red light. She slams on the brakes. Now the horn of the Nissan is honking. Finally she looks over and the driver is saying something she can't make out.

He's pointing at her tire, with an alarming look on his face. Wendy rolls the window down. "Just trying to tell you it looks like the oil pan is dragging on the ground."

Wendy's face turns flush. She feels quite stupid, believing he was trying to push up. "Is it?" she asks with a cheesy smirk. Not knowing anything about cars she asks, "What should I do?"

"Just pull over and I will see what I can do," he says. "Turn right here," he advises.

Wendy turns onto Seventh Street and pulls close the curb. The Maxima pulls right behind her. The passenger, a young man dressed in thug gear, hops out quickly. Wendy leans forward to put her shoes on her feet before getting out. Through the rearview, she notices the driver hop out.

She looks around at the darkness and solitude of the area and thinks maybe it's not a good idea to get out. Instead she hangs her head out of the window. "I didn't lose it did I?"

"Nah, it's still hanging," the man from the passenger seat says. He leans over, looking under the car. Just as his head lowers, he pops back up with the quickness. With one hand he reaches into the car and grabs the steering wheel and with the other he pulls at the door handle.

Wendy steps on the gas pedal nervously. The engine races but the car doesn't move. The door is pulled open. She quickly looks down and slams the gear into drive. She speeds off, door swinging wide open.

The man runs side by side the car with a gun aimed in the car. Blocka! Blocka!

The windshield shatters. She ducks low from the glass particles, still speeding.

Blocka! Blocka! Blocka!

The back window is now shattered as well. She busts a wild right turn back onto West Market and melts the asphalt at one hundred miles an hour. Never has she driven so fast. A getaway is the only thing on her mind.

* * *

One hour later, Wendy sits on the couch in her apartment a nervous wreck. She's shivering with fear, still shook up. Once the call was made all business was ordered to be shut down, from the business Breezy conducts on the street to the business that Toy and Storm conduct. The Mami house was closed early tonight and all are present for the emergency meeting.

Surprisingly it's Beeba who shows the most compassion for Wendy, who has always been so cold to her. Wendy's head rests on Beeba's shoulder, with Beeba stroking her hair like a child. Toy sits on the arm of the couch, petrified while Storm paces around, not saying a word. Mud, Breezy, and Mud's partner all sit in the backdrop in deep thought.

"So, you didn't get a license plate or nothing?" Storm asks.

"Storm, no. How could I get a plate when they trying to snatch me out of the car and shooting at me?"

"I don't believe you fell for that shit anyway," Storm says with no compassion. "You don't be on point, yo." Wendy rolls her eyes with disgust. A great birthday has ended in chaos, the same chaos that she always seems to have in her life. When good happens for her, bad always seems to sneak in. This is the story of her life.

"I hate Newark niggas!" Toy shouts. "Instead of carjacking and robbing people of their hard earned money, why don't they just get out there and make their own money?"

"We need answers," Storm says while staring into space. She's quite calm about it all. "We will get to the bottom of it though." She looks to the men who are all in a pack. "We need to get out on them streets and find out who got that Maxima," she says with authority. "And when we do, y'all know the rest."

71

DAYS LATER

A FTER DAYS OF rolling through the streets, they have seen no
sign of the Nissan Maxima that Wendy described. Breezy and
the fellas have reached out to every lead they have on the streets
that could possibly know something. Everyone says they are on the
case, but no one has gotten back to them as of yet. In the meantime,
Storm is not letting up. In no way will she let this go unsolved.

On another note, after still not hearing from Mr. Antonelli,
Storm finally broke down and called him. To her surprise, he didn't
answer. She called for two days straight, still getting no return call
from him. What hurts her the most is that he didn't call her to
even wish her a happy birthday. Ignoring her only made her furious
which led her to his house to do a drive through.

This isn't like him at all. She decided to drive past his house
to see if his cars are in the driveway. She believes the only way he
wouldn't get back to her is if he may be out of town. She's even considered the worse like maybe he's in the hospital sick. With him being such an old man, she can't count out that he even could be dead.

As she sits parked in front of his house she notices that not only
are all of his cars present, but there's another vehicle there which
doesn't belong. The red BMW X5 sits parked as the last car in the
row. In all her years of coming here, she's never seen this vehicle.

She gets out and walks over to the car. Her heart races with each step. She plants her hand on the hood to see if the engine is hot, but it's cold as if it's been sitting. The pink bow hanging from the rearview mirror tells her the car belongs to a woman. Now her fury kicks in.

She stomps up the stairs and rests on the bell. No one answers fast enough for her, so she starts to bang on the door. When that doesn't happen fast enough for her she kicks on the door.

Finally it opens. The housekeeper stands there with a perplexed face. "Yes?"

Storm forces the door open wide enough so she can enter. The housekeeper tries to block her. "Is Mr. Antonelli aware of your arrival?" she asks as she holds the door.

Storm pushes the door open with all of her might, and the housekeeper stumbles backwards a few steps. Storm pushes her a few more steps backwards. "The fuck outta my way!" She walks past the housekeeper who trots behind her. "I can't let you in without his permission."

Storm turns around with both fists clenched. "Try to stop me." She's tempted to give the woman the beating that she so rightfully deserves. She decides not to because that will only stall her. "Touch me and I will beat the fuck outta you in this motherfucker!"

The woman stops in her tracks, not wanting any physical altercation. "Fucking black savage," she mumbles under her breath.

Not able to contain herself, Storm swings a wild haymaker at the woman. She ducks just in time to prevent herself from being struck. She backpedals away with fear. Storm continues on with her mission.

She forces the door open and she sees exactly what she was expecting. There in the middle of the room is Mr. Antonelli and a woman. They dance together to the sound of Frank Sinatra's "My Way" which plays softly. The woman whose back is toward the door, is butt naked while Mr. Antonelli is in his signature robe. Storm is surprised to see the woman with skin as white as his, but still it doesn't make her feel any better about it.

He spots Storm in the doorway, and he damn near has a heart attack. The woman turns to the door, and she becomes paralyzed with fear. The woman appears to be Storm's age if not younger. A devilish smile spreads across Storm's face. "So, this is why you're not answering my calls?"

Her smile widens, but she's really crying on the inside. As she looks at the beautiful young woman, her heart melts. She feels a sense of betrayal that she's never experienced when it comes to a man. She's never invested enough emotion into a man to ever care. That is until now.

It's all surprising to her because she never knew that he meant this much to her. This is a wake-up call that, as much as she denied it in the past, she really loves the old man. To see him here with another woman brings out feelings and emotions that she never knew she had. For the first time in her life, she's heartbroken.

Storm pulls her gun from her waistband. "Owww!" the woman screams as she runs for cover.

"Hey, no!" Mr. Antonelli screams as he runs toward her.

"It was the first time that I ever experienced anything like this. I was hurt and felt like he betrayed me. I didn't know anything else to do but get even."

The man shakes his head, eyes wide open with suspense. "Please, tell me you didn't kill the old man. Young lady, before you go any further, please tell me you didn't do that."

Storm aims the gun at his head. He stops short with his hands high in the air. "Please, no."

Storm squeezes the handle of the gun tighter, preparing to fire. The woman with her arms filled with her clothes makes a run for the door. Storm aims the gun at her head. "Sit the fuck down, bitch. You ain't going nowhere." The woman stops. Storm walks toward her. "Down!" she commands as if she's talking to a dog. The woman drops to her knees obediently.

"Mr. Antonelli, is everything o?" the housekeeper asks before seeing the gun in Storm's hand.

Storm races over to her. "No, bitch, everything ain't okay," she says as she snatches the woman by the collar. "You get the fuck in here, too." She slams the housekeeper onto the floor. She locks the door and makes her way back over to Mr. Antonelli, who is holding his chest, hyperventilating. She pushes him onto the floor. She aims the gun at his head. "So, that little bitch is the reason you haven't called me? She's been taking up all of your time, huh?"

"Angelica, please, just listen."

"Fuck listening," she replies. "I'm doing the fucking talking." She grabs the naked woman and flings her. She lands almost on his lap. Storm then aims the gun at the housekeeper. "Get the fuck over here!" The housekeeper runs over and drops to her knees right next to them. Silence is in the air.

Storm and Mr. Antonelli lock eyes for seconds. She can picture the bullet spiraling into his head. Mr. Antonelli has that picture in his mind as well. Blood gushing from his head is the only thing that would make her feel better right now.

"What? I got too old for you?" she asks, while biting onto her bottom lip. "Had to go out and find you a new young thing, huh? Is that it? Did your attorney friend get her for you to get your mind off me?" She places the nose of the gun onto his forehead and holds it stiff. Mr. Antonelli shakes uncontrollably as he keeps his eyes on her trigger finger.

"How much you pay her a week to have sex with your old wrinkly ass? I know she not doing it for free. Oh, my bad, you can't have sex because your lil, old-ass, dick can't get hard. She got the fountain of youth to drink from like me?"

Storm is making herself angrier the more she talks. "How you keep her interested? Did you promise her you'd sign her into your will, too? Is that your weak ass game? Old ass think you a player, huh?" she asks before nudging his head. She palm grips his face and bangs his head against the wall.

Her facial expression transforms from fake cool and calm to satanic. Her eyes are bloodshot red from anger. She looks like the devil himself, just minus the horns. "You old limp dick slick ass bastard! You know what? I got something for your ass!" She pushes him over before snatching the house phone out of the wall. He lays there in a fetal position. Storm then checks the housekeeper and takes her phone from her apron. She digs into the girl's pocketbook and takes her phone as well. She snatches the old man from the floor. "Come on!"

She looks to the women who are scared for their lives. "You bitches move a muscle and I will slaughter both of you." She pushes the old man to the door. Once they get to the door, she reaches up to the ledge and grabs a key. She steps out with him in front of her. She uses the key to lock the women inside.

She forces the old man down the corridor until they get to his library. "Angelica, why are you doing this?"

"Shut the fuck up and just walk!" she says, shoving him into the room.

She drags him to the wall in the corner of the room. He watches as she grabs the Bible from the shelf. He knows exactly what she's looking for. He feels like a fool to have exposed her to so much of his life. In a zillion years, he would've never thought they could ever be at odds with each other. With all that he's done for her, no way would he believe that she could ever be his enemy or bring him any type of harm. He questions if she has had him fooled all this time or if the signs were there and he fooled himself.

She flicks through the pages until she finds what she's looking for. She hands it to him while holding the gun to his head. "You promised me that you would write me into your will, right? Now write it motherfucker!" She grabs the twenty-four karat gold pen from the mantelpiece and shoves it in his hand.

With his hands trembling, he looks up at her. "What do you want me to write?" She shoves the gun under his cheekbone. "I don't know motherfucker but be creative." She reads over the wording of the rest of the will and comes up with her own clause. "I want two million dollars. That's fair for all the years I suffered being with your old ass. Write, in case of death, I will be awarded two million dollars. Oh, and I keep my cars."

He looks at her with a dumbfounded expression.

"You think I'm bullshitting with you? Don't write it and you will be the seventh murder that they will be trying to charge me with. You know I don't have no problem murdering. I will kill you just like I killed the other six motherfuckers they are trying to charge me with."

Mr. Antonelli can't believe his ears. As much as he wanted to believe her innocence he knew better. He's shocked that she now has the guts to tell him the truth. "Write it, motherfucker!"

Before now he would try to picture her standing over dead bodies but he couldn't. Right now the vision is crystal clear in his mind. His hands shake barely able to write but he does. After writing her in, he holds the pen afraid to sign. He fears if he does, she will end his life right now.

"Sign it!"

"If you kill me after signing this, you will never get away with it." He feels giving her warning may save his life. "Angel, this is not the right thing to do," he says in a sweet tone. He prays his tone will change her mind.

"Motherfucker, how many times have I told you not to call me that?" She places the barrel of the gun into his wide open mouth. "Do I look like a fucking angel?" She smiles devilishly. "Nah, I'm nobody's angel, but I was a good bitch to you. You fucked that up though. Now sign it."

He signs it with his best penmanship. "Listen I promise you if you change this will or even report any of this to anybody I will find you and murder you. You hear me?" He nods his head. "Yes, I hear you."

She pushes him back to his bedroom, and when she opens the door, she slams him onto the floor. "Both of y'all get the fuck out!" The housekeeper jumps up and leaves with no hesitation. The young woman scrambles to get her clothes. "No, you skeezer bitch. Leave as you are before you can't leave," she says while aiming the gun.

The woman runs out of the room stark naked and empty handed.

Storm looks to the old man. "Your attorney friend warned you about me, but it was already too late. I been nothing but straight up with you for all these years, but you wanna play me? I showed you nothing but respect, but now you gon' see that other side that your bootleg-ass lawyer warned you about. He called me a pretty monster, right?" she asks with a smile. "You brought her out, and if you even think about calling the cops about this, you won't live to see your seventy-ninth birthday. And I mean that shit!"

Storm walks briskly through the corridor, with the will and testament in her hand. She left the old man in his bedroom shivering in fear.

Storm steps onto the porch and looks both ways before closing the door behind her. She slams the door shut and takes off down the steps. Midway down the flight, she catches a glimpse of a shadow to her left. She drops back and draws her gun, preparing for war. Through the darkness, she spots the young woman who is hiding her nudity behind the huge bushes. Storm aims her gun at her. "Bitch, you still here?"

The young woman raises her hands high. "My car keys are inside."

Storm tucks her gun and runs to her car. She gets inside and peels off with no hesitation. At the other end of the block, she busts a U-turn. With a perfect view of the house she sits and watch, wondering if the girl has plans of staying.

Seconds go by and she starts to come down off her high. She notices how wet and swishy her panties are. Her panties are so soaked, she realizes she must have reached a few orgasms in the midst of the action. The way her jeans cling to her legs is indication that the magic fountain had sprouted without her knowing it. With it all happening so fast she didn't notice. The fear that she put in Mr. Antonelli as well as the sense of submission from the woman and the housekeeper has obviously turned her on.

Once it was just her and the old man alone, she realized his fear was getting her excited. She hadn't been this sexually aroused since the night of the robbery/triple homicide. She was getting so hot and horny that she wanted to stay and continue on with instilling fear. She also wanted to force-feed herself to him.

This time it wouldn't have been for him or for the money. It would've been for her own pleasure. In all the years of them indulging, she's never been horny for him, until tonight. The only reason she didn't stay is because she's not sure if the women have called the cops yet.

For once, for as far back as she can remember, her tough exterior has melted. Tears drip down her face. She cries silently before she can no longer hold it in. She's heartbroken. She feels she's been played. She realizes that she's fooled herself all these years into believing that she didn't love him. She would always jokingly say to herself that he sucks her of her youth and she sucks him of his money. Today she understands that it was more to it. Love is involved, and after tonight she can no longer deny it.

Along with the pain from the betrayal, she also feels like an idiot. All these years of protecting herself from men who she felt were only playing games she rarely caught feelings for any of them. No matter how strong their game was, she went into it with her heart guarded, never getting weak. To get played by a no game having, old man is a slap in the face to her. All her life she's strategically dealt with men that she knew she could never fall in love with, just so this would never happen.

> *"The only reason I didn't kill him that night is because I knew I wouldn't get away with it. With all the charges I had against me, I knew the finger would be pointed at me. And that would've meant I wouldn't get my two million dollars. I felt that I was more than deserving of that money and I was going to get it one way or another.*
>
> *"I had been waiting patiently for over five years. Wouldn't be long now. Just had to practice a little more patience. Either he would die of old age or I would pull some strings. One way or another, I wasn't gonna let that money get away from me. I worked for it."*

Storm watches as the young woman, who is now fully dressed comes running out of Mr. Antonelli's house. She gets into her car and backs out of the driveway recklessly. She shoots up the block like a speed demon. Storm is tempted to take off behind her.

Someone has to pay for this pain and heartache that she feels right now. Maybe running her off of the road will take away some of the pain. Killing her will also keep her out of the way. Through her rage she couldn't help but notice how beautiful the girl was. He definitely has great taste.

She also can't deny the amazing body she has. Envisioning her in that house naked in his arms has her jealous and her blood boiling. She's really ready to chase behind her, but she refrains only because she's in the Bentley. She doesn't need anything to lead back to her. Had she been in a rental, she would be trailing the woman ready to get her out of the picture.

The BMW disappears into the darkness. Storm digs into her pocketbook. She stares at the driver's license she holds in her hand. She reads the address over and over until it's locked into her memory bank. She looks to the date of birth and sees that the girl is a couple years younger than her, not even twenty-one.

As she looks to the address again, she begins to think of a plan. At this point, she's ready to remove anything that can get in between her and that two million dollars. She feels she has wasted five years with him. That's in the past and she can't change that, but she can set up the rest of her life. She will be damned if she lets anything get in the way of securing her future.

72

TWO WEEKS LATER

B REEZY HOPS INTO the tinted-out black Cherokee. Upon entrance, he greets Storm with the peace. She bought this Cherokee two days ago. Ever since the incident with Wendy, she has put both of her cars up. She refuses to bring them back out until they get to the root of their problem.

She looks to Breezy with hopes that he has good news for her. This has been a long and drawn out process with them searching for the culprits of that night's activity. Seems as if no one knows anything about it. One thing she knows is the streets will always talk, but for some reason this has been a quiet situation.

"Finally," Breezy says as he sinks into the seat.

Storm sits up with excitement. "What's the deal?"

"My man from Georgia King Village put me up on the scoop," he says as he leans his head onto the headrest. "Said his lil man was posted up right in front doing what he do, when they saw the Maxima and a Cherokee sitting there, just parked."

Storm listens attentively, careful not to miss a word. "Uh-huh."

"So he make the call for his lil niggas to get right thinking niggas about to move on them. Before his lil niggas could get to him, the Maxima pull off. Later on the word get back to him that the niggas tried to carjack a Benz. He found out later the Max was on some stolen shit."

"Please tell me he know who had it?" she asks with desperation.

"Nah, he don't know who had the Max but he got the word of who the Cherokee was."

"Who?" she asks anxiously.

"The homie Big Face," he says as he looks to her for the first time since speaking.

Storm's jaw drops open. "Motherfucker," she says with a smile. "So, that wasn't no carjacking at all, huh?"

Breezy nods his head slowly. "Exactly. They must have spotted your car and followed her there or something, thinking it was you."

"That's what it is then," she replies anxiously. "The war is on."

"Nah, slow your role, Sis. This shit can get crazy. We gotta think this one all the way out. You know if we set it off with him we will be beefing with damn near the whole city. Nigga got hands all over. More arms than an octopus. This shit gotta be done smart."

"Listen, Breeze, that could've easily been me in there. If they would've had it their way, I wouldn't even be here today. This nigga pressed the button. It's go time. No time for all your *48 Laws of Power, 33 Strategies of War* shit. It's just all-out war from here!" she sits in silence for a few seconds. "I don't even know how this nigga look. I need to see his face."

"Slow down. I got this. Just let me handle it. I got the perfect plan to reel him right on in. Just promise me you gon' follow my lead and not do nothing crazy that can cost us all in the end?" he asks. He looks to her pleading for a promise.

Storm is furious. She really hates to give him her word, knowing that she is ready to retaliate the first chance she gets. She shakes her head from side with the rage building up by the second.

"Have I ever let you down before?" he asks.

"Never, but…"

"No buts. Everything after but is bullshit. Give me your word."

"All right. You got my word, but this thing gotta happen ASAP. It's already long and drawn out enough. I ain't gon' be sitting around waiting for them to bust a move to take me the fuck outta here. You gotta couple days to put together whatever plan you think you got. After that time is up, I gotta go for what I know."

Breezy shrugs his shoulders, palms up. "Fair enough. I got this."

73

THE NEXT MORNING

B REEZY AND STORM sit in the upstairs apartment of the work house. While the Mexican women are downstairs busy at work, Breezy is working on his plan. He scrolls through his phone before he finally gets a spark in his eyes. "Got it," he says happily.

He hands the phone over to Storm. "That's him right there." On the phone screen is an Instagram photo of Big Face and a few of his boys. "He the ugly motherfucker in the middle.

Storm's eyes stretch wide open. "Yo, that's the motherfucker from Slicks."

"Huh?" Breezy questions.

"One night, we was over there and this nigga bumped me, was staring at me crazy as shit like he was ready to make a move. I just thought he was on some drunk shit." She sits back for seconds, realizing how it all could've went down differently that night. She would've had no clue of what it was about. "Damn. I was slipping."

"So, how it end though?"

"We just got in the cars and left." It all makes sense to her now. "That's how the fuck he knew about my car. Motherfucker," she says with a smirk.

"I just wonder why he ain't move on you then?" His question leads her to thinking as well. "He could've easily gotten it over with that night."

"Word," she agrees. "That's his Myspace page?" she asks.

"Myspace?" Breezy says, laughing in her face. "Girl step into the new millennium. Nobody got Myspace no more."

"Shit, you know I don't know." Storm may be the only young woman without a social media presence. She can't imagine posting pictures of herself for people to like. For one her low self-esteem won't allow it and of for two, she feels like gangsters on social media is taboo. Breezy taught her that many years ago and she never forgot it.

"I bet you we can catch him there any night of the week," she says with certainty.

"Indeed. I did the homework already. That's their spot. They be heavy in there, like it's their house. We gotta catch him away from there. I got it all figured out though." He pulls out a phone, still in the box. "We gon' have to reel him in."

Storm sits back, wondering what his plan is. "I found out the ugly nigga love them bitches. Just like all ugly niggas do." He cracks a grin. "That's his weakness. I figure we put your homegirl on him and bring him right to us, instead of going looking for him."

"My homegirl who?" she questions.

"The Ethiopian joint. She perfect for this. She not from Jersey, so nobody knows her." As always, Storm loves his way of thinking. "You think she will do it?"

"Do I think she will do it?" Storm replies with arrogance. "She will do whatever the fuck I tell her to."

"Say no more."

* * *

One hour later, with a throw-away, burn out phone that Breezy bought for the occasion, he works away diligently. Beeba sits back with doubt as Breezy creates an Instagram profile for her. They snapped a few random pictures of Beeba for the profile. The photos show very little of her face, purposely. Breezy understands that the face is the last thing a thirst bucket will be looking for.

Most of them are of her locs, her butt, and her long legs. She also has one photo where she's nude, laying on her side. The picture tastefully shows her curves and just the side carriage of her breast, no trace of nipple showing. Overall the profile looks sexy and classy as Beeba really is and not raunchy like the most of the accounts.

Breezy jumped from profile to profile of the people that were tagged in the initial photo and even some of the comments. Eventually he was led to Big Face's page. That is where the obstacle presented itself. His page is blocked and a request has to be sent for him to approve.

"Check it all out before I press the button," Breezy says as he hands over the phone to Beeba. Beeba doesn't like the idea of this, yet she keeps that to herself. She never wants to tell Storm no, with all that she believes Storm has done for her.

Beeba examines her profile until Storm snatches the phone out of her hand. She doesn't like being involved in this. Storm scrolls through the few photos that are posted. "Yeah, you look good as shit in these pictures. He's sure to fall for you." Beeba blushes crazily. "African Goddess," she says as she reads the name that Breezy has given her. "I like the sound of that." She hands Breezy the phone. "It's a go."

"Yeah, sounds clean and classy. Use a ghetto name and he may be cautious. Have her looking like a square from nowhere and he will have his guard down," Breezy says right before he presses the button. He sends the request for Big Face's approval. "Done. Now all we have to do is wait on him. Could take days or weeks but when it happens. We in there."

An alert sounds off in the notifications almost instantly. A smile pops onto Breezy's face. "Or, it could take seconds. He accepted us. These niggas way too easy. They not even a challenge. Chasing that fame got these niggas posting their whole life and their whereabouts, making their life an open book just for likes. Ain't no money involved. These niggas don't wanna be rich. They just wanna be famous," he says while shaking his head.

"Motherfucker got seven thousand photos posted," he says as he scrolls through every photo looking for a lead. "What part of the game is that when gangbanging killers feel comfortable enough to take pictures for the world to see?" He studies the houses to see if maybe he can find where he lives. He studies the faces of every woman he's in pictures with. He studies the faces of any old person and any baby in the pictures. "And this is why you will never catch me on social media," he says as he continues searching. "This gon' be fun, too." Back to back alerts sound off. He reads the notifications and sees that Big Face has liked every picture posted under the profile. "Yeah we got him. Just liked them all."

"Go in for the kill," Storm says.

"Not yet. We don't want to come across as desperate as he is. Let's slow roll with this, and rock him to sleep. Patience. This won't take long at all."

74

ONE WEEK LATER

A TTORNEY TONY AUSTIN sits in the courtroom in front of the honorable judge, Figari. For the very first time in a long time, Tony is early for court. He realizes this case is one of his tougher ones and doesn't need his huge ego to get in the way and mess things up by pissing the judge off. He needs to everything to be in the proper perspective for this one if he expects a win.

Tony has been working hard on this case, for the old man's sake. Despite his personal feelings toward Storm, she's still a client. On top of that, just like with any other case, his reputation is on the line. He will never let personal feelings get in the way of business.

Just a few days ago he was able to get a speedy court date for a status conference. Today he will be putting in a motion to suppress the initial murder case for lack of evidence. With Kirah being dead, they have no witnesses. Although the prosecutor and a host of others feel that Storm has murdered her to keep her from coming to court and testifying, they don't have proof.

Regardless of anyone's personal beliefs, everyone knows without proof or a witness, there is no case. One thing that Tony has on his side when it comes to this motion is he's sure the prosecution fears going to trial with him. In trial is when he makes a mockery of them and really shows them what he's made of.

Tony sighs with frustration as he looks at his watch again. The first time in history that he's ever beat his client into the courtroom. He's angered believing that Storm is not taking his time seriously. He looks over his shoulder at Mr. Antonelli who shrugs his shoulders.

Mr. Antonelli has been calling her since last night and hasn't gotten an answer or return call. He fears that she may have skipped bail on him. He would hate to lose two million dollars but can't help but to think that maybe that will get her out of his life. If the bail money will buy her out, then he's willing to take the loss. Something tells him that even if she doesn't show up, she still won't leave him alone. He's been living in fear of her for what seems like an eternity and he just wants it to end.

Tony plays it cool like he has everything under control. The last thing he wants is for the people to know that he hasn't heard from his client. He looks to the young man sitting next to him with a confident smile. The young man, his protégé, wouldn't be recognized by his own family due to his transformation.

The thuggish-looking young man with the wild afro is no longer. Today he sits in a suit almost as fine as the one that Tony is wearing. The curly afro he wore until yesterday is now the typical wavy top, tapered side haircut that the Wall Street brokers sport. Tony has even lent him one of his classiest watches and best briefcases for the occasion.

"So, you ready, young fella?" Tony asks.

"I don't know, man," the young man admits.

"What you mean, you don't know? We don't deal with doubt. Listen, in my days as an amateur boxer, my trainer told me that most fighters who lose, lose in the locker room long before the fight. If you think you can't win, you won't win."

Tony plants a comforting hand on the young man's shoulder. "I know you're a winner. I saw that in you from day one, and that is why I took you up under my wing. That and you come from good stock.

"You come from the Banks brothers' bloodline, so I already know how you built. They don't breed mutts. When the book writer put his stamp of approval on somebody, I know not to question it because he and his brother rarely stamp anybody. You're their younger cousin, so y'all share the same blood. Correct?"

"Yes, sir," the young man replies. Tony's speech makes him feel a hundred percent more confident.

"Now that's what I want to hear. Remember this… I'm getting old. I'm teaching you everything I know because, when I fall back, I want to feel comfortable that you will hold down the firm. I'm passing the torch to you. You got next."

"Mr. Austin, I thank you for this opportunity. I promise you. I won't let you down."

Deep frustration sets on the judge's face. "Uh, Attorney Austin. We can't wait any longer. Are you ready to proceed?"

Without the presence of his client, he hates to start, but his arrogance won't let him admit he doesn't know her whereabouts. Tony taps his protégé underneath the table. The young man stands up with all the confidence he has. "Your Honor, my name is Anthony James, I represent, Austin Law Group, who represents the defendant Angelica Hill." He stands tall and firm.

"All fine and well," the judge says. "I see no sign of your client though. Is Ms. Hill present?"

Ironically at the mention of her name, the double doors swing open wildly. Everyone's attention is captured by Storm who struts down the aisle, dressed in a classy skirt suit and high heel pumps. The ruffled satin blouse has her looking more like the first lady of the United States than the cold killer that she really is. Storm looks so amazing that the man that she's accompanied by is barely noticed.

Tony is the only one who pays notice to the man and knows exactly who he is. The young, Caucasian man is quite shabby in appearance in Tony's eyes. A traditional Brooks Brothers blue blazer, crisp white dress shirt, beige khakis and turned over Rockport, soft bottoms makes him look like a pauper. His hair is full of curly locks and his face is clean shaven. He appears to be no older than thirty years of age.

The young man looks to Tony with a viciousness in his eyes. Tony smirks as if he's a joke. At the sight of this man, Tony has already read the play. Tony has nothing against the man but for some reason he hates Tony's guts.

The young man is an up and coming attorney that wants Tony's spot. He's only been practicing for a few years, but already he's been compared to Tony with his relentlessness in the courtroom. The young attorney has climbed the ranks positioning himself as the second best attorney in the state, with Tony being the number one guy. The young man has plans of taking that spot and has told Tony on many occasions. When Tony hears the young man compared to himself, he feels like Michael Jordan does when the younger players are compared to him. He feels with all the work that he's put in the game of law, there's no way a kid who hasn't made his bones should be mentioned in the same sentence. He understands it all though. There comes a time in life when the people get tired of watching the same man win. They will get so tired of the champ's name that they will be quick to replace him with just anyone.

Tony smiles as he thinks to himself. "Dirty, bitch," he mumbles under his breath.

The young man speaks as he's walking. "Your Honor, Aharon Levy, I've recently been hired as legal representation for Ms. Angelica Hill. May I approach?"

The judge, the prosecutor and even the court stenographer all look at Tony with disbelief. This can't be happening to the great Tony Austin. The man digs into his briefcase and hands over documents.

The judge flashes a smile, loving what is happening right now. He hates Tony so much and loves the opportunity to get one up on him. The judge calls the prosecutor over and they include him on the details of their conversation. At this point, it's Tony who is the outsider. Still he plays it cool as a fan.

The judge speaks. "Attorney Austin, can you approach for a sidebar conference?"

Tony leans back in his seat with his normal amount of cockiness. This is quite surprising to the people, under the circumstances. "Your Honor, I respectfully ask you to read it for the record. As there is no need for a sidebar," Tony says loud and clear.

After thinking long and hard, Storm decided it's at her best interest to find an attorney that she trusts. She feels the way the old man has been acting toward her shows how they feel about her. She feels she would be a fool to have her life in their hands at this point, especially with her not knowing if Mr. Antonelli has told Tony about the incident at his house and her forcing him to sign the will.

She truly doesn't believe he would risk his life by telling, but she can't take a chance like that. After researching the best attorneys in Jersey, this man's name came up as number two. She already has the number one guy who she hates and doesn't trust so she feels the number two guy will be her best bet. She's already paid the new attorney fifty thousand for her defense.

The entire courtroom is shocked at what's going on. They are all expecting to see Tony pitch a fit. Tony's protégé looks to him quite baffled. Tony looks to him and flashes a wink of reassurance.

"Mr. Austin, I have a letter of representation superseding Austin's Law Group as representation of the defendant Angelica Hill. You have been dismissed off the case," he says with satisfaction. "Do you wish to add something onto the record?"

"Nah," he replies nonchalantly. "It's all been said."

"Okay, Mr. Austin, you are free to go," says the judge.

Tony stands up from his seat and grabs his briefcase from the table. He taps his protégé. "Let's go." He looks to the judge. "Have a great day, Your Honor." He walks over to Storm and her new attorney who are both watching his every move. They are expecting him to be irate, but he's quite the opposite.

He places his hand over his brow and salutes the young attorney. He shakes the attorney's hand firmly. "Good luck." He looks to Storm. "I wish you well," he says like the good sport that he is not. Storm rolls her eyes without even a thank you. Tony diddy bops up the aisle with his protégé at his heels.

* * *

Minutes later, Tony and his protégé wait in the parking lot for the car. The young man seems to be taking this matter harder than Tony. His head hangs low in defeat. It hurts him to have witnessed his idol crushed in this manner.

"Mr. Austin, can I ask how you were able to take that loss so well? Like didn't it bother you that you were fired in front of all those people? I know you saw the smiles on their faces."

Tony chuckles. "Young fella, as long as you're in the game, suited up and prepared to play your hardest, you can never take a loss. Fuck what the scoreboard says," he says with passion. "In the game of life, we can't win them all and we won't win them all.

"What separates us from losers is our mindset. Losers fear losing and they play with doubt. We play to win, determined to win, but if by chance we don't, we learn. You win like a man, and you lose like a man. The best part of falling like a true man is the ability to stand back up like a man and still have the respect and honor of the people. More important, to still have respect for yourself. Honestly, I don't even pay attention to the scoreboard. I just play the game. Let the people on the sideline keep score. That's what they are there for."

The young man sits back slowly sipping on the drink that Tony has dropped on him. The parking attendant pulls up in the black Maserati Gran Turismo Spyder. The car is stopped short right in front of them. The top is dropped, giving all the privilege of viewing the black interior which is piped out in subtle red trimming.

All the people standing around waiting for their cars watch in admiration. Tony signals his protege to take the wheel. The young man diddy-bops to the driver's side, trying hard to conceal his excitement. They pull their suit jackets off and place them onto the back seats before getting in.

Tony looks to the young man who has a spark in his eyes. He feels Tony has passed him the baton. "You like the attention?" Tony asks. "I can see it in your eyes."

"I love it," the young man replies.

"Get used to it. This is just the beginning." Tony immediately pulls two cigars from the console and hands one to the young man. After Tony lights the stick for him, he doesn't hesitate to spark up his own. He inhales and blows a huge ring into the sky. "A celebration stick," Tony says with a smile. The young man takes a small but cautious puff.

"You, young fella, saw it as a loss, but I saw it as her doing us a favor. No doubt in my mind, with us on the case, she would've beat the charges, no matter the odds. But to beat that case and have her around to torture my good friend for the rest of his life, who would be the winner? My good friend is late into the last quarter of the game.

"We are young and fly and we got time to lose and learn. Him, he's too old to learn. At this late second on the shot clock, he can't learn from his mistakes. He can only lose. I'm glad she kicked me off the case, so I wouldn't be the cause of his losing streak and witness his legacy be destroyed by getting blown out in the last quarter."

By now the young man is dizzy and drunk from the back to back drinks Tony has dropped on him. He sits back comatose. Tony fiddles with his radio until he finds his selection of music. He raises the volume and Michael Franks's "Tiger in the Rain" rips from the speakers and seeps into the air as the young man cruises through the parking lot, marinating in the beginning of his own success.

"He's a tiger in the rain!" Tony sings along with happiness. Even in defeat, today has been victorious for him.

75

11:30 P.M.

B EEBA STANDS IN the hallway of the raggedy apartment building here on Fourth Avenue and Oraton Parkway. The glass front is shattered so badly that she has to peek outside through a small corner of the window. Behind the glass, she looks amazing, dressed in a long white linen dress that accents her curves. On her head, she wears a silk scarf that covers her locks as well as shields her face. The scarf adds a lovely sense of mystique to her exotic appearance.

A Jeep Cherokee pulls up and parks right in front of the apartment building. Beeba inhales deeply. Today is the day that she's been dreading. In the Cherokee is Big Face. After many weeks of online chatting, today is the first time they will see each other in person.

Breezy operated the page for Beeba all the while. A few likes of his pictures with a few kissy face emojis, and he fell for the bait. He dove into the inbox head first. He made several attempts for them to link up, but Breezy was careful to stall, so he would become eager. Last night he decided the time is now and he had Big Face where he wanted him; well, Beeba had him where she needed him. They set up the date and here they are.

Beeba steps out of the building looking way too elegant to be walking out of such a dump. Big Face believes this is where she lives, but this is really her first time ever seeing this place. Breezy chose this place for several reasons. The darkness of the area is perfect. Also, it's convenient being that the highway is two hundred feet away.

Big Face watches in awe as she moves down the path toward him. In all of his life, he's never seen a woman who looks so godly. She's so much different from the rest of the girls he deals with. As he sits here, he doubts if he's even on her level. Either way, it's way too late for doubt because he's here now.

He hits the power lock and Beeba stands there with a disturbed look on her face. He rolls the window down. "Get in."

"I'm used to doors being opened for me," she says with a hint of attitude. She gets in and slams the door. The smell of her perfume fills the truck immediately. Big Face just stares at her in awe of her beauty. Her skin glows like a chocolate angel.

"Damn! We finally face to face. I was starting to think you was catfishing me," he says as a joke.

"Catfish?" she asks as if she has no clue of the term. "What is that?"

"Never mind," he says, laughing it off.

"So do I look like my pictures?" she asks. "It's hot in here," she says as she cracks the window. "So do I?" She holds her arms open for him to view all of her.

"You look better. Your pictures don't do you no justice. Damn," he says.

"Why, thank you," she replies.

Beeba's heart speeds up as she thinks of all that is expected of her. Suddenly he makes the move that was predicted. "Can I get a hug? Damn! You had me waiting for you for weeks. It's the least you could do."

He hugs her tightly and goes on to rubbing all over her back, romantically. Beeba moans as if his petting is soothing. Just as he's about to pull away, she tightens her grip on him. "Damn, you smell good," she says. She takes a huge sniff of his neck.

Four car lengths behind is Storm's Cherokee. In the driver's seat is Mud, and in the passenger's seat, there's Breezy. Storm is seated in the back. Both Storm and Breezy have their guns gripped in their hands. They watch closely as Beeba's hand hangs from the passenger's window.

"Showtime," Breezy shouts. "There go the sign."

She throws two fingers up, and Mud pulls out of the parking space with the lights out. In three-seconds flat, the Cherokees are parked side by side. Breezy dashes out of the passenger's seat gun in hand and Storm is at his heels.

Big Face, in the middle of the hug, peeks over his shoulder. His heart skips a beat as he attempts to get out of hug. Beeba grips him tightly. She lets go once the door is opened and the gun is aimed at Big Face's head.

Storm snatches the door open for Beeba to exit. Before she's out of the Jeep Breezy's gun sounds off.

Boc!

Blood splashes everywhere including the back of Beeba's white dress. Beeba stops at the curb, not able to look away from the sight.

Big Face's body lays over the console, head on the passenger's seat. It's obvious that he's already dead, but of course that's not enough for Storm. She places the gun onto his temple and lets the shots rip.

Blocka! Blocka! Blocka!

"Let's go!" Breezy shouts, snapping Storm out of her zone. Beeba, still in a trance, has to be dragged away from the Cherokee. Breezy hops back into the front seat while Storm forces Beeba into the backseat in front of her. Once they are in, Mud speeds off. At the top of the hill, he turns onto the parkway and heads onto the perfect getaway.

* * *

An hour later, the crew cruises through Branch Brook Park in Breezy's car. With it being so late, there's almost no traffic in the park. They ride in silence as they all entertain their own thoughts.

Beeba, thinking the hardest, hasn't said a word since the incident. It baffles her how she managed to get caught up in all of this. She prays that this doesn't come back to haunt her. Her newfound life of adventure seems to be getting crazier by the day. It's hard to believe that just a few months ago she lived an almost regular life with her husband.

While Storm drives, Breezy is busy on the phone, deleting Beeba's Instagram account. Once he's done, he speaks. "Pull over right here," he commands.

Storm stops the car on the dime. Breezy hops out and runs over to the ledge of the lake. He draws back and throws the phone as high as he can. He watches as the phone makes a huge splash in the water a couple hundred feet away from him. He races back to the car, gets in and Storm cruises off moderately.

He looks to Storm as she's driving. "Patience and strategy wins the war," he says before looking away from her. "No war is ever won fighting with emotion."

76

LAS VEGAS NEVADA
DECEMBER 8, 2012

APPROXIMATELY FOUR MONTHS have passed, and things have only gotten better for Storm. Business has picked up drastically. As far as the situation with Big Face, nothing has ever come back to them. The streets have charged his murder as a revenge for the dirt that he's done in them. With all that he's dished out, it's impossible for anyone to track his death down to one culprit. Like many deaths in the hood, his will go unsolved and charged to the game.

The only thing that could make Storm's life better is if those charges were not hanging over her head. No matter how much she's enjoying her life, those charges always have a way of raining on her parade. Not a minute of the day goes by without her being reminded that one day all of her good times could possibly come to an end. Her trial starts in a couple of weeks and knowing that is quite stressful for her.

The biggest damper on her spirit comes from Mr. Antonelli. Things haven't gotten any better between them. He's even more distant with her these days. She's sure that, if she wasn't forcing him to see her, he wouldn't. She stays at his house more than she ever did. Her reason for being there is to keep him close and keep watch on him. She continuously drops threats on him, so he doesn't forget that she's promised to end his life if he ever went to the authorities on her. He only deals with her out of fear.

As far as business goes, Toy has been doing a great job at getting her consistent work through the casinos. Storm has a total of twenty Mexican women on her team and that's enough to rake in the dough. She has two houses to work from now and they both are doing well. Outside of having to switch apartments ever so often, she has no complaints. A few times local police have gotten onto them where they had to pick up and move.

Luckily, only three of her girls have been arrested. One morning the police kicked in one of her spots and caught the two girls dead in the act. The girls and the tricks were arrested and taken into custody. The girls held up well under pressure, never giving her up or the traffickers.

They knew what trouble they would get in if they opened their mouths, so they said not a word. After being released on petty charges, Storm sent them back to Esto just to keep them cool. He traded her three girls in their places. Storm believes they were sent back to Mexico, but they could have easily been just shipped over to New York to work. Once they get shipped her they get shuffled through the pipeline.

Storm and her Angels as she now calls them, just arrived here this morning. With this being the weekend of the Manny Pacquiao versus Juan Manuel Marquez fight, she's sure the money will be flowing in abundance. All walks of life will be present, and she has something for everyone.

She has Toy and Wendy, her faithful riders with her, and she has full confidence that they will get to the money as they always have. She also has Beeba with her. Beeba is now her top earner. Beeba has found a way to put that murder she was an accomplice to behind her. She has accepted her new life and can't imagine going back home to her husband.

From day one, Storm knew Beeba had it in her to be great. Beeba has reached a level of productivity that Storm is even surprised by. Storm doesn't even have to play the mind games with her to keep her onboard. Addicted to big money and a luxurious life that her husband once provided, she works her hardest to maintain her prestigious lifestyle.

It's been six months and she hasn't missed a beat. Through their network, she's able to provide more for herself than her husband ever provided for her. He still calls and begs her to come home every now and again but never once does he step foot anywhere near them. Although she's still married to him on paper, their marriage is over. She's now married to the game.

Storm only brought half of her stable of Mexican women with her. The other half she left divided in her two whore houses. She has Mud and his boy in the houses to watch over them. She has faith that they can hold it down without her.

Just in case those women aren't enough to fulfill every man's sexual cravings and desires, she's brought along five strippers. Normally she wouldn't entertain such raunchy and ghetto talent, but she's sure the young drug dealers will eat them up. She made sure to bring the biggest booties she could find in the city of Newark. All in all, with eighteen women on deck, she's positive this will be the most profitable weekend of her career.

She is sure that anybody who is somebody will be here this weekend and she couldn't come short handed. She packed her best attire, her finest jewelry, and even had her car shipped down here for the occasion. This weekend she plans to show her ass like she's never done before. She tells herself this could easily be her last big event with her murder trial starting soon. If by chance it goes against her favor, at least she will have lifelong memories.

With Mr. Antonelli hating her guts now, she often thinks that he's just waiting for her to go away to prison, so he can go on with his life without her. She believes she made the best decision by firing Tony and hiring the new attorney. She can't help but wonder if Tony would have done a better job at her defense. She couldn't take that chance though. That little voice in her head tells her that Tony was just waiting to throw her to the wolves, and would have lost her case intentionally. Whenever she thinks like that, she's tempted to reach out and touch him. A few times she's thought of seeking revenge for what she thinks he may have had planned for her and her future.

The bright lights on South Las Vegas Boulevard are hypnotizing. Storm walks from her hotel on her way to the MGM Grand. She's draped in her thirty-thousand dollar, black sheared mink, swing jacket, which is accented by Chinchilla. The Vegas weather is way too hot for fur but she couldn't resist. This coat is the most expensive coat that she's brought for herself, and this is the perfect occasion for her to show it off. Just to not look way extra, she dressed the fur down with a basic black sleeveless jumpsuit and black Chanel sneakers.

At ten o'clock at night, the sidewalks are crowded with barely enough space for her to walk. The streets are still busy because the undercard fights are still going on. The traffic on the streets is bumper to bumper with exotic cars. She would love to be in that lineup of traffic, gracing the streets, but it's senseless being that her hotel is a few doors down. Besides, she's played the scene so hard earlier that she's sure many will remember.

She noticed many Bentleys filled with women drivers and has charged most of the women as merely wives of celebrities. The others who were extra in their demeanor, she charged off as the wives of the drug dealers. As many of them as she's seen, she doubts if any of them are bosses in their own right, who made their money off their own muscle. That makes her proud be one of the biggest boss bitches of them all.

A few steps away from the MGM Grand, she slides in between a group of people walking toward her. Unsuspectedly her hand is grabbed from behind. This is nothing new to her being that men having been tugging at her ever since she got here. She snatches away as she turns around, expecting it to be another man trying to push up on her, she's wrong in her way of thinking.

The face she sees is one that she never expected to see again. "Small world," the man says with a sarcastic smile. "Never thought we would run into each other again, huh?"

Never in a million years did she expect this. Her heart pounds as the man from Ohio, Money Sal stands face to face with her. She's caught by total surprise. So much has happened in her life since then that she's forgotten all about him and the thirty grand that she stole from his house. It's obvious that he hasn't forgotten.

He links his arms around hers and shoves her along. "Told your little funny looking ass I would eventually catch back up with you. Didn't think you would ever see me again, did you? You said it though, 'life is funny like that,'" he says with a grin. "Now walk, bitch. Make a false move, and I will blast your ass right here," he threatens as he shoves a gun into her side. With their bodies being so close, the gun can't be seen.

As she's being shoved along, she peeps game. Two other men are behind them at their heels. She walks along with her heart racing. The further they get from the MGM Grand, the lighter the foot traffic becomes. She's sure they are trying to get her away from the crowd to do whatever it is that they plan to do to her.

She looks around, hoping that someone sees what's going on, but everyone seems to be moving along about their merry own business. She inhales deeply just to regulate her pounding heart. She looks into the distance and can only see less than a handful of people. That to her is a sign that she's doomed.

She peeks behind her and the two men behind them are even closer. "Walk bitch. Don't turn around. Keep your eyes in front of you," Money Sal says while shoving his gun into her ribs. The handful of people pass them without looking their way. Seems like there's not another soul in front of them.

With no other alternative for safety, she slides her hand into her left pocket. She realizes the chance that she's about to take but feels hopeless to the matter. She can either submit and let them take her somewhere to finish her off, or she can take her chances and go for what she knows. She chooses the latter.

"Now," she mumbles to herself. She peeks over to the man to the left of them who is stepping with his eyes ahead of him. She quickly peeks over her shoulder at the men behind them just to see how close they are. She realizes they are so close that she has no room for error.

Her reasoning for having her car shipped here wasn't only to show the car off. She had the car shipped with two guns in her stash box. From the looks of it, that may be one of the smartest decisions she's made in a long time. If she's lucky that decision will save her life. If not...

She quickly plans her move and realizes it's now or never. She squeezes the trigger of the gun while still inside her coat pocket.

Blocka! Blocka!

Money Sal lets her go and stumbles backwards. Caught by total surprise he doesn't know where the gunfire has come from. She draws the gun from her pocket and fires again quickly.

Blocka!

The sight of the gun leads the man in the front to flee. Money Sal stumbles backwards clumsily as he grabs hold of his abdomen. From his hands falls a cellphone in which he was bluffing to be a gun.

She spins around to the men behind her, and to her surprise they flee away with fear. She fires at them as they are running away from her.

Blocka! Blocka! Blocka!

One man tumbles forward while the other continues running for his life. Storm is so caught up in her zone that she doesn't hear the screams of the people who are scattering like roaches. She doesn't hear or see them. She takes a few steps toward the man who lays flat on his face. She dumps two shots into the back of his head.

Blocka! Blocka! Blocka!

She sees Money Sal attempting to crawl away and runs over to him. As he's on all fours, she has a clear shot at the top of his head. She aims… she squeezes.

Blocka!

The impact of the bullet makes his neck swing forward like a sling shot. His head and body fold onto the concrete.

Just as she's about to make her getaway she hears, "Freeze!"

That word snaps her out of her zone. She stops in her tracks, and all she can think of is going to jail for another double homicide. With lightning speed, she turns around into the direction the voice came from, with her finger already mashing the trigger. Before she can even see his face, she squeezes.

Blocka!

The young white cop falls to his knees before, crumbling over.

The sirens are coming from every direction, but she can't hear them. The dead bodies lying at her feet has her adrenaline racing.

She shakes her head to gather herself, and when she comes to, she finds herself surrounded by police in every direction. No way does she plan to be captured. She realizes she's in too deep. She's come too far for it to end like this.

She takes a few steps back to find a wall to place herself against. This is war, a wide open battlefield and she's a warrior. She takes a few more steps backward, aiming her gun from side to side to keep the cops at bay. Totally and unsuspectedly, she's blindsided by an impact that feels like a Mac truck. She's tackled to the ground from behind by a hero cop that she never saw.

The cop wrestles her, overpowering her. He pries the gun from her hand, and that is when they all come in. All she can see from the ground is police shoes, which seem to be about a hundred of them. She puts up some resistance but that doesn't stop her arms from being placed behind her back. Once she's handcuffed, she receives the worse beating of her life.

Loud sirens roar in the air. With her eyes swollen shut, she can't see a thing. She's picked up from the ground and dragged away. She's thrown into the back of the police car and the door is slammed shut.

Everything seems to be moving in slow motion. Through bloody, swollen shut eyes, all she can see is flashing lights. The flashing lights ricochet and bounce off the many lights that illuminate the huge buildings of the Vegas skyline. Even through partial vision she can see that her freedom is gone.

The police have the area roped off. White sheets covering three bodies tells Storm that she's added three more murders onto her jacket. Swarms of people are everywhere. The feature attraction is the cop car that she sits in. They peek nosily into the car, trying to see who is responsible for the mayhem. She knew this would be a big night but never did she think she would be the main event.

77

"No one could've ever told me I would've ever ended up living this type of life. I'm the daughter of a pastor, the granddaughter of a pastor. As a child I wanted to be a pastor. I was groomed to be one in my early childhood."

ELEVEN-YEAR-OLD ANGELICA STANDS at the pulpit dressed in her best Sunday dress. She paces back and forth as she wipes the perspiration from her forehead with a handkerchief. She daps the corners of her mouth with the handkerchief as she looks down at her bible. She peeks up, staring at the congregation.

"Y'all don't hear me though," she says, smiling from ear to ear.

"Preach!" a woman shouts from the back of the small church.

"Every first Sunday, in Sunday school, they would let me preach a sermon that I prepared myself."

Young Angelica has one hand in the air, finger pointing to the ceiling. The congregation are all standing to their feet and clapping.

Angelica continues on with her sermon. "For I am persuaded that neither death, nor life, nor angels, nor principles, nor powers, nor things to come, nor height, nor depth, nor any creatures shall be able to separate us from the love of God which is in Christ Jesus Lord!"

"Amen!" a man shouts from the first row.

Angelica jumps for joy excitedly, hands stretched upward before falling backwards. She stumbles over the few chairs that are lined up behind her before falling onto her back. All the members of the congregation become hysterical. They run to the front of the church, crowding her.

"And it all went blank from there. The next thing I know I woke up in a hospital hooked up to many machines with my whole family surrounding me. I didn't know what happened, but from the looks on their faces it couldn't be of any good."

Angelica lays in the hospital bed, barely conscious. Her mother sits at her side, holding a bible close to her heart. Her father and her little brother sit on the other side of her.

Angelica looks up into her father's eyes. "Daddy, what happened?" She looks to the machines that are hooked up to her. "What's wrong with me?"

"My Angel, you have suffered a heart attack."

Angelica doesn't know much about heart attacks except that everyone she's ever heard of having one has died. Fear settles in her bright and innocent eyes. "Heart attack? Am I going to die?"

"No, baby," he replies. "You are an angel protected by God."

A doctor enters the room and Angelica's father and mother bum-rush him. Their conversation is not loud enough for her to hear, but the sadness on their faces speaks volumes.

"Doc, will she ever be the same?"

Sadness covers the doctor's face. "Sir, I'm afraid that she has suffered severe heart failure. The only thing that will save her young life is a heart transplant."

"Heart transplant?" her mom asks. She breaks out into tears.

"I'm afraid that is the only answer," the doctor replies.

"From that point on my whole life changed. I felt as if my childhood had been stolen from me. No more basketball or bike riding or even running. My parents tried to protect me from every little thing. Their overprotecting and crowding later led me to run away and never look back.

"For the life of me, I couldn't understand why that was happening to me. I was always told that I was one of God's Angels, so if I was, why was God putting me through that? I started resenting God and I hated to be called Angel from that point on. To me an Angel was just a reminder of the torture that I had gone through and how when I needed God most he wasn't there for me. I felt that he abandoned me.

"A few months passed and finally our prayers were answered."

Angelica's mother and father sit at a desk across from a woman dressed in a tailored fit, pin-striped business suit. The woman is hospital administration. Angelica's mother looks up to the ceiling. "Thank you, Jesus!"

Her father lowers his head in humility as he drops a silent thank you to God. He looks up with a huge smile on his face. The woman wears a stone cold look on her face but she smiles with her eyes. "So, when can we get on with the procedure?"

"I remember it like it was just yesterday. I was terrified and confused as they rolled me down the hall on the stretcher. I remember looking into my daddy's eyes looking for confirmation but the look in his eyes didn't give me any."

Angelica lie on the stretcher as she's being wheeled through the hospital hallway. She's wearing a hospital gown and bouffant cap on her head, prepared for surgery. Her mother on one side of the stretcher holding her hand as her Dad walks along with his hand on her shoulder. The stretcher is stopped short at the double doors. Angelica's mother bends over and kisses her on the forehead.

Her father leans over close to her. "My daughter," he whispers. "I know that you're afraid right now, but you must be brave. This is for the better. After this you will be like new again and we will live happily ever after."

"You promise?" Angelica asks with no sign of hope or faith in her eyes. The uncertainty on his face is a look that she will never forget.

"I promise."

* * *

Hours later, Angelica lays in the hospital bed, in the recovery room. She's hooked up to machines. Her mother sits at the foot of the bed reading from her Bible while her father paces back and forth around the room. Angelica opens her eyes slightly in a groggy state just as the doctor is walking into the room.

Her mother looks up from her bible and finds Angelica's eyes open. She double takes at Angelica before looking up to the ceiling with her hands in a praying position. She thanks God over and over again.

"All I remember is waking up in a dreamlike state hooked up to machines. For the life of me I couldn't figure out why or even how I got there. It was all a blur."

Angelica looks down at herself as her mother kisses her gently on the forehead. Her father holds her hand with a tight grip. "My Angel, you pulled it through," he says.

Angelica's little brother comes into the room, leading a pack of a few of the members of the church. Her brother curls up next to her, wrapping his arms around her neck. He's so happy to see his big sister. She's his idol. The members of the church surround the bed, hands clasped together in prayer.

After the brief prayer session ends, the doctor walks over to the bed and stands over Angelica. "Congratulations, Angel. You pulled it through successfully. You're such a brave and courageous young lady." He extends his hand for hers. They lock hands. "Here's to new life!"

"And then it all started coming back to me. I realized that the heart transplant had just taken place."

As the priest wipes his eyeglasses, he peeks up at Angelica with a look of true concern. "And how did you feel about all that had taken place?"

A confused expression crosses her face. "Well, at that time I was too young to actually understand how blessed I was. But it was all so strange. I felt weird, like cold and empty inside. I didn't feel like myself."

The priest listens attentively before interjecting. "The donor of the heart, by chance do you know who he or she was? Did you ever meet the family?"

"You know, those thoughts I lived with all of my adult life. For some strange reason, the information was never revealed. I've always felt like I was living with a stranger inside of me. I always wondered what type of person he or she was. It wasn't till I got here in this place that I did some research." A starry look fills her eyes, coupled with a grin. "And this is what I found out. Listen closely because this is where it gets good."

NORTH PHILADELPHIA, 2005

A shabby, blond dread head albino steps out of an abandoned house. He stops short with a shocked expression on his face. The house is surrounded by police whom all have their weapons drawn. "Calvin Collins, don't move!" is shouted through the bullhorn.

The dread headed albino backs up with caution, peeking around attentively. He stumbles clumsily over a row of garbage cans that are lined up behind him.

"Calvin Collins, we have you surrounded! It's over! Put your hands in the air and slowly drop to your knees!"

"I learned that a string of robbery/homicides led the detectives back to him."

The albino ducks behind two garbage cans as he draws his gun from his waistband. He lifts his head up slightly, peeking over the lid of the can. Two detectives run toward him with their weapons drawn. The albino raises his gun in the air and fires.

Boc! Boc! Boc! Boc!

The first detective stumbles backward from the impact of the bullet crashing into his bulletproof vest. The second detective stumbles over onto his side, holding his thigh. A detective standing off to the side, behind an open car door has a clear shot in the alley and takes it. He fires three consecutive rounds.

Blocka! Blocka! Blocka!

The albino stands up and quickly fires a shot of his own.

Boc! Boc! Boc!

He quickly ducks low for his safety. The detective ducks low behind the car in a nick of time. The car window shatters into pieces.

The albino peers around and notices that the street is now swarming with police with riot gear on. That doesn't scare him one bit. In fact it excites him. He stands up and fires two shots.

Boc! Boc!

As he's ducking down three shots come back at him.

Blocka! Blocka! Blocka!

The bullets whiz past his head and ricochet off the wall behind him. He looks over his shoulder at the chipped aluminum siding which is only inches away from his head. He peeks around quickly, looking for a better shield. He spots an old refrigerator on the other side of the alley.

"Calvin, drop your weapon!"

The albino's eyes peer from side to side, in between two garbage cans. "Never!" he shouts back at them with determination.

The detective places the bullhorn to his mouth. "You will never," he manages to say before the sound of gunfire rips through the air.

Boc! Boc!

Both bullets bounce off the hood of the car. The detective ducks for safety.

The albino runs across the alley as he squeezes two shots.

Boc! Boc!

He makes it to the refrigerator where he hides behind it, standing tall. The sound of a helicopter hovers in the air. He looks up and sees it's a news helicopter but in his sick and deranged mind, he believes it to be the opposing army's copter. His days as a Marine veteran are relived. He aims at the copter and fires.

Boc! Boc! Boc!

After firing, he rolls over and lays flat on his stomach. He reaches over and pulls a sink closer to him, using it as another shield. He has himself boxed in.

In his mind, bombs sound off. He clasps both hands over his ears with his eyes closed. He has a history of suffering from post-traumatic stress disorder from the war he was in. "Aggghh!" he screams as he relives it. A huge explosion takes place only in his mind. He envisions his soldier buddy a few feet from him step onto a landmine. "No!" he screams as he attempts to shake away the vision. He screams out names and code words. Before his eyes he sees a war battlefield, with the opposing army and not the police that are actually here. He leans against the wall, gun in the air. He hits the lever and the cartridge drops into his hand. He quickly counts the rounds that he has left before slamming the cartridge back into the gun. He peeks to the front of the alley and the back, and in his mind he sees soldiers coming at him, instead of the cops. They have him trapped. He peeks back and forth nervously.

"It's all or nothing," he says to himself. "They'll never take me alive." He stands up and fires a shot at the front of the alley and one to the back of the alley.

Up overhead, two snipers lie on their bellies on top of neighboring buildings. Both of their assault rifles are aimed downward. Just as the albino is looking around planning his next attack, the sound of two shots from the rifles rip through the air. The albino collapses, falling onto his face.

* * *

Hours Later, two doctors stand across from each other in an operating room. On the stretcher in between them is the dead albino. One doctor shakes his head in pity as he explains the details to the other doctor, "An all-out war for fifteen minutes before snipers took him out." He points to the hole in the corpse's head.

"Oh! Is this the wack job, Killer Cal, that was all over the news? Oh and how many dead women did they find in his home?"

"In total, seven. One being his ex-wife who apparently cheated on him ten years ago. He just decided to repay her after all those years. Abducted her from her home after murdering her current husband. He slept with the corpse in the bed with him for months. Even had sexual intercourse with her. The other six women were crack whores whom he murdered after sex, all by strangulation. Some of them had been in the closet dead for close to a year. They all had one thing in common."

"And what was that?" the doctor asks curiously.

They all shared the same complexion. All high-yellow complexioned women. It's apparent that because of his wife he had a thing against all women of that complexion."

"Wow," the doctor sighs in disbelief. "Yeah, a real wack job. So, what are you doing now?"

"Extracting the heart. Upon enlisting into the Marine Corp, he signed on as an organ donor. I guess that's the only good that he has done in his whole life. After God knows how many lives he has taken at least he will save one."

"Or end many more," the other doctor replies with sarcasm. "I'm not sure if I would want the heart of a serial killer. It's like you're doomed from the start."

"Try telling that to the many people who are waiting in line for this heart. They will be so ecstatic to have the heart they may not even ask whom it originally belonged to."

The doctor shakes his head sadly. "Well, God bless the individual who gets that heart. They will need it. They're getting a gift and a curse."

78

LAS VEGAS, NEVADA
FLORENCE MCCLURE WOMEN'S
CORRECTIONAL FACILITY DEATH ROW
MARCH 14, 2016

TWENTY-FIVE YEAR OLD Angelica Hill, dressed in an orange prison jumpsuit and shower slippers, sits at the end of an old steel table. Her hair drapes down in two long Pocahontas braids. Currently she's the youngest woman on death-row in the entire country. She's been on death-row for three years, one month and twelve days, but her time is now up. She's broken another record as well. Before her the shortest amount of time spent on death-row before being executed was held by a thirty-nine-year-old man from Alabama for killing his own six-month old son. She has him beat by a little less than a year.

She holds her shackled wrists over the table, hands clasped together. Underneath the table her ankles are shackled together as well. Her head is hanging low with her face wet from tears. "Well, Father. There you have it. That explained my hatred for lighter skinned women. It also explained how the city of Philadelphia was not foreign to me. Also, my change of hair color after the transplant. I'm sure no one would ever believe me if I told them it was like he was living through me. So I never told anyone until now. It's like no matter how hard I've tried in life to do the right thing that uncontrollable force inside of me managed to always bring the worse out of me."

Across from her sits the elderly Caucasian priest in his late seventies. Father John's wrinkled, baggy face looks like that of a hound dog. Tiny, oval shaped spectacles cover his low, sagging eyes. He stares into Angelica's eyes for seconds before speaking.

His face is wet from tears as well. Hearing this story has him heartbroken. From the bottom of his heart he now believes what she says about the uncontrollable force but he's quite helpless. He really doesn't know what to tell her at this point. "My dear child, the biggest war that man and woman has ever had to fight is the war with their self. You, my child, have allowed the wrong to overpower the right and now you sit here to pay the consequences for your actions. Such an expensive price to pay."

Angelica shakes her head from side to side with despair. Her face lights up when the door opens. There her parents stand accompanied by her younger brother. She hasn't seen them in many years. They all hug her tightly, weeping hard.

Father John reaches over the table and claps his hands over Angelica's forearms. "My child, my job here is done. You are in God's hands. Let us bow our heads."

The four of them bow their heads as Father John leads the prayer. Her brother says a prayer of his own and so does both of her parents.

* * *

One hour later, Angelica sits strapped in an electric chair. In the room there is only her and the person who is administering the procedure. The many witnesses on the other side of the two way mirrors, include her brother, her father, Toy, Beeba and Wendy. Mr. Antonelli is present as well.

Her mother couldn't bear the sight. The only reason her brother, her father, and her friends are watching is because they promised her they wouldn't leave her side. Mr. Antonelli's presence is not for the support,but wanting to witness and be sure that she is dead. The fear that she has instilled in him the past few years has him trauma-tized. The witnesses wait with anticipation as they watch through the window. Angelica's loved ones watch through crying eyes.

Thirty minutes ago, she was fed her last meal. The access of any meal she could think of and all she requested was her favorite, chicken wings and shrimp fried rice from the local Chinese store, a bag of Swedish Fish and a can of C&C cola.

It wasn't the big filet mignon or lobster that most ask for. She's had enough of that and has never really been impressed by it. With all the fine dining and exquisite cuisine that Mr. Antonelli exposed her to, that isn't what she missed over the years. What she misses the most is the junk food and the small things in life that she over-looked and took for granted.

"Are you ready?" the man asks Angelica with no compassion.

Angelica looks at him with an arctic blast in her eyes. Her heart is thumping with fear, but she refuses to show it. "It's gotta go down, so let's get it over with." She braces herself and tries hard to prepare herself for the unexpected.

The lights are shut off and Angelica sits in the darkness. The man hits the button and the sound of electricity sounds off.

"Aghhhhhhhhhhhhhhhhhh!" she screams with agony for what seems like forever. Her body jolts violently. The screaming ceases and so does her movements.

Close to a minute passes and the lights are turned back on so her death can be witnessed and recorded. Angelica sits strapped in the chair, stiff like the stuffed animals that hunters post in their homes as trophies. Her hair stands straight up on her head from the bolt of the electricity. Her eyes are stretched wide open with the look of shock still in them. Her mouth, stretched open has blood and foam seeping from both sides. With no sign of compassion, the man looks at his watch and records her time of death onto the legal document.

The End...

Rest in peace, Angelica "Storm" Hill — the indirect offspring of the infamous Killer Cal from *Caught 'Em Slippin'*.

Book Order Form

Purchase Information

Name: _____

Address: _____ City: _____

State: _____ Zip Code: _____

$14.95 - No Exit _____
$14.95 - Block Party _____
$14.95 - Sincerely Yours _____
$14.95 - Caught 'Em Slippin' _____
$14.95 - Block Party 2 _____
$14.95 - Block Party 3 _____
$14.95 - Strapped _____
$14.95 - Back 2 Bizness (Block Party 4) _____
$4.99 - Block Party (Comic) _____
$14.95 – Young Gunz _____
$14.95 - Outlaw Chick _____
$14.95 – Block Party 5k1.1 Book 1 _____
$14.95 – Block Party 5k1.1 Book 2 _____
$14.95 – Heartless _____

Book Total: _____

Add $5.75 for shipping of up to 3 books.
Add $1.00 for each additional book. Free shipping for orders of 6 or more books.

Total included: _____

Make Checks/Money Orders payable to:
True 2 Life Publications - PO Box 8722 – Newark, NJ 07108

Got Distribution?

Do you know what separates you from the major publishing firms? Distribution. And what does distribution equal? Distribution equals access to a wider audience which can ultimately lead to more sales and a sales force engine behind your title(s).

True 2 Life will place your books in the world's most comprehensive distribution system through our very own network that was built on business relationships forged with top wholesalers and retailers in the industry.

True 2 Life also offers distribution packages that include, editing, typesetting for print and eBook, and cover design.

For more information, about True 2 Life distribution and distribution packages, please email:

True2LifeMedia@yahoo.com

or by correspondence

P.O. Box 8722
Newark, New Jersey, 07108

Made in the USA
Middletown, DE
21 November 2021